W9-CDG-484

12 02 03
$ 3.00

THE
SHADOW
WAR

THE SHADOW WAR

GLEN SCOTT ALLEN

Thomas Dunne Books
St. Martin's Press
New York

This is a work of fiction. All of the characters, organizations, and events portrayed in this novel are either products of the author's imagination or are used fictitiously.

THOMAS DUNNE BOOKS.
An imprint of St. Martin's Press.

THE SHADOW WAR. Copyright © 2010 by Glen Scott Allen. All rights reserved. Printed in the United States of America. For information, address St. Martin's Press, 175 Fifth Avenue, New York, N.Y. 10010.

www.thomasdunnebooks.com
www.stmartins.com

Book design by Rich Arnold

ISBN 978-0-312-57655-4

First Edition: December 2010

10 9 8 7 6 5 4 3 2 1

For Inna

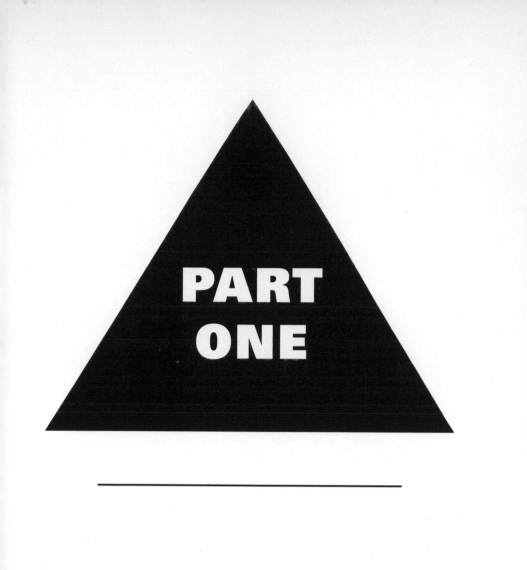

PART ONE

PROLOGUE

WESTERN MASSACHUSETTS, OCTOBER 1675

The man ran across the clearing as though the devil himself were at his heels. He stumbled and fell more than once, but each time picked himself up and struggled on, glancing furtively over his shoulder. Plunging into the tree line, he hid for a moment, crouching behind the wide trunk of a huge, gnarled oak tree. Panting heavily, he looked back toward the stockade walls of the encampment visible in the bright moonlight. And what he saw there was a scene out of hell.

The flames had spread from the outside walls to the dozen buildings inside. A storm of sparks and smoke writhed over their peaked roofs, roiling and billowing as if feeding off the pandemonium of war whoops from the Indians and the wails of their victims. Rising highest was a wooden steeple topped by a large cross, which stood out against the glare of the fire that even now was reaching upward to engulf it. And over it all shone the sterling moonlight, casting grotesque shadows against the smoke, as though the struggling figures hidden from his view were dancing in ecstasy rather than agony, celebrating some perverse Witches' Sabbath.

He silently murmured a few words of what might have been a prayer, then turned his face away and rose with effort, pushing his way farther into the tangle of thornbushes and vines. The moon was hidden for a moment by the thick clouds scudding by overhead, and in the sudden darkness his vest caught on the twigs of a small sapling. He was wearing only a night-shirt beneath the vest, barefoot and bareheaded, his long white hair flying loose; against his chest he clutched a loose leather wrapping, cradling it as he struggled with the twigs, protecting it as though it were a child. Finally he freed himself from the sapling and continued stumbling on, pushing aside the underbrush with his one free hand. He paused, listening for the rushing sound of a nearby river, then struck out with renewed vigor, certain of his direction.

Moments after he left, two other figures entered the spot, moving more slowly, cautiously. As the first proceeded, he pushed aside the low branches with a small stone-and-wood hatchet, the other following in his footsteps. In the darkness their faces weren't visible, but against the background glare of the burning encampment, the profile of the first was distinct: his head was bald except for a narrow strip of hair in its center running from his forehead to the nape of his neck and rising straight up several inches above his skull. The figures both stopped, crouched, listened for a moment, then followed the sounds of breaking branches and crackling leaves a few dozen yards ahead.

The man with long white hair reached a small clearing, or rather a meadow, a natural amphitheater surrounded by woods on all sides. The floor of the meadow was interrupted here and there by mounds of earth, each mound topped by stones piled in small pyramids. He stood on the edge of the clearing, uncertain whether to leave the relative cover of trees; then, with a final glance over his shoulder, he ran quickly to the nearest mound.

He immediately fell to his knees at the small monument of stones and, carefully setting aside his leather bundle, began to dig frantically beneath them. He scooped out a small cave beneath the stones. When it was large enough, he shoved the wrapping and its contents into the recess, then began to throw and pack dirt over the opening.

Suddenly he heard something behind him—a distant scream—and stopped his frenzied activity, looking back at the tree-lined boundary of the meadow. The moon was behind the clouds for the moment, and he saw nothing there. He turned back to his work, scraping more earth and then some leaves over the hole, then patted his handiwork one final time.

He stood and began to run to the other side of the clearing; then, pausing, he looked again at the mound, at the woods, at the moon overhead—and instead turned and ran back the way he had come.

He had worked his way only a short distance into the trees again when he saw the outline of the two men who had been following rise up before him. With the moonlight obscured he could make out no details of their forms, but the black shadow of the first, his arm raised high overhead, was clear; then suddenly a break in the clouds allowed moonlight to stream through the branches, and he saw the necklaces of teeth and beads around the man's neck, the simple leather loincloth, the hide moccasins . . . and the glint of stone in the small hatchet held ready to strike.

Frozen, he raised his right arm in defense, or perhaps to block the moonlight streaming through the window in the clouds. His assailant came closer, and leaned over him, bringing his face fully into the moonlight. It was then the crouching man's expression turned from one of simple terror to utter astonishment, and his mouth gaped open in silent surprise.

"Judas," he whispered.

Then the second man came closer, and his face, too, became visible. Beneath the crude stripes of war paint and smudges of smoke, above him was a face that shone in the moonlight, a face with blue eyes. A face as white as his own.

SOUTHEASTERN SIBERIA, OCTOBER 1968

The man walked briskly down the hallway, glancing back over his shoulder occasionally. His footsteps made no sound, as he was wearing low rubber slippers pulled over his black shoes. He came to a door—oval-shaped and with a large metal wheel in the center. He stood for a moment, his hands on the wheel, looking back the way he'd come.

The hallway's ceiling and walls were curved, and at irregular intervals the entire corridor bent first right then left at sharp angles, like some huge, painfully contorted snake. Parallel rows of pipes and conduits ran along the walls. Ceiling, walls, floor, pipes—all were painted a uniform pale gray. Harsh fluorescent lights in the ceiling made everything shine, as if slightly wet. A stenciled word over the door read офицерекие казармы (Officer Barracks).

He turned the wheel and pulled the door open with some effort, stepped into the small room, then pulled the door closed behind him, locking it with a spin of the wheel. The room's walls and ceiling were curved, too, making it cramped. There was only enough room for two small metal cots, two upright metal wardrobes, and a small metal desk. He went to the cot next to the wardrobe marked леворотов (Leverotov) and sat down.

He was wearing a military uniform: a sea green jacket over similarly colored tunic and pants, a blue beret, and a brown leather gun belt buckled around his waist. The only insignia on the entire uniform were brass pins, one on each collar: two crossed cannons, the symbol of the artillery.

Reaching inside his tunic pocket, he extracted two objects: a green-and-blue pack of cigarettes and a small wooden box of matches. The cigarette pack read шипка (Shipka) in white letters against a green background, with a picture of a square monument rising in exaggerated perspective into the sky. The number 1877 was printed on the side of the monument. The matchbox cover displayed a simple drawing: two raised hands, one with a hammer and the other with a sickle, and a miniature rocket arcing over them.

He sat for a moment looking at the cigarettes and matches.

The faint squeaking of footsteps in the hallway brought his head up, his eyes concentrating on the wheel of the door. The footsteps grew closer—then passed by.

He opened the matchbox, dumped the matches on the cot, and removed the box's cover. He took a small pencil from his pocket and began carefully drawing something on the inside bottom of the box—lines, some in sharp wriggles, others straight, a tiny dot and rectangle, some other symbols. It was painstaking work, and soon he was sweating, even though the room was chill with recycled air.

Finished, he turned to the matches. He began putting them back into the box, counting as he did so. When he reached thirty-three, he took another match and, inserting it into his mouth, bit off the blue-colored tip—and swallowed it. He put the beheaded match into the box; the matches inside now covered his tiny sketch.

Taking up the pencil again, he wrote 34 on the box cover, beneath the tiny rocket. There were six matches left on the cot. He shook a filterless cigarette from the pack and pulled it out with his lips, then lit one of the remaining matches on the side of the box, brought it to the cigarette. He inhaled deeply. Then he picked up the remaining five matches and brought the burning match against them. The matches flared, bringing his face into sharp relief, reflecting in his brown, grim eyes. He watched them burn, then blew them all out. He reached over and took a metal ashtray from the desk. Putting all six spent matches into the ashtray, he stubbed out the cigarette and placed it on top of the matches, then returned the ashtray to the desktop.

He tucked the matchbox inside the nearly empty cigarette pack. He stood and crossed the narrow aisle to the cot opposite his: орлов (ORLOV) read its wardrobe. He opened the thin metal door and, parting the front of a dress tunic identical to his draped on a hanger, slipped the package into the tunic's inside pocket. Then he carefully straightened the tunic and closed the locker's door.

Returning to his own cot he sat down. He looked at his hands, which were trembling, and closed them into fists. The trembling stopped. He removed a small black-and-brown automatic pistol from the gun belt's holster. Embossed on the grip was a tiny five-pointed star. The pistol looked surprisingly light for something made of metal, something so lethal. He removed his beret and placed it carefully on the pillow of his cot. Then he raised the pistol to his temple and pulled the trigger.

The sound, in such a confined space, was deafening.

CHAPTER 1

WESTERN MASSACHUSETTS, OCTOBER 200-

The low, rolling, thickly wooded hills of western Massachusetts passed by the windows of Benjamin's car. The leaves were just beginning their transition to browns and golds and reds, and as Benjamin rounded another curve in the winding country road, his passage sent up a colorful, swirling wake that settled with a soft rustling behind him. The sky was a clear blue, the air crisp with a hint of the winter chill to come. . . . All in all, a beautiful day for a leisurely drive through the country.

But Benjamin wasn't feeling leisurely. And while the sights and sounds were those of a Thanksgiving television special, Benjamin's gut told him a Halloween thriller would be more appropriate.

Until late afternoon the day before, Benjamin Wainwright had been a happy-if-obscure postdoctoral fellow at the Library of Congress, pursuing his research on Colonial Native Americans with the pure focus of a scholar who had found his little bit of heaven in the bowels of the most extensive library on earth, a modern-day Alexandria. He would have been perfectly content to be left alone for the next two years rooting among historical detritus that hadn't been important even when it was new, and now was important only because it was so very old.

And then he'd received the phone call from Jeremy Fletcher.

Benjamin hadn't heard from Jeremy for nearly ten years; not since they'd been undergraduates together at Harvard. They'd been occasional friends back then, but too different to become more than that: Benjamin the bookworm, Jeremy the computer whiz kid; Benjamin raised in a solidly middle-class family of scholars, Jeremy from the titled British upper crust. Even their physiques were a contrast: Benjamin was above-average height, with short, curly black hair, his body fit and solid, whereas Jeremy was short and thin, as though his body fed on itself to supply his brilliant, methodical intellect.

Benjamin had always felt slightly intimidated by Jeremy's brilliance. But then, so did most people. Jeremy simply saw the world differently than other people did. For Jeremy, life wasn't random and haphazard; it was a complex network of interrelating causes and effects.

"Take your favorite subject, history," Jeremy had said late one night as they sat on the steps of Widener Library, the neatly trimmed grass of the Harvard quad a checkerboard of dark trees and pools of light. "It's created by people, not some disembodied 'forces.' And people are, as the saying goes, creatures of habit."

"That's an old theory, Jeremy," Benjamin had objected. "Or are you becoming a conspiracy nut?"

"Oh, I'm not talking some drivel about who killed JFK," Jeremy replied. "I'm talking about the fact that people do things for the same sorts of reasons, century after century. There are decidedly patterns there, patterns made up of millions of individual acts, like dots in one of Seurat's pointillist paintings. The dots may not know the whole picture, but it's bloody well there, just the same. One merely has to find the proper perspective from which to see it."

"And you're going to find that perspective buried in one of your computer programs?" Benjamin teased.

"Perhaps," he'd said enigmatically. "Just perhaps."

Benjamin hadn't seen history that way. To him, the past knew things the present had forgotten, and one didn't kill that wisdom by autopsying it. The true wonder of the past lay in the ineffable complexity of human minds. And the key to those minds was to be found in books.

He remembered standing in front of his father's floor-to-ceiling bookshelves, inhaling the smell of leather and age, and feeling as though he were praying at an altar. Thus, when the opportunity for a postdoc at the Library of Congress had presented itself, it seemed to him those prayers had been answered.

After college, Benjamin followed in his father's footsteps, taking a degree in Colonial history at Georgetown University; meanwhile, he'd heard that Jeremy had finished MIT and then taken a postdoc at the RAND Corporation, doing some sort of supersecret work for the government with computer modeling. And they hadn't communicated in all those years since.

So when an intern at the Library had interrupted Benjamin—he'd been preparing a lecture he planned on calling "Savage Art: Civilization Confronts Chaos in the New World"—telling him there was a Jeremy Fletcher on his office phone, at first he couldn't believe it.

Why would Jeremy call him, after all this time?

After the usual shallow pleasantries of a friendship gone stale with the years, Benjamin had finally asked Jeremy if what he'd heard was true: Was he doing some sort of supersecret work for one of the "spook factories"?

"Not exactly," Jeremy had replied cautiously. "Actually, I'm out here at the American Heritage Foundation."

"*The* Foundation?" Benjamin had whistled appreciatively. "Even better. They're richer than the spooks."

"Well that actually brings me to why I'm bothering you." There'd been an uncomfortable pause, then, "Benjamin, I'd like to share some of that wealth with you. I wonder . . . do you think you might be enticed into coming out here for a few days?"

Benjamin had been stunned. Nothing he knew of either Jeremy's work or that of the American Heritage Foundation would seem to relate in any way to his own expertise. "Not that I don't appreciate it," he finally managed, "but what on earth could I do for you?"

"Well, it's difficult to explain, but you see, some of my own research . . . well, it's gotten tangled up in that Indian Wars muddle you love so much."

"Native Americans," Benjamin said reflexively, but really thinking about the curious, almost artificial breeziness of Jeremy's tone. "We colonials don't call them Indians anymore."

"Yes, quite right. Anyway, I could use that musty encyclopedia you call a brain to help me sort it all out. It would only be for a few days, a week at most. But it would have to be now, Benjamin. Tomorrow, actually. Think you could make the slog out here to the wilds of western Massachusetts?"

For a moment Benjamin had no idea what to say, but after a bit more hedging, Benjamin had allowed himself to be . . . seduced seemed like the right word. But not by Jeremy's promise of exorbitant reward; rather, it had been the mystery of the thing, the sheer *eccentricity* of Jeremy's offer.

Of course Benjamin had heard of the American Heritage Foundation; it was one of the most prestigious and most secretive "think tanks" in the entire country. Young obscure scholars went into the Foundation—as it was known with a certain instinctual awe—and came out to appointments in the corridors of power that would otherwise have required decades of thankless service to obtain. And while the occupants of those corridors were elected officials and therefore merely passing through, the overseers of the Foundation were answerable to no one—or at least not anyone so lowly as a mere voter.

Ergo, any young academic would kill to gain entry into that world, and here Benjamin was being handed his opportunity on a silver platter.

But why him? And why *now*?

Thus had Benjamin's mind spun around the problem ever since he'd boarded a flight to Logan, rented a car, and begun his long journey across the length of Massachusetts, out to where the wealthy Boston Brahmins kept summer cottages the size of boarding schools and listened to classical music under the stars.

He glanced at his briefcase sitting on the seat beside him. Inside it were a few reference books to the Colonial Indian Wars—general stuff, as Jeremy hadn't been specific about his "muddle"—and his father's notebooks. Whereas Benjamin's area was early Native Americans, his father had instead concentrated on what he called "non-Native Americans"—the Puritans. He'd spent his entire career tracing the Byzantine sects and schisms among America's spiritual founding fathers, and just when he was completing work on a book, he and Benjamin's mother had been killed in a car accident, leaving Benjamin a small inheritance, and the large collection of his father's notes, which he treasured as a sort of family heirloom. And, while he doubted those notes would prove useful to Jeremy's work, bringing them along made him feel as though his father were along for the ride in this unlikely adventure. They were a kind of comfort—even though the ache he felt when he thought about his parents, about their sudden, violent erasure from this world . . . that ache knew no comfort.

Finally Benjamin found the exit, and thirty minutes later he sat at the end of a narrow, winding road, facing the Foundation's formidable entrance.

Nestled in a natural bowl of small, rounded hills, the Foundation was separated—or perhaps protected was a better word—from the outside world by acres of woods. The nearest settlement was a good half-hour drive away; even the summer mansions Benjamin had passed seemed vulnerable and déclassé by comparison.

The Foundation was an expanse of manicured lawns, geometric flower gardens, strategically placed copses of oak and sycamore and maple trees, all with their leaves now glowing in the earthy tones of early fall, and a dozen buildings, most in a Colonial-style architecture of red brick, white trim, and copper-gabled eaves. It all looked more like an exclusive private school than a secret research institute.

Until one noticed the ten-foot fence that stretched around the grounds. A fence Benjamin was sure was electrified.

After passing through imposing wrought-iron gates and parking his car in a graveled driveway, Benjamin stood on the portico of the large, mansionlike edifice to which the gate guard had directed him. His briefcase clutched in one hand, he wondered again what on earth he was doing here. But then Jeremy would explain all that to him in a moment.

He squared his shoulders and entered the building.

Benjamin felt dizzy.

The circular foyer of the building was enormous, open all the way up to the domed ceiling some fifty feet overhead. A grand spiral staircase wound around the wall of the foyer, up to the second floor.

And then he noticed the mural.

Beginning where the dome joined the foyer's walls and stretching all the way down to the floor, the mural covered every inch of the walls. It reminded him of the WPA Depression-era murals that adorned the lobbies of so many American post offices, but the scale of this one was tremendous, overwhelming. He could make out people and machines and landscapes, all interlocked in ways both intricate and yet heroically simple. He saw light bending along the curve of muscle and polished steel surfaces, faces fixed in transports of calm determination.

He felt simultaneously proud and insignificant.

He wrested his attention away from the mural and looked around the foyer. Just opposite him was an office door with ARTHUR TERRILL, A.D. on a brass plate in its center. That was the person the guard had directed him to see.

He walked over to the door. Inside, he could hear voices, raised and apparently arguing. He hesitated, then knocked.

The voices stopped, there was a pause, and then the door opened. A short, thin man with large-rimmed glasses and carefully styled silver hair stood looking at him quizzically.

"Yes?" he said.

"Excuse me," said Benjamin. "I'm Benjamin Wainwright. I'm here to see Dr. Jeremy Fletcher?"

The man looked nonplussed for a moment, then shook his head.

"Of course, of course," he said, backing up, "I forgot all about you. Come in, come in."

Benjamin entered a large office with a great block of a desk to one side, armchairs here and there, a small couch, a Persian rug, walnut wainscoting, floor-to-ceiling bookshelves. . . . He imagined now he was in the principal's office of this "private school."

"Arthur Terrill," the man said, somewhat perfunctorily shaking Benjamin's hand. He motioned for Benjamin to sit in one of two unoccupied chairs before his desk, then returned to his seat behind it.

"This will only take a moment, Mr. Wainmark," he said. "Please sit down."

"It's Wain*wright*," Benjamin corrected. "Benjamin—"

"Excuse *me*," said another voice behind Benjamin.

Turning, he saw a man sitting on a small couch that had been hidden by the open door. He was dressed in a light gray suit and matching tie, and in one hand was a glass containing amber fluid and ice.

"Benjamin Wainwright?" the man asked. Benjamin nodded. "Good." He took a sip from the drink. "I hoped we'd meet."

The man rose, came over and stood beside Benjamin, looking down at him. He seemed amused. He also seemed slightly drunk.

In all the time Benjamin was to spend with Samuel Wolfe, he never quite gained a single, fixed idea of his overall persona. Samuel was tall, and held himself so erect one's impression was that his manners came from another century. He could appear patrician and imposing one moment, relaxed and mischievous the next. His face had gone out of style in the thirties: a curving beak of a nose and large, intelligent eyes; eyes that encouraged an instinctual confidence. It suddenly came to Benjamin that Wolfe was a dead ringer for that actor he'd seen in an old black-and-white detective film . . . something about a "thin man"?

And then Benjamin realized Wolfe was extending a hand toward him, still with a drink in the other. He took it and felt the firmness of Wolfe's grip. Wolfe sat down in the other chair before Terrill's desk.

"This is Mr. Samuel Wolfe, a . . . security analyst," Terrill said, tapping a pencil on his desk and looking down at a fan of papers spread across the desktop's green blotter, "here to help us with an . . . unfortunate incident." He sighed. "And it's because of that incident that your services will not be required."

Now Benjamin was the one nonplussed. "Not required?"

"I'm afraid there's been a significant change of plans—"

"Significant!" Wolfe snorted, shaking his head.

"And unfortunate," Terrill continued. "I'm terribly sorry, but in any case the Foundation will cover your expenses for the trip and, let's say, two weeks?"

"Christ on a crutch, Arthur." Wolfe frowned at Terrill, as if scolding him. "This young man hasn't the foggiest idea what's happened here. Toss him a line, for godsake." And for emphasis he recrossed his legs, rather elegantly.

"Yes, of course, I'm sorry." Again Terrill tapped and rifled. "If only Jeremy had spoken to me sooner. You see, I didn't know he'd contacted you until this very morning, well after the . . ."

"The incident?" Benjamin offered.

"A hit," said Wolfe, raising his glass in a toast. "Give the lad a drink."

"Oh, yes, I'm sorry. Would you care for a drink?" Terrill asked.

"No," Benjamin said. "Well, perhaps some water—"

"And the whiskey you don't give him," Wolfe said, handing his empty glass across the desk to Terrill, "put in this."

Terrill took the glass and went to a small bar by the fireplace, and as he made another drink and poured a glass of water for Benjamin, he continued.

"Anyway, as I said, there's been a terrible . . . event. Jeremy Fletcher—the man who requested your services, a resident fellow here at the Foundation, in fact a very accomplished scholar in his own right—Well . . ." Terrill returned and handed both of the men their glasses, then sat back down. "Well, he's dead."

"There," sighed Wolfe, "you said it." He saluted Terrill and took a sip of his refreshed drink.

"Dead?" Benjamin exclaimed. "But he called me at the Library of Congress. Just yesterday. He asked me to come out and help with some work he was doing." They both looked at him in silence. "He . . ." Benjamin realized he'd run out of things to say. "Dead?" he repeated.

"Decidedly," said Wolfe. Then he looked sharply at Terrill. "You say this 'incident' occurred sometime yesterday afternoon?"

"Well, it must have happened after Dr. Fletcher's afternoon meeting with Edith, certainly," Terrill said nervously. Then he glanced at Benjamin. "But there's no reason to go into all that now, taking up Mr. Wainwright's time, when we've wasted so much of it as it is."

Benjamin turned to Wolfe. "You're a policeman?"

Wolfe shifted those lidded eyes as if Benjamin had insulted him.

"A miss," Wolfe said. And then he smiled—and again Benjamin felt both charmed and irritated by his expression.

"In any case," Terrill continued with some effort, "as Mr. Fletcher was the only member of the Foundation doing that sort of research, we simply don't need—"

"What sort of research?" Wolfe interrupted.

"What? I told you—"

"No," said Wolfe, turning to face Benjamin. "I'm asking Mr. Benjamin Wainwright. Why do *you* think Dr. Fletcher requested your illustrious presence?"

"You mean, what sort of work was Jeremy . . . was Dr. Fletcher doing?" Benjamin shook his head. "I know almost nothing about it. I hadn't spoken to him in years, and then suddenly, out of nowhere, yesterday—"

"You *knew* Dr. Fletcher?" Wolfe asked sharply.

"Well, yes, back in college. But—"

"And then, after a long interval without any contact, he called you yesterday, asked you to come out here?"

Benjamin felt like he was being interrogated. "He said something about working with the Colonial period, and, as that's my field—"

"Then," Wolfe interrupted him again, "you do know of Dr. Fletcher's research."

"No, not really. I mean, I know his degree was in statistics—"

"*Inferential* statistics," corrected Wolfe. "You know, to draw *inferences*."

"Samuel, really," Terrill protested, exasperated. "I feel I must put my foot down here. This is the very sort of thing that we wish to remain confidential. And confidentiality, need I remind you, determined our course of action in bringing *you* here."

Wolfe stood and crossed to Terrill's desk as if to confront him; but instead he merely smiled tolerantly at Terrill, then turned and addressed Benjamin.

"Doesn't it strike you as odd, Mr. Wainwright," Wolfe said, "that a statistician, inferential or otherwise, would need the services of a Colonial historian?"

Benjamin entirely agreed with Wolfe, but for some reason he didn't want to say so.

"Well . . . not necessarily. Jeremy and I used to discuss Colonial history back in college, and—"

"Fletcher's *current* work was all on nuclear war theory," Wolfe said heavily. "Hardly the stuff of Puritan religious dogma, wouldn't you say?"

Benjamin looked to Terrill, who was now jotting notes furiously, resorting to the pretense that neither of them existed. And then an answer seemed perfectly obvious to him.

"Jeremy knew my dissertation was on the Native-Settler wars. Perhaps his work on war game theory had something to do with those wars and . . . well, modern guerilla warfare?"

Wolfe looked at him silently for a moment, turned to Terrill.

"How much were you going to pay him, Arthur?"

Terrill looked up from his papers. "What? Him?" He glanced at Benjamin. "Well, I don't see how that's really relevant, given the circumstances."

"As much as my assistant?" Wolfe said.

"Your *assistant*?"

"If I'm to explore this incident thoroughly in no more than three days, I'm going to need some help, Arthur. And there's the not inconsequential issue of who's to be trusted. Wasn't that your point in dragging me away from my cozy little loft in Boston this morning? To guarantee a little discreet nosing about before the big-footed detectives arrive?"

Terrill roused himself. "And *confidentiality*, Samuel. At least you were once already employed by the Foundation, thus the proper security checks—"

Wolfe leaned over and patted Benjamin's shoulder. "And our congressional librarian here works for the government, too, don't you?" He turned back to Terrill. "The government that writes your checks, Arthur. The same government that's not going to write you that very fat check, unless—"

Terrill held up his hand. "Samuel, *please!*"

Wolfe smiled. "My point is that you can spare no one, I need someone, and someone has just very propitiously arrived. Someone whom poor Jeremy thought could help *him*. Well, perhaps he was right, Arthur. Perhaps Mr. Wainwright can help *us*."

"Really, now, Samuel . . . ," began Terrill.

But Wolfe suddenly cursed as his glass slipped from his hand and fell with a crash to Terrill's desk. Ice and liquid spread everywhere across the papers there. Terrill first looked stunned, then horrified, then began grasping willy-nilly at folders and papers.

"Oh dear," Wolfe said—and began dabbing at the expanding rivulets of scotch with the end of his tie.

Terrill sat back, exasperated.

"I think," he said, speaking slowly and carefully, "this discussion's usefulness is concluded for the evening. Mr. Wainwright, we'll decide in the morning what, if any, your continuing role with the Foundation will be. And Mr. Wolfe . . ."

Wolfe looked up, grinning ruefully, and handed Terrill the one folder he'd managed to snatch from the deluge, a shard of glass perched in its concavity. And then without another word he turned and, nodding to Benjamin, walked out of the room.

When Wolfe was gone, Arthur looked at Benjamin. "I have to apologize for Mr. Wolfe," he said. "He's been through a . . . well, a recent shock. You haven't seen him at his best."

Benjamin realized that Terrill's schoolmaster tone of earlier was tempered with the concern of an elder colleague for a promising friend—someone whose promise was vanishing before his eyes. "Go upstairs, Mr. Wainwright," Terrill continued, "and there you'll find an empty guest room. You can use that for the night. We'll sort all this out in the morning."

"Thank you," Benjamin said. "Then . . . good night." He gathered his briefcase from the floor and crossed what seemed an immense distance to the office's doorway.

"Close the door, if you please," said Terrill behind him, and Benjamin did as he requested.

When he entered the foyer, he looked around for Wolfe, and decided he must have gone upstairs already. Then he realized that if he were to stay overnight he would need his suitcase from the car.

The night sky outside was perfectly clear, the stars bright and undimmed by city lights or smog. It had been a very long time since Benjamin had seen them so brilliant, so ideal. The only sound was that of his footsteps on the gravel.

Back on the portico, suitcase retrieved, he stood for a moment letting the silence surround him. He could make out black lumps of trees, behind them darkened hulks of other buildings, and the lighter blackness of the sky overhead. And then, perhaps a hundred yards away, on one of the footpaths, he saw someone walking. Someone with a dog. A dog that was straining at its leash.

Benjamin hurried back into the building.

CHAPTER 2

"Ya uverna," Natalya said. "I am certain. He's lying."

"Pravda?" The man in the small booth next to her smiled. "And how do we know this, oh great seer Natashka?"

Of all the men at the Russian embassy who had a crush on Natalya—and there were several—she liked Yuri the best. Not only was he the most handsome, he was also the most . . . useful. So, she tried to keep him interested.

Natalya returned the smile, somewhat wryly, then pointed through the one-way mirror.

"Look at his eyes. Up and to the center is thinking. Up and to the left or right is fabricating. And he's touched his nose twice and pulled on his ear three times. He's lying through his teeth." She turned her back to the window, leaned against the console, folded her arms, and looked down at Yuri. *"Da?"*

"Harasho," Yuri said, adjusting the dials of the console before him. "One course in psychology, you are now an academician?"

"Isn't that what your little blips tell you about him?" She nodded toward the one-way mirror in front of Yuri.

Two men sat in a small room on the other side of the mirror, across a table from each other. One held a clipboard upon which he was writing notes; the other was leaning back in his chair, apparently at ease. And as the two men continued to talk, the computer screen in front of Yuri displayed traces that jumped abruptly, expanding and contracting. There was a super-imposed grid on the screen, and when the traces labeled *Interviewiruyemiy* jumped above or below those lines, they turned red. They were red now.

Yuri laughed. "*Da, da.* So, all this expensive equipment is completely useless, and all we need is Natalya Orlova, Cultural Attaché and Eye Move-ment Master."

Now Natalya laughed. She knew Yuri was teasing her; she accepted it as part of the price of being where she wasn't supposed to be, witnessing inter-rogations—no, interviews—she wasn't supposed to witness. It was a deli-cate balancing act, keeping Yuri's interest active but harmless. And she needed that interest. Occasionally she required Yuri's assistance in obtain-ing fast access to the restricted archives, where the documents all had num-bers instead of titles, and were all written by the same author: *Otdel,* for "official department." Hanging out with Yuri was a small taste of that world of secret, anonymous documents.

She leaned over and planted a kiss on top of Yuri's thick, closely cropped brown hair.

"You will have to continue without Madame Natashka," she said. "I have real work to do."

Yuri took her hand for a moment. "And you owe me one drink," he said.

"*Da.*" Natalya pulled her hand free. "Soon, Yuri Alexandrovich, very soon."

Once in the hall, she turned right and walked past the interview room, glancing once more at the man inside. He was applying for a license to do business in Russia. Smuggler, she thought. But of what? Cigarettes, music CDs, computer software, drug formulas? But not military secrets. Not these days. Now the enemies of Russia were most often the same as the enemies of the United States: money launderers, drug dealers, software thieves. And in these days of the global market, the difference between the American Mafia dons and the Russian *vor v zakone* was gray and indistinct. And of course there were the terrorists, people once trained and supplied by her former government, but now embarrassments to be hunted down and eliminated. Cooperation was the watchword, détente on a scale unimaginable only a decade ago. In the New World Order, this only made sense.

Then why didn't it make her feel more secure?

As she headed for her small desk on the third floor and the pile of paper-work she'd been avoiding by playing spy with Yuri, she wondered once again about her career choice.

She might, like Yuri, have joined the Federal'naya sluzhba bezopasnosti, the FSB—the theoretically licit and more civilized successor to the notorious Komitet gosudarstvennoy bezopasnosti (KGB). She'd even been interviewed by them when she'd graduated from the Moskovsky gosudarstvennyi institut mezhdunarodnykh otnoshenii, the Moscow State Institute of International Relations.

Had she so desired, her credentials certainly could have earned her entrance into the ranks of the FSB: both of her grandfathers had been clever and nondescript enough to survive in the secret service while nearly everyone around them was consumed by the homicidal paranoia of the thirties and forties; and her own father had been a political officer in one of the first divisions of the Raketnye voyska strategicheskogo naznacheniya, the Strategic Rocket Forces, the most elite corps of all the Red Army.

She herself had even served as leader of her school's Komsomol, Communist Youth Union, in a secret military city hidden in plain sight in the vastness of Siberia. And finally, with a degree in international cultural relations from MGIMO, Natalya Orlova should have been the perfect candidate for a life of privilege that was the lot of the new *FSBeshniky*.

But she'd been idealistic when she'd graduated, flush with enthusiasm for the perestroika and promises of the New Russia. More important, she'd felt the need to atone for the crimes of her family during their long history with those secret services; a history she'd known as a child only through family gossip and the sinisterly suggestive gaps in her relatives' recounted biographies.

And then there had been her father's own deep disillusionment with the "worker's paradise"; a disillusionment hardened on an almost daily basis as the *samizdat* press published one heretofore repressed history after another, and the truths that had always been denied, but which in revelation seemed all too blatant and indisputable, made swearing allegiance to the Security Services, however "modernized," unthinkable.

Through those years of revelations, Natalya had watched as her father's eyes became sad, quiet, angry. Distant.

And there'd been something else to his silence—some secret more sinister, it seemed, than all the terrible revelations about her grandfathers and the regime they served. A secret that created a small, dark space between them which even to this day had never been breached, and which she had since decided he would take to his grave.

So she'd chosen instead to become a simple cultural attaché, a job she thought would perhaps actually serve the fledgling state and help it atone for all the buried transgressions of its history—and hers. But every time she found an excuse to shadow Yuri or one of the other "special attachés," she took it. Perhaps it was in her genes.

So she split her time between her official duties at the Russian Cultural Center—ironically housed in a grand edifice on Phelps Place that had once belonged to the archcapitalist Evalyn Walsh McLean, one-time owner of the Hope Diamond—and a small, nondescript desk here at the embassy on Wisconsin Avenue. Even though the embassy's squat, gray architecture was far more reminiscent of the Soviet-era government buildings back home, she instinctively felt this was where the *real* identity of the New Russia was being formed—or at least where it was created for its American audience. And she wished to be an insider in that seductive drama.

But then Natalya had always been an *outsider.* Her looks reflected her mother's lineage—Finnish, not Slavic—with her high cheekbones, brilliant, almost white-blond hair, and blue-green eyes, she was unique among all the brown-haired, wide-faced, flat-nosed children in the military town's state school. *"Rusalka,"* mermaid, the teachers had called her: something exotic, foreign. Suspect.

Even the way she had dressed marked her as an exception. "It's the nail that sticks up that gets hammered down," her mother's father had warned her. Exhibiting a taste for Western styles back then was considered almost tantamount to treason: the short skirts, the bright colors, the high-heeled shoes. Not the tastes of a true *sovok,* a loyal Soviet citizen. She still remembered vividly the old *babushkas* on the street, shouting after her when she walked by in such clothes. *Zapadnaya,* they called her: Western girl. And much worse.

Now of course everything had changed. Down was up. What had been foreign and bad was now stylish and good.

And Natalya used it to her advantage. Her looks, her Western manner, her command of colloquial English—all had gotten her a posting in the Washington embassy of the Russian Federation in Washington, D.C., at a time in her life when she should still have been stamping visa applications in a gray basement office somewhere in Moscow. And there were perks.

For instance, before she'd stopped in to "advise" Yuri in his monitoring of "interviews," she'd been headed to make final arrangements for the coming reception for the Bolshoi Ballet. The social event would certainly be a break in her routine—but she didn't relish the thought of being patronized by Madame Zenova, the aging *ballet prima,* complete with purple-feathered boa.

Zenova had already visited the RCC that day, whisking around with her trailing entourage, looking at everyone through lowered eyelids, playing the part of fickle diva to perfection. And Natalya knew she would be just one of many nameless functionaries at the reception, invited more because of her looks than her importance; all part of the show for the American Washington insiders, all a demonstration of just how thoroughly over the bad old gray days of the Soviet era were.

But to keep the perks she had to occasionally do her actual job, regardless how tedious.

Muttering a curt greeting of *"Privet"* to a few colleagues—it was four thirty and most of the staff had left for the day—she wound her way to a small desk set in a corner.

Before her was a stack of mail she'd brought with her from the RCC; somehow going through it at the embassy made it seem more important. It was work that demanded little of her training and provided few opportunities for her powers of "creative interpretation"—the kind she'd demonstrated for Yuri.

Working her way through the stack of mail and messages on her desk, she found them to be for the most part the usual sort of communiqués: a request for access to archives of the Organization of Security and Cooperation in Europe by a student at Harvard's Kennedy School of Government writing a dissertation, "Cultural Schisms and the Deformation of International Law by National Codes of Justice"—it made her head ache just to read the title; a letter from a museum in Philadelphia asking for slides of the new exhibit in the RCC's "Russian-American Room"—a stultifying display of joint agricultural projects she thought better suited to the 1950s; a letter addressed to Ambassador Extraordinary and Plenipotentiary Vasily I. Schastny—she had no idea how that one had found its way into her pile; it should have gone to the ambassador's secretarial pool.

Then she came across an envelope that immediately struck her as strange. It was an ordinary enough eight-by-eleven white envelope, but it bore no institutional return label—just a P.O. box number somewhere in Massachusetts—and held a U.S. postal stamp rather than the usual machine mark of bulk mail. And it was hand-addressed to her personally: *Ms. Natalya N. Orlova, Cultural Attaché, Russian Cultural Centre.* She noticed the British spelling of the word "centre."

Using one of her stylishly long red fingernails—she was forever misplacing the silver Imperial Russia reproduction letter opener Yuri had given her after he watched her opening her mail this way—she slit open the envelope.

The letter inside was strange, too.

It was handwritten in Russian. Not particularly good Russian, but at least the writer was making an effort; nearly all American correspondents just assumed a cultural attaché would read and write English. The writer (it said) was looking for any information regarding a book, published sometime between 1960 and 1970, titled *Stzenariy 55,* or perhaps *Borba s tenyu.* But he wasn't certain of that title, he wrote; it could be some other version of those words.

Script fifty-five? she thought. *That could mean almost anything. And the second is . . . very strange indeed.*

Borba had many possible meanings: fighting, struggle, conflict. And *tenyu* wasn't any more specific, referring to twilight or shade, or simply dim light.

Fighting with Shade? Fighting in the Twilight?

But those translations were literal, and Natalya knew that literal translations almost never caught the real meaning of a phrase, especially a literary phrase.

In fact, she couldn't think of any English phrase that captured the real sense of the Russian: a weaker combatant struggling against a stronger and invisible force.

Now Natalya was intrigued. . . . But it was late on a Friday evening, and she had a hectic, crowded subway trip ahead of her to her apartment near Dupont Circle. As curious as the request was, it would have to wait until Monday.

But before she put the letter away, she glanced at the bottom of the page, to the signature.

Iskrenne vash, the letter concluded. And it was signed in steep, angled writing difficult to read; but she finally made out the signature.

Jeremy Fletcher.

CHAPTER 3

Benjamin reentered the main building, passed through the darkened foyer and up the spiral staircase. The details of the gigantic mural were now even murkier, and vaguely threatening. When he reached the second floor, he saw a light coming from an open doorway down the hallway to the left. He went to the room, found Wolfe standing inside.

"This should do," Wolfe said, motioning him to enter. "All the perks of a private estate, none of the expenses. To say nothing of the first-class security."

"Yes," Benjamin said, "I noticed the fence and cameras on the way in."

"I wasn't talking about the fence," Wolfe replied. "But, here, we need provisions. I'll go scour the kitchen."

As Wolfe started to leave, Benjamin extracted his cell phone from his pocket, flipped it open.

Wolfe stopped. "What on earth are you doing?" he asked.

"I thought I'd better call a friend who's watching my cat, tell them I might be back tomorrow."

"Not on that, you won't," Wolfe said. "Cell phones don't work here. The whole campus is blanketed by a filter. You can only make a call through the landline," he pointed at the phone next to Benjamin's bed, "and if it's off campus, even that has to be scheduled."

"Oh," said Benjamin. "I didn't know."

"As I said," Wolfe smiled, "very secure." Then he turned to go. But as Wolfe reached the doorway, Benjamin said, "Before you go, may I ask, what happened to . . . to Jeremy?"

"Heart attack," Wolfe answered bluntly.

"Heart attack?" echoed Benjamin. "My god . . . But then, why—" Benjamin waved vaguely at Wolfe.

"Why a security analyst instead of the county medical examiner?" He smiled. "You know how submariners can be sure there are no leaks?" Benjamin shook his head. "They can't," Wolfe said, patting his shoulder. "So they're always checking. *Always.*"

And then he went off in search of food.

Benjamin put his few things away—the room was very well apportioned with armoire, bookcase, several chairs, a small table he imagined could serve as a desk, everything in the dark, polished wood and satin of the Federalist style—and then looked about the room, wondering how long before Wolfe returned with food, as he hadn't eaten since the morning and was in fact starving.

It was then he noticed three books placed on one of the nightstands.

The first two were *The European & the Indian* and *1676: The End of American Independence*. Both were books he recognized from his own work in Colonial history. Perhaps these were the "bit of a snag" Jeremy had referred to?

But the third was a slim volume, roughly eight by eleven inches, clearly very old, bound in thick red water-stained pasteboard. The title—*A Brief History of the Reverend Harlan Phlegon Bainbridge: His Vision and His Tragedy*—was stamped onto the cover.

Benjamin went suddenly white.

He recognized the name—how could he not? His father's book—his uncompleted book, and all those years of research—had partially been about the Reverend Hessiah Philadephia Bainbridge. And Harlan, he knew, was Hessiah's son. But while Hessiah had been the subject of several books on Colonial Puritan history, almost nothing was known of his son, Harlan. And in all his studies, in all his father's studies, Benjamin had never heard of *this* book.

How on earth had Jeremy come across it?

At that moment Wolfe returned. He was carrying a tray with small plates of sliced turkey and ham, some yellow cheese, and a bowl of black olives. He'd also brought a pot of coffee, as well as a full bottle of Glenlivet scotch.

As Wolfe set the tray down on a little round side table near Benjamin's bed, he saw Benjamin eyeing the coffee and whiskey. Wolfe poured himself a tumbler of the scotch.

"Nightcap?" Wolfe asked.

"Uh, no, no thanks," said Benjamin. "I just wake up later and—"

"Capital," said Wolfe. He poured another tumbler and handed it to Benjamin. "I hate to nightcap alone."

He tapped Benjamin's glass with his own, then downed half of his at a single gulp. Benjamin sighed, lifted his glass to his lips, and sipped. It was very strong scotch, and Benjamin had always preferred gin. But then as the aftertaste faded it left a warm glow going down. He took another sip.

"Attaboy, Benny," said Wolfe. He sat down in a chair beside the bed, crossed his legs, again in a move of almost antique elegance.

"Uh, Mr. Wolfe, could we get one thing straight?" Benjamin sat down on the bed, the slim red book still in one hand, and began picking at the meat and cheese from the plate.

"What's that?"

"Could you stop calling me Benny?"

Wolfe smiled broadly. "Do you have a middle name?"

Benjamin sighed. "Franklin."

Wolfe's eyes went wide. "*Mein Gott!* Benjamin Franklin Wainwright?" Benjamin nodded. Wolfe raised his glass. "Here's to Ben Franklin, Colonial scholar." This time Benjamin joined him in drinking. "How on earth did that happen?" Wolfe asked.

"My father was an historian, too, and a fan of the Founding Fathers. He always said it that way, capitalized. When he spoke of Thomas Jefferson, sometimes I could swear there were tears in his eyes." He took another sip of the scotch. Winced.

"But then why aren't you *Thomas Jefferson* Wainwright?"

Benjamin laughed. "My father admired Jefferson tremendously, but he thought Franklin a little more . . . human."

"Human?" asked Wolfe.

"Maybe colorful is a better word. There was this letter my father showed me when he thought I was of the . . . proper age; a letter Franklin had written to a friend who'd asked his advice about the best way to conduct 'discreet affairs.' The letter wasn't published until the 1920s, for fear it would damage the reputation of so respected a Founding Father." Benjamin took another sip of the scotch. "In the letter, Franklin lists eight reasons it is best to have such affairs with older women, the last one being 'because they are so *grateful!*' "

Wolfe laughed sharply. "Very strategic thinking."

Wolfe was exhibiting his ingratiating smile, and Benjamin couldn't help feeling a growing affection for the man. He thought of what Terrill had told him downstairs. He decided the circumstances were ripe for a little prying.

"Strategic thinking . . . that's what got you into the security business?"

Wolfe looked at him and the smile disappeared.

"Vietnam," he said. "I was too eager for the Canadian option, too bright to sling an M-16. So they put me into military intelligence. God," Wolfe laughed, drinking again. "There's the mother of all oxymorons."

"But how does that lead . . ."

"Here?" Wolfe indicated the room, the grounds, the situation with a whirl of his empty tumbler.

Which brought his attention to his glass. He leaned over to pour another drink—then put the cork back into the bottle.

"Another time, Benjamin. It's getting late, and you have some homework to do." He pointed to the book in Benjamin's hand and the two on the table. "I found those in Fletcher's room. They seemed distinctly different from the bulk of his reading material, all that nuclear apocalypse gloom and doom. I thought you could take a look at them, give us a head start in the morning." Then Wolfe stood up to leave.

"But how do you know Arthur will keep me around now that Jeremy . . ." Again he couldn't bring himself to say it.

"He was a good friend?"

Wolfe's sympathy sounded sincere, so he gave a sincere answer. "Not for years now. But once, yes."

"Don't worry about Arthur. I think I managed to . . . divert him from a precipitous decision. And tomorrow is another day." He smiled broadly.

Again Wolfe made ready to leave, and again Benjamin stopped him.

"Divert?" he asked. "You mean that spilled drink, that was . . ."

Wolfe smirked. "Distraction. All the best illusionists use it."

"Uh-huh," replied Benjamin. "But even if I stay, what exactly is it we're supposed to *do* tomorrow morning?"

Wolfe smiled at him. "Like I said, look for leaks," he said. "Beginning, like all good detective novels, at the scene of the . . . crime?" Then Wolfe gave him a curt salute, said good night, and pulled the door shut.

Benjamin sat for a moment, wondering what Wolfe had meant by "leaks." Or, for that matter, "crime." Terrill had introduced Wolfe as a security analyst. . . . Was there some suspicion Jeremy had been leaking information? That seemed unthinkable.

He shook his head. He was accustomed to the hard reality of print, not this conjecturing out of thin air. Perhaps a little of that black-and-white certainty of print would set him right.

He moved the food tray off the bed, scooted back so he could lean against the headboard as he looked through Fletcher's books.

He picked up the slim volume about Bainbridge, the book he'd never heard of before. He turned it back and forth. The ornate binding, the thick pages . . . it seemed like the sort of book custom-produced for rich bibliophiles. On the first page, below the title, was the author's name: Warren Ginsburg. And under that was typed, *Fellow of the Heritage Institute for Good Government.*

Heritage *Institute*? Some earlier incarnation of the Foundation? If so, he hadn't realized the Foundation had been around that long, all the way back to—he checked the date on the title page—1929.

Then he noticed beneath that a stamp, the sort of seal placed in valuable books by people who collect such things. With some difficulty, he read the embossed letters printed in a circle.

The Library of Seymour H. Morris.

The name sounded vaguely familiar, but he couldn't quite place it. He turned the page. Here, Ginsburg had quoted from Hobbes:

> *By art is created that great Leviathan, called a Commonwealth*
> *or State—(in Latin, Civitas) which is but an artificial man.*

And beneath this, written in purple ink now faded with age, was written *To Cecil, our modern Bainbridge, with concern & hope on this Brave New Century's longest day—Warren, 10/29/1929.*

Benjamin turned the page and began reading about the "Vision and Tragedy" of the Rev. Harlan Phlegon Bainbridge, 162?–1675. And for a while he was engrossed in his reading, but eventually his eyes began to droop, his head began to nod. . . .

As Benjamin fell asleep, the book slipped from his hands and fell off the side of the bed. And as it fell, a slip of paper—small, yellow, with ruled lines—fluttered out of the center of the manuscript and dropped lightly to the floor. When the book landed next to it, the gust of air sent the paper floating sideways a foot or so, so that it came to rest under the bed.

CHAPTER 4

Jeremy Fletcher's room was tidy to the point of obsession. *So like Jeremy,* Benjamin thought. Which made the overturned chair and computer keyboard on the floor all the more surprising.

Wolfe had awakened Benjamin at the ungodly hour of 6:00 A.M., thrusting a cup of hot coffee under his nose.

"Get changed and meet me in the hall," he'd offered by way of a morning greeting. "Those leaks won't plug themselves."

Once Benjamin had washed his face and put on some fresh clothes, they'd walked down the hall and through the manse's expansive foyer—in the early morning light the mural was more visible, but Benjamin hadn't time to make out any details—and down a hallway until they stood before Jeremy's door. Wolfe was neatly dressed in a suit and tie, and showed no evidence of a hangover. He was carrying a small black briefcase in one hand.

"Haven't you already examined his room?" Benjamin had asked, sipping the coffee.

"I just glanced in yesterday, before you arrived. Then after we met . . . well, I decided to wait until we could examine it together, when both our impressions would be fresh."

"But I don't even know what I'm looking for."

"Exactly," Wolfe had said. "Unbiased eyes are the best detectors of fraud."

When they'd reached Jeremy's doorway, Wolfe had stopped and examined the space where the door met the jamb. Finding what he was looking for—a small, transparent piece of tape—he'd ripped it from the jamb before unlocking the door and ushering Benjamin into the room.

It was furnished almost identically to Benjamin's room: bed, nightstand, mahogany secretary-bookcase, small round tables, a cherry chifforobe-armoire. Set in front of the window in the left wall was a small mahogany Philadelphia card table, also much like the one in his room.

But upon this table was a laptop computer. And several feet in front of the table, lying on its side on a Persian throw rug, was a Chippendale chair. It was then Benjamin had noticed the detachable computer keyboard, also on the floor.

"I don't understand," Benjamin said. "If the laptop has its own keyboard, then why . . . ?"

"Exactly," said Wolfe. "And why is it on the floor."

"So this is where he had his heart attack?" Benjamin asked. Wolfe nodded. "And who found him?"

"Another excellent question," Wolfe said, smiling. "You've a nose for this sort of thing, as I suspected. Anyway, Terrill told me it was one of the other fellows, a Mrs. Gadenhower. She was apparently bringing him some books, something about a topic they'd discussed earlier the day of the . . . incident."

"And then she notified Mr. Terrill?"

"She didn't have to. From what Arthur told me, close on her heels was Hauser."

"Hauser?"

"Eric Hauser. In charge of security here at the Foundation. Most providential, his timely arrival. He prevented anything from being touched. Except, of course, the body."

"And where . . . ?"

"There's a fairly complete biology lab, with a storage freezer. Dr. Fletcher is laid out, very respectfully I might add, in there."

Benjamin frowned. "But isn't that . . . illegal? Shouldn't they have left his body here, for the police?"

Wolfe gave Benjamin one of his hooded, slightly disappointed looks.

"Given the Foundation's standing in the local environs, and the confidential nature of much that goes on here, Arthur assumed he would have a certain leeway in dealing with, as he so delicately called it, the 'incident.' However long is the arm of the law, the Foundation's reach is longer still."

"Well, I know the Foundation is influential, but this is a man's life. Well, a man's death."

"If you can't exercise influence over life *and* death, Benjamin, what good is such power?"

Benjamin had another question. "And why isn't this Hauser dealing with the investigation?"

Wolfe smiled again. "The Foundation may have some entitlement to do things in their own way and their own time, but there are limits. It's not some banana republic. Arthur understood that the government's going to want some assurances. There's a very large contract about to be finalized soon, and now's not the time for scandals."

"Who watches the watchers?"

"Something like that," said Wolfe.

"But Mr. Terrill said something about you already working for the Foundation. Isn't that—"

"That was some time ago, Benjamin," Wolfe cut him off. "Now, let's have a look around."

Wolfe stepped over to the chifforobe, opened it. There were two suits and half a dozen button-down shirts hanging neatly, another hanger with two almost identical ties, a pair of brown Florsheim shoes on the shelf. "Not exactly a *bon vivant*," he said. He opened the lower drawers of the chifforobe, shuffled through small, neat stacks of underwear, white T-shirts, argyle socks.

All this time Benjamin had been staring at the laptop computer. Finally Benjamin said, "Excuse me, Mr. Wolfe—"

"Samuel," said Wolfe, still rifling the drawers.

"I don't mean to be telling you how to do your job, but all this . . ." He waved vaguely toward the chifforobe, the rest of Fletcher's room. "I just don't see how this relates to finding leaks."

Wolfe answered him without standing up. "My dear boy, leaks come in all shapes and sizes, but ultimately they're like pets: they tend to wind up looking a lot like their masters. First we have to complete our portrait of the good Dr. Fletcher. Or the bad Dr. Fletcher, depending on what sort of picture emerges here," and he waved about the room.

"So that *is* why you're here," Benjamin said half to himself. "Look, Mr. Wolfe—"

"Samuel," Wolfe insisted again.

"I may not have talked to Jeremy in a while," Benjamin said skeptically, "but I just can't imagine him being some sort of . . . traitor. Is there any evidence he was?"

"None whatsoever," said Wolfe, finally finished with the drawers and standing up. "In all his work for the Foundation to date, Jeremy Fletcher seems to have been meticulous, insightful, dedicated. The one word that keeps cropping up about him is 'brilliant.'"

"I know." Benjamin frowned. "So you're saying if he *did* breach security, such an indiscretion would be . . ."

"Yes?" Wolfe looked at him quizzically.

"Well, meticulous. Brilliant."

"Give the lad a hand. And ergo, any such leak will be damned difficult to spot. So, the more careful we are now, in the beginning, the less likely we are to make false assumptions later on."

Benjamin looked down at the laptop again. "Well, if we're looking for leaks, shouldn't we examine his computer?" He reached out a hand to its keyboard.

Wolfe reached over and stopped his arm.

"Fingerprints?" asked Benjamin.

"Sort of," said Wolfe.

Benjamin looked to the keyboard on the floor. "And that one, too?"

"Yes. Let's get a pristine keyboard in here before we continue."

Wolfe went to the phone next to the bed. Using his handkerchief to pick up the small black receiver, he dialed a few digits, spoke to someone for a few moments, hung up, looking a little puzzled.

"Interesting," he said. "I just spoke to someone in technical services, asked them to bring a keyboard to the room."

"Don't they have one?" asked Benjamin.

"Oh, yes, they do," said Wolfe. He looked at Benjamin. "But he complained. Wanted to know what had happened to the other *two* they'd sent over."

"*Two?*" asked Benjamin. He looked about the room again. "But there's only the one on the floor."

"As I said, interesting."

Wolfe went into the hallway, brought back the small black briefcase Benjamin had noticed earlier. As he opened the briefcase, he pointed to the windows. "If you wouldn't mind, the curtains."

As Wolfe extracted something from the briefcase, Benjamin went to the two windows and drew the curtains closed. When he turned back, he saw that Wolfe was leaning over the laptop's keyboard with a small aerosol can.

He moved the can back and forth above the keys, a fine, white mist coming from the can's top. He put the can back in the briefcase, then brought out a small flashlight, but a rather strange one, with a rectangular blue plastic screen affixed over the lens.

"I thought that only worked for blood."

"The spray reacts to perspiration, not blood, but the principle is the same. Now," and Wolfe switched on the flashlight.

The laptop's keyboard reflected the black light dimly, the letters appearing as stark blue outlines against the dark keys.

"Nothing," said Wolfe, disappointed. He reached over and pressed the Power key of the laptop. There was a quiet whir as its hard drive spun up and the system messages moved across the screen. After a moment, a message appeared.

ENTER PASSWORD it read.

"Ah," said Wolfe. "The plot thickens."

At that moment there was a knock at the door. A young man was standing in the darkened doorway, a detachable computer keyboard in his hands. He looked around the room curiously. "Somebody called for this?" he asked.

"You said you'd already sent over two others?" Wolfe asked, accepting the keyboard.

"Well, yeah," the young man answered. "Dr. Fletcher said he didn't like using the laptop's. Said his wrists crimped on the edge. You know, carpel tunnel." The young man held up an arm, drooping his hand limply at the wrist.

"But he'd been using this," Wolfe pointed to the laptop, "for some time. Didn't he already have a detachable keyboard?"

"Yeah. But then yesterday afternoon he called over, said it was missing, could I bring him another one."

"That one?" Wolfe asked. He pointed to the keyboard on the floor.

"I guess so. I'd have to look at the serial number."

"All the keyboards' serial numbers are logged?" Wolfe asked.

"Computers, too. You know, Hauser—"

"Yes," interjected Wolfe. "And what time did Dr. Fletcher call you?"

"Uh, maybe three, three thirty, some time around then."

"One other question before you go. Did Dr. Fletcher's computer have access to the Internet?"

The boy smiled. "You're kidding, right?"

"Not at all," replied Wolfe coldly.

The boy looked nervous. "Sorry, I just thought everyone knew. Too much hush-hush stuff going on for just anybody to plug into the Internet.

You have to put in a special request, use a special computer, one with these hardened firewalls and protocol filters and 128 encryption—"

"All right," said Wolfe, patting the young man's shoulder. "Well, thank you very much. That's all we need for now."

The techie shrugged, went off down the hall.

Wolfe went to the table, set the new keyboard carefully in front of the laptop, and plugged its USB cable into the side of the computer.

"Well, now all we need is the password." He looked to the keyboard on the floor.

"You still haven't explained why it's on the floor," said Benjamin.

"Imagine Fletcher sitting in that chair." Wolfe motioned toward the tipped-over Chippendale. "Now imagine him typing. Suddenly his left arm goes numb, his chest cramps, he jerks back, knocking over the chair. . . . It must have been a massive coronary, to kill him so quickly. He's still gripping the side of the keyboard, and as he falls from the chair—"

"He takes the keyboard with him?" said Benjamin. "But that," he indicated the aerosol can in Wolfe's hand, "shouldn't work. If Dr. Fletcher had been using the keyboard all this time, wouldn't *all* the keys have fingerprints on them? How can we possibly know which ones were the password?"

"If Young Master Techie is telling the truth," said Wolfe, "and this isn't the keyboard originally registered to Dr. Fletcher, then yesterday would have been the first time he used it. And if I'm right about the most curious aspect of this entire incident, then perhaps his password was the only thing he managed to type."

"The *most* curious aspect?" asked Benjamin skeptically.

"Fletcher's age," Wolfe responded absentmindedly.

"His age?"

"Patience," said Wolfe, as if that answered Benjamin's question.

Wolfe hunched down over the keyboard and took the aerosol can, held it a few inches above the keyboard and, pressing the red tip down with his thumb, ran it slowly back and forth as he had with the laptop. As Wolfe shined the flashlight over the keyboard, several of the keys responded with a shiny smudge of eerie blue.

"Ah," he said. "We're in luck." He leaned back to the briefcase, took out a small spiral notepad and a felt-tip pen, handed them to Benjamin. "Write down what I dictate." Scanning the keyboard from left to right and top to bottom, Wolfe read off the glowing keys: "I, O, P, S, N."

"That's all?" Benjamin asked. "Nothing else? No numbers?"

Wolfe ran the black light over the keyboard again. "No, that appears to be all. Of course," and he switched off the flashlight, stood up, "that doesn't give us the order of the letters."

"Well, it's like a game of anagrams, isn't it," said Benjamin. He sat down on the bed, stared at the letters in the notepad. "I-O-P-S-N. Well," and he began writing combinations in the notepad, saying them out loud as he wrote them down. "Sopni, sonpi, sipno, sinpo, nospi, nopsi, nispo, nipso . . ."

"We're methodical, aren't we," said Wolfe.

Benjamin smiled nervously. "Frankly that's the only way I know how to do these things. The answers never jump out at me. I can't stand crossword puzzles . . . where was I . . . posni, pisno . . ."

Wolfe leaned over and took the notebook and pen from his hand. He wrote something, handed the pad back to Benjamin.

Benjamin read what he'd written.

"Poisn?" he asked.

"The fingerprints give us the letters, but not their order. Or their *frequency*."

"So . . ."

"So he might have used one of these letters more than once. And if he did . . . say the O," Wolfe added a letter to the last word Benjamin had written, gave the pen back to him.

"Poison," Benjamin read. He laughed. "Isn't that just a little too Agatha Christie?"

Wolfe shrugged. "It's the only combination so far that's actually a word. And there's only one way to verify it."

He stepped over to the small table, switched on a banker's lamp next to the computer, and raised his hands above the new keyboard like a maestro over a piano.

"Of course, three wrong entries and the computer will lock out his account, perhaps permanently. Well, here goes." And Wolfe tapped out the word P-O-I-S-O-N on the keyboard, placed his finger over the Return key—then struck it.

INVALID ENTRY—PLEASE ENTER PASSWORD read the screen.

"That's one," said Benjamin.

Wolfe turned to the window, threw open the curtain, and stood staring out.

Benjamin moved over to the table. He looked from the keyboard to his little notepad. He began writing combinations again, and after a few more attempts sighed.

"That's really the only word that makes sense. If he didn't use a word, just those letters in some random combination that only he knew . . ." He began scribbling again.

Meanwhile Wolfe was still staring out the window. "Unless it wasn't his password," he said faintly, almost to himself.

"Damn!" exclaimed Benjamin. He slapped his forehead. "Idiot!"

Wolfe didn't turn. "I hardly think that's called for, I'm just speculating . . ."

"No, no, not you. Me. What was Jeremy's profession?"

Wolfe turned and looked at him, as though Benjamin was a very slow child, indeed. "I told you, a statistician. But what does that—"

"As you said, we know the letters, just not their order. Or their *frequency.*" Then he held the pad up to Wolfe's face. "What do you think?"

Poisson was written there.

"Why would the O be the only multiple letter?" Benjamin asked. "And what better word to choose than the name of one of the most famous statisticians of all time, Siméon-Denis Poisson."

Wolfe smiled broadly, stepped aside from the table. "Be my guest," he said.

Benjamin leaned over and slowly tapped out the letters: P-O-I-S-S-O-N. He looked at Wolfe. Wolfe shrugged. Benjamin hit the Return key.

The screen went blank for a moment—then a desktop appeared with several icons. The black-and-white picture on the desktop was of a distinguished-looking gentleman with the flat, curled hair and stiff, formal clothes of the Empire period.

"Greetings, Monsieur Poisson," said Wolfe, patting Benjamin's back.

Benjamin looked at the single icon on the desktop, a folder labeled "TEACUP-6."

"Teacup?" Benjamin turned to Wolfe. "Whatever that is, it's the only thing here."

"Well, open it."

Benjamin shrugged, double-clicked on the TEACUP-6 icon.

After a short delay, a splash screen appeared that read *Text Entry, Analysis, Conversion and Utilization Program—Version 6.0.*

"TEACUP 6," said Wolfe, smiling. "Fletcher was British, after all."

Benjamin was watching a small progress bar that was slowly expanding. "I remember Jeremy talking about this, back in college. A program that could convert text to a kind of mathematics. But I had no idea he'd kept with it . . ." And then he stopped. "I don't believe it."

Wolfe stepped over behind him. "What?"

Benjamin was pointing to the computer screen.

ENTER PASSWORD FOR TEACUP INITIALIZATION it read.

And beneath it was a small box with a cursor that was blinking steadily. Patiently.

Wolfe sighed, walked over and sat down heavily on the bed.

"Didn't Dr. Fletcher also have an office here at the Foundation?" Benjamin asked.

"Yes," said Wolfe. "I looked over it first thing I arrived. There were some books, mostly reference materials, a blackboard filled with equations. But nothing so convenient as a little Post-it note with 'Teacup password' written on it in bright red letters."

Then Benjamin noticed the icons on the bottom menu bar. The one for the Trash was bulging.

"Here," he said. "He threw a file away, but didn't delete it."

He opened the trash. Inside its window was a single file, marked "Untitled."

"Open it," Wolfe said eagerly.

Benjamin clicked on the "Untitled" file.

Four lines of text appeared, divided neatly into a table.

Contact Name	Contact Date	Contact Response
F. Myorkin Free Russia News SP	10/1	10/16 — Cnfrmd Sznri 55. Ck CSA archv.
N. Orlova Russian Cultural Center DC	10/17	
B. Wainwright LoC DC	10/20	10/20 — arrvs tmrrw. TG.
A. Sikorsky Georgetown U. DC		

"I'll be damned," said Wolfe.

"My god," Benjamin said. "Those Russian names." He swallowed hard, turned and looked at Wolfe. "It appears I was wrong about Jeremy."

"It's not that," Wolfe said absently.

"What do you mean? Isn't this list pretty much a smoking gun?"

Wolfe smiled down at him. "So *you're* part of a Russian spy ring? And this F. Myorkin is, I would hazard, a journalist working for the *Free Russia News*. And Orlova at the Russian Cultural Center? Hardly FSB headquarters in Moscow."

Benjamin looked back to the list. "And this Sikorsky?"

"Ah," nodded Wolfe, "*that* one I most definitely know. Anton Sikorsky, of Georgetown University. His name on this list guarantees it has nothing to do with Russian spies."

Benjamin turned back to the screen. "Then what do you make of these notes? Is that a code?"

"A crude one, perhaps. Fletcher was, among other things, a computer programmer. Programmers have a habit of condensing text by eliminating the vowels. That line by Fyorkin could be something like 'Confirmed *Something* 55.' And if FRN is still operating in St. Petersburg, then that's the SP. And if *that's* correct, there is a particularly interesting archive in St. Petersburg, the Central State Archives, where they house all the KGB's records."

"Jesus," exhaled Benjamin. "What was Jeremy doing?"

"Whatever it was," Wolfe said, "this Fyorkin's response seems to have sparked his interest in contacting other people. It's immediately after he hears from him that he contacts this Orlova at the RCC. And then you. But apparently not Anton. Not yet anyway. Perhaps he simply ran out of time . . ."

Benjamin glanced back at the screen. "So if you're reading his code right, his note by my name would read as . . ."

" 'Arrives tomorrow,' " said Wolfe.

"And the TG?" asked Benjamin.

Wolfe smiled ruefully. "I would suspect it meant 'Thank god.' "

With that, Wolfe reached down, closed the file, carefully removed it from the computer trash, and shut off the laptop.

"Well," he said with finality, "I believe we've extracted everything we can from the scene of the . . . incident, that is without this TEACUP password. We need sustenance. After all, empty stomachs make for empty brains."

He bent and began packing the can and flashlight back into the briefcase. When he was done he turned to Benjamin and said, "Ready?"

Benjamin nodded, then said, "I was just wondering."

"What?"

"At that last moment, as he died. I wonder what Jeremy was feeling."

Wolfe snapped the briefcase closed. "Regret, I imagine."

"Regret?" Benjamin asked.

"Yes." Wolfe moved into the hallway. "That he hadn't finished his work."

Benjamin followed him. Wolfe pulled the door closed and locked it. He took a small roll of transparent tape out of his pocket, tore a one-inch strip from it, and pressed it firmly against the top of the doorjamb.

"Now," he sighed, "let's see about a little eye-opener, shall we?"

CHAPTER 5

The rather large man sat on the bed, reading a brochure. This seemed an odd thing to do, given that there was a smaller man on the bed next to him, lying faceup, struggling to breathe.

The brochure was all about the Winter Ice Festival in St. Petersburg. It explained to visitors the history behind the commemorative Ice Palace that was being constructed in the square near the Mars Field.

> In 1740, the Empress Anna Ivanovna, Ruler of All the Russias, decreed that a palace was to be constructed in her capital of St. Petersburg. But this was to be a very special palace; a palace made entirely of ice! Complete with miniature rooms, furniture, statues—even a royal bedchamber with bed. All made of ice! And when it was finished, its first occupants were nearly also its first victims. Displeased with the conduct of one of her ministers, the empress had forced him to marry a female serf in that very ice palace, and then demanded that they spend their wedding night on that bed of ice. They both nearly froze to death!

The large man snorted, as though amused at such a deadly caprice.

Meanwhile, the struggles of the man on the bed had grown considerably weaker, his breath now coming in sharp, infrequent gasps.

The large man sighed, stood up, walked to the window. His round head and rounded shoulders made him seem bearlike. He was dressed in a nondescript blue nylon leisure suit and white sneakers. His only distinguishing feature, other than his bulk, was a streak of white in otherwise dark brown hair.

Beyond the window, the modern St. Petersburg skyline was still beautiful. One could see all the way down Nevsky Prospekt to the dual snakes of lights lining the Neva River. During the day, from this vantage, one could make out the Winter Palace, sometimes even the Peter and Paul Fortress across the Neva.

The bearlike man stepped over to the bed, lowered his bulky frame onto it, which made the mattress bounce—as well as the now-quiet body lying across it, which now looked merely passed-out drunk; an impression reinforced by the near-empty bottle of Koskova vodka on the nightstand. The heavyset man reached into his pocket, took out a pair of latex gloves, slipped them with some effort over his thick hands. Then he reached over and took the vodka bottle and the half-full glass next to it. He stood, walked with them into the bathroom, where he poured the remaining vodka from both down the sink. He used a washcloth to wipe them clean, then, holding the bottle and glass gingerly, walked back into the room and set them carefully back on the nightstand.

He surveyed the room: a suitcase on top of the dresser, a small valise leaning against the closet.

He went through the suitcase first. Finding nothing of interest, he indifferently repacked the clothes, set the suitcase where he'd found it.

Taking the valise to the bed, he unzipped it. Tucked in a pocket was a Russian passport. The name there was just as it should be.

Fyodor Ivanovich Myorkin.

Behind the passport were press credentials in Fyodor's name from *Svobodniye Rossia Novosti*, the *Free Russia News*.

He found the journalist's notebook, flipped it open. It was filled with notes from Fyodor's visit that day to the Tsentral'nyi gosudarstvennyi arkhiv Sankt-Peterburga, the Central State Archives of St. Petersburg, housed in its squat, Soviet-style blockhouse on Varfolomeevskaia.

He nodded, satisfied, and pocketed the notebook. He was about to zip the valise closed when he noticed a letter, tucked down inside a pocket. He extracted the envelope, pulled out the single page, careful not to wrinkle it.

It was handwritten in Russian. He scanned the text quickly. It was from an American academic doing work on the Holodnaya Voyna, the Cold War. The academic wrote that he'd read some of Myorkin's earlier articles exposing secrets of Soviet policies; then he asked politely if Myorkin had ever, in his own research, come across any references to something called *Borba s tenyu*?

The man read the contents again, his lips moving as he read, committing the important parts to memory. He was about to tuck the letter back into its envelope when he thought to check the signature at the bottom of the letter and find out who this Americanski was, writing to the late Mr. Myorkin.

Jeremy Fletcher, it read.

He repeated the name to himself. Then he replaced the letter in the valise, glanced about the room once more, and, with a last nod to the peaceful Fyodor on the bed, he opened the door, checked the hallway, and left.

CHAPTER 6

Natalya hadn't been able to resist. She'd puttered around her apartment in the morning, watering plants, cleaning dishes, looking through mail . . . all in an attempt to distract herself from thinking about the strange letter she'd received from Dr. Jeremy Fletcher. All to no avail.

But before she'd left her apartment, Yuri had called to invite her to dinner with some of the embassy staff. They were going to the Russkiy Dom restaurant, over on Connecticut. Was she interested? Under pressure and wishing to stay in Yuri's good graces, she finally said yes, perhaps.

So eventually she found herself at the embassy, almost alone. The white walls and shining stone floors created a sense of cavernous emptiness. Yet once there and with Fletcher's letter before her, she still wanted to postpone her investigation. She decided to check on some of the details for the embassy's reception for the Bolshoi the coming Monday evening.

They were using an American caterer rather than the embassy's own kitchen—money had changed hands there, she was sure—and as soon as she looked at the menu faxed over from the caterer's the day before, she knew there was a problem.

Borsch was on the menu. Which for Americans, she knew, meant a watery beet soup with a mass of sour cream dumped on top.

That wasn't borsch. At least not Russian borsch.

Russian borsch was more of a stew, with beef, onions, potatoes, peppers. . . . How, she wondered, did Americans think Russians had survived on beets in hot water?

And then she saw that caviar was also on the menu—no doubt served with chopped eggs, onions, chives, black olives, and probably half a dozen other garnishes, all of which were another American invention—like chop suey—and there for people who actually didn't like the taste of fish eggs.

But true Russians did, and enjoyed their caviar with nothing more complicated than hard bread and butter. And they probably would serve red caviar as well as black, but unless the red caviar was sevruga, it would be an insult at such an important dinner.

A half hour later she hung up the phone, having tactfully if forcefully explained all this to a Mr. Foy, the manager of the catering service.

"Well, of course," he'd said finally, exasperation evident, "if that's what you want. We strive to be ethnically authentic."

Ethnically authentic? The Soviet Union may have fallen, but she was sure Mr. Foy thought of Russians with the same old Cold War clichés: borsch-slurping, vodka-swilling, caviar-snob savages who just happened to possess nuclear weapons.

Would Americans and Russians ever truly understand one another? Was that even *possible* between two such vastly different cultures, one formed by Enlightenment logic, the other steeped in centuries of Pagan mysticism?

She realized she was still distracting herself from Fletcher's letter.

She carefully unfolded Fletcher's letter and read it again. Perhaps she was reluctant to dive into it because he had provided so very little to go on: he was doing research on the Cold War period, specifically 1960–1970; he was particularly interested in documents concerning Russian nuclear war strategies—a word, curiously, he'd translated as *stzenariy,* which meant something more like screenplay, rather than the more literal *strategija*; she shrugged and read on—and he wondered if Natalya had any knowledge of a particular book about such *stzenarii*, something called *Borba s tenyu* . . . though, he admitted, he wasn't sure if it was a book, a report, a memorandum . . . or even if that was the title at all.

Well, the subject and period provided her with at least one clue: if whatever Fletcher was after had been published in the Soviet Union between 1960 and 1970, and it was about Soviet nuclear arms strategy, then it couldn't possibly have been an *official* Soviet publication. So it could only have been *samizdat*: something produced unofficially by one of the dozens of small illegal presses run from basements by brave, idealistic dissidents—which would only make tracking it down all the more difficult.

The first reference she discovered wasn't a book at all, but rather a film; a silent film at that, titled *Borba za Ultimatum,* a title translated into English as *The Fight for the Ultimatum Factory.* But it was much too early, 1923.

Natalya thought for a moment. The word *borba* was old Russian; in fact, its roots could be traced to the Serbo-Croatian Борба, which meant simply "struggle." So she tried the search from that angle.

This soon revealed that *Borba* had been the title of a newspaper in Belgrade, printed by the League of Communists of Yugoslavia. Nuclear secrets published in a Party paper in Belgrade? Unlikely. But then perhaps *tenyu,* shadow or shade, was the pseudonym of a dissident writer for the paper, someone using the Party organ to expose its own secrets?

She wasted a full hour looking through the archives of the newspaper *Borba,* searching for any mention of *tenyu.* But most of the archived material was either numbingly routine or the raving paranoid fantasies that passed for commentary during those dark, suspicious years: articles about Americans needing to buy their oxygen from vending machines, being thrown out of the windows of hospitals for not paying their bills . . . amusing stuff, but hardly Cold War intrigue.

She sensed this was a wild-goose chase, as the Americans put it—though she'd never been able to understand why the goose had to be wild; was there such a thing as a tame goose? Did early Americans keep such geese as pets, teach them tricks, put them in circuses, like Russians with their bears?

There was so much cultural history beneath almost every colloquialism— so much meaning that was simply taken for granted—it sometimes astounded her that people from two different cultures could communicate at all. And then sometimes, too, she wondered if they ever truly did.

She thought back to her one brief affair with an American. He'd been a speechwriter for the White House. She remembered one very early morning in particular, a discussion that had seemed unimportant at the time, but had by now become a symbol for the cultural gulf between them.

They'd been lying in bed after making love, smoking, the ashtray set on the gold satin sheet—she brought them out especially for his visits—when he'd started complaining about his job.

"It's difficult to keep coming up with phrases that say much but mean nothing."

She'd smiled. "Mr. Gorbachev was a master at such speech. We called it *sotryasat vozdukh,* shaking the air."

"Well, he's much admired in this country," said her lover, exhaling smoke.

"And hated in Russia," said Natalya.

He had suddenly grown serious. "The Soviet Union was rotten to the core. It had to collapse. He was just trying to limit the damage."

"And of course the Americans did not benefit from this 'damage control.'"

He sighed. "There you go again, with those paranoid theories. Did you ever consider that sometimes there is no *plot*? Sometimes, as we say, shit happens?"

And sometimes, she'd thought, *shit very* conveniently *happens.* But she hadn't said anything, not wanting to start another argument.

And eventually it was such arguments that ended the affair.

To her mind, most Americans were naïve children, playing at world politics as though the Bad Guys always wore black hats, like in their cowboy fairy tales. Growing up during Soviet times, even in their sunset years, had taught her that enemies were not always so clearly identifiable; that, more often than not, the hats they wore were gray, not black.

"Gray Cardinals" they were called in her culture; the true power that stood always behind the throne, whispering into the ears of those seemingly in charge, all the while remaining invisible.

The faint bluish glow of the computer screen suddenly seemed irritating, her eyes unable to focus on the multicolored symbols.

Natalya leaned back and stretched, trying to work some of the tension out of her back. No one had returned to work in the last hour. Apparently the weekend staff was taking a more traditionally Soviet lunch break. She remembered what a friend had said of those days: "We pretend to work, and they pretend to pay us."

She walked out of the small glass-walled office, saw no one, then wandered over to the window and gazed out on Wisconsin Avenue. Even on a Saturday it was filled with taxicabs and heavy traffic. She looked up to the clear blue sky, a crisp early fall day. The row of maple trees across Wisconsin were crowned in fall colors, the distant pinnacle of the Washington Monument a stark intrusion into the cloudless sky.

The scene made her want to give up the search now and leave, perhaps walk over to the Mall, visit the Lincoln Memorial, a diversion she always found refreshing. There was something so comforting, yet so tragic, in that immense statue's face that she always felt both inspired and humbled in its presence.

Of course tragedy was something Russians knew a great deal about. In fact, she'd often thought that was what most mystified Americans about her countrymen: their ability, even their *need,* to treat sadness as an emotion like any other, as something necessary to life, like joy or determination. She'd voiced that idea once to a counterpart in the American embassy, and he'd replied, "Oh, I see. So Russians aren't happy unless they've got something to be depressed about?"

Perhaps there was something to that. She felt in her own heart the need to know and appreciate both sides of her emotions, both the light of pleasure as well as its shadow.

And at that thought her mind suddenly went back to her search. So far she'd been focusing on the word *borba.* What if she took *tenyu,* "shadow" or "shade"—there was really no distinction in Russian—as the key?

With renewed energy she went back to her desk. She sat down and immediately began typing.

And immediately she got a hit: another film, this one titled *Бой с тенью* (*Boy s tenyu*). But it wasn't the film itself that had caught her attention, it was the English translation of the title.

Shadow Boxing.

"Shadow boxing" made a lot more metaphorical sense than "fighting with shadows" or "warring with shade."

Or did it?

After all, besides fighting and struggle, *borba* could just as easily be interpreated as "war." *Borba s tenyu.* Warring with shadows? Or, given that the word "warring" didn't exist in Russian, what about the simpler version?

Shadow war.

It occurred to Natalya she should scour the archives for a Russian book that had been translated into English as *Shadow War,* regardless of its original name in Russian.

She glanced out the window and saw that the outside light was fading as evening approached. Her second wind of curiosity was wearing off. But she had time for one more attempt.

She tapped at the keyboard until *English Title = Shadow War* was glowing in green letters on her screen. She hit Return.

Immediately there was a result. At first she was surprised by what she read; but then she realized it confirmed her first intuition.

Доступ в архив ограничен read the screen.

Restricted archives.

In bright red letters. Blinking bright red letters.

"Everything all right, Natalya Nikolayevna?"

The voice startled her. She looked up to see one of the guards standing in the doorway. He looked quite threatening in his gray-and-olive camouflage uniform, a small pistol strapped at his waist.

"Yes. Just working." She smiled, and shifted so her shoulders would cover the computer screen.

"On a beautiful Saturday afternoon?" said the guard. "A pretty woman like you should be out enjoying herself, not cooped up in this mausoleum with an old fossil like me."

"Is there a problem?" she asked somewhat curtly. She didn't want him to linger long enough to become curious.

He looked confused. "No, of course not. I just—"

"I am very busy," she said.

He nodded. "Of course." He decided to counter her frostiness by asserting his authority. "But be certain to sign out when you leave. In these days—"

"I will." Now she smiled, hoping that would satisfy him. "You have my word."

He nodded at her, continued on his rounds.

She turned back to the computer screen. The red "Restricted Archives" message was still blinking. She canceled it out, then began filling out the form on the screen that would submit a request for access to the restricted archives; permission that could only come from the Ministry of Internal Affairs, but which would really come from the FSB. Which could take anywhere from a week to forever.

She thought of Yuri. Now she would *definitely* have to accept that dinner invitation.

And then she thought of one additional source to which she might turn for help.

Her father.

If this book—if it was a book—had something to do with the Cold War, and *if* it had in fact been somehow leaked to the *samizdat* press . . . well, then, it might be something her father had found in his own searching. Not that he would necessarily tell her about it. But she had nothing to lose by asking—other, that is, than suffering another of his inscrutable silences. And she hadn't called him in two weeks. This would give her an excuse.

She logged off and watched the screen go black. She put Fletcher's letter back in her desk drawer and locked it, then reached over and switched off the lamp on her desk.

She had taken her purse and coat and turned to leave when she paused.

Taking her keys out again, she unlocked the drawer, took out Fletcher's letter, and put it in her purse.

She had no idea why she did this; it just felt right. Then she shrugged on
her coat and walked down the hall to the elevator, her very non-Soviet high-
heeled shoes creating echoes as they clicked on the white-and-brown-veined
marble floor.

CHAPTER 7

Benjamin and Wolfe were sitting in the dining hall—a one-story brick building behind the manse and across a collegelike quad of open grass, trees, and cobblestone footpaths. Wolfe called it "the Trough." He'd brought Benjamin here after their examination of Fletcher's room so that he might listen to Benjamin's account of his "homework" with "some modicum of civilized comfort," i.e., a glass of orange juice laced with bourbon.

"Well, to begin with the most interesting, the book on Bainbridge, you need first to know that Hessiah Philadelphia Bainbridge was either a fanatic, or a visionary." Benjamin paused to sip his own black coffee, still feeling the effects of his nightcap. "Depends on which of the Puritan factions you asked."

"Factions?" Wolfe raised an eyebrow. "I think of the Puritans as all equally . . . well, puritanical."

"Not so." Benjamin shook his head. "There were left and right wings, just like political parties. Puritans like Cotton Mather, for instance, were ultraconservative and demanded absolute adherence to doctrine. It was Matherites that conducted the Salem witch trials. But on the other hand, there were Puritans like Jonathan Edwards, who believed in a certain individual liberty when it came to knowing God. And then on the far left were the Antinomians, sort of hippie Puritans, who believed in all sorts of things—

almost all of which the Boston Elders called anathema. Which is why they were eventually exiled from Massachusetts."

"And this Hessiah Bainbridge, he was one of these Antinomials?"

"Antino*mians*. Not exactly. But when Anne Hutchinson and the other Antinomian leaders were sent packing, Bainbridge and his congregation went with them, to New Jersey. It isn't exactly clear why, except that he was a passionate advocate of the Prayer Town movement."

"Prayer Towns?"

Benjamin warmed to his topic.

"Prayer Towns were a revolutionary idea, at least for the period. You've heard of Eleazar Wheelock?"

"Well," Wolfe demurred, "if he had anything to do with Wheelock College in Boston, I have."

"Yes, same family. You know the little ditty about him? 'Oh, Eleazar Wheelock was a very pious man, he went into the wilderness to teach the Indian'?"

"Uh, no," said Wolfe, "can't say as I do." And he raised an eyebrow as though Benjamin had gone slightly mad.

Benjamin saw he was being kidded, smiled, went on.

"Anyway, he and Robert Gray and Hessiah Bainbridge all shared a dream: to build a whole town where the Native Americans could come to learn the English language and customs—and of course be converted to Christianity."

"Of course," nodded Wolfe.

"But Bainbridge was a lot more enlightened than most. He once wrote the Puritans should 'give the savages Civilitie for their bodies before Christianitie for their soules.' He even dared suggest they weren't just savages, that the Puritans might learn something from *them*."

"Heresy!" pronounced Wolfe.

"Listen, it was all a helluva lot more enlightened than what the Matherites had in mind for the Natives. They preached about converting them, but it was no secret they'd have been just as happy to see them simply disappear. And if they had to help *make* them disappear, well, that was God's will."

"So that's what this Ginsburg book is about, this conflict between Bainbridge and those other Puritans in favor of genocide?"

"Well," Benjamin shook his head, "no, not exactly. That's just background. The book is about Hessiah's son, Harlan Phlegon Bainbridge."

"*Phlegon?*" Wolfe whistled. "My, they certainly had a way with names back then."

"It's a powerful name indeed. From the book of Romans, for 'burning zeal.' And according to Ginsburg, the name fit. Harlan kept at his father's work until he actually convinced a wealthy New Jersey merchant, Henry Coddington, to finance his father's idea."

"And where was this utopia constructed?"

Benjamin frowned. "No one's really certain, that's part of its mystery. It was completely wiped out some time in 1675, burned to the ground, by Wampanoag Indians. But it was somewhere out here, in western Massachusetts."

"And now the sixty-four-thousand-dollar question: whoever this Bainbridge was, why was Fletcher interested in him? Still think it had something to do with the Indian wars?"

"Native-Settler wars," Benjamin corrected, then frowned. "Ginsburg's book does make reference to one John Sassamon, someone connected to both Bainbridge and King Philip's War."

"King Philip's War? My Colonial history's a little rusty. Which king was that?"

"It wasn't really a king, it was the settlers' name for Metacom, chief of the Wampanoags, the most powerful tribe in the region. And King Philip's War was the bloodiest of the time. More people per capita were killed than in any other American war, even World War II; and it was the death knell for Native Americans, their Waterloo. They never recovered that kind of power or unity again. And this Sassamon and the destruction of the Bainbridge Plantation were involved in starting that war. So yes, *normally* I'd say that's why Jeremy was interested in Bainbridge."

"Normally?" Wolfe pried.

"Well . . ." Benjamin chose his words carefully. "There are several very strange things about this book. For one, I'd never heard of it, and as far as I know, neither had my father, even though he was much more the expert on the early Puritans. I need to read it again more carefully. I was falling asleep last night and—"

"Well, enough strangeness for now," Wolfe interrupted him, rising. "Let's deal with something definite."

He reached into his pocket and extracted a small appointment book that he tossed on the table in front of Benjamin.

"This was in Fletcher's office," Wolfe said. "It's a list of the people Fletcher had met with here at the Foundation. Or planned to meet with, before his . . . accident."

Benjamin opened the book, flipped past dozens of empty pages until he came to the pages for that week.

- *Monday, 10:00 A.M.—E. Stoltz*
- *Thursday, 1:00 P.M.—E. Gadenhower*
- *Friday, 10:00 A.M.—G. Soderbergh*

"Gadenhower," read Benjamin. "Isn't that the woman who found his . . ."

"Yes," said Wolfe simply.

"And these other names?" asked Benjamin.

"Here, read for yourself." Wolfe handed him a brochure about the Foundation that listed the various fellows in residence with brief summaries of their credentials and research.

Benjamin discovered that Dr. Edward J. Stoltz was an historian and the official curator of the Foundation's collection of rare manuscripts, paintings, and other art; that Dr. Gudrün Soderbergh was an expert on "international relations and counterterrorism policy"; and that Mrs. Edith Gadenhower (no "Dr." before her name) was reported as "working on an innovative research project involving the social matrixes of bee colonies."

"While I can possibly understand his interest in Ms. Soderbergh," Wolfe said, staring intently at his empty drink, "I find an art historian and a bee-keeper hard to explain. But that isn't the question I find most perplexing."

"No?"

"Fletcher's research, whatever it was, apparently didn't involve the necessity of interviewing *anyone* at the Foundation in the entire six months he was working here. And then suddenly, upon receipt of this letter from Myorkin, he hurriedly arranges three interviews, writes to this Orlova, and discovers a burning need for your rather limited expertise. No offense."

"None taken. That's the question I've been asking ever since he called. Why me?"

Wolfe shook his head. "As central as that question may be to you, it is still *not* the most important question. In fact, none of these curious connections are."

"Then what on earth is?"

"As I said, Fletcher's been hard at work at the Foundation for six months, and prior to that, for many years. Yet among his things in his office or on his computer there isn't a half-finished white paper, notes for a journal article, an unfinished book . . . nothing." Wolfe raised his eyebrows. "You see? Where on earth are the fruits of all that labor?"

CHAPTER 8

Wolfe decided it was best they begin interviewing Jeremy's appointments, to see if the focus of his discussions could shed any light on either his sudden interest in art, bees, and Puritans or the direction (or for that matter whereabouts) of all his important work.

They decided to begin where Jeremy had ended, with Mrs. Gadenhower. They learned she had a laboratory in the biology building—one of the few modern structures on the Foundation's campus: a low, functional, nondescript, white stone edifice that appeared to have been constructed in the 1960s. They entered and, tracking the laboratory numbers down black-and-white linoleum-tiled hallways, eventually came to room 133.

Edith Gadenhower was an older woman, at least seventy, her face and manner of expressing herself graced with wonderful continuity. Yet, for all her tea-and-crumpets charm, Benjamin felt there was something undeniably *predatory* about the small, rotund old woman. Simply put, she gave Benjamin the willies.

Or perhaps it was her surroundings. Oddly, given the modern fixtures—the aluminum counters, Plexiglas cabinets, even racks of electronic equipment Benjamin didn't associate with bee research—the atmosphere in Mrs. Gadenhower's lab was somehow Gothic. Perhaps it was all the test tubes, vials of colored liquids, and specimen jars containing the preserved dead bodies of various kinds of bees.

After showing them several large hives that were intimidating in their frantic and indifferent activity—all from behind the safety of Plexiglas shields—she invited them to sit down. They pulled up two nearby lab stools.

"I can offer you tea," she said, "or there is a regrettable imitation of coffee." She pointed to a small automatic pot jammed in between test tubes and Bunsen burners. They both declined. "Well, then," she said, settling herself on another small stool that seemed hardly able to support her bulk, "how may I help you?"

Wolfe explained that her name had been on Jeremy Fletcher's appointment list, and they were interested in what they'd discussed. Especially as she was the one who'd discovered his body.

"Poor boy," she frowned. "So very young for heart troubles."

"I agree," Wolfe said with a certain harshness. "But we're particularly interested in what he might have said of his own research."

"Nothing," said Edith simply.

"Nothing?" echoed Wolfe.

"I didn't ask. One becomes so focused, you see, on one's own interests. And there really wasn't time. The lad was so very interested in my little fellows, we talked of nothing else."

"Well, perhaps you could hazard a guess, then, Mrs. Gadenhower."

"Edith," she prompted.

"Edith. Excuse me. What have bees to do with nuclear war?"

If Wolfe had hoped to shock her, he was disappointed. She took the question quite in stride. "Oh, a very great deal, I suppose. If you look at it from the right angle."

"And what angle is that?"

"Why, Dr. Fletcher's angle, of course."

"You mean, statistics?"

"What are statistics but a way to tidy up disorderly numbers?" she said firmly. "To the uninitiated, a bee colony looks quite disorderly. But if one stands back, as it were, for perspective, then one sees the method in that apparent madness."

She settled herself in preparation for a short lecture. "The analytical study of bees goes back quite some time. As early as 1705, a Mr. Bernard Mandeville wrote a wonderful book called *The Fable of the Bees; or, Private Vices, Publick Benefits*. Mr. Mandeville suggested that bee colonies thrive as long as they are organized around *in*equity. The workers only work, the gatherers only gather, the queen only lays . . . you see?"

"Well, yes, but how does this . . ."

"Dr. Fletcher had his own name for Mr. Mandeville's organized inequity. He called it 'swarm intelligence.'" She paused to take a sip of her tea. "And apparently there are those in the Pentagon who believe this idea holds some promise for, what do they call it? Nanotechnology?"

"You mean," interjected Benjamin, "what appears to be random behavior really isn't?"

"Quite the opposite," corrected Edith, smiling sweetly. "What *appears* centrally organized is often in fact merely the result of thousands of tiny, overlapping little routines. There is no controlling mind—counter to what most people think of the queen—but still an overall purpose is achieved. It's really quite remarkable. Would you like the same demonstration I gave Dr. Fletcher?"

They both nodded. Edith roused herself from the stool, led them to one row of hives behind their Plexiglas shields. The bright fluorescent lights in the ceiling made everything seem abnormally white, and the hum of activity from behind the shields was like a muted dynamo.

Arriving before one of the bee chambers, Mrs. Gadenhower turned to them.

"After studying the dance that bees perform when they return from finding a food source, what is called their 'waggle dance,' I decided to see if the bees could give flight instructions for the colony to navigate to a fight as well as a find. Could this honey-dance serve as a bee warning system, a kind of communal radar?"

They nodded and she continued.

"Actually, I must give credit for the idea to what happened in Poland, immediately following Chernobyl. Beekeepers there began to notice that foraging bees were being stung to death by their *own* colonies, immediately after they returned home. The other bees could somehow sense they'd been irradiated, you see, and were a danger to the colony. Well, if looked at politically, it seemed a lesson in the creation of enemies to benefit the community. The radioactive bees became a threat that the colony organized to fight, in order to survive. So I decided to re-create those conditions. But without the radiation, of course."

As she spoke she set a container on the counter that contained a single live bee. She took a pair of forceps from the counter and, lifting the lid of the container slightly, inserted the forceps and very gently grabbed the bee with them and took it out of the container.

"Now, my methods may seem rather gruesome, but I assure you, bees have absolutely no equivalent to our sensation of pain."

She paused, the bee struggling in the grip of the forceps. Then she took a pair of tweezers and, one at a time, neatly plucked the wings from the bee. She stepped over to the shield and placed her hand on the handle of a small trapdoor set into the shield. She opened the trapdoor about an inch, put the forceps and bee into the chamber, dropped the bee so that it landed squarely in the middle of one of the honeycombs, then snapped the trapdoor closed.

"You see the poor fellow moving across the backs of its fellows?" They could see the wounded bee crawling across others in the hive, in great agitation. "This is much as any worker does when returning with the report of a find. And, just as in that dance of honey, this dance of, well, dismemberment includes pauses where, normally, the bee would stop and hum." Here, she emitted a quite cheery little hum. "You see?

"But of course this bee has nothing to hum with, which makes its dance quite exceptional . . . see there, now?" She pointed again into the chamber. She noticed their reluctance. "Come closer, gentlemen. I assure you there's no danger."

They moved closer to the shield and leaned in. The bee she'd placed in the hive was scrambling around now in awkward figure eights, and the other bees seemed to be taking notice of it. They formed an uneven circle around the wounded bee, a small space cleared of contact.

"Now, there certainly is no denying the vigor of the wounded bee's dance. I was looking for some indication of how the communal sense of bees would respond to a purely individual situation: a single, wounded bee, speaking energetically, if somewhat ungrammatically, of its own dire predicament."

She turned to face them, held up a finger in emphasis.

"*But* what I had failed to take into account was Mr. Mandeville's book and his idea that there *is* no individual among bees. A thing exists to them as something that either benefits the entire swarm or threatens it. There is no in between."

By now the circle around the wounded bee was growing smaller, tightening around the space in which it frantically gyrated.

"You see, gentlemen, how they first move away, then close in? Well, at first I was so taken by this response of the swarm, I forgot about my wounded bee. And when I remembered him again, he wasn't there. He had simply disappeared."

As she said this, the two men looked into the chamber—and indeed, the wingless bee was nowhere to be seen among the swarm.

She leaned toward them.

"Here," she said. "Have a look." She handed Wolfe a large magnifying glass. He placed it against the shield, put his eye close.

"I don't—," he said.

"Look carefully," she said.

Wolfe paused, then. "Is that—?"

"Yes, indeed," said Edith. "Mr. Wainwright, would you care to see?"

Wolfe backed away, handed Benjamin the magnifying lens. Benjamin placed it against the shield, as he'd seen Wolfe do.

It took a moment for his eyes to adjust to the magnified bees, their compound eyes enormous, the thousands of hairs along their bodies and legs. Then he noticed something alien in the mandibles of one bee. He looked to Edith.

"What I saw then is what you see now," she said, looking into his eyes. "Bits and pieces of my wingless sacrifice in the mandibles of other bees: here a leg, there a section of stripped fuzz . . ."

Benjamin handed the glass back, not wishing to look again.

"You see, gentlemen? They've quite literally torn him limb from limb."

She crossed her hands against her white lab smock, waiting for their response.

They were both silent for a moment. Then Wolfe asked, "And you gave this same . . . demonstration to Dr. Fletcher?"

"Oh yes. He was *intensely* interested. Which is why later, when I thought of the Mandeville book, I decided to trot it over to him. And that's when I discovered the *corpus delicti.*"

"Well," began Wolfe. And then he seemed to have nothing to say, still shaken by the demonstration. "Well, Edith, thank you for this . . . enlightening session." They started to leave, then Wolfe stopped and turned to her.

"One other question." He flashed that charming smile. "What kinds of bees are you working with?"

"Why, *Apis mellifera scutellata,* of course. They're such an . . . energetic species. One tends to get results faster."

"Apis . . . ?" said Wolfe vaguely.

"*Mellifera scutellata,*" completed Edith. "For *Africanized* bee. Of course they're popularly known as killer bees, but that name, as regards their dealings with human beings, is quite ridiculous. Of course, in this instance," and she motioned toward the chamber where they'd just witnessed the almost ritualistic cannibalization of the de-winged bee, "it seems appropriate, doesn't it?" She smiled.

"Doesn't that . . . ," Benjamin began. "Well, aren't you a little . . . frightened to be working with them?"

"I've been working with these little fellows for quite some time, young man. And just in case—" She pointed to a large red button set into the wall next to the lab door.

"An alarm?" asked Wolfe.

"That button activates an alarm, yes, but it also causes a gas to be sprayed into the laboratory. From those." She pointed to the ceiling, to what looked like fire sprinklers.

"But wouldn't the gas—," began Wolfe.

"It's instantly fatal to the bees, but merely irritating to humans. A bit like tear gas, I understand." She saw the looks of doubt on their faces. "Don't worry about *me*, gentlemen. I respect my bees, but I don't fool myself that they respect me."

"Yes," said Wolfe. "Well, thank you, Edith. Thank you for your time."

"Not at all," she said, already turning back to her work.

Nodding good-bye, Benjamin followed Wolfe out the swinging doors of the laboratory.

CHAPTER 9

A few moments after speaking with Edith, Wolfe and Benjamin were outside in the quad, sitting on a bench beneath a tremendous sycamore tree.

Benjamin looked farther out to the west, to the low, rolling hills, covered with similar trees in their fall splendor. The trimmed hedges, bright flowers, warm-colored leaves all seemed a world away from the metal and plastic and methodical cruelty they'd just left.

"Well, that was . . . ," Benjamin began.

"Yes," agreed Wolfe. "It was indeed."

"But useful? She said Jeremy told her nothing about his work. Bees and nuclear war? Swarm intelligence? Despite what she said about the Pentagon's interest, I still don't see how they connect."

Wolfe frowned. "Apparently Fletcher did. If we could get at his computer files, perhaps we would, too."

Benjamin squinted over at Wolfe.

"Look, I'm certainly not telling you how to do your job, but it's just . . . well, you seem to be investigating this incident as though it was a murder, not a security leak."

Wolfe looked at him without reaction. "And?"

"And why do I get the feeling you don't really believe Jeremy leaked anything to anyone?"

Wolfe frowned at him. "Oh, but he did," he said. "Just not yet."

"Not *yet*?" The grotesque session with Mrs. Gadenhower had left him little patience for playing games. "What does that mean?"

"Ah," Wolfe observed, ignoring Benjamin's question and looking down the path. "Here's someone who probably agrees with me."

Benjamin turned, saw a figure approaching them on the path. The man was very tall, very solidly built, with closely cropped *very* blond hair. He was dressed in a dark suit and tie and wearing sunglasses. He strode purposefully but without hurry toward them.

"Samuel," he said, extending his hand. Wolfe stood and took it and they shook hands somewhat abruptly. "And this must be Benjamin." Benjamin rose and shook his hand also. "Eric Hauser," he said. His grip was strong, brief. "Campus security."

"Campus?" Benjamin asked.

"That's what we call our little community, the campus," said Hauser, smiling broadly.

"An ivy-covered retreat, far from the strife and worries of the civilian world," added Wolfe. "Out where a man can hear himself think."

Hauser looked at him. "That's what they're paid to do, Samuel."

"And paid very well," Wolfe answered. "And, I assume, they carry full life insurance?"

"Look, Samuel," Hauser glanced nervously at Benjamin, "I know we've had our differences in the past. But I'm sure you understand why Dr. Fletcher's . . . untimely death, as tragic as it was, can't be allowed to tarnish the reputation of the Foundation. Why we need this all settled as quickly as possible." Wolfe didn't respond. "If there's anything I can do to help your inquiry along—"

"Now that you mention it," Wolfe said, "there is. We'd like to get a list of all the computer registration numbers on the . . . campus. Who has what shiny toys, that sort of thing."

"Everyone?" asked Hauser. "I don't see how that's possibly relevant."

"Wouldn't you say a missing computer would be relevant? I know it would certainly worry other government beneficiaries."

Hauser looked dubious. "Dr. Fletcher's computer is missing?"

Wolfe smiled. "How do we know what's missing until we know what everyone's supposed to have?"

Hauser stared at Wolfe, his friendly manner of earlier evaporated.

"I'll have to check with Arthur about that," he said frostily.

"Fine," said Wolfe. "And tell him, every hour you're checking with him is an hour closer to our deadline. And his."

Hauser seemed about to say something to Wolfe, but stopped himself. He smiled at Benjamin and said, "Good to meet you, Mr. Wainwright," and continued on down the pathway.

After he'd left, Benjamin turned to Wolfe.

"You two have a history?"

"In a manner of speaking," Wolfe said, still looking after Hauser's retreating figure.

Benjamin lost his patience.

"Look, everyone we've met, everywhere you go here, there seems to be *history*. How can I help you sort something out when I don't even know what it is we're looking for? Or why they picked *us* to look for it."

Wolfe looked at him, suddenly very serious.

"Not why us, Benjamin. Why *me*."

Benjamin looked slightly hurt. Wolfe patted his arm.

"I'm sorry. Don't take me too seriously. Not until I tell you to, anyway." He smiled that charming smile.

Benjamin suddenly felt quite fond of Samuel Wolfe; he also felt for the first time that he could trust Wolfe, completely.

"I need to check on a few things with Arthur," said Wolfe. "I'll meet you back in your room in, say, an hour?"

Benjamin nodded, and Wolfe walked off in the same direction Hauser had taken.

When he got back to his room, Benjamin was surprised to find a maid there. The bed was made, the room looked straightened up—but he wondered why the maid was there now, rather than in the morning. She had a vacuum cleaner out and was pushing the sweeper back and forth across the bare floor. She was just about to shove it under the bed when he entered.

"Excuse me," he said.

She turned, frightened and caught off guard.

"I'm sorry," he said, "but could you do that later? I'd really like to take a nap."

"Of course," she said. She switched off the vacuum, rolled the cord up, and, with a "Good afternoon, sir," she left.

Benjamin retrieved his briefcase from the dresser, opened it. Inside was a thick, leather-bound journal. Its neatly ruled pages were filled with notes in a small, precise handwriting, and the journal itself was stuffed with sheets of paper, Xerox copies, pictures . . . it looked just like what it was: a fanatically methodical academic's scrapbook. Or, as his father had called it, his "treasury."

Benjamin took the journal, sat down in a chair at the small table, opened the cover.

Journal of Dr. Thomas Woodrow Wainwright was written there in the same precise hand.

The writing was so like his father: solid, staid, respectable. And slightly obsessive in its neatness.

Yet, for all his compulsiveness, there'd been nothing arrogant about his father. In fact, the two things he disliked most in others were arrogance and intolerance.

"They go hand in hand, Benjamin," his father had said once. They'd been discussing one of his colleagues at Georgetown, an academic with a brilliant career—one built almost entirely by demolishing the careers of others. "Believing you have the flawless answer," he'd said, "is perhaps the biggest flaw of all."

Benjamin felt the usual twinge of regret that his father hadn't lived to see him complete his own degree, start his own career. . . .

He shook off the sentiment. He began flipping through pages, looking for the copies of the few known letters of Harlan Bainbridge which he knew his father had copied verbatim into the notebook.

The first was a letter Harlan had written to his aunt soon after his group arrived on the land Coddington had purchased where they might begin their "New Jerusalem," their utopian Prayer Town, a place far beyond all other English settlements of the time. Above the letter his father had written *Establishes claim to land; chronicles exodus from New Jersey,* and then the text of the letter:

> *Honor'd Aunte—*
> *—I've sent this with Elder Sassamon in greate haste, and he is trusted and that God's Speed did see him to you is my prayer— for the papers here be disposed as quickly as you mighte seeke a counsel with the Capetown Elders, that they may Recognise and Grante our Claime.*
> *—Nosce teipsum reade the Scriptures, and this done, and trusting in the Wisdome of the Lord, so with my few and trusted people this Lent just passe'd fled much as Brother Bradford fled*

*the Dutch truse with Spain, the Inquisition promising too near
and hot a fire for his heels—and, passeing through the County
of Mattekeesets and thought to abide meantimes in the Plantation of Providence, onely to find there no reall peace from Perse-
cution and in feare of Salus Populi and againe, as the wandering
Israelites, faceing West—so made discovery of this place by the
Savages called Pettaquamscutt, but with the agreement of the
whole community drawne as the Christian settlement of Bainbridge Plantation.*

    [an entire half page was illegible]

    *. . . but the Savages revere this place as welle, and their pa-
gan gods be of a like not so tamne as weake, and they did in
tragick form reape the Smallpox this winter laste as great as
that of 1634.*

    *—Unto you I commit theese papers, and so do I here note on
this day of Our Lord, March 15th, Sixteen Hundred and Sixty-
Six.*

Your Trusted Nephew
The Right Reverend Harlan P. Bainbridge
At Bainbridge Plantation, his sign

How typical of the Puritans, Benjamin mused, to assume a smallpox
epidemic was a punishment visited upon the Natives by a Christian God
offended by their pagan forms of worship; when in fact the smallpox, Benjamin knew, had come from infected blankets given to those Natives by those
same "righteous" settlers. Also typical was Harlan's portrayal of himself as
a latter-day Moses leading his small congregation to the Promised Land.
How frustrating it must have been for him to discover that the Wampanoags thought the land had already been promised to *them*.

The journal continued with entries about further communiqués between Harlan and his aunt, most reporting the slow-but-steady progress as
Harlan's group established the Bainbridge Plantation and began to work
toward Harlan's utopian goal. His father had noted, for instance, that Harlan's group was one of the first in the region to actually sign treaties with
the Natives and to begin bartering with them on a regular basis.

The second full Bainbridge letter was the last one he'd ever written,
penned sometime before the plantation's destruction. Above this letter, his
father had written *Fears sabotage—from C.E.P.?* Benjamin had never deci-
phered what his father had meant by that abbreviation. Thomas had all

sorts of shorthand symbols he employed in his notes, working always to be more efficient, but he kept no glossary or index of them. He shook his head in frustration at his father's unique obsessions and read on:

> *Honor'd Aunte—*
> *—Despite all the Perfidies practiced upon us by those who beare the marke of Puramis as Satan beares the Trident forke, The Lord has ordained that we shoulde establishe the Command-ments of Piety and Efficiencie in all acts stemming frome and displaieing their respecte for God and His selfe-made workes, which, in their echo of our Creater, canne be not but sensicall, propere, and prosperous.*
> *—The heathens may worshipe their god 'neath any randome sycamore, but a Christian knows Nature to be a chapel, which conceals not the ugly face of Death, but the abundante mani-festations of a Supreme God, in whose Bosom we freely place our Truste and Fate; and we suffere not to be disheartened nor dissuaded from our Course by those who hide in Shadow and sow Feare on all Mankinde. . . .*
> [rest of the letter missing]

And that was it. While there were still many entries about the Puritans and their growing success in the New World, Benjamin knew there was nothing further about Bainbridge, either pater or fils. But as he was closing the journal he noticed, for the first time, a single, very faint mark in the margin next to the word *Puramis*. It looked partially erased. Leaning down so his face almost touched the paper, he saw that it was a small triangle, with what might have been a single dot in its center.

It might have been another of his father's shorthand codes, but Benjamin couldn't remember ever having seen this one anywhere else in his notes.

It was then a knock came at his door. He looked at the clock on the table—almost an hour had passed while he was reading his father's journal. Before he could say anything, the door opened and Wolfe entered. He was wearing an immaculate white dinner jacket.

"Chop chop," he said. "We're wanted for dinner."

"Dinner? Uh, why don't you go on without me. I'm a little busy here. And I haven't changed . . ."

"You're fine. Hurry, we don't want to miss the cocktail hour. I'll wait in the hall."

Benjamin went into the small bathroom, splashed some water onto his face, combed his hair and straightened his tie, then went back into the bedroom. He found his shoes where he'd tossed them next to the bed, put them on.

As he bent down to tie his shoes, he saw something under the bed. He squatted down and reached, slid it out from under the bed with two fingers.

It was a yellow piece of paper with blue lines—a page from a small legal pad, folded in the middle. He was about to open it when Wolfe shouted from the hallway.

"Benjamin! I hear the ice clinking!"

Benjamin threw the paper, still folded, on the bedside table, switched the lamp off, and left.

CHAPTER 10

The dozen or more round tables in the dining room had been set with white tablecloths, gardenia centerpieces, candles, and white china. At the head of the room the massive antique table was covered with a deep red tablecloth. The crystal chandeliers were aglow, there was a modest fire in the fireplace, and light reflected from the gilt-edged mirror over the fireplace and the deep brown walnut wainscoting.

"Eureka," said Wolfe, ignoring the elegance of their surroundings. He guided Benjamin to a bar on one side of the hall, somewhat forcefully elbowing his way to its edge. He handed Benjamin a drink, something amber.

Benjamin took a sip, winced. "Scotch again?"

"Yes," said Wolfe, looking about the room. "Because you liked it so much last night."

Benjamin surveyed the room, noticed the "grandees" table at the front. He saw Arthur Terrill there, and on his left Edith Gadenhower. On Arthur's right was an extremely well-tanned gentleman with thick, shining, impeccably styled silver hair.

"Who's that?" Benjamin asked, pointing.

Wolfe turned, looked, chuckled. "Ah. That particularly well-preserved monument is George 'Former' Montrose."

"Former?"

"Former secretary of state, former chief of staff, former director of the CIA . . . From what I understand, he's a genial idiot, but with first-class connections. Montrose is the Foundation's front man for this new contract."

"Contract? You mean that 'paycheck' you mentioned in Arthur's office?"

Wolfe didn't seem to hear him. He was scanning the room as it filled with people, everyone standing around sipping their cocktails and chatting before dinner began.

Suddenly Wolfe started out through the crowd, saying to Benjamin, "Let's try this direction, shall we."

Stepping between the chairs and groups of people—Wolfe nodded to one or two but kept Benjamin moving forward—they arrived at a mismatched couple: a very tall woman and a very short man.

Benjamin couldn't help but stare at the woman. She was a striking blonde with her hair up in a French twist and dressed formally in a low-cut black evening dress. She smiled when she saw Wolfe, as though she knew him; her smile was brilliant, cool, enticing—almost fierce. Benjamin hardly noticed the man she was with.

"Dr. Gudrün Soderbergh," Wolfe said, making introductions, "this is Benjamin Wainwright." She nodded at him as she raised a cocktail—something clear and with ice—to her lips. She kept her eyes on Benjamin even as she drank, and Benjamin had to pull his gaze from her as Wolfe continued the introductions.

"And here we have Dr. Edward Stoltz." He indicated the short, very well-dressed man in his midfifties with black hair and a small, well-trimmed mustache. Stoltz nodded and said, "Greetings."

Benjamin gave Wolfe a quizzical look.

"Yes, I called them," Wolfe said. "I thought we might save some time."

"So, Benjamin," said Gudrün, "you're Mr. Wolfe's protégé?"

"Not at all, Dr. Soderbergh," Wolfe replied for him. "Dr. Wainwright is a gentleman and scholar in his own right. I've merely commandeered his talents for the duration."

"The duration of what?" asked Dr. Stoltz. He was drinking a cocktail in a frosted glass with sprig of mint in it.

"Their investigation, of course," said Gudrün. "Of Jeremy's unfortunate demise. Isn't that why you asked us to dine with you?"

"Well, that and the stellar company," said Wolfe. He saluted Gudrün with his empty cocktail glass—which he immediately held up, looking to catch a waiter's eye for a refill. "You see, I believe you were among the last people to see Dr. Fletcher alive."

"And how do you know," Stoltz said with a certain irritation, "that we were the *last* people to see Dr. Fletcher alive?"

"Well . . . ," began Wolfe. Then he saw a waiter passing, said "Excuse me," and hurried off in pursuit.

"I think what Mr. Wolfe meant," said Benjamin uncomfortably, "is that you were his last appointments. He met with you this week."

Gudrün shook her head. "Not with me," she said.

"No, no," Benjamin said hurriedly, "but he wanted to. I mean, he'd scheduled you for Friday, yes?"

Again Gudrün shook her head. "Not that I know of," then said, "I hope that doesn't mean you don't want to speak with me."

"Oh," was all Benjamin could think to say.

"With you, Dr. Soderbergh, most of all," said Wolfe, returning, his glass full again. "Gudrün," he said thoughtfully. "Wasn't that the name of some Norse Amazon in the tale of Sigurd? The one he spurned, and who then enacted terrible revenge upon him?"

Gudrün didn't flinch. "Amazon," she replied coolly, "is really just a word for a strong woman. And strong women tend to make men . . . uncomfortable. So they make up terrible stories about them."

Wolfe smiled but didn't respond. Benjamin couldn't see how any of this was serving as an interview and decided to take the lead.

"So, Dr. Stoltz, you *did* speak with Jeremy, yes?"

Stoltz looked at him as though he were a slow child. "Yes," he said, "and a most interesting conversation it was." Wolfe used that moment to steer Gudrün a few feet away and begin a conversation with her, Benjamin couldn't quite hear about what, but Stoltz was going on.

"But first tell me, Mr. Wainwright, what do you think so far of our little community?"

Benjamin wasn't sure whether Stoltz was referring to the Foundation or its people, so he decided to assume the former, as it was easier to categorize.

"It's beautiful. The buildings and grounds . . . and that extraordinary mural, in the manse?"

"Ah," said Stoltz, nodding. "The Bayne *panorama*. Odd you should bring that up. That was what brought Dr. Fletcher to me."

"Really?" said Benjamin, trying to conceal his surprise. "And what did you tell him?"

"Well, I began by telling him that it's from the late 1920s. It isn't quite a Gropper, he was too busy doing post offices and banks, that sort of public welfare thing. But I told him it's an excellent representation of Gropper's style:

the heroic poses, the slick surfaces, complete lack of corners, even in the faces. And the enormous scale. It's no *Man at the Crossroads,* of course, but it's quite interesting."

"I haven't had time to really study it yet."

"Oh, you should," enthused Stoltz. "Some of the scenes date back to the 1600s, back to when this whole area was part of the Quincy Homestead, one of the first—"

"*Edmund* Quincy's homestead?" Benjamin interrupted.

Stoltz looked surprised. "You know of him?"

Benjamin tried to recover some of his disinterested manner. "Wasn't he a partner with a . . . Henry Coddington? I seem to remember that one of their investments had to do with a Puritan compound, something called the . . . the Bainbridge Plantation?"

Stoltz beamed. "Then you *know* all about that sordid little chapter of our past?"

"Sordid?"

"Well," began Stoltz, "what with the Quincy Homestead, and then the Bainbridge Plantation practically on top of that ancient Indian burial ground, and then the Foundation's various predecessors—"

"Excuse me?" Benjamin couldn't contain himself. "This . . . plantation, it was *here*? I mean, exactly . . . here?"

Stoltz smiled. "We're practically eating over Bainbridge's grave."

"Really?" Benjamin took a sip of his drink to give himself time to calm down.

"Indeed. Our august institution occupies the very same plot of land as the Coddington Estate. Which was, before that, the Bainbridge Plantation. You see, the plantation was wiped out, by Indians, back in the 1600s. Burned to the ground, not a stick left, everyone massacred."

"Then how," Benjamin said, keeping his tone calm, "could they know that the plantation was here? There were no . . . I mean, I would imagine there were no surviving records or anything?"

"Well, yes, they never actually found Bainbridge's body, that's true. But when they discovered his diary here during the excavations in the twenties—"

"*Diary?*" This time Benjamin couldn't keep his voice from rising.

"Yes. The late twenties were when the Foundation first became *The Foundation*—as one of those populist institutions for good government, or something dreadfully idealistic like that—and they were digging to expand the manse, when they came across this small stone crypt. Inside that, they found a sealed lead box. And inside *that,* they found this diary." He paused for a moment, took a long drink of his wine. "Remarkable story, though it rather got lost amongst the more . . . commanding events of that year. It was, after all, 1929. In fact, about this very time of year. October."

"Extraordinary coincidence," said Wolfe.

Stoltz smiled broadly. "Odd you should call it that," he said. "That's exactly how Dr. Fletcher reacted when I told him the same story."

Benjamin could feel himself holding his breath. "Did Dr. Fletcher know any of this *before* you spoke with him?"

"No, of course not," said Stoltz. "But after we spoke about the mural he was asking all sorts of questions about that episode—which I thought rather strange. For a mathematician." He shrugged, took another sip of wine. "Oh, and especially the scandal that transpired *after* they found the diary, when—"

"Ah," Gudrün said, stepping back to them and interrupting Stoltz, "Eric, please, don't bore poor Benjamin to death." She turned to Benjamin. "I'm sorry, you get any one of us started, we forget other people don't share our . . . obsessions." Gudrün put her hand on Benjamin's forearm. "I think they're about to start serving. Shall we find a table?"

Benjamin glanced around for Wolfe, didn't see him, and let himself be led to a nearby table with four empty seats.

While wineglasses were being filled and plates set down, Benjamin thought about what he'd learned from Stoltz. What struck him as strangest of all was that Jeremy, after residency at the Foundation for several months and probably passing through the manse's foyer on a daily basis, should suddenly take an interest in the mural. In all the time he'd known Jeremy at Harvard, never once had he expressed an interest in art. He'd always imagined that to Jeremy art, being unquantifiable, didn't really exist; not in the certain way of numbers and patterns.

Benjamin realized Gudrün was introducing the others at the table.

"And this is Dr. Morton Cavendish," she was saying, pointing with her wineglass to an older gentleman with full white hair and beard. "Our resident expert on international relations."

Cavendish frowned. "Don't let her mislead you, Mr. Wainwright. Gudrün isn't taking proper credit. Her white paper on the Middle East . . . well, it wouldn't be inaccurate to say it helped point this administration in the right direction." He saluted her.

"Really, Dr. Cavendish." Gudrün smiled, but Benjamin noticed she did not demur.

"Yes, a remarkably successful invasion, as invasions go," said Wolfe, rejoining the group. He was greeted by stares and silence. He scanned their faces, smiled. "I'm sorry, is that word out of season now?"

"You can't possibly suggest," began Cavendish, "that we should have done nothing and let our enemies—"

"Please, Morton," Gudrün said, smiling sweetly at Wolfe, "let Mr. Wolfe finish."

Wolfe bowed slightly to Gudrün. "What would you say regarding enemies, Ms. Soderbergh? Thanks to our doing *something,* do we now have fewer? And does this splendid little war make the next big one less likely?"

"I'm more interested in what happens *before* a conflict begins," she said steadily. "Napoleon said a battle is won or lost before it ever starts. That's when victories are made."

"And those victories," said Wolfe, looking very pointedly at Gudrün, "they're made here?"

She didn't flinch. "Those in power have always recognized the value of innovative thinkers to advise them."

"To think the unthinkable?" asked Wolfe, quite calmly. "Like Kahn?"

"Kahn?" asked Benjamin, struggling to understand the tension between Wolfe and Gudrün—and, he realized with some embarrassment, trying to find a way to reenter the conversation, perhaps to get Gudrün to turn those luminous eyes toward him again.

"Herman Kahn," replied Cavendish. "Wrote on nuclear war theory. Practically invented it."

"Or invented the notion that it was 'thinkable,'" amended Wolfe, still looking at Gudrün.

"Wasn't he merely being realistic?" said Gudrün. She leaned toward Wolfe, the cynicism of earlier replaced by what appeared to be sincere commitment. "Most people don't really know *why* they believe as they do. They require . . . call it direction. Or purpose. And history has taught us that purpose is usually found in the face of one's enemies."

"Then I alter my question slightly," said Wolfe, now looking quite serious himself. "Those enemies, are *they* made here?"

Before Gudrün could respond there came a tapping of a fork on a wineglass from the head table. Arthur Terrill was standing and attempting to get everyone's attention. Finally, when the murmur of conversation and clatter of silverware had died down, he spoke.

"While I have you all gathered together like this, I believe it's an excellent time to acknowledge the supreme effort of one of our own. All of you know him, but I think few of you appreciate how absolutely vital his efforts are to the survival of the Foundation and its mission. I'm speaking of course of Mr. George Montrose."

Arthur turned toward Montrose, and there was a round of applause. Terrill continued.

"Without his work in the lobbies of the Capitol, every bit as important as the work that goes on in the laboratories and studies here on campus, we wouldn't have the luxury to pursue our precious researches. Here's to George Montrose." He raised his glass to a chorus of "Here, here" and "Good work, George."

Everyone at the table drank, Wolfe draining his glass. Then Montrose stood and began to speak, beginning with something about the "unsung heroes here in the wilds of Massachusetts," and there was general laughter . . . but at that moment Gudrün leaned in closer to Benjamin and spoke in low tones.

"I can't stand these speeches. I'm going outside for a smoke. Mind keeping me company?" She placed her hand on his shoulder in a gesture he couldn't quite define. Friendly? Flirtatious? Maybe he was drunker than he thought.

Benjamin's first impulse was to look to Wolfe, but Wolfe was engaged in an intense whispered dialogue with Cavendish.

"Wouldn't it be rude, to leave in the middle of . . . ?" and he waved his hand toward Montrose and the head table.

"They'll assume we're off to be naughty," Gudrün said, and before Benjamin could reply she'd lifted his hand and led him, winding through tables, out the doors, across the foyer, and into the empty quad outside.

CHAPTER 11

Once outside, Gudrün immediately extracted a cigarette and lighter from her purse, lit up, and inhaled with undisguised relief. Then she looked up at the night sky. The chilled air made Benjamin pull his jacket closed.

"Amazing out here, isn't it?" she said. "Away from the city lights. They're so much . . . clearer. But then, so many things are."

He looked upward, if for no other reason than to prevent himself from staring at her face shining in the starlight—and noticing the way that same starlight emphasized the contours of her breasts above the low-cut neckline of her dress.

She threw the cigarette to the stone pathway, ground it out beneath the toe of a black high-heeled shoe, looked back to him. Smiled that radiant, rapacious smile.

"We never really got a chance to have our chat at dinner, did we. Look, I have some very nice brandy in my room—what say I bring it to yours, mine is an absolute mess, and I'll answer any . . . inquiries you might have had for me."

When he hesitated, she placed her hand on his arm, and said, "I'll be nice, I promise."

"Enjoying the night air?" said Edward Stoltz loudly, approaching them from the dining hall.

Gudrün said, "Saying good night. So I will. Good night, Edward." She turned to Benjamin. "Mr. Wainwright." And, her high heels clicking on the cobblestones, she walked off down the path and into the manse.

"A remarkable woman," said Stoltz. "Not my type, of course."

Benjamin nodded, said nothing. He was about to say good night himself when he remembered their earlier conversation that had been cut off.

"Dr. Stoltz, you mentioned there was some sort of . . . scandal after they discovered this diary?"

"Scandal with a capital S," said Stoltz, smiling wickedly. "Seems the painter of that mural we were discussing, Cecil Bayne? Seems he was having an affair with one of the fellows here. A Warren Ginsburg. An historian, like you, I believe."

At first Benjamin was so surprised to hear that Stoltz knew he was an historian that the name of Bayne's lover didn't strike him. Then he realized it sounded familiar.

"*Warren* Ginsburg," repeated Benjamin.

Now Stoltz's eyes went wide in surprise. "You know of him?"

"Well . . . as you say, he was an historian, so . . ." He let his voice trail off, then added, "But an affair, even a homosexual one . . . that was a scandal?"

"Oh, no," said Stoltz. "They weren't that provincial, even back then and even out here."

"Then why—?"

"It was the *termination* of the affair." Stoltz smirked as though he'd made a particularly clever joke. "Messy. One of those murder-suicides that's supposed to happen in dens of iniquity like Hollywood, not staid Massachusetts."

"So they both . . ."

"Died, yes. Bayne murdered and Ginsburg . . ." Stoltz held a finger to his temple, pulled an imaginary trigger. "You see? Needless to say, Bayne never completed the mural. Pity."

Benjamin nodded. He shivered as if cold. "Well, I think I'll say good night too, then." He began to leave, then turned back as if he'd remembered something. "And that diary you mentioned, is it still here?"

"No, no, it was donated long ago," said Stoltz, waving his hand, apparently now bored with the whole story. "To the Morris Estate."

As in 'the Library of Seymour Morris'? Benjamin wondered. But he dared not ask.

"Well, good night then. Pleasure meeting you," Benjamin said.

He turned and started off down the path to the manse—not certain whether he wanted Gudrün to keep their rendezvous in his room or not. He had a lot to tell Wolfe, and wasn't sure he could wait until morning.

CHAPTER 12

By the time Natalya got back to her apartment, it was almost 12:00 A.M., or 8:00 A.M. in Dubna, Russia. Her father would be awake soon. On weekends he liked to spend the mornings working in his *ogorod,* his kitchen garden, a small plot of ground in a communal square down the street from his apartment building. If she called in perhaps thirty minutes, she could catch him before he left. So she just had to stay awake until then.

Which might prove difficult. Going over the Bolshoi reception menu with Mr. Foy had in fact made her quite hungry, and she'd skipped lunch while working at the embassy, so when she met Yuri and his friends at Russkiy Dom she'd opted for a full-course dinner: *soleniye ogurscy,* sliced and salted cucumbers, for an appetizer (Yuri had tried to tease her by ordering *seledka pod shuboy,* as he knew the name alone made her cringe: salted herring in a sheepskin "coat"). For a main course she'd ordered veal *pelmeny,* what she called "Siberian ravioli." Perhaps she'd hoped to capture some memory of childhood, when her mother would make and roll the thick, salty dough for the wrap and grind a mixture of veal and beef for the filling. She'd even had a dessert, which was quite unusual for her: *tvorog,* cottage cheese with honey. Yuri had watched her eat with some appreciation—and a certain horror.

"Natashka," he'd said, "how do you eat like such a *obzhora,* and still look like a ballerina?"

She'd then surprised Yuri further by agreeing to go with them for a drink afterward. Yuri had said something about Natalya finally becoming a "party girl"—though he'd said it in English, and with Yuri's accent it sounded like "party ghoul."

Later, when they were ensconced in the noisy discomfort of the Sibir lounge, she'd finally felt he was relaxed enough to bring up her request.

She'd told him she was doing research for an American academician; it wasn't of any real consequence, she said dismissively, but he was a friend of someone at the embassy. She hadn't been able to find one of the books she needed, so she'd turned in a request for permission to access the restricted archives. But that normally took months. Could Yuri be a dear and see if there was anything he could do to speed things along? It probably wasn't important, there were so many books and magazines tossed into that immense trash heap labeled "State Security."

Yuri had smiled and said of course, for Natashka the Great Seer, he would do anything. She'd leaned across the table and kissed him—on the cheek. He'd smiled, in a tolerant, disappointed sort of way. But then she'd agreed to dance with him, and he seemed satisfied.

Natalya looked at the clock above her refrigerator: 12:15. Still too early to call.

She opened the fridge and took out a plastic bottle of water, went into the living room, and sat down in a large, overstuffed chair near the window. She didn't really like the furniture—modern, squarish, all in earth tones—but it had come with the apartment.

Everyone thought her apartment was too small, but in fact it made her feel secure, as though she were invisible—another sign of trying hard to be the nail that didn't stick up.

Yet oddly enough here, in America, she finally felt at home.

She'd always been fascinated with all things Western. One of her father's cousins, Svetlana, belonged to Beriozka, a folk dance troop that was allowed to travel abroad—her own father's position as an officer in the *rocketchiki* meant he wasn't allowed to leave the country, *ever*—and when Svetlana visited she would bring Natalya the most wonderful presents: chocolate from Germany, magazines from France, toys from Sweden. Natalya was particularly eager to tear through the magazines. Of course she couldn't read the words, but that didn't matter; she was looking for pictures of anything

American: American cars, American clothes, American cities; but most of all American people. To her, they looked universally confident, handsome, happy—like people from another planet.

One day back then, when she was perhaps seven, she began speaking in a language all her own, and her mother asked, "What is that? Have you lost your mind?" And she'd answered, "Don't you know? This is English."

She simply hadn't fit in Uzhur, not in any sense. In a town where tanks sat at the entrances like squat, metal dragons; where soldiers were more common than children; where the boundaries were marked not by the usual fields of wheat and barley, but by a huge fence topped with electrified barbed wire; a town that, had she looked on a map, she wouldn't have found listed . . . in the midst of all this regimentation and sense of constantly being scrutinized, she was an utterly foreign free spirit.

She remembered one day her father came home from a ten-day duty at his base—what he called his "time in the hole"—to find her doodling on a photo of Lenin. It was an old black-and-white picture in one of the Party-published biographies her father kept above the desk he called his study, and she'd drawn a clown nose, gogglelike glasses, and a full beard on the Father of the Soviet Union's sacred face.

Her father had reacted in horror.

"Do you want a chance to become an orphan?" he'd said, snatching the book away.

Later, she saw him feeding it into the fire he started in their tiny, rarely used fireplace. But she also saw that he was smiling.

And so she'd learned something all the other children seemed to know instinctively: there were things you didn't draw, didn't say, didn't *do*.

Thinking now of that time reminded her of the tremendous pride she'd always felt in her father, even when he punished her for her independent ways. She remembered the ritual of him polishing his high, shiny black boots, the spitting and rubbing that would continue for an hour. "Can you see yourself, Natashka?" he would say, holding the boot beneath her face. She remembered the strong, musky smell of boot polish and leather, the way the boots made Nikolai seem a foot taller when he finally pulled them on. And then he would disappear for ten days or two weeks at a time. When he returned he was always very hungry, very happy, and very tired.

She snapped awake. She looked to the clock: 12:45. She cursed. Her father might already be gone for his morning's puttering at his garden.

She went to the end of the living room where she had her desk, a small study area that, she realized now, was a copy of her father's back in the apartment in Uzhur. She picked up the handset and dialed the prefix for Russia, and then the area code for Dubna.

She listened to the metallic buzz of the first ring. And then the second. Then she heard her father's voice.

"*Alloa?*" he said.

"Nikolai," she replied. She had addressed him with his first name since leaving the university, feeling it was the truly adult thing to do. "*Privet.* This is your daughter."

"Natashka." She could hear the pleasure in his voice. "*Privet.* You caught me just as I was leaving. I have to put my time in as a peasant, you know."

She laughed. "I won't keep you long, Father. I just wanted to know how you are."

"Ah," he said. She could hear the reticence in his voice. "I survive. That's the most important thing."

"You are well?" she asked.

"Better than some," he replied. Then he went on to list the troubles of various relatives and friends: divorces, drunkenness, unruly children, poor wages. It was all something of a ritual with them. "And poor Dmitri Sergeivich. His leukemia is very stubborn."

Dmitri was one of her father's oldest comrades from his days as a *rocketchiki*. Natalya knew that the incidence of all sorts of cancer and blood diseases was extraordinarily high among the former *rocketchiki*; her father attributed it to "sitting like a hen on nuclear eggs" for years at a time. Fortunately, her father was as yet free of such "souvenirs of service," as the ex-soldiers called them.

"And you, Natashka? How is my little diplomat?"

"I am fine, Father. I had lunch with the president just yesterday," she joked. "He agreed to see about increasing your pension."

She knew her father's so-called military pension was a ridiculously small amount, given his years of dedicated service. He worked now with a branch of the State Bank in Dubna, looking after their security and planning for various emergencies and disasters. He described the difference in responsibilities this way: "Once I held the fate of the planet at the tip of my finger. Now I use that finger to plug leaks."

She spoke for a few minutes about her work at the Cultural Center, trying to make it sound more glamorous than it really was, as she knew this made her father feel a sense of pride. She mentioned the Bolshoi reception, and he responded that she was living the life of an aristocrat.

"How things have changed," he said, somewhat wistfully.

She laughed again. "An aristocrat that works like a dog," she said. And, since she knew he was about to say he had to leave for his garden, she finally broached the subject she'd been working up to.

"Nikolai," she tried to keep the increased tension and formality out of her voice. "You know I am contacted from time to time by American professors, seeking help with books from the archives." She waited for a moment, but he didn't respond. "Well, I received a very curious request the other day, about such a book. But I cannot find anything about it in the places I usually look. I thought perhaps it was a book you might have encountered in . . . your extensive reading."

Now her father's silence was palpable. "Yes?" he said finally.

"It is a book with a strange name. Or actually, it might not be the book's name at all. The American was not certain about that. He knows only that it was published sometime between 1960 and 1970." She waited.

"And this book's maybe-name?" her father asked.

"Something like *Stzenariy 55*. Or perhaps it is *Borba s tenyu*. You see? Very confusing."

Again, there was silence.

"Have you ever heard of a book with either title?" she prodded.

"No," her father said finally.

She waited again, for some question, some comment. But he said nothing.

"Are you certain," she said, though she already knew his answer. "Nothing like that at all?"

"I've read so many books, Natalya," and she noticed his return to the formal address, "it's hard to remember them all. But a title like that . . . and who is this American academician who is asking about this maybe-book? A boyfriend?"

She laughed, even though she felt the joke was forced. "No, I've never met him." She was about to tell him Jeremy Fletcher's name, when for some reason she decided not to. "Just someone at an American university. Probably someone whose Russian is very bad, and he simply mixed it all up."

"Yes," her father said. "I'm certain that's it. Probably best just to leave it alone. You know how persistent these Americans can be." He paused for a moment. "Probably someone you should not contact."

Then they exchanged a rather awkward *"pakah,"* too informal a farewell for the tension she suddenly felt; and then, instead of hanging up, her father had added, "Natalya, you know I love you very much."

She was surprised. He wasn't usually this emotionally forthcoming in their phone chats. "And I love you too, Father," she said.

And then they hung up.

Natalya sat for a while in the overstuffed chair, looking out the window, and wishing desperately for a cigarette. In all the years of her rebellions, her alien tastes and desires, her difficult marriage with Sander, her parents' separation and divorce . . . through all those years, she'd never suspected that her father actually ever lied to her.

But he was lying to her now. Of that she was certain.

It was nearly 1:30, far past her usual bedtime. Perhaps she would try to do something different on Sunday, something away from the center and the embassy, away from this search that was leading nowhere. Perhaps tomorrow she would go to the Mall, visit the Lincoln Memorial, and find some sort of wisdom there. Or at least comfort.

She turned out the light by the chair and made her way through the darkened apartment into the bedroom, where, as soon as she'd undressed and stretched out on the bed, she immediately fell asleep.

CHAPTER 13

Once back in his room, Benjamin had looked around for glasses for Gudrün's brandy. He was nervous, and felt silly for being nervous. There was always the chance she'd change her mind and not show up. Or maybe he was making too much of this. Perhaps she really *did* want to talk to him about Jeremy. Which, he reminded himself, smiling, was what he was supposed to want, too.

As he was washing two glasses he found in the bathroom a knock came at his door. Holding the glasses, still dripping, in one hand, he went into the room and opened it.

"As promised," announced Gudrün, holding aloft a squat bottle of brandy. She was still in her evening dress, though she'd let her hair down, so that it shone like a mane against her bare shoulders. Once again, Benjamin thought she was one of the most striking women he'd ever seen. "Are you going to invite me in?" she asked.

"Oh, of course." He pointed to the two chairs set next to the small table, but Gudrün sat down unceremoniously on the bed.

"Is one of those for me?" she asked, pointing to the wet glasses.

"Yes." He shook the water from it. "Sorry, all I could find." As he held forth the glass she tilted the bottle, poured a healthy portion into it, then motioned for the other, did the same. She set the bottle on his nightstand, took one of the glasses from him, and tapped glasses.

"To making new friends," Gudrün said.

"And absent old ones," Benjamin answered.

"Yes, of course." She took a sip of her brandy. "So tell me, Benjamin, how do you . . . sorry, *did* you know Jeremy Fletcher?"

Benjamin sipped his own, found it pretty strong stuff. "In college," he said. "But I hadn't heard from him in years."

"But then he called you to come out here? To help with his work?" Benjamin just nodded. "And your field is Colonial history?"

"How did you—?"

"Samuel told me." Gudrün leaned back on the bed. "Though he didn't explain why Jeremy suddenly needed a Colonial historian."

Benjamin paused. "Why do you say suddenly?"

"Well," Gudrün smiled, "you arrived late yesterday afternoon with a single suitcase, you weren't on the roster of new fellows sent around last week, and there wasn't a single rumor about your coming." She laughed lightly at Benjamin's look of surprise. "The Foundation is like a village, Ben. Everyone knows everyone else's business. Oh, do you mind if I call you Ben?"

Benjamin was beginning to feel uncomfortable still standing over Gudrün. He perched at the head of the bed, on a pillow. "Not at all," he said, lying. "But now let me ask you something. Why do you think Jeremy suddenly needed you, an expert in counterterrorism?"

"I'm sure I wouldn't know," she said. She leaned over him, took the brandy bottle from the nightstand and held it toward him.

"I'm fine," Benjamin said. "I had a lot of wine with dinner, and . . ."

Gudrün set the bottle and her own glass on the nightstand. She turned back to Benjamin, reached forward, and took his hand.

"You're really quite handsome, Ben. Are you used to hearing that from women?" She put her right arm around his neck and began caressing the back of his hair with her fingertips. When he just sat, staring at her, saying nothing, she leaned forward and kissed him.

The taste of the brandy was like an aphrodisiac. Benjamin felt his head reeling. Gudrün kept her mouth against his, her lips slightly parted. Benjamin was surprised at how tender the kiss seemed, how sincere. He was intensely aware of her perfume—something both sharp and musky—and the sound of her dress pressing against his shirt, her fingers on the back of his neck. . . .

She moved her head back a few inches.

"Let's dispense with this jacket, shall we?" she said.

Almost instinctively, Benjamin started to shrug off his jacket, then realized he would have to set his drink down first. He leaned awkwardly over to the nightstand. As he did so, the glass bumped the side of the yellow sheet of folded paper he'd set there. It fell to the floor, where it lay almost beneath the bed, half open. Even as Gudrün was helping him out of his jacket, he couldn't help glancing down at it.

When after a moment she realized he wasn't helping her, she stopped.

"Cold feet?" she asked, arching an eyebrow.

Benjamin looked at her. His first thought was that she was indeed a very beautiful woman: her blond hair, dark eyebrows, bright red lipstick . . . like something out of a 1950s movie. And he was about to turn her out.

"No, no," he said. He ran his hand through his hair, then stood up so that his shoe was covering the yellow paper. "I think I've had too much to drink after all," he said. "That damned scotch of Samuel's." And then he gave her a look he hoped was both guileless and slightly drunk.

If she was insulted, she hid it well. She stood as well, put her hand on his chest.

"Well, there's still time to . . . get to know each other. I think you'll be around for a while." Before he could ask what she meant by that, she gave him a very kind peck on the cheek, said, "Do you mind?" and took the brandy. Then she left, closing the door softly behind her.

It was only after she was gone that Benjamin wondered *why* he was hiding the paper from her. From what little he'd seen of what was written there, he didn't have a clue what it meant.

Benjamin crouched down and took the yellow paper gently by one corner. When it had fallen partially open, he'd seen only the word "TEACUP" written across the top in neat, block letters. Now that he saw the entire half-page, he knew he had to show it to Wolfe, regardless of the late hour.

He went into the bathroom, splashed cold water over his face and hair, and ran a towel over his head. Then he went back into the bedroom, grabbed the yellow paper, and hurried out of the room and down the hall.

CHAPTER 14

"I'll be damned." Wolfe was holding the small yellow paper Benjamin had brought him. "What on earth does it mean?"

Benjamin had found Wolfe still awake and reading in bed, some sort of scholarly journal, and listening to a radio; somehow he'd found a station with oldies from the 1930s, the kind of music that he thought suited Wolfe perfectly. He also had the ubiquitous tumbler of scotch on his bedside table.

The half sheet of notepad paper had small figures on it, and a single word:

TEACUP

58-42-54-33-23-31-21-33

"Tell me again, slowly, *where* did you find this?"

"On my nightstand." Benjamin said, then corrected himself. "I mean, that's where I'd put it. But it must have fallen out of the Ginsburg book, the one about Harlan Bainbridge."

Wolfe stood up. He studied the paper in silence for a moment, turned to Benjamin.

"Care for a drink?" he asked, as if nothing extraordinary had happened.

Benjamin frowned in frustration. "Drink? No, thank you, I've had quite enough for one night. And I have a feeling I'm going to need a clear head—that *we're* going to need clear heads—if we're going to figure this out."

Wolfe gave him that infuriating smile. "Quite the nanny, aren't you?"

"Samuel." He stopped, controlled his frustration, began again. "Would you mind telling me what the hell is going on here? This is most likely some sort of note Jeremy placed in that book. But why would he go to all the trouble of putting it in *code*? Why all the passwords on his computer? Why this cloak-and-dagger about who he spoke with? I just practically chased Gudrün . . . Dr. Soderbergh out of my room because I didn't want her to see this. And I'm not even sure *why*, except that your paranoia is contagious."

Wolfe raised an eyebrow. "Gudrün? You're on a first-name basis?" Benjamin started to protest, but Wolfe waved him silent. "It doesn't matter. It may even be of benefit. Anyway, you did the right thing by not letting her see this. You were acting on instinct."

"Then they're instincts I didn't know I had," said Benjamin, sitting on the bed. "And you haven't answered my other questions."

Wolfe waved the yellow paper at him.

"I think *this* may answer your questions. And I have a feeling you *do* know what it means, or it wouldn't have been in the Ginsburg book, a book Fletcher knew you would want to examine."

"But why not simply tell me when I arrived? Why put it in code?"

"Perhaps he had a premonition he might not be able to tell you in person," Wolfe said heavily. "Here, take another look at it."

Benjamin took the paper and studied it again.

"Well," he began tentatively, "offhand I'd say it looks like Franklin's pyramid code. Perhaps it's a coincidence . . ."

"To hell with coincidence," insisted Wolfe, "just tell me what you're thinking."

"You know what a pigpen code is?"

"Yes," said Wolfe. "As does every Boy Scout. It's the code the Masons used for some of their documents." Wolfe shuffled through papers on his nightstand, found something to write on and a pen, spoke as he drew on the paper. "You make two simple tic-tac-toe grids and two Xs, then distribute the letters of the alphabet across them, and then use symbols that represent the position of the letter in its grid. Like this, correct?" He showed Benjamin the sketch he'd made.

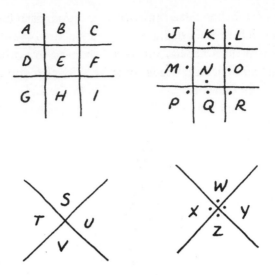

"So for instance 'Samuel' would be rendered as . . ." Again he drew on the paper. "This."

"Yes," said Benjamin, "that's the basic code."

"But," Wolfe objected, "I don't see any of those kinds of symbols there. It's all these little pyramids."

"Well," said Benjamin, "the pigpen code actually predates the Masons. There's even a record of a seventeenth-century gravestone in England, in Cheshire—one Thomas Brierley—with that code carved into it. Franklin felt the code was compromised by its very popularity. He thought he could do better. And he was a printer, after all, used to playing with letters and texts. He'd been experimenting with simple Caesar substitution codes for years; you know, where you simply shift letters so many places to the right or left?" Wolfe nodded. "But then that interest collided with one of his other manias, which was for *pyramids*. The Masons were quite mad about pyramids. They thought their 'perfect symmetry' held some ancient wisdom."

Benjamin lifted up the paper again. "So Franklin decided to combine the two codes, to construct a *tabula recta*—you know, Blaise de Vigenère's alphabet grids?" Wolfe nodded impatiently, and Benjamin hurried on. "But with *pyramids* rather than grids. Here."

Benjamin took the notepad from Wolfe and made his own sketch.

"So. If you construct a pyramid of small triangles, you get something like this."

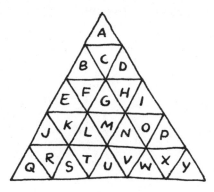

Wolfe looked down at the sketch. "But there's only twenty-five triangles, no room in it for Z," he protested.

"Wait, I'll get to that. Of course, if the code is always the same, with the same letters in each triangle, then it isn't a very good code, is it. So there's a first key that tells the recipient which letter to put in the top triangle. Then, once you have the letters distributed in this pyramid of triangles, you assign a two-digit number to each letter. The first digit is the row, the second digit is the triangle within the row. So in this pyramid the A becomes 11, B becomes 21, C becomes 22, and so on. And whatever the missing letter is, like Z in this instance, becomes—"

"Zero?"

"Exactly." Benjamin placed the small yellow paper with TEACUP at the top next to the notepad. "But remember the first symbol here, the little triangle with a B in it? Well, *that* must be Jeremy's first key, which means the letter to place at the top of the pyramid is a B, so . . ." He rapidly drew another pyramid and began filling it in with letters. When he was finished he leaned back and pointed with the pen.

"Then 58 is fifth row, eighth triangle, which is Y, and the rest . . ." He worked silently for a minute. "There," he said finally, leaning back in the chair.

Wolfe looked down at what he'd written.

"Y-L-U-H-E-F-C-H?" Wolfe frowned. "Well, that may be a code, but it certainly isn't easy to remember. He would have had to go through this operation every time he wanted to enter his password. And what about this symbol at the end?" He touched the inverted triangle with the little dot in the upper right-hand corner.

"Ah," said Benjamin. "*That's* what put me on this track. The traditional Masonic code couldn't handle numbers, so Franklin created *another* pyramid of triangles just for numbers, like this." Again Benjamin worked at the notepad.

"Then he used the dots from the traditional pigpen code, rotating the dots around the corners and midpoints of the triangles, so you get this." Benjamin jotted on the pad.

"And as with the alphabet pyramid, zero would simply be an empty triangle."

"But why use any numbers here at all?" Wolfe asked. "Why not just a word or phrase?"

Benjamin smiled. "Franklin *did* use it for numbers with the older Masonic code. But with his *own* pyramid code, it took on a different function: the function of the second or *shifting key* in a Caesar substitution code."

"To shift letters so many places to the right?"

"Well, to shift the letters so many triangles ahead in the *tabula recta* pyramid. This symbol at the end of Jeremy's code would decode as a six. So if we go back to the pyramid and add six places to these letters we get . . ." He worked on the notepad for a moment. When he finished he sat back, grunted.

"What?" Wolfe leaned down closely over his shoulder. The converted message was written at the bottom of the page.

F-R-B-N-K-L-I-N

"Not much better," said Wolfe. He laughed. "I'm afraid you don't quite have this—"

"Of course!" Benjamin erased the B and wrote in an A. Now the line read:

F-R-A-N-K-L-I-N

"Jeremy was new to all this," Benjamin explained. "He forgot he'd shifted the A to the zero triangle, which isn't in the pyramid proper. Franklin had a special notation in those cases, but I guess Jeremy didn't know that, and . . ."

"Yes, yes, very interesting," said Wolfe, taking the paper from Benjamin. "Well, I suggest we don't wait until morning. Let's go and try this on Fletcher's computer right now."

Benjamin nodded, but as Wolfe retrieved his shoes and put them on, then moved to the door, Benjamin hadn't yet risen from the bed.

"Benjamin?" Wolfe prodded.

"It's just strange," he said.

"That someone as precise as Dr. Fletcher would make such a mistake?"

"No, not that. It's just very odd that Jeremy would choose this code, from all possible codes."

"Think where you are, Benjamin," Wolfe answered. "There's a cryptologist here, a Dr. Karl Bennett, one of the best in the field. I'm sure Fletcher was resourceful enough to seek him out and find out whatever he needed to know about codes."

"Perhaps." Benjamin shook his head. "But it's still strange. Franklin scholars had discovered these numbered codes in his correspondence and some of his business papers, and they'd assumed it was based on the Masonic code. But they'd never been able to decipher it before, until a particular letter was unearthed just last year."

"And who unearthed it?" Wolfe asked.

Benjamin looked up at him. "I did."

"*What?*"

"I wrote a paper about it. That discovery was responsible for my appointment at the Library of Congress."

"So in other words," said Wolfe, remaining in the doorway, "Fletcher knew that quite probably the only person who would be able to recognize this and decode it would be one Benjamin Franklin Wainwright."

Benjamin looked up at him, not quite comprehending.

"Isn't it obvious, Benjamin?" He smiled broadly. "He didn't leave this for himself. He *knew* the password. He left it for *you*."

Wolfe came over to the chair, put his hand on Benjamin's shoulder.

"That's what I meant when I said Fletcher had leaked information, just not yet. He *intended* to leak something, that much is clear. To *you*."

CHAPTER 15

Wolfe immediately led Benjamin off down the hall to Fletcher's room. Once there, again Wolfe performed the ritual of examining the strip of tape on the doorjamb; once again he seemed satisfied that it had not been tampered with. He unlocked the door and they entered Fletcher's dark room.

Everything was as they had left it. Benjamin walked in and almost stumbled over the keyboard on the floor, as Wolfe had insisted on closing the curtains before turning on the small banker's lamp on the table. Then Wolfe switched on the laptop computer.

This time when it asked for a password, Wolfe immediately typed in "poisson," and the desktop with its few icons appeared. Then, as Benjamin had before, Wolfe double-clicked on the icon that read TEACUP-6. And as before, a small window appeared with the message ENTER PASSWORD FOR TEACUP INITIALIZATION.

Wolfe bent his fingers over the keyboard, then stopped.

"What do you think, 'franklin' with a small or capital F?" he asked.

Benjamin looked at the yellow paper where Wolfe had set it in the circle of light from the lamp. "Just small F, I think. He knew there was no way to designate capitals in Franklin's code."

"I agree," said Wolfe. He tapped the name, all in lowercase letters, into the waiting rectangle.

Nothing happened.

"Damn," Wolfe said. "If this doesn't work—"

"Wait," said Benjamin. "Look."

On the laptop screen, a new window had opened. It was a list of file names—but before they could read any of them, another window appeared on the screen.

CONVERT GADENHOWER DATA? (Y/N) it read.

"Gadenhower data?" said Benjamin. He looked at Wolfe. "Mrs. Gadenhower?"

Wolfe nodded. "He had spoken to her just that day, remember. And told her he was going back to his room to type in notes from their conversation. And I suspect we want to continue where he left off, don't you?"

Benjamin nodded.

"Very well then." And Wolfe extended his index finger and very gently hit the Y key.

The window disappeared—and another window replaced it.

CONVERTING TEXT it read. And then a progress bar appeared beneath it, with the message above it: *Time Remaining: About 30 minutes.*

"Apparently," Wolfe said, "we have half an hour before our next revelation."

He bent and turned the Chippendale chair upright, then motioned to Benjamin to drag the other chair over to the table. Once seated, he offered Benjamin the bottle of scotch he'd brought from his room.

"Without a glass?" Benjamin asked.

"You've conquered your fear of scotch," Wolfe said. "Now take the final plunge, my boy."

Benjamin shrugged, took the bottle and tipped it very slowly. Despite his caution, a glut of scotch rushed into his throat. He pitched forward, coughing. When he had himself under control, he handed the bottle back to Wolfe.

"Consider yourself initiated," said Wolfe, taking a swig himself.

Benjamin wiped the tears from his eyes. He sat looking at Wolfe, silent for a moment, then apparently made a decision.

"Arthur said something to me the night I arrived," he said. "Something about you. About a loss." He hesitated a moment, then went on. "Is that why you drink?"

Wolfe sighed. He looked at the bottle.

"Arthur was talking about my wife, I imagine," he said very quietly. "Cancer."

"I'm terribly sorry," Benjamin said. "I didn't mean to—"

Wolfe shook his head. "Actually, it was quite gentle, as such things go. Fairly rapid. Relatively painless." He paused. "Relatively," he added, and took a drink.

Benjamin felt the need to change the subject. "But you also said something about Vietnam?"

Wolfe looked up at him. "That was a long time ago," he said, looking suddenly serious, the typical smirk entirely absent, his eyes not focused on Benjamin.

"I was assigned to SIG-INT, signals intelligence. We were stationed in Saigon. At first, our job was to listen to the Vietcong's radio transmissions."

"And that's where you learned cryptography?"

Wolfe nodded, but provided no further details.

"And afterwards?" Benjamin prodded.

"There aren't many things a man can do with that kind of experience. Not that I wanted to do, anyway. I kicked around for a while with various security firms, you know, for banks, corporations with offices abroad, that sort of thing."

"But how . . ." Benjamin accepted the bottle from Wolfe, waved its neck around the room.

"How did I come to work for the Foundation?" He laughed. "What does it mean to be secure, Benjamin?"

"I'm not sure what you—"

"That's the first question a security analyst must ask. What does the client wish to 'secure'?" He sighed heavily. "It's always about fault lines. And I learned that, paradoxically, the best place to look for those fault lines is typically in whatever the client considers their greatest strength."

Benjamin noticed that the lean lines of Wolfe's face had become tense, hard; that the humor that usually lurked in his eyes and at the corners of his mouth was gone.

"For instance, there are those who consider their love of freedom to be their greatest strength. I worked, here at the Foundation and other places, with such people. I know what they fear, what makes them insecure. And more often than not, it's the threat of that selfsame freedom. Only in others."

Suddenly there was a little *beep* from the computer. Immediately Wolfe rose and went to the table. "It appears our cake is done."

Benjamin joined him at the table. The progress bar on the computer screen had disappeared, and in its place was a new window.

In the window were two lines, like graphs—the one on the left blue, the one on the right red—rising from opposite sides of the window, like two halves of a bell-shaped curve. But where the top of the curve would be, there was a gap. Underneath the curve were a series of complicated mathematical formulae, leading up to a final one in red:

$$\forall i, x_i \in S_i, x_i \neq x_i^* : f_i(x_i^*, x_{-i}^*) \geq f_i(x_i, x_{-i}^*) = \mathbf{80\%}$$

"Now it's my turn," said Benjamin. "What on earth is that?"

"It's a formula for a concept in game theory," said Wolfe, still studying the graphs. "Something called a Nash equilibrium." Wolfe began tracing the lines with a finger, as if touching the screen would somehow communicate to him something intimate about them.

"And what's that?" prodded Benjamin.

"Oh." Wolfe looked up at him. "It's when, in a game, there's no advantage to a player changing his strategy as long as the other player keeps doing whatever he's doing. It's a complicated way of saying they're at a stalemate. Do you know a game called The Prisoner's Dilemma?"

"I've heard of it. Something about two prisoners trying to decide whether to rat on one another?"

Wolfe nodded. "They're told that the first one to betray his fellow will receive a lighter sentence, and the one betrayed will receive a harsher sentence. But if neither one betrays the other, they both receive moderate sentences. In such a game, the best strategy is for both players to remain silent. While neither really wins, it guarantees neither completely loses. It's the best *aggregate* result possible."

"But what if they don't know what the other one will do?"

"Exactly. That's the random element. That's why the police—and other security workers," here he smiled, "always keep the two suspects separated, and try to convince each one that the other is turning snitch. If they collude, they might agree to stonewall it out and stymie the interrogators. In that case, all three parties will have reached a Nash equilibrium."

Benjamin looked at the computer screen. "Well, I have two questions. The first is, what does the eighty percent sign mean?"

"And the other one?" asked Wolfe.

"What has that game got to do with Dr. Fletcher's research on nuclear war?"

"Let me answer the second question first." Wolfe pulled the chair over to the table. He took the bottle of scotch, studied it as if contemplating another drink, then set it with some finality on the table.

"You heard Herman Kahn mentioned at dinner." Benjamin nodded. "Cavendish was right, Kahn practically did invent theorizing about nuclear war. He worked out dozens of scenarios: What if the Soviets strike first? What if we do? What if they use only half their missiles in such a strike? Every conceivable variation of mass death. He was the one who argued that, however horrific the idea might be, it was better to come out of such a war with twenty million dead than a hundred and fifty million dead."

"You're right," said Benjamin. "It does sound horrific."

"He called it 'thinking the unthinkable.'" Wolfe pointed at the computer. "Kahn didn't really bring this level of sophistication to bear on such thinking. That came with computer wizards like Fletcher. And, in his day, Arthur Terrill." He saw Benjamin's look of surprise. "Yes, in his early days, Arthur was quite the whiz kid of Armageddon."

"But he said he knew nothing about Jeremy's research."

"Apparently Arthur's also become adept at an administrator's most useful skill: lying."

"But how do *you* understand this stuff?"

"I told you I recognized the name Anton Sikorsky from Fletcher's list?" Benjamin nodded. "Well, Anton and I worked together, some years ago, for the Foundation. On this 'stuff.' Not at Fletcher's level. His whole career had been devoted to examining Kahn's scenarios, the assumptions behind them, and subjecting them to rigorous statistical analysis. To establishing the probabilities of such unthinkable events."

Benjamin turned, walked to the bed, but didn't sit down. Suddenly he turned.

"You mean his program calculates the probability of the Cold War?"

"Yes."

Benjamin laughed. "But isn't that like predicting rain *after* a flood?"

"Not quite." Wolfe knitted his eyebrows. "From what I've been able to understand of Fletcher's work, he simply didn't believe it."

"Believe it?" asked Benjamin, confused. "How can you not *believe* in the Cold War?"

"It's more about questioning the fundamental logic of the MAD doctrine—Mutual Assured Destruction—that supposedly kept the Cold War from turning hot. He doesn't come right out and say so, but he seems to imply that, at least statistically, it simply doesn't make sense. Or put in Fletcher's terms, that it has a high probability of such a doctrine being unstable. And if I'm reading this right, the TEACUP program is calculating that probability at 80 percent."

Before Benjamin could say anything, Wolfe moved the pointer on the screen and slowly dragged the window with the graphs aside, so that the list of files underneath it was now visible. "And I would assume this is the list of his data points from which to calculate that probability."

Benjamin stepped closer, leaned down over Wolfe's shoulder.

There were three columns of file names. On the right, Benjamin recognized a number of books about King Philip's War. In the middle was a single file name: "Gadenhower Data." And on the left was a list of titles he didn't recognize, but they were clearly all about nuclear war: *The Effects of Global Thermonuclear War, Thinking About the Unthinkable, The Fallacies of Cold War Deterrence* . . . and a long list of journal articles and white papers.

Benjamin saw that each of the titles had a little X in front of its name . . . or so he thought until Wolfe suddenly placed his hand on Benjamin's arm.

"Look there," said Wolfe, pointing to the bottom of the list.

"Bainbridge Data," said the bottommost file name on the left. And there was no little X before its name. "And there," said Wolfe, pointing to the last entry in the column on the right.

Stzenariy 55, it read.

"Well, here goes," said Wolfe. He clicked on the "Bainbridge Data" file, and it opened . . . to reveal nothing.

"Obviously he hadn't gotten that data yet," Wolfe said.

"But he had the Ginsburg book, we know that," protested Benjamin.

"Then 'Bainbridge Data' must refer to some *other* information about the good Reverend," Wolfe said, sounding frustrated.

Benjamin thought for a moment. "Like his diary," he said.

"Diary?" asked Wolfe impatiently.

"Something Dr. Stoltz told me about at dinner. It's an amazing story. I can't understand why my father never mentioned it, as it surely would have been referenced—"

"Benjamin!"

"Yes, sorry. Anyway, according to Stoltz they discovered something he called the Bainbridge diary here, on the grounds of the Foundation, back in the 1920s."

"And Stoltz told Fletcher about this discovery?"

"Yes. He said Jeremy came to speak to him about the mural in the foyer, but that he was also very interested in anything about Bainbridge, including this diary."

"Then why is the file empty?"

"Because the diary isn't here. Not anymore. It was donated to the Morris Estate."

"The *Seaton* Morris Estate?" Wolfe asked.

"Stoltz didn't say," Benjamin said. Then he thought of something. "But there's a stamp in the Ginsburg book that identifies it as part of the *Seymour* Morris library."

"Do tell." Wolfe turned back to the screen. "Well, let's see if this other file is more revealing."

He clicked on the "*Stzenariy 55*" file. And when it opened, it did indeed contain something more. But only three words.

Borba s tenyu.

CHAPTER 16

Once again, Benjamin found himself driving through the wooded hills of Massachusetts. The good weather had given way to a typically overcast New England fall day and, though it wasn't raining yet, the threat of a downpour lurked in the low clouds overhead.

Benjamin and Wolfe were headed for the Morris Estate, not far from the Foundation's campus, for a hastily arranged interview with one Seaton Morris: son of the late tycoon, philanthropist, and bibliophile Seymour Morris, now guardian of the original Bainbridge diary—and wealthy benefactor of the American Heritage Foundation.

"On a Sunday?"

"Arthur implied the Morris family owes the Foundation a favor, or many favors," Wolfe said. "But he suggested we arrive no later than ten o'clock. Apparently they're hosting a charity art auction this afternoon, and they want our little tour group out before then."

So, still groggy from too little sleep and too much wine, brandy, and scotch, Benjamin had followed Wolfe outside. He'd noticed Wolfe was carrying his briefcase, and when he'd asked, Wolfe had told him yes, Fletcher's laptop was inside, as he no longer felt Fletcher's room was a "secure site." But he hadn't explained why.

Soon the narrow road was again bordered by rows of maple and sycamore trees, with the occasional paved driveways leading up to stately, isolated mansions. As they drove, they discussed the files they'd discovered the night before on Fletcher's computer.

"I recognized most of the ones about nuclear strategy," Wolfe said, "but not the one titled *Stzenariy 55*. Which I translate as 'Script 55.' Which means nothing to me."

"And that Russian phrase that was inside?"

"Borba s tenyu?" said Wolfe. "Not a clue."

"Well, I was paying attention to those other files, from the Colonial period," Benjamin said. "Did you notice the one called 'Newburgh Data'?"

"No. Why, does it mean something to you?"

"Well . . ." Benjamin hesitated. "I believe it refers to the Newburgh Conspiracy."

"Who was Newburgh?" asked Wolfe.

"It's not a who, it's a where. Newburgh, New York, where the Continental Army was camped at the end of the Revolutionary War. And actually it's not really an accurate name, as their camp was closer to New Windsor, and—"

"For godssake, Benjamin," Wolfe interrupted him, "stop being the historian for a moment and just tell me why this Newburgh-whatever is important."

"Well," said Benjamin, "it might be important because it was *almost* the only military coup ever attempted against the United States government."

"*Coup*?" replied Wolfe in surprise. "You must be joking. There's never been a coup against the U.S. government."

"I said *almost*," corrected Benjamin.

And then Benjamin told Wolfe the story of the infamous—and for many years utterly secret—Newburgh Conspiracy of 1783, when the United States of America almost fell before it ever existed.

General George Washington, Commander in Chief of the Continental Army, was miserable.

He was cold. The winter of 1783 was proving to be as bad if not worse than that of 1782. The small hut that served as his headquarters in the camp at New Windsor was little more than a log cabin, and the bitter New York wind entered through a hundred chinks. And this was a windy March, indeed.

He was in pain. The latest set of wooden false teeth fit poorly, stretching his jaw and forcing him to at all times grit his teeth, as though in the extremity of rigor mortis.

He was downcast. Before him on the small rickety wooden table lay two letters: the first was from Superintendent of Finance Robert Morris in the Continental Congress, expressing in polite if adamant terms that there simply was no money in the treasury to pay his freezing, hungry soldiers; just as there'd been no money last month, or the month before.

The other letter was from Thomas Jefferson, appointed but not yet seated in the Congress, and therefore, to Washington's mind, a reliable observer of events there. He complained that the Treaty of Paris with the British had still not been ratified by the squabbling Congress, and that the young Articles of Confederation government was proving just as fragile and powerless as they'd feared it would be: unable to agree on even raising taxes to pay its army, and locked in bitter argument over a fundamental issue of their new government that Washington believed was the heart of everything they'd fought and suffered for: the principle of "one man, one vote." Jefferson wrote that the aristocratic members, like Hamilton, were fiercely and apparently unmovably against surrendering any of their power to what they called "rule by ignorant mob." It more than made the general angry; it was disheartening in the extreme to think that some of the rebels and patriots who had been most passionate about independence and democracy in the beginning of the fight did not, when the crucial time came, actually believe in either.

Thus, on the verge of victory and after seven years of bitter struggle for independence, all his dreams for the new Republic seemed to be unraveling.

At that moment there came a knock at the door.

"Yes," he said, not raising his head.

The tall, lanky figure of his longtime aide-de-camp, Lieutenant Colonel Tench Tilghman, entered the room. He strode to the table and threw a parchment down in front of Washington.

"Have you seen this?" he said, barely able to contain his anger.

Washington picked up the parchment. It was a letter, addressed to "All good and patriotic soldiers of the Continental Army, fellow sufferers at the hands of an indifferent and feckless Congress." He read the opening paragraph.

> *Have you not more than once suggested your wishes, and made known your wants to Congress, wants and wishes, which gratitude and policy should have anticipated rather than evaded? And, have you not lately, in the weak language of entreating memorials, begged from their justice, what you could no longer expect from their favor?*

"What is this?" Washington asked, not looking up from the paper.

"This . . . perfidy was distributed in the camp this very morning," Tilghman said through tight lips. "Read on."

Washington continued reading.

> *Can you then consent to be the only sufferers by this revolution and, retiring from the field, grow old in poverty, wretchedness and contempt? Can you consent to wade through the vile mire of dependency and owe the miserable remnant of that life to charity, which hitherto has been in honor? If you can, go, and carry with you the jest of tories and the scorn of whigs; the ridicule and, what is worse, the pity of the world!*
>
> *Go, starve and be forgotten! But, if your spirits should revolt at this; if you have sense enough to discover and spirit sufficient to oppose tyranny under whatever garb it may assume, whether it be the plain coat of republicanism or the splendid robe of royalty; if you have yet learned to discriminate between a people and a cause, between men and principles: awake, attend to your situation, and redress yourselves! If the present moment be lost, every future effort is in vain, and your threats then will be as empty as your entreaties now.*

Now Washington looked up, his eyes heavy and sad.

"It's an incitement to *treason*," Tilghman said. "They're calling for a meeting of all officers tomorrow, in the temple. They mean to march on Philadelphia, demand their blood money, and, if frustrated in that claim, disband the government and replace it with a military tribunal." He leaned forward, his hands on the table. "And we know who's scheming hand puts these words to paper."

"Gates," Washington said, with a sigh.

Tilghman nodded vigorously. "He has been hungry for your commission since the war began, we both know this. And he has been hard lobbying at Congress to replace you. Even after his marathon retreat, better to call it flight, from Cornwallis at Camden, he has Hamilton's favor. He sees final power in this maneuver."

"But what proof—," Washington began to protest, though weakly.

"Look at the letters!" Tilghman answered. "If that isn't the imprint of the press in Gates's quarters, I'm an English bulldog. And these sentiments, they're the constant cry of his aide, that artillery man with lead shot for brains, Armstrong."

Washington leaned back, ran a hand through his hair—hair that had once been a vibrant red, but which had gone a steel gray in the course of the long, frustrating war; a war that had been a much nearer thing, and a much longer campaign, than he'd ever imagined.

"The fools," he said finally. "The British are but sixty miles away, warm and content in New York. If they caught wind of such dissension . . ."

"Arrest him," Tilghman said with vigor. "And Armstrong. In fact, put his entire staff in chains. They must know of this."

Washington frowned. "And fulfill the slander of 'tyrant'?" He shook his head. "The men are ragged enough, Colonel. One of the officers was hung in effigy in the Sixth Regiment just Tuesday last. Mass arrests would put match to powder."

"Then what would you have?" asked Tilghman, exasperated. "Let them march? Toss out the Congress? That would bring civil war, and the redcoats would happily sup up the leavings. All would be lost!"

Washington pushed back from the table, stood up, walked to the small potbellied stove in the corner upon which steamed a small porcelain pot of tea. Offering a cup to Tilghman, who declined, he poured himself one and sipped at it, his eyes unfocused, thinking.

Finally, he turned to Tilghman. "Do nothing to impede them for now," he said.

"What!" Tilghman could barely speak. "But then—"

"Let them assemble," Washington said. Then he smiled. "It's addressed to *all* officers, isn't it?" Tilghman looked at him blankly. "The last time I glanced at my shoulders, Colonel, I was an officer in this army, too."

Washington's lamp burned late that night, and anyone looking through one of the frosted windowpanes of his modest quarters would have seen him at the table long into the cold darkness, writing with a steady and energetic hand.

The next morning dawned as bleak and chill as any of that March. Rising even earlier than usual, Washington dressed slowly, putting on his full dress uniform, complete with red sash and bright rows of medals. When he was ready, he threw on his greatcloak—the same he'd worn that fateful Christmas night in the crossing to Trenton, though now considerably more frayed and patched—and left his quarters, walking slowly across the crunching ground to the long, narrow wooden building his men had completed just a month before; a place meant to serve as the one warm sanctuary in camp where men might gather to drink and play at cards, and which had been named, with a certain ironic military humor, the Temple of Virtue. Adjusting the coat upon his shoulders, he opened the door and entered.

The room was warm from the large stove in the center, and musky with the scent of canvas and leather and men too long from the niceties of bath and soap. Rows of churchlike pews faced a small lectern set at the front of the hall; the pews, he was distressed to see, were full with all ranks of his officer corps.

There was a cacophony of voices as he entered, men shouting, declaiming, some standing as if ready to come to blows. And then a few saw him at the doorway, and nudged their neighbors, and so on until the hall fell almost silent. All heads turned as he walked slowly down the center aisle of the hall, and most displayed a look of shock. Other than the hiss and crackle of wood in the stove, for a moment the only sound was the slap of his boots on the floorboards.

Behind the lectern stood, of course, Major General Horatio Lloyd Gates, also in full dress uniform. Clearly, Gates was as shocked to see him as anyone else in the hall. He'd been about to speak when Washington entered.

"General Gates," Washington said, standing next to him.

Gates was at first flustered, then remembered himself and saluted. "General Washington," he said nervously.

"General," Washington repeated, "do I have your permission to address this assemblage?"

Now Gates looked terrified. "Of course, General Washington," he said. "Uh . . . please," and he moved aside from the lectern.

Washington moved behind the podium and surveyed the room. He waited until he had every pair of eyes upon him. And then, with a movement deliberate and graceful, he reached into his greatcloak's pocket.

"Gentlemen," he said, "you will permit me to put on my spectacles, for I have not only grown gray but almost blind in the service of my country."

There was absolute silence. He realized most of the men in the room didn't even know he wore spectacles. And he saw that his comment had had the desired effect, their faces expressing shame in the face of Washington's humble admission of all he'd given to the Cause these past seven terrible years. As he looked around the room, here and there men dropped their gaze, unable to look him in the eyes.

He then drew his speech from his pocket, the one he'd labored all night to produce. But even as he read from it, he knew it was unnecessary; he could feel the shift in the room's sentiment. He knew that when he finished, thanked them for their attention, and left, they would never be able to pledge themselves to open rebellion again.

CHAPTER 17

"Astounding," Wolfe said when Benjamin had finished the story. "That certainly wasn't covered in *my* high school history of the Revolutionary War."

"Nor anyone else's," said Benjamin. "For decades after the war, it simply wasn't spoken about, by either side. Once the Treaty of Paris was signed and the war successfully over, certainly the conspirators didn't want their names associated with such a betrayal. And for Washington's side . . . well, he thought the country too fragile to know it had survived its birth by a pair of spectacles.

"And years later, when some of the facts came out, the argument was it had all been something of a joke, a tempest in a teapot. Other historians, however, my father for instance, have taken it more seriously. He thought Hamilton's group didn't necessarily want a *real* coup, just the threat of one, a 'crisis' that would allow them to establish martial law, get the money the army was owed, and establish a more powerful and restrictive central government, and not the general democracy of Washington, Jefferson, Franklin . . . well, the majority of the Founding Fathers. But true democracy was something Hamilton and a few others had been opposed to ever since the Revolution began."

"And who besides this Gates was definitely involved in this *almost* coup?"

"That's always been a little vague, though one of the ringleaders was almost certainly Hamilton."

"But there's no proof?"

"Well, not what you would call proof. You see, the group that supported Gates—a General Alexander McDougall, a Colonel Walter Stewart, and a Major John Brooks—had exchanged letters during the whole affair. Some of them came to light years later, and in them they'd used code names to refer to one another. McDougall's was 'Brutus.'"

Wolfe laughed. "How appropriate."

"And there were mentions in some of their letters to another group, or club, whatever you want to call it, which supposedly included Gates and some other proaristocracy types, a sort of *anti*-Masonic society. These letters made reference to another code name, someone they called 'the Indian Laird,' in a way that suggested he was either the founder of this anti-Masonic group, or a very prominent member."

"Indian Laird?" asked Wolfe.

"Alexander Hamilton was born in the West Indies. And he was the illegitimate grandson of a Scottish laird."

"All right, that gets us Hamilton's connection to the conspiracy perhaps. But not Fletcher's interest in it."

"A prominent New Englander was also implicated in the plot. One Gouverneur Morris. He was famous—or perhaps infamous is a better word—for stating that no successful country ever existed without an aristocracy, and that voting should be restricted to those who owned property."

Wolfe chuckled, then a thought struck him. "Morris?" Wolfe said with surprise. "As in *Seaton* Morris's family?"

"I'm not sure," said Benjamin. "But it would be quite a coincidence, wouldn't it."

"Like Freud, I don't believe in coincidences," Wolfe said. "So you think Fletcher's interest in the diary led him to Morris, and Morris led him to this Newburgh plot? But still, what does either have to do with Indians or Puritans?"

"I don't know," said Benjamin. "I don't understand it yet, really." He was quiet for a moment. "But the other night I read over my father's notes about Bainbridge, and there are extracts from two of his letters. In one of them, Bainbridge used this word 'Puramis' in a rather odd context. And my father had made a very curious mark by that word. I'm not certain, but—"

"Here we are," Wolfe interrupted him, turning into a side road. "Soon we'll have this precious diary in front of us and we can settle all these questions."

Wolfe turned the car through the gates of the Morris Estate—and Benjamin decided the word "palatial" was perhaps an understatement.

CHAPTER 18

Samuel drove through two redbrick pillared gates into the long, graveled driveway of the Morris Estate. As they passed down a lane of overarching oak trees, Benjamin's first reaction was that the grounds looked remarkably like the Foundation—the same Colonial architecture of red brick with white trim, the same carefully arranged flower gardens, the same sense of protected privilege.

But here there was also a sense of immense personal rather than public power. As they pulled up near the front door, Benjamin noticed that, rather than the typical bull's-eye window in the attic far overhead, there was a stained-glass rendering of a coat of arms.

As they got out of the car and approached the front porch, he could see a glassed hothouse set apart to the left, and some other smaller buildings farther back, on the right. Benjamin counted two Mercedes, a BMW, a Jaguar, and a champagne-colored Bentley parked in the driveway.

Before he rang the front door chimes, Wolfe turned to Benjamin.

"Let's be a little circumspect about what we're here to see," he said. "Seaton knows we're interested in the Bainbridge diary, but there's no reason to focus primarily on just that." He smiled, and once again Benjamin noticed the trace of a certain craftiness in his smile, as though Wolfe was rehearsing his role for Seaton Morris. "In other words, we know it's important, but Mr. Morris doesn't need to. Understand?"

Benjamin smiled, nodded.

The door before them was a massive, dark-wood, Gothic portal, bookended by two enormous urn-shaped flowerpots, which conflicted with the otherwise Colonial architecture of the house. They pressed the bell and, after a two-minute wait, were admitted by a small, thin, and absolutely stone-faced butler.

Before Wolfe could utter a word, the butler said, "Mr. Morris is momentarily engaged. If you would kindly wait in the library?" He indicated a room through sliding French doors left of the enormous foyer.

The Morris library was a cross between a typical library from a country estate and a museum. The floor-to-ceiling bookcases, walnut wainscoting between them; a wallpaper with a Zuber Cie Chinese design above that; a tall bay window in the center of the wall opposite the French doors; the wingback chairs, couch, and coffee table neatly arranged before a large marble fireplace, above which was a portrait of an elderly gentleman in Colonial garb . . . all suggested the mix of intimate comfort and grand display one expected in such a well-pedigreed house. The furniture was an impressive, if eclectic, assemblage of bright, silk-upholstered Chippendale chairs and dark, Sheraton Federal-style tables, with the requisite Hepplewhite bird's-eye maple grandfather clock standing guard in one corner.

But the real treasure of the room was obviously not its furnishings. Displayed in several long cases set in the middle of the room, with several others along one wall, that treasure was proudly displayed beneath the transparent protection of curving glass.

Books. Dozens, perhaps hundreds of books. Everything from enormous volumes in heavy leather bindings to small pamphlets and broadsheets to woodcuts and engravings set in tiny frames or displayed simply, unadorned, as if lying about on their printer's desk; all of them arranged with apparent care—and a certain pride of ownership.

Wolfe went to one of the cases containing over a dozen leather-bound books and began walking slowly along its length, studying the pages to which they were opened.

"My god," he said. "Benjamin, look at this. Here's an illustrated Bible, dated 1751. And a copy of Newton's *Philosophiæ Naturalis Principia Mathematica*! And here's one for you, *Institutio Christianae Religionis,* by one John Calvin. *Collected Sermons of Richard Clyfton,* whoever he is. And

Magnalia Christi Americana, by Cotton Mather himself. Ha! And it's cheek by jowl with a first edition of *Paradise Lost* . . ."

Wolfe turned around, saw that Benjamin wasn't behind him, but instead had crossed the room and was standing in front of a mahogany secretary. Wolfe walked over and stood beside him.

"Did you hear me?" he said. He pointed back toward the display case. "There's Newton's *Principia Mathematica* over there, in perfect condition. And god knows what else." He noticed Benjamin didn't seem to be listening to him. He looked at the piece of furniture Benjamin was studying.

"What's so interesting about this bookcase?" he asked with some irritation.

"Secretary," Benjamin corrected. He was looking intently at a small brass plate set above the glass window of the right-hand door.

"All right," sighed Wolfe. "What's so damn interesting about this secretary?"

"Look at the name," said Benjamin, pointing to the brass plate.

Wolfe read it out loud. "I. Winslow." He looked back to Benjamin. "And what is so extraordinary about Mr. Winslow's . . . secretary?"

"It's one of a kind," said a voice behind them.

They turned and saw a man standing in the open doorway. His face was that of a man in his late twenties, firm and tan and confident. But by his receding hairline, the wrinkles in his neck above the tight, button-down shirt collar, even the way he stood, with one hand in his trouser pocket, they could tell he was more likely in his late forties.

He was exceptionally well dressed in a dark and very subtly pin-striped suit, coal-black alligator shoes, banded tie, and pale blue shirt. His tanned face was clean shaven, his light brown, medium-length hair immaculately groomed. In some superficial ways he reminded Benjamin of George Montrose. But there was none of the sense of bright celebrity here that Benjamin had felt with Montrose. This man didn't invite attention, though he was probably used to receiving it; rather, Benjamin suspected that he would prefer to be the quiet observer in any group of people. It occurred to Benjamin that he was the silent hawk to Montrose's loud peacock.

"I'm Seaton Morris," the man said.

He took a step into the room, turned, and pulled the two French doors closed with an almost inaudible thud. Then he turned again and walked toward them—or strode might be a more accurate description. His clothes, manner, style, the apparently permanent and friendly slight smile on his face—everything about Seaton Morris exuded confidence and precision.

He shook first Wolfe's hand, then Benjamin's. Then he turned to Wolfe and said, "I believe what the young man is trying to tell you is that this one piece of furniture is as important, at least historically, as many of the rare books in this room."

"Winslow made furniture for the 'who's who' of America's patriots," explained Benjamin. "Including this secretary, whose first owner, if I'm correct, was—"

"Alexander Hamilton," finished Seaton. "In fact, it was built to his specifications, during the Revolution. So it has a number of unique features. Here, let me show you."

Seaton stepped closer to the secretary and lowered the small writing table, then reached into the exposed recess.

"This little compartment that would typically hold an inkwell is in fact a detachable box, which you remove by pressing on a hidden spring." He gently pressed his thumb against a concealed button, and the compartment popped out an inch. "Now, if you look inside," and Benjamin and Wolfe leaned down to gaze into the revealed space, "you'll see several additional small boxes, all attached by a chain, which can be used to store special . . . correspondences." Seaton replaced the box, pointed to the secretary's side panels. "And those panels slide open, for other papers of a sensitive nature."

"Ingenious," said Wolfe. "The perfect desk for someone writing seditious letters."

"Of course, the secretary was acquired from Mr. Hamilton's estate after his death. But this house saw its share of just such clandestine activity," said Seaton.

"You see that fireplace?" He pointed toward the large, tile-bordered fireplace in the wall to their right. "At one time, there was a crawl space inside it, accessed by tilting the brick wall that forms its back on a hidden pivot, which led to a concealed room. Just like in those terrible novels of haunted mansions. But also perfect for hiding attendees of illegal meetings quickly, should there come an unexpected knock on the door. And upstairs," he pointed to the ceiling, "you would discover that not all the rooms seem to be on the same level, what with many risers and steps where they don't seem strictly necessary."

"More secret spaces?" asked Wolfe.

Seaton nodded. "And there's a closet in the master bedroom. Move a particular pane of the paneling aside, and you find a ladder that leads down, behind that chimney, into the secret room. And a door in the room leading outside—though from the outside it appears to be an alcove for a statue."

"A statue of whom, I wonder," said Wolfe.

Seaton smiled. "At the time the house was built, I believe it was Socrates. Now it's a very bad imitation of Rockefeller's *Aphrodite*. But it hasn't roused nearly the controversy here it did for him in 1905."

Seaton pointed to the chairs and couch in front of the fireplace. "Here, please gentlemen, sit down."

Even as Seaton invited them to take seats, the downpour that had been holding back outside let go. There was a series of terrific flashes of lightning and, a few seconds later, peals of thunder. Rain came lashing against the panes of the tall bay window, washing down in waves across the glass.

"Looks like you got here just before the deluge," said Seaton. Again, he motioned toward the chairs and couch set before the fireplace.

The three of them moved to the chairs, Benjamin and Wolfe taking their seats on the silk-covered couch, and Seaton sitting in the rightmost wing-back chair. "Can I get you anything to drink?" he asked. "Coffee? Bloody Mary? Mimosa?"

"Well . . . no thank you," said Wolfe, catching a look of surprise from Benjamin.

"This house may date to the Puritans," said Seaton, smiling broadly, "but believe me, we dispensed with their prohibitions a long time ago."

Wolfe leaned back and fixed Seaton with what Benjamin recognized as one of his supercilious stares.

"Just how old is this house, Mr. Morris?" he asked.

"Well." Seaton leaned back, looked about as though taking in the room for the first time. "Actually, it's not the site of the first Morris estate. As I imagine Arthur has told you, that distinction belongs to the Foundation. The manse, as I believe they call it?" Wolfe nodded. "That was the original ancestral hall of the Morris family."

Benjamin leaned forward. "But wasn't that Henry Coddington's estate first?"

Seaton laughed. If Benjamin's comment had discomfited him, he didn't reveal it.

"Yes, that's right. Poor old Coddington put his eggs in the wrong basket, I'm afraid. And paid the price. His entire estate was awarded to Gouverneur Morris in recognition of all his work on behalf of the new American nation."

"Then how—?" began Wolfe.

"Did we wind up in *here*?" finished Seaton. "There was a great deal of

millennial activity after the war. You know the sort of thing, utopian societ-
ies, eager to expand on the ideal of the new America; or in some cases I
suppose convinced it wasn't ideal enough. Anyway, one of Gouverneur's
daughters—Rebecca Morris—became involved with one of them. It was
called New Cairo, or New Egypt, something exotic like that. When she
died, childless, she bequeathed the property and everything on it to the
group, and so it passed out of the family holdings, and we were forced into
this more . . . humble abode. The old manse has had a great many incarna-
tions since then, as I'm sure Arthur informed you." Seaton smiled. "But
you're not here for the family history lecture, are you. What you're interested in is over there."

He rose and walked to one of the display cases in the middle of the
room, and Benjamin and Wolfe followed him. He led them to the middle of
the case.

"The Bainbridge diary," he said, softly touching the rounded dome of
glass.

Beneath his hand and a thick layer of glass, and supported on a wooden
bookstand, was a book a little over a foot high and perhaps almost as wide.
Open as it was, the cover wasn't visible.

What was visible was the first page of the book. Its edges were blackened
with age, and the paper appeared to have been damaged in spots by damp
and mold. Age had also faded some of the black ink lettering on the page,
which was written in a careful, flowing script.

As Benjamin and Wolfe gazed down at it, Seaton asked, "Do you know
the story?"

Benjamin started to nod, but Wolfe said rather abruptly, "No, not all of
it. Would you mind?"

"Not at all," Seaton said. "It's fascinating."

"The Foundation, and before that the Coddington Estate, stands on the
grounds of what was, in the 1600s, something called the Bainbridge Plantation. It was one of those religious communities—from what I've been told,
Harlan Bainbridge, the founder, was something of a fanatic, a thorn in the
side of the other Puritans. So, like Moses—or I guess Brigham Young and his
Mormons—Harlan led his followers out into the wilderness. Back then, that
was anything west of Deerfield, I guess. And they built a compound. It was
extraordinary, really. But then the entire camp was wiped out by Indians—"

"In 1675," interrupted Benjamin. "By Wampanoags." He was looking at
Seaton, not the diary. "Or so the story goes."

Seaton returned the look. "Yes," he said. "Exactly. It was tragic. Not a soul survived."

Seaton looked back down at the diary. "Anyway, after the Indian 'troubles' were settled, Coddington built his estate there—apparently he had provided some sort of financial support to Bainbridge's group, and the deed was in his name. He built the main house that's still there, what they call the manse, and the family lived there for a hundred years. Until my ancestors came into the site after the Revolutionary War. But nothing much was really known about the Bainbridge Plantation, as it was apparently called, after their extermination." He looked up at them again.

"The Morris family also inherited the Indians' displeasure with the 'White Man's' presence," he continued. "Seems there was a sacred burial ground nearby. They continued to agitate about it, bothered the commune when they were there, and the women's institute after them. Never let up, really. Until finally there were no official Wampanoags left to complain."

"And how exactly—" Wolfe pointed to the diary.

"Oh, yes. Well, as you know, the Foundation—though it was called the Heritage Institute for Good Government back then—was officially established there by the 1920s. They undertook some excavation to expand the main building. Imagine their surprise when they encountered a tiny, buried crypt, and inside the crypt a box, and inside that box," he pointed, "this book."

There was a short silence as all three of them contemplated the diary. Benjamin thought it seemed completely indifferent to their scrutiny: ancient, weary, eternal.

Seaton leaned over the case and began reading out loud the carefully inked lines weaving across the dull, yellowed page:

> "And the kings of the earth, and the great men, and the rich
> men, and the chief captains, and the mighty men, and every
> bondman, and every free man, hid themselves in the dens and
> in the rocks of the mountains; and said to the mountains and
> rocks, Fall on us, and hide us from the face of him that sitteth
> on the throne and from the wrath of the Lamb; for the great
> day of his wrath is come; and who shall be able to stand?"

Seaton looked back up at them. "It's from Revelation—," he began.

"Six fifteen," said Benjamin. He looked up at Seaton. "I remember because it begins with the lines everyone always quotes from Revelation. You know." And he recited, still staring directly at Seaton.

"And I beheld when he had opened the sixth seal, and lo,
there was a great earthquake, and the sun was as black as
sackcloth of hair, and the moon was like blood."

"Well, yes," Seaton said. "But of course it's also written there, at the bottom of the quote."

Just beneath the block of text, in the same flowing, faded script, was a single line.

R 6:12—HPB

Seaton paused, looked at Benjamin. "R 6:12. Revelation six, verse twelve. And the HPB is, of course . . ."

"Harlan Phlegon Bainbridge," finished Benjamin.

"Of course," echoed Wolfe. Then he hurried on. "And exactly when was it your family obtained the diary from the Foundation?"

"Some time later," said Seaton. "They felt we had the resources necessary to preserve a treasure like this. And fortunately it was one of those that survived the fire."

"Fire?" asked Wolfe.

"I'm sorry," Seaton said, smiling. "I forget not everyone is as familiar with the family history as most of the folks around here. In the sixties my father decided to donate a portion of our collection to the Library of Congress. But just before those books destined for the library were to be shipped off, there was a terrible fire on the grounds. One of the old gardeners' cottages and a storage shed were completely destroyed, parts of this house were badly damaged, and some of our books were lost. But fortunately not this one."

He looked down at the diary with the undisguised pride of an ardent collector, and added, "It is, after all, one of the most magnificent hoaxes ever produced."

Benjamin was about to say something when Wolfe gently touched his arm.

"I'm sorry, Mr. Morris," Wolfe said carefully. "Dr. Stoltz was a little . . . vague on that aspect of the story. Could you—"

Seaton smiled, as though he'd heard this before.

"Yes, Edward doesn't like to emphasize that part. Diminishes the glamour. Well, it's quite simple, really. Such a find was of course submitted to the foremost antiquarians of the day. And, while whoever the perpetrators were certainly knew their stuff, after close examination, inconsistencies and flaws were found. Eventually they established that the book couldn't possibly have been written more than a year or two before it was unearthed. It was probably all part of some elaborate joke someone was playing on the Institute, perhaps an attempt to embarrass them. The Institute's principles weren't as . . . mainstream back then as they are today. There were those who wished to strangle it in the crib, as it were."

"Remarkable," said Wolfe, leaning closer to the glass. "It looks so . . . well, *old*."

"As I said, a magnificient deception." Seaton's manner changed, becoming even more condescending. "But after all, think about it. What are the chances a book would survive all those decades, two hundred and fifty years, no matter how well protected, in the earth? Or that it wouldn't have been discovered long before?" He shook his head. "No, I'm afraid, as much as I'd like to be the possessor of something so rare, I must satisfy myself with owning the diary equivalent of the Piltdown Man." And he smiled at his own joke.

Benjamin finally felt calm enough to speak.

"I'm curious," he said. "The forger, what sorts of entries did he create in the diary? Would it be possible to, well," he looked Seaton straight in the eye, "to obtain a printed copy of its contents?"

Seaton's composure didn't waver. "What an odd request," he said, smiling. "I suppose, from when it was studied, we might have something like that. I could look, send it over to Arthur should I find anything."

Benjamin started to speak and Wolfe interrupted him again.

"That would be fine. Most appreciated. Well," Wolfe said, nodding, "we don't want to keep you any longer. I know you have important people coming this afternoon."

Benjamin was still looking very closely at the diary. Suddenly there was a knock at the French doors.

"Come in," Seaton said. The doors slid open and the butler stood there.

"Your first guests for the auction have arrived," he announced.

"Tell them I'll be right there," Seaton said. The butler bowed slightly, turned on his heel, and left.

Seaton turned back to Wolfe. "Well, I hope this information somehow helps your . . . inquiry, though I'm not certain I see how it can."

Wolfe smiled broadly. "We really don't know, you see. This is all just an attempt to be thorough. It probably can add nothing to what we already know about Dr. Fletcher's death."

"Yes, Arthur told me," said Seaton. "Terrible. I understand he was brilliant."

"Apparently," said Wolfe. He extended his hand, and Seaton shook it. "So, thank you very much for your time and all your help, Mr. Seaton. We've intruded long enough. And I'm sure Arthur will be very grateful."

"Anything we can do for the Foundation," Seaton said, shaking Benjamin's hand. "And very good to meet both of you."

Again Benjamin seemed on the verge of speaking, but before he could Wolfe took him by the arm. "Time to vamoose," he said, smiling, "before we wind up buying a painting we can't afford."

They both nodded to Seaton, and then followed the butler through the foyer and out the front door. They declined the offer of an umbrella from the butler and, after he'd said a curt "Good day" and shut the door, Wolfe and Benjamin made a dash to the car.

Once past the gate, Wolfe carefully pulled over to the side of the road, stopped the car, and, with the rain pounding down on the roof of the car, turned sideways to face Benjamin.

"Now . . . *what*?" he demanded.

"It's a fake," Benjamin said calmly. "A forgery."

"Yes, of course it is, we know that. Seaton *told* us it was a hoax."

"You don't understand. I mean, it's a *fake* hoax."

Wolfe was absolutely silent for a moment. When he finally gathered his breath, he asked, "What on earth does that mean?"

"What it means is, it would only be a real hoax if there were no real diary, right? But there *is* a real diary."

"How could you possibly know that? Seaton didn't let us examine it closely."

Benjamin smiled, paused, enjoying the fact that for once he was about to surprise Wolfe.

"Because whoever created that one *had* seen the real diary," he said. "And so have I."

CHAPTER 19

Again Wolfe stared at Benjamin for a moment. The only sound was the rain beating against the car's windows and roof.

"What do you mean," he asked, speaking very slowly, "you've seen the *real* diary? Why wouldn't you have told me that much sooner?"

"Because I didn't *know* I'd seen it!" Benjamin answered. He sat back, calmed himself. "At least, I'm fairly certain I have seen it."

"My god, Benjamin, a book that old? How could you not be sure whether you've seen it before or not?"

"Because the book I now believe is the original diary . . . well, it's not an exact match to the book Seaton showed us. Which is precisely why I think it was the real diary. Look, it's hard to explain. It would be much simpler just to show you. But I need to wait until we're back at the Foundation to be certain. They have a library?"

"An awfully good one," said Wolfe, "for so remote a spot."

"Good," Benjamin said firmly. "Let's get back to the Foundation, so I can be certain."

Wolfe started the car and eased it back onto the road. The rain was letting up slightly, but it was thick enough to make driving on such a narrow and winding road dangerous, and Wolfe devoted his attention to navigating the twists and turns.

After they'd been driving for a few minutes, Benjamin spoke again.

"Oh, and something else. Did you notice that portrait over the mantel?"

"You mean the rather stiff-looking gentleman?" asked Wolfe. "I just assumed he was a Colonial paterfamilias."

"Me, too," said Benjamin. "At first I thought it was a portrait of Gouverneur Morris. Then I realized I'd seen that painting before. It's a portrait of Major General Horatio Lloyd Gates."

"The *Newburgh* Gates?"

"One and the same," answered Benjamin. "I'd bet my career that painting is based on a sketch done during the war, a sketch I *am* sure I've seen. It was used as an illustration in a pamphlet he had distributed at Congress, part of his publicity campaign to replace Washington as commander in chief of the Continental Army. But what would a portrait of Gates be doing in the Morris mansion?"

"Ah," sighed Wolfe. "There's no 'X marks the spot' to all this. Not yet, anyway. I said we've been following Fletcher's bread crumbs. Let's keep on the trail and see where it leads. Though these seem dark and tangled woods, indeed."

Benjamin laughed.

"You find that funny?" Wolfe asked, surprised.

"No," said Benjamin. "It's just that the whole 'trail of bread crumbs' theme comes from Hansel and Gretel."

"Yes," said Wolfe.

"Well," said Benjamin, "I was just thinking about what nearly happened to them."

When they returned to the Foundation, Wolfe suggested that he would talk with Arthur while Benjamin pursued his research in the library, and they should meet in the dining hall in an hour.

"About Arthur," Benjamin asked, "you'll tell him about the fake diary?"

Wolfe smiled. "Nothing quite so precipitous. No, I'm largely interested in the first question he'll ask me about our visit to the Morris Estate."

"And what will that be?"

"How should I know," Wolfe said impatiently, "until he asks it?"

With that rather cryptic comment, Wolfe patted his shoulder and headed off to Terrill's office.

Wolfe had told Benjamin that the Foundation library was back behind the laboratory building, so he walked through the manse's foyer and on out into the quad.

The rain had stopped as suddenly as it had begun, but the downpour had left puddles in the grass and on the cobblestone walkway. The copper gables of the dining hall and manse glistened faintly in the dim, gray light.

Benjamin felt a sudden sense of oppression, and realized that his deepest desire was to return to his room and get some sleep. He couldn't believe he'd been at the Foundation for only two days—not even that—and already his life before this seemed a distant memory.

As he crossed the quad, he saw Gudrün sitting on one of the benches. She smiled as he walked up to her. She was dressed in a tailored beige corduroy jacket, crisp white blouse, and tight black slacks, the toes of shiny black dress boots visible beneath the cuff of the pants. Her blond hair was fastened at the back in a ponytail. Benjamin thought she looked every inch the wealthy country gentlewoman out to stroll the grounds of her weekend estate.

"So," she said, rising, "you and Samuel visited the Morris digs?"

"Yes," said Benjamin, surprised. "But how did—"

"I told you, the campus is like a small town," Gudrün said. "So, what did you think?"

"Impressive," he said, keeping it simple.

Gudrün smiled at his understatement. "At the very least. There was a reception there some time ago for the Foundation fellows." She stopped, looked him in the eyes, smiling now as he'd seen her do at dinner the night before—but this time it seemed more genuine. "I imagine their book collection is like King Solomon's treasure for someone like you?"

"Well, we certainly didn't see all of it, but what we did see—"

"Benjamin," she interrupted him, "I know I came on rather strong last night. I just wanted you to know . . . I do like you, Benjamin. Under other circumstances . . . well, I just mean, with all this going on, this can't be the best impression of the Foundation for you."

"What do you mean?"

"I'm just saying, Benjamin, you might . . . what we do here, we believe in it, all of us. Do you understand that?"

"Well, yes, I imagine you do." He hoped he didn't sound too critical.

Gudrün reached into the breast pocket of her jacket, extracted a pack of cigarettes and lighter. She pulled out a cigarette, offered one to Benjamin—he declined—and she lit up. She took a long drag on the cigarette and then turned to him.

"I mean it's easy to become cynical. When your whole life people have treated you as some sort of prodigy..." She took another drag on the cigarette. "Well, you must know that feeling of infallibility."

"Infallibility?" he asked. He shook his head. "Hardly. I'm good at memorizing names and dates, that's about it. That doesn't come close to what Dr. Fletcher did. His work, it's—"

"Benjamin, I lied to you," she said abruptly.

"What?"

Gudrün threw the cigarette to the ground and stamped it out.

"I *did* make an appointment to speak to Jeremy," she said. "I don't know exactly why I lied, I just..." She shook her head. "Anyway, I'm sorry. I just didn't want to be associated with anything...potentially embarrassing. My career is very important to me. This fellowship at the Foundation, it could mean...anyway, I am sorry." She smiled. "Do you believe me?"

"I...understand," Benjamin said.

"Do you?" she asked, sensing his hesitation. "Do you have some time now? We really didn't get a chance to talk last night."

Benjamin hesitated. "Well, I was just on my way to the library..."

"Then later perhaps? This evening, after dinner? We could take up where we left off?" Again she smiled a bright and what seemed to Benjamin an utterly sincere smile. And again he felt flattered by her attention. He nodded.

"All right then," she said. "I'll let you get off to your musty books." She leaned closer and kissed him briefly on the cheek. And she walked off slowly, as though deep in thought.

CHAPTER 20

An hour later Benjamin was retracing his way across the quad, two books under one arm. His trip to the library had been successful, and he couldn't wait to show Wolfe what he'd discovered—which was that he'd been absolutely correct: Seaton Morris's "hoax" was itself a hoax.

As he passed the biology building he saw a light on in the window of Edith Gadenhower's laboratory. He thought Wolfe must have finished with Arthur sooner than he expected and come to Edith's lab to ask more about Jeremy's visit, and he figured he might as well join him there.

When he entered the building it was almost preternaturally quiet. The only sound was his shoes squeaking on the linoleum hallway. He came to Edith's laboratory, saw that indeed a light was on inside, and entered.

He expected to hear Wolfe and Edith speaking, but silence reigned here as well.

"Mrs. Gadenhower?" he called out. There was no response. "Sam?" he tried again. Still nothing.

He rounded the corner into the area where Edith kept her hives behind the Plexiglas shields. At first, he saw no one. One of the fluorescent lights over a workbench was on, which accounted for the light through the window. And then he did hear something.

It was a low, muffled hum—like someone had left some electrical equipment on.

He stepped forward to the large lab bench that divided the room. As he did so, his shoes crunched on something. He looked down and saw broken glass scattered across the floor.

"Edith?" he called again.

And then he saw them.

Moving across the cabinets on the other side of the room, drifting up to the ceiling and around in irregular spirals, clumped together here and there along a workbench . . . bees.

Hundreds of them.

He stood frozen.

Out of the corner of his eye, he saw that one of the trapdoors in a Plexiglas shield was open. And now he could make out bees in twos and threes exiting through the small open door, moving in lazy tangents across the room, to a spot on the floor hidden from his sight by the lab bench.

He realized this was the spot from where the hum was emanating.

His first impulse was to turn and flee for the door, but he felt instinctively that any abrupt motion would attract the bees' attention.

He rose on tiptoe, trying to peer over the bench, to where the bees were congregating.

What he saw made him gasp—and then immediately catch his breath.

It was Edith Gadenhower.

She was lying on the floor, in her white lab coat. She was utterly still. And across her coat, in her hair, along the one bare arm that lay awkwardly out across the black-and-white tile . . . bees. Crawling, hovering, alighting and flying off again, dozens of them. She was surrounded by an aura of bees.

Mellifera scutellata, he thought suddenly. Africanized bees.

Killer bees.

Reflexively, Benjamin took a step backward. His shoe landed on a shard of glass, cracking it.

It was as if a wave passed across the surface of all those crawling, circling, floating spots of yellow and gold; almost as one, like faces in a startled crowd, they turned to him.

Benjamin spun around and ran. But as he did so he tripped over one of the high stools, and went crashing to the floor.

He nearly screamed—but then stopped at a horrifying vision of hordes of bees flying into his open mouth.

And then several things happened at once. Even as he raised his arm to shield his eyes from the first descending bees, he heard a shrill alarm—and then a sort of strangled hiss. A yellowish vapor began spraying from the ceiling. As its first tendrils reached him, his eyes and throat went icy hot with pain, and he found himself on his side, coughing and retching simultaneously.

The next few minutes were a blur. His eyes felt scalded, and a misty veil of tears obscured his vision. . . . But he saw someone come into the lab, someone with a handkerchief over his mouth . . . Samuel Wolfe.

Wolfe grabbed Benjamin by his shoulders and began dragging him across the floor, toward the laboratory doors.

CHAPTER 21

"Here," Wolfe said, "have another." He was holding a glass of water toward Benjamin. Benjamin thanked him, accepted it, drained the glass.

"Sure you don't want something stronger?" Wolfe asked, grinning.

Benjamin shook his head.

"Well then, allow me." And Wolfe rose and went into the kitchen at the back of the dining hall.

Though his eyes and throat still burned, Benjamin was finally beginning to believe he might survive. Thanks to Samuel Wolfe.

Coming to Edith's lab after speaking with Terrill, Wolfe had pushed open the door, only to discover Benjamin sprawled on the floor with a cloud of angry bees descending upon him. Immediately he remembered about the emergency button, rushed back to the door and pressed it, and then returned to extract Benjamin from the fearsome cloud of yellow gas and dying bees.

The alarm had brought almost everyone at the Foundation to the laboratory. Benjamin didn't recall clearly what had happened over the next hour or so. He remembered someone bringing eyedrops and an inhaler from the medical office and ministering to him as he lay on the wet grass outside the lab. It might have been Gudrün. And soon thereafter he remembered hearing the wail of an ambulance—apparently Arthur had called the nearest hospital, which was some thirty minutes away.

He also remembered someone saying that Edith Gadenhower was dead.

Once the ambulance had left with Edith's body, Wolfe had shooed everyone away, saying he would take Benjamin to the dining hall to get him some "medicinal libation." When Terrill had objected that he should speak to Benjamin first, Wolfe had said with firm authority, "Later, Arthur. He's in no condition to be interrogated now."

"Feeling better," Wolfe said, returning from the kitchen. He had a glass of wine in one hand—"Apparently they won't open the real liquor cabinet until dinnertime"—and some food on a tray for Benjamin: a green salad and some clam chowder.

"Eat up," Wolfe said sternly. "Get something inside you besides that damn gas."

"The . . . laboratory?" Benjamin managed to get out between dry coughs.

"Quite a mess," said Wolfe. "Apparently in trying to defend against the swarm, Edith knocked over a good deal of equipment. Glass everywhere. And of course dead bees. Hundreds of the little buggers. I was a little concerned. You know, they say a dead bee can still sting." He greeted Benjamin's look of surprise with a smile. "And that damn gas, still enough of it there to make one cough up a storm. But there was Hauser, tromping about, so I thought it was safe enough. By the way, he's still 'putting together' that list of computer serial numbers for us."

"Poor Mrs. Gadenhower," Benjamin said. "It must have been . . ."

"Yes, it must have," Wolfe said. He drained half the wineglass. "Ah, that's better. Anyway, it was impossible to tell anything about what happened to her."

"It just seems strange," Benjamin said. "She seemed so careful . . . yesterday. I can't imagine how she . . . could have been careless enough . . . to let them out."

"No, that does seem out of character," Wolfe said, eyeing him with some concern. Then he looked down to the books on the table, the ones Benjamin had taken from the library and had with him in Edith's lab. "I saved these from the shambles. I hope they were worth it."

"You have no idea," said Benjamin, wiping his eyes. "It's exactly as I thought. You see—"

"Not now," Wolfe interrupted him. "I must talk with Arthur about how Edith's 'incident' effects our . . . arrangement. The police will be coming out tomorrow. They have to now. And they'll be bringing the county medical examiner with them. For Fletcher. I don't see how they can delay an official investigation into his death any longer."

Benjamin looked disappointed. "You mean, our work here is over?"

"Not yet it isn't," Wolfe said, shaking his head. "But we don't have much time, at least not . . . unchaperoned time. Let me talk to Arthur. Then I'll meet you back in Fletcher's room."

Wolfe gulped the last of the wine, then stood, preparing to leave. Benjamin stood up as well, tucking the books under his arm, and, as they walked to the foyer, he turned to Wolfe.

"Gudrün spoke to me," he said.

Wolfe stopped. "Oh?" he said. "Anything . . . relevant?" Benjamin ignored the smirk in his tone.

"Just that, well, she admitted she'd lied to me."

Wolfe nodded thoughtfully, led him out through the doors into the quad.

"Anyway, get some rest. I'll see you in an hour."

Benjamin turned to cross over to the manse.

"Oh, and Benjamin." Wolfe turned to him. "Let's not talk with anyone else—especially Gudrün—until then, all right?"

Benjamin nodded, then watched Wolfe enter Arthur's office. He crossed the foyer and went to the staircase to go up to his room. Then he stopped.

He had an hour, he thought, and he already knew the parts of the books he wanted to show to Wolfe. Perhaps this was finally a good time for him to take a closer look at the mural.

The foyer's chandelier wasn't yet lit, and the dim light coming through the glass dome overhead didn't provide much illumination. Still, it was enough for him to make out the larger details of the mural. He began to study it, standing in the center of the foyer and turning to follow its narrative.

For narrative it was. He could see immediately that the mural was a historical panorama. And the story it told was the making of America.

One began on the left with a rather clichéd (and politically incorrect) version of the discovery of America by Christopher Columbus. Heroic figures in full fifteenth-century garb stood at the top of a hill, greeting Native Americans in loincloths and feathers, while behind and below them the three ships of Columbus's fleet floated serenely in a vast, fading, turquoise-colored ocean. Next, and seemingly crowding them out of History's sweep, came the Pilgrims, dressed for a formal Thanksgiving feast, again accompanied by stock Native American figures. But in the midst of these typical scenes was a rather strange one.

It depicted a grove in some dense forest. In the center of the grove a preacher stood atop a tree stump, a copy of the Bible raised in one hand. He had long white flowing hair and a fanatical light in his eyes. Around him were gathered his pious flock, all kneeling, heads bowed. But what was most strange was that amongst the worshippers were some Native Americans, dressed as Europeans, but with dense black hair; one or two even wore bead necklaces. Benjamin had never seen a rendering quite like this, with Puritans and Natives mixed, praying together.

Then of course came a group of soldiers from the Revolutionary War era; but Benjamin was surprised, given the traditional depictions of the other eras, that there was no figure representing George Washington among them. Instead, there was a figure in a general's uniform—someone who bore a faint resemblance to the representation of Horatio Gates in the portrait over the Morrises' mantel. Next to this was a scene depicting the signing of the Constitution, but once again, none of the figures were recognizable. Where, he wondered, were Jefferson, Franklin, Adams? Or the father of our country, George Washington?

After that, there was another curious scene of some group gathered at a stream in the act of baptism—but into what religion? And what was the historical event represented?

As the panorama moved into the nineteenth century, the scenes became more typical: a farmer plowing rolling fields of yellow wheat, railroad workers laying iron tracks, a miller driving his mules at an enormous grindstone. But in the center of them all was a scene depicting what appeared to be a college campus, with small figures of scholars in academic robes crossing its green squares of common; a campus that bore an uncanny resemblance to the Foundation's oldest buildings.

And then, moving into the Industrial Age, there were factory workers emerging from squat, gray buildings topped by busy smokestacks, steamboats on a wide river, long snakes of trains loaded with cattle and iron and coal. . . . The only Native Americans here were small, indistinct figures perched on the top of hills, vaguely threatening.

As Benjamin continued to turn, he saw more groups of workers— miners, lumberjacks, blacksmiths, cowboys—always with their faces aglow with dedication and purpose, and always pointed toward the right of the mural, as though straining to see the final realization of the true America that lay just over the cloud-covered horizon.

Next, the mural's pale blue sky became crowned with airplanes—the Wright biplane, a tri-motor mail plane, even a flying boat—while down on the earth the factories multiplied, their halos of black smoke apparently indicating the building power of America's industrial might. And it was with this section of the mural, the last, that the faces became somewhat blanker, more generic and idealized. In one or two small scenes he saw what appeared to be strikers or protestors, with signs and torches—but always surrounding them were indistinct figures shrouded in a kind of gray fog. . . .

Finally, the mural reached its near climax with the depiction of the building of a mighty skyscraper: steel girders were suspended in the air, while in the foreground a giant, blond-haired steelworker, stripped to the waist, gazed outward from the mural, directly into the viewer's eyes, as though challenging that viewer to put on some work gloves, climb into the painting, and join the great communal effort depicted there.

And there it ended. There still were another five feet of blank wall space. As Stoltz had said, Bayne hadn't completed it. Given the year he was working in, 1929, Benjamin wondered how on earth Bayne would have rendered the collapse of the American economic system—especially as so much of the mural seemed a tribute to America's economic stability and power— though in places he sensed a strange undercurrent to that tribute, as though it were all an immense parody. Benjamin noticed how, in the background, people seemed to coalesce out of the smoke and clouds and dust, as though the landscape itself was producing Americans.

Benjamin moved closer to make out these background figures, and he began to discern other details in the painting: smaller figures whose clothes and faces were clearly intended to represent historical personages: that was probably Lincoln, that was Edison, here was Teddy Roosevelt. . . . But why were they in the background, as though they were unimportant, mere supporting characters in this historical theater?

And then one of these details caught his attention—a tiny, almost invisible mark which at first he took to be a mere shadow. He looked closer, and saw it was some sort of symbol, painted as though it were carved in the keystone of a granite gate over the entrance of what he took to be a Depression-era university. Then, when he looked back to the left, back in time, as it were, he saw it again. And then again.

After some careful searching, he found it on the architectural plans spread across a drafting table in the section about skyscrapers; again on an X-ray machine in a paean to what was obviously a modern clinic; again on one of the standards being carried by Union soldiers on the charge, the pennant almost obscured by the smoke of battle; then again, scrawled as though a doodle in the notebook of a woman student seated amidst other women students, in what was probably a women's finishing school of the early nineteenth century.

After further searching, he located the strange symbol again as a shaded area in the aura of light above the preacher in the woods where the mural began; in fact here it was most distinct, once one knew what to look for. And then, after poring over the odd tableau representing the signing of the Constitution, he found it yet again: very subtly set into the seal of a letter sitting on a table by the elbow of one of the anonymous delegates.

Benjamin stepped back, slightly out of breath, rubbing his eyes. With a little distance, these symbols and other details quickly melded into the overall complexity of the mural, and for a moment he wasn't even sure he'd seen it at all. These tiny, indistinct marks might easily be taken for mistakes of the brush, shadings, small details. . . .

He looked again over that representation of the Continental Congress signing the Constitution. And now he realized the scene was meant to refer to John Trumbull's famous *Declaration of Independence,* though without the famous personages that populated that painting. It was as if the painter had replaced every famous delegate with a figure in the same posture and clothes, but a nondescript Everyman, without features or personality.

Except one.

He leaned in closer again, brought his face to within a few inches of the part of the scene depicting a particular seated delegate. The delegate's right elbow was propped on a small table, and upon that table was what looked like a group of letters. On one of those letters was a wax seal, and set into that seal—unless his eyes were playing tricks on him in the dim light—was that same symbol. Then he looked to the face of the delegate seated at that table.

He felt a chill spread down his back.

He quickly looked over his shoulder, saw that the foyer was empty. But for some reason he took small comfort in being unobserved.

After a last glance at the mural, Benjamin hurried up the staircase to find Wolfe as quickly as possible.

CHAPTER 22

When Benjamin got upstairs to Fletcher's room, he found Wolfe waiting for him there. Wolfe had Fletcher's computer set up on the small table, opened and turned on. There were lines of strange text displayed: words, but also mathematical formulae, lines, and symbols. Wolfe seemed frustrated and testy.

"What are you looking at?" Benjamin asked, seating himself and folding his arms on the books in his lap.

"One of the data files for Fletcher's program," Wolfe answered. "But it might as well be Sanskrit for all I can make of it." He looked at Benjamin. "I'm sorry," he said, rubbing his eyes.

"That's all right, we're both tired. What did Arthur say?"

"His first question was, as I expected, very telling. He wanted to know if we'd uncovered any evidence of Fletcher sharing his work with anyone outside the Foundation."

"And what did you tell him?"

"Well." Wolfe leaned back in the Chippendale chair, smiling. "I told him that it was entirely possible Dr. Fletcher had indeed leaked sensitive information to someone outside the Foundation's anointed circle."

"What?!" Benjamin nearly dropped the books. "Excuse me, but I was under the impression you didn't want anyone here to know what we were discovering. Not yet anyway."

Wolfe nodded. "Then your impression was as perceptive as usual, Benjamin."

"Then why—"

"I couldn't very well have said everything was hunky-dory with Fletcher's research, as that doesn't square with whatever Arthur already knows that he's not telling us. So I told him just enough of the truth to keep him interested and satisfied. For now."

"For now?"

"He also said, as I expected, that, what with Edith's fatal encounter, there was simply no way he could keep Dr. Fletcher's death from being investigated by the local police." He looked intent. "He's in an absolute panic about how all this will affect that new contract, the one Montrose negotiated. He's afraid to expose the Foundation to too much scrutiny, but equally terrified of being accused of covering up. He's in a very neat dilemma. And," Wolfe raised a finger for emphasis, "that's a dilemma I believe we can exploit. Depending, of course," and he nodded toward the books in Benjamin's lap, "what you discovered in the library."

"Oh." Benjamin looked down at the books. "I hardly know where to begin."

Wolfe interrupted him by standing up. "That sounds as though I'm in for a bit of a lecture."

He walked over to his briefcase leaning in the corner, opened it, and extracted a half-empty bottle of scotch and two empty glasses. He carried them back to the table, set the glasses down, and half filled both of them with the amber liquid.

"And now," Wolfe said, sitting back down and crossing his legs, making himself comfortable, "why don't you begin with your extraordinary claim that Morris's hoax is itself a hoax."

Benjamin's eyes sparkled. "I was *right*. Let me show you what I went to the library for."

Benjamin opened the books then placed them side by side.

"Here, look," he said.

Wolfe leaned over so he could read the pages Benjamin was pointing out. On the opposing pages, set next to each other, appeared the following text:

And I beheld when he had opened the sixth seal, and lo, there was a great earthquake, and the sun was as black as sackcloth of hair, and the moon was like blood. And the stars of heaven fell unto the earth, as a fig tree casteth her green figs, when it is shaken of a mighty wind. And heaven departed away, as a scroll, when it is rolled, and every mountain and isle were moved out of their places. And the kings of the earth, and the great men, and the rich men, and the chief captains, and the mighty men, and every bondman, and every free man, hid themselves in dens, and among the rocks of the mountains, and said to the mountains and rocks, Fall on us, and hide us from the presence of him that sitteth on the throne, and from the wrath of the Lamb. For the great day of his wrath is come, and who can stand?

And I beheld when he had opened the sixth seal, and, lo, there was a great earthquake; and the sun became black as sackcloth of hair, and the moon became as blood; and the stars of heaven fell unto the earth, even as a fig tree casteth her untimely figs, when she is shaken of a mighty wind. And the heaven departed as a scroll when it is rolled together; and every mountain and island was moved out of their places. And the kings of the earth, and the great men, and the rich men, and the chief captains, and the mighty men, and every bondman, and every free man, hid themselves in the dens and in the rocks of the mountains; and said to the mountains and rocks, Fall on us, and hide us from the face of him that sitteth on the throne and from the wrath of the Lamb; for the great day of his wrath is come; and who shall be able to stand?

Wolfe spent a few minutes looking over the two passages. Finally, he said, "They're both from Revelation, yes?"

"Yes, just as Seaton said. Revelations six, verses twelve through seventeen, to be exact."

Wolfe looked up at him. "They're almost identical."

"*Almost,*" said Benjamin. "That one on the right, that's from the King James Bible. It's the phrasing most people recognize. And the one in Seaton's hoax diary."

"And the other one?" Wolfe asked.

"Ah," Benjamin said, apparently very pleased with himself. "*That's* the Geneva Bible."

"Geneva Bible?"

"In 1553, when Mary Tudor, who was a devout Catholic, became Queen of England she banned the printing of the Protestant version of the Bible. So two of the leading Protestant scholars of the day, William Whittingham and Anthony Gilby, fled to Europe—to Geneva, actually—and started work on their *own* Bible. They wanted to produce one free of any 'Catholic taint.' They used original Greek and Hebrew texts to produce their Bible, and it was considered the most accurate translation of its time. And it came to be known as the Geneva Bible."

"Well and good," interrupted Wolfe, "but how does that—"

"*And* it was the one all good Puritans used. It was tantamount to blasphemy for a Puritan to use the King James Version. Let alone," and he gave a significant look to Wolfe, "to quote from it."

"And the quote in the front of Morris's diary . . ."

"Is from the King James Version. The Reverend Harlan P. Bainbridge, the most devout of devout Puritans, would certainly not have quoted from King James. He would have used the Geneva. Therefore, he didn't write that epigraph. Therefore, that's *not* his diary."

Benjamin sat back, quite pleased with his chain of logic; pleased enough to sip his scotch. And wince.

Wolfe looked askance at Benjamin. "But we already know Bainbridge didn't write it. Seaton told us this supposed Bainbridge diary was a hoax, so I really don't see—"

Rather than look chagrined, Benjamin smiled even more broadly.

"Because," he said, "that quote wasn't in the book *I've* seen."

"You've seen? What are you talking about? *Where?*"

"At the Library of Congress, of course." Benjamin took another drink, wondered whether he was developing a taste for scotch.

"It was soon after I arrived at the library. They had me down in the 'dungeons,' where they keep stuff that hasn't been cataloged yet. There was a crate with a dozen or so books and manuscripts, all of them old. There was no label on the crate, no identifying cards with the books. Which actually is more common than you'd expect. The library has so much material, there are thousands of documents they haven't properly identified yet.

"Anyway," Benjamin continued, "there was one book in that crate, without a cover, that struck me as something that ought to be in the preservation room. And it was clear there had once been a block of lines on that page, an epigraph; but over the years it had worn or been eaten away. The only readable line of text was underneath the quote. And guess what it said?" Benjamin was rather enjoying teasing Wolfe, now that he was the one with the answers.

But Wolfe was up to the question. "R six-twelve HPB?" he asked.

Benjamin looked a little disappointed, but he recovered quickly. "Yes, exactly. The attribution was still readable. When the forgers created the fake diary, they tried to make it as similar to the real one as possible. But with this quote, all they had to go on was chapter and verse, and as a consequence—"

"They quoted from the *wrong* Bible," finished Wolfe, nodding. "Very neatly reasoned."

"And the very presence of that same attribution in the book I saw means there *was* a real Bainbridge diary and somehow it wound up in the Library of Congress."

Wolfe pondered for a moment. "So the real diary is discovered at the Foundation during the excavations in the twenties, but for some reason we don't yet know the Foundation doesn't want it made public. They have a fake diary constructed, create the story of a hoax, and the whole episode is forgotten." He thought this over for a moment. "But how on earth did the diary get from the Morris Estate to the Library of Congress's basement?"

"I've been thinking about that, too," said Benjamin. "Remember the fire Seaton told us about? He said they had other books to be donated to the library, crated and ready to be shipped. When that fake diary was created, the original was probably put away somewhere safe. Probably the same safe place as the collection was put during the fire. And afterwards, in the confusion . . ."

"The real diary was sent off to the Library of Congress, to fifty years of obscurity." Wolfe laughed. "Still, that doesn't tell us *why* the Foundation, or the Morrises, whoever is behind this, needed a fake diary in the first place."

"That I cannot answer," said Benjamin. He decided it was time for his next revelation.

"I went to the library to get the two Bibles. While I was there, the librarian asked if we were done with the books Jeremy had checked out. She was particularly interested in the one by Warren Ginsburg. She said it was quite valuable, and she was eager to get it back where it belonged, in the rare books collection—especially as it had been missing all those years."

"Missing?"

"Until Jeremy found it, rooting around for books about King Philip's War. Apparently it had been filed there, in the Ws, probably for Wampanoag." He laughed, but Wolfe didn't, so he hurried on. "She said it was particularly valuable because, according to the official Foundation history, Ginsburg had been commissioned to write it to commemorate the discovery of the Bainbridge diary. That's why he was *here*."

"But then," Wolfe's eyes narrowed, "Ginsburg had to have seen the diary. The *real* diary. Was there any mention of it in his book?"

Benjamin shook his head. "No. As I said, the book was . . . strange, disconnected . . . as if whole sections of it had been lifted out. It's especially . . . sinister, given what happened to him and his lover, Bayne."

"Who the hell is Bayne?"

"Oh that's right, I hadn't had a chance to tell you. According to Stoltz, Ginsburg and Bayne—Bayne painted that extraordinary mural in the foyer—were lovers. And their affair ended with Ginsburg murdering Bayne, and then committing suicide."

Wolfe tried to make a joke, "I had no idea the Foundation had such a high mortality rate among its fellows," but his face remained grim. "And when did the librarian say Fletcher made this discovery?"

"This past Wednesday."

"The day before he called to request your services?"

Benjamin nodded. "Yes."

"Well then," said Wolfe, rising from his chair and beginning to pace back and forth. "Where does this leave us?"

"Fletcher came here to complete work on a computer program, one he designed to do some sort of analysis of the Cold War. He contacts this Fyodor Myorkin, and something he learns sets him off on a hectic bout of investigation. Something he learns from *that* piques his interest in these Indian . . . excuse me, Native American wars. He interviews Dr. Stoltz, and then decides to contact this Orlova at the Russian Cultural Center. And you. And in the middle of all this he decides he simply must talk to Edith Gadenhower about bees."

Wolfe stopped pacing and turned to Benjamin.

"Does that about sum up what we know so far?"

"Well . . ." Benjamin was thinking of something, a missing link in the series of events as Wolfe had laid it out. "We also know Dr. Stoltz told Jeremy about the diary's discovery, so we have every reason to believe Fletcher knew that the original diary was supposedly at the Morris Estate." Benjamin looked up at Wolfe. "So wouldn't it be logical to assume that he reacted the same way we did? That he asked to visit the estate and *see* what he thought was the original?"

Wolfe looked quite steadily at Benjamin, smiled appreciatively.

"Perhaps he did just that," he said. "Sometime late last Wednesday, would be my guess."

"The day before his heart attack?" asked Benjamin.

"Precisely," said Wolfe. He took the glass and walked away from the table. He poured a drink, took a sip, then changed his mind and set the glass down.

"Which brings us back to why," Wolfe said. "*Why* was that diary so important to Dr. Fletcher?"

But Benjamin's mind was wandering, thinking about what he'd seen—or thought he'd seen—in the mural. Perhaps Wolfe could make sense of it. Then he began to wonder just how he would explain his unease: a tiny, *indistinct* symbol? *Possibly* familiar faces? A vague *feeling* about something not quite right in the mural's depiction of American history?

It all started to sound too fantastic, something he might well have imagined. He decided it would be best to wait until he'd had a chance to actually examine the real diary, go over his father's notes again—and have another look at the mural.

Wolfe noticed his concentration, asked impatiently, "What?"

Benjamin shook his head. "Nothing. Look, shouldn't we take all this to Dr. Terrill? Get his permission to travel to D.C. so I can look at the *real* Bainbridge diary? And then you could consult with this Anton Sikorsky. In fact, we could also find this N. Orlova, at the Russian Cultural Center. We can kill three birds with one stone."

Wolfe frowned at him. "Poor choice of clichés. And that, Benjamin," he said ponderously, "is the one thing in all this confusion that I am absolutely certain we should *not* do. Not yet, anyway."

Wolfe seemed to come to a decision.

He switched off Fletcher's computer, put it into his briefcase. He surveyed Fletcher's room carefully. Satisfied, he took Benjamin by the shoulder and steered him out of the room, closing and locking the door behind them.

"Let's set this," and he held up the briefcase with Fletcher's laptop inside, "in your room for now. Then let's you and I join the throng in the dining hall. And Benjamin," he grabbed Benjamin's arm, and Benjamin noticed his grip was tense, almost painful, "let's keep it to chitchat at dinner, shall we? Should we run into anyone. Like, for instance, Dr. Soderbergh?"

Benjamin looked at him, nodded.

And then they walked off down the hall, toward Benjamin's room. But Benjamin noticed that Wolfe hadn't bothered to put the strip of tape at the top of Fletcher's door, as though there was no longer any reason to keep it secure.

CHAPTER 23

Wolfe and Benjamin sat on the same bench in the quad, beneath the giant sycamore tree, where'd they been only a day before. Now, however, instead of the bright afternoon sun scattering light across the tops of trees spread out across the low hills beyond the Foundation grounds, it was late evening. The first stars were beginning to appear in the deep purple western sky, and there was a nip in the air that had caused Benjamin to turn up the collar of his jacket.

They'd arrived at the bench after a long walk around the Foundation's grounds; a walk that had seen Wolfe remain almost completely silent and deep in thought; a walk that had followed their very brief appearance in the dining hall.

And Benjamin had felt it was just that: an appearance. As though Wolfe wanted them there for everyone to see, chatty and happy, exchanging hellos with some and a few quiet words of grief over Edith's death with others.

Benjamin had seen Gudrün there, sitting at a table with Stoltz. She'd waved him over, but Wolfe had subtly if forcefully steered him toward another table, with Arthur Terrill and George Montrose. Once seated and with an entrée before them, Wolfe had very skillfully kept the conversation to neutral topics: the grandeur of the Morris Estate, the tragedy of Edith's accident. And as soon as the coffee had been served, Wolfe had risen to excuse himself and Benjamin.

"We've still got some tidying up to do," he said, "and we'd best get to it before it gets too late, especially if the police will be here in the morning."

Benjamin said good night to Terrill and Montrose, even as Wolfe was practically dragging him out of the dining hall and into the chill air of the quad outside. But then, instead of explaining his silence during dinner or his haste to leave when it was over, Wolfe had simply led him on their walkabout of the grounds.

Benjamin noticed that they seemed to circumnavigate the area, taking the outmost pathways; in several places Wolfe had left the path to walk toward copses of trees, in some cases only a dozen yards or so from the surrounding fence.

Eventually they found themselves back in the quad, sitting on the bench beneath the sycamore.

And finally Wolfe broke his long silence.

"I'm afraid, Benjamin," he said, sounding quite serious and without any of his usual glib undertones, "perhaps I should have let Arthur give you that severance pay and let you go."

"If you're worried about my talking with Gudrün again . . ."

Wolfe shook his head. "Look, Benjamin, I said the Foundation had influence. Perhaps I should have used the word 'power'—though in Washington, the first is the most effective expression of the second." Wolfe thought again for a moment, continued, again with a deadly serious tone.

"Most citizens of this country don't realize how our modern government functions, which is only on the advice and counsel of thousands of technical experts, like these." He waved a hand around the Foundation's grounds. "If there's need for a new telecommunications bill, or energy policy, or foreign policy, who do you think plots that all out? All the technical details, the intricacies? Do you think your average senator is up to that task? They're lawyers, for the most part, not technocrats. And half the time they're out raising money to remain senators. So by and large such laws and policies are written by people like these, here at the Foundation. People like your new friend, Gudrün, for instance."

He stood and put his hands in his pockets, apparently against the cold air, then looked down at Benjamin and continued.

"These are ideologues of the first order, Benjamin. People who are absolutely *convinced* they are right. And they will do any and everything necessary to exercise their . . . rightness."

Benjamin realized this was the most impassioned speech he'd heard from Wolfe since he'd met him.

"So you're telling me the Foundation is a sort of . . . shadow government."

Wolfe sat back down on the bench, sighed. "Whatever you choose to call them, they have enormous power. And they are very *protective* about that power. Very protective."

"Which is why Arthur is so worried that Fletcher might have shared his work before his heart attack?"

"Heart attack?" Wolfe smiled grimly. "Are we still calling it that?"

Benjamin sighed. "I suppose not." He shook his head sadly. "When I said earlier you were conducting this like you were investigating a murder instead of a security leak, I just hadn't wanted to admit I was thinking along those lines myself. But since we're being honest about it, I have two questions. The first is, *how?*"

"I know of at least three substances that can induce a heart attack if ingested," Wolfe said, quite matter-of-fact. "One needs only add DMSO to the mixture to assist in uptake through the skin, and then apply it to almost any surface. Such as, for instance, a computer keyboard?"

"But why the extra keyboard? Why not simply put this substance on the keyboard Jeremy was already using, on the laptop?"

"Not precise enough. Such things evaporate rather quickly. Our assassin had to know *exactly* when Fletcher was going to use the keyboard. Obviously he knew Jeremy was in the habit of using a detachable one, so while Fletcher was talking with Edith, he stopped by his room and removed it. Then, when Fletcher called for another keyboard, he could prepare it and . . ."

"So you're suggesting that computer guy, the one who brought us the keyboard, that *he* killed Jeremy?"

"Or someone with access to the computer equipment," said Wolfe.

Benjamin went silent again, then said, "That raises my second question. What could Jeremy have discovered that would be so potentially damning that someone would kill him to keep it secret? And for that matter, why bring you in to investigate his death? Why not simply let the police come, see it as a heart attack, and when it's all over destroy his research?"

"Well," said Wolfe, sitting back and staring up into the sky, "I can think of two responses. Either whoever is responsible for his death isn't in a position to prevent an investigation. Or, they are in a position to *want* an investigation."

"What do you mean?"

"Perhaps they want the incident investigated for the same reason we do: to find the truth. A truth they don't yet know, one they hope *we* will discover for them. Remember what I told you about security and fault lines? Perhaps they're waiting for a signal that we've stumbled across the fault line to all this, so they can better disguise it from others." Then he turned and looked at Benjamin, his eyes again expressing sincere concern. "And perhaps today, you did exactly that."

"*Me?*"

"When you realized that Seaton's hoax diary was a fake and perhaps, *perhaps* let slip to Seaton that you *knew* it was a fake. And if the real diary has anything to do with whatever Fletcher discovered . . ." Wolfe let the implication sink in.

Suddenly Benjamin felt a band tightening across his chest.

"But we don't have proof of *any* of this."

"You're right there," Wolfe said. "Under normal circumstances, I'd say we'd next like to talk to one F. Myorkin and N. Orlova. Find out what their relationship is, or rather *was,* to Fletcher."

"But these aren't normal circumstances?"

"I don't mean to further excite you, my boy, but do you realize that just by taking Fletcher's computer with us today, off the Foundation's grounds, we violated their confidentiality requirements? That they could, if they wished, arrest both of us right now for security violations? Don't you think that's exactly what our dear friend Hauser is aching to do?"

"Then why doesn't he?"

"Well, that brings us back to a question I asked you soon after we first met. 'Why me'?"

"Why you, what?"

"Why would they bring *me* in on this? Someone who hasn't worked for them for years? Someone not of their 'inner circle'? Someone who, as you seem fond of pointing out, has spent too much of the last year nursing a bottle?"

"I didn't—," Benjamin started to protest, but Wolfe waved him silent.

"No, you were right. And Arthur *knows* it. So isn't the answer obvious? They want the truth, but from someone they think too incompetent—or, to put it finely, too drunk—to recognize it when he sees it. I was to be a foxhound, someone who could tree the secret of Fletcher's research, then be pulled off so they could catch it. And kill it."

He rose and stood next to Benjamin so he could look him in the eyes.

"But they didn't count on you," he said. "They couldn't have known Fletcher sent for you. *You're* the random element here, Benjamin Franklin Wainwright. And we need to take very good care of you."

Wolfe put his arm around his shoulders, seemed on the verge of saying something else, then changed his mind. "You should get some sleep."

"And you?"

"I'd like to take another look at Edith's laboratory without Hauser hanging over my shoulder. I still don't see the connection between Edith's research and all this, if connection there is. After all," he shrugged, "accidents do happen, even in the midst of conspiracies."

"Conspiracy?" Benjamin said. " Do you think *everyone* here at the Foundation is involved?"

Wolfe smiled that glib, infuriating, charming smile of his.

"Yes and no," Wolfe answered cryptically. "The most effective conspiracy," he said, patting Benjamin's shoulder, "is the one you don't know you're part of."

And then he wished Benjamin good night and walked off toward the biology building, his shoes leaving a trail in the chilled grass.

Benjamin was reluctant to let him go. For one thing, after what Wolfe had told him, he didn't particularly want to be alone. He also had the thought that in the morning he might awaken to find himself arrested and hauled off to jail in handcuffs. Hardly the sort of boost he'd originally imagined his stint at the Foundation would provide his career.

Thus Benjamin reached his room dejected and nervous. He doubted he would be able to sleep. He saw Wolfe's briefcase where he'd left it, propped against the far side of the bed, with Fletcher's computer inside. Oh, good, he thought. More incriminating evidence.

He sat on the bed, staring at the Ginsburg book and thinking back to how it had all started, so quietly and apparently innocently, just two nights before.

And, despite his anxiety that at any moment he would hear Hauser pounding on his door, a police van with flashing red and blue lights waiting in the cold night air outside, he found himself nodding off to sleep.

CHAPTER 24

The first sound that woke Benjamin up wasn't someone pounding on his door, but rather what he took for a clap of thunder. And his first thought was that it had started raining again.

Still half asleep, he listened for the rain on the windows, or another peal of thunder. He heard neither.

As he slowly roused himself, he began to hear other sounds: people running in the hallway, and then voices outside, down in the quad.

He shuffled over to the window, pushed the curtain aside. He expected to stare into the dark night—there weren't many outside lights on the Foundation grounds—but instead found that he could see people in the quad, a dozen or more. They were standing in the center, on the grass and some on the pathway, and they were looking off to his left, to something beyond the dining hall.

It was then he realized that the scene was being lit by a flickering light, something that waxed and waned in intensity, a pulsating yellow glow.

And it was *then* there came a knock at his door.

He immediately looked to Wolfe's briefcase. He walked over and picked it up, looking around for somewhere to hide it. And then someone outside the door called his name.

"Benjamin," the voice said. "Benjamin, are you awake?"

It was Gudrün.

He tossed the briefcase under the bed, gave the room a quick look, then went to the door and pulled it open.

Gudrün was in jeans and a sweatshirt, slippers instead of shoes. Her hair was mussed, she wasn't wearing any makeup—and yet her face still shone with a kind of clear, confident beauty.

But she didn't look confident; she looked frightened.

"Benjamin," she said. She pushed past him into the room. "Close the door."

He did so, turned around. Gudrün went to the window, looked down at the scene below.

"Did you hear it?" she asked.

"I heard something," he said, coming to the bed. "I thought it was thunder."

She turned around. "It wasn't thunder," she said. "It was an explosion. In Edith's lab. There's a fire down there now. The whole building is burning." She put her hand on his shoulder. "I thought perhaps you were in there."

"No," Benjamin said. His head was still blurry from sleep . . . and then he realized. "But Samuel!" He hesitated for a moment. "Sam Wolfe went to Edith's lab. To take another look at the scene."

Gudrün didn't flinch, and Benjamin realized she wasn't surprised.

"Gudrün," he started, "what do you know about all this?"

"I can't—," Gudrün began. She turned her head aside, looked out the window again, then back to him. "You need to leave," she said bluntly.

"What? I can't do that. What about Sam? Did anyone see him come out of there?" He went to the bed, began to put on his clothes. "Did anyone call the fire department?"

She came over to him, took his arm.

"There's nothing you can do," she said. "Not now. And not here."

He stopped with his shirt half on. "What are you talking about?"

She touched his cheek. "I wish—," she said.

Benjamin shook himself free, continued to get dressed, putting on his shoes, his jacket. He moved to the doorway. "Whatever is going on here, I need to find out whether or not Sam is alive."

Gudrün stopped him at the door.

"No one can get near the lab now. The only thing you can do for him is get away from here. Take your things and just go. *Now.* The fire department will be arriving any minute. I'll go and ask the gate guard to help with the fire so you can slip out. But you'll only have a few minutes."

She looked into his eyes, then moved into the hallway, glanced up and down its length. Then she turned back to him.

"I'll . . . I'll try and get in touch with you, let you know what happened."

She leaned in, kissed him briefly on the lips, and then turned and ran off down the hallway.

Benjamin stood indecisive for a minute. Then he went to the bed, bent down, and retrieved Wolfe's briefcase. He looked about the room, thought about gathering up his few other clothes, but left them and went into the hallway.

The foyer's chandelier wasn't on—in the rush outside no one had turned on the inside lights yet—so the mural passed by as indistinct, shadowed scenery as he wound his way down the spiral staircase, though it now seemed more populated with ghosts than ever.

He reached the ground floor, still without seeing anyone. With a last glance at the darkened foyer, he stepped outside.

Though the fire was on the other side of the manse, its pulsating glow reflected against the low, gray clouds overhead. He could hear the sounds now of breaking glass and the crackle of fire; and, rising in the background, the wail of approaching sirens.

He stood for a moment. Then he glanced down at the briefcase in his hand.

He quickly went to his car, opened the trunk, and tossed Wolfe's briefcase inside. He slammed the trunk closed, went around to the front, and got in. He started the car up and pulled quickly down the gravel driveway.

Even as he approached the gate, which he saw was open to admit the fire trucks, he could see the approaching flashing red-and-white lights. He gunned his car to get out of the gate before the fire engines could block his way. Even as he turned sharply, two engines roared past him down the driveway, sirens blaring.

A few dozen yards from the gate the darkened country lane proved too hazardous for him to drive very fast. He slowed down; even then, the hedges and trees seemed to leap out of the darkness with discomforting speed.

Benjamin wasn't sure exactly where he was. When he saw a sign indicating a road to the Massachusetts Turnpike, he avoided it. He realized he would have to stop soon, at a gas station or a food mart, and buy a map of the local area. He needed to find a way, somehow keeping to back roads and minor highways, to get from where he was to where he wanted to be.

Benjamin was headed, as quickly if indirectly as possible, toward N. Orlova, of the Russian Cultural Center, in Washington, D.C.

Even as the fire trucks pulled up in the gravel driveway before the manse and disgorged a dozen bulky figures who began extracting equipment and running toward the fire, two people emerged from the shadows by the door. Both were tall, both had blond hair.

"Nicely done," said the man, looking out through the gate where Benjamin's car had just fled. "And you're sure where he's headed?"

"Of course," said the woman, taking a drag from a cigarette. "He's more motivated now than ever. He's on the scent, and he's got his newfound friend to avenge."

"Um-hm," the man replied noncommittally.

"Speaking of his friend," the woman said, her tone harsher now, "couldn't you have been a little subtler?" The man didn't reply. "And how can you be sure, in all that mess?"

"I'm sure," he said.

"I hope so, for your sake," she continued. "We've set one hound loose. They wouldn't like discovering the other has gone astray, too."

She threw the cigarette to the ground, stamped it out, left without another word.

After she left the man pulled a cell phone from his pocket, flipped it open. He dialed a special extension that would cut through the communications blanket, and then dialed long-distance. The area code was for Washington, D.C.

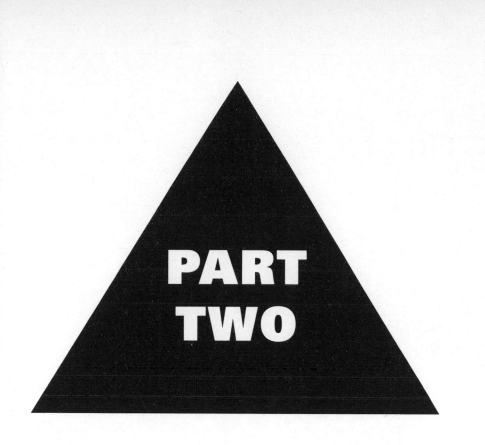

PART
TWO

CHAPTER 25

Benjamin stood in the main concourse of Union Station in Washington, D.C. Behind and around him throngs were streaming by, all of them intent on their destination, and all of them apparently late. High overhead the immense arched roof of the station, with its frescoed inset panels and dramatic lighting, gave him the feeling he was in an enormous underground bomb shelter.

Which matched his other mood: watchful paranoia. He was certain at any moment men in dark coats would converge on him out of the crowd, quickly flipping open wallet badges they didn't really expect him to read, and lead him away to a black van waiting outside, after which he would never be heard from again.

He'd had that feeling of imminent danger ever since he'd driven recklessly out of the Foundation gates and barreled on down the country lanes of western Massachusetts as fast as his frayed reactions could allow.

Soon after leaving the grounds, he'd found a small service station where he'd filled the gas tank and purchased a road map for the Mid-Atlantic Region. Sitting in the car pulled off to the side of the road a half mile away, sipping his first of many cups of coffee, he'd traced a route that bypassed 95 and the glut of cities along the coast, and which instead led through meandering connections and small towns. He'd driven a constant five to ten miles over the speed limit of the back roads. But the closer he got to Washington, the more he worried about what would happen once he entered its permanent traffic jam. If they were looking for his car, it would be easy to spot and easier to seize.

So he'd decided to drive to Silver Spring, park his car in the MARC lot there, and take the train into Union Station. He figured he'd be just another anonymous commuter among the tens of thousands arriving for their Monday work. Once there, he found the saturating roar and bustle comforting, as though it made him invisible.

Which, right now, was his deepest desire.

He was exhausted. He needed to find somewhere to sit down and think.

He found a coffee kiosk, bought a mug of latte and a croissant, though he doubted he could stomach yet another dose of caffeine. Making his way to a small table, he sat with Wolfe's briefcase on his lap, almost superstitiously afraid to open it. But finally he did, took out the yellow pad—the same one they'd used that first day in Fletcher's room—and the same pen he'd used to figure out those first snatches of Franklin's pyramid code.

He thought about Samuel Wolfe, about their initial jousting in Terrill's office, and felt a wave of nostalgia—and something not quite yet grief.

The roar of the crowds around him brought him back to his immediate situation. During his nighttime drive, he'd thought about what he would do when he got to D.C. He instinctively felt that contacting any authorities, the police or the FBI, was out of the question. Besides, with Fletcher's computer sitting like radioactive material in the briefcase, he doubted they would believe anything he had to say.

Stuffing the remainder of the croissant into his mouth, he gathered up the briefcase and his coffee and went to the nearest bank of telephones. He fished some change from his pocket—he had avoided using credit cards for gas, and he didn't want to use one now for the phone—then dropped some into the slot and dialed Information.

He was told there was indeed an Anton Sikorsky listed in Georgetown—the only one in the directory.

He dropped the requisite amount of change into the phone, dialed the number provided, and listened while it rang once, twice, three times.

"*Alloa,*" said a voice on the other end. "This is Anton."

The voice had a thick accent that Benjamin couldn't quite place.

"Hello," said Benjamin. "Is this Anton Sikorsky? The Anton Sikorsky that teaches at Georgetown University?"

"Yes," said the voice. "Who please is asking?"

Now that he had Sikorsky on the phone, Benjamin wasn't sure what to say. As far as he knew, Wolfe hadn't contacted Anton since he'd arrived at the Foundation, perhaps hadn't spoken to him in years. How much would the mention of Wolfe's name gain either Anton's trust or his ire? After all, Benjamin had the distinct impression that Wolfe wasn't in the habit of endearing himself to people.

"Mr. Sikorsky," he began, "my name is Benjamin Wainwright, I'm a . . . colleague of Samuel Wolfe. He suggested that, well, that I contact you if I had questions about . . . about a project he and I are working on."

"Samuel Wolfe?" said Anton. There was a long silence, and Benjamin began to wonder if he'd made a fantastic mistake. There was a cough, and then Anton said, "And how is that son of a bitch?"

Benjamin laughed. It sounded like Anton knew Wolfe quite well. "He's fine," he said, wincing at the lie. "He sends his regards."

"And you're, what, colleague?"

"Yes. Mr. Sikorsky, I have something I'd like you to look at, a computer program, that Samuel thought you might be more . . . familiar with than he is. It's the work of someone named Fletcher, and—"

"Jeremy Fletcher?" Anton interrupted. "Bright young man. Genius, maybe. How the hell Sam work with him? Last time I read about Fletcher, he's at American Heritage Foundation. Samuel wouldn't go near that place again." There was a pause. "Are you government bastard?"

This was all becoming more difficult than Benjamin had anticipated.

"No, I'm not," he said. "I'm an historian. An academic." He didn't want to tell Anton anything more specific until he could meet him. "Mr. Sikorsky, I wonder if I could see you today. Perhaps at Georgetown?"

"Today off," Anton said. "Thanks god. Are you in Washington?"

"Well," Benjamin couldn't see the harm in telling him that. "Yes, yes I am."

"Come to house, then. Show me what's so important, Sam sends you all the way to me." Anton gave him an address to write down, and Benjamin told him that he could be there in half an hour, if that was all right.

"I'm up," said Anton. "Hardly sleep anymore anyway. I'll make coffee."

Oh, god, Benjamin thought as he said good-bye and hung up. Please, no more coffee.

CHAPTER 26

Benjamin stood outside Anton's town house in Georgetown. It was typical of the neighborhood, with an undersized front door—a relic left from a time when apparently people were shorter—and the black shutters on the windows fronted by black wrought-iron fences and short hedges. He noticed there were cornstalk decorations in front of some of the doors, and a few houses had already placed pumpkins outside on their steps.

He lifted the brass knocker, tapped it on the door three times, and waited. He heard footsteps coming, someone fumbling with a lock, then the door swung open.

He was greeted by the sight of a short, rounded older man dressed in a thick sweater, and baggy pants drooping over well-worn slippers. His thick white hair sprouted up stiffly in a dozen different directions. The man peered at him over the rims of large square glasses.

"Mr. Wainwright?" Anton asked.

"Yes," he said. He extended his hand. "And you're Anton Sikorsky?"

"Of course," he said. Anton stepped forward a little, took his hand. "Come in, don't let cold air in house. Drafty as hell. Americans know nothing about drafts."

Benjamin stepped into the foyer and Anton shut the door behind him. The layout was as typical as the house's façade: a staircase extended upward from the foyer, with a narrow hallway running to its left, back to what Benjamin knew would be the kitchen. To the left out of the foyer was a drawing room, and it was into this room that Anton showed him.

The first thing Benjamin noticed were the books.

Everywhere.

Not only on the floor-to-ceiling bookshelves but also stacked on a large round table in the middle of the room. Here and there on the floor were more stacks, some of them tilting precariously, as though the slightest nudge would send them toppling over.

Benjamin had to thread his way carefully around the towers of books, wending his way to an open spot on a large overstuffed couch. Anton sat down in an armchair to his left. He picked up a cup of coffee from a round end table next to the chair, took a long, loud slurp, and then looked again at Benjamin over the tops of his glasses. But Benjamin noticed he was looking not at him, but rather at Wolfe's briefcase perched on his lap.

"So, Mr. Wainwright," Anton began. "How can old fart like me help smart guy like Sam Wolfe?" He smiled. Then he seemed to remember himself. "Oh, and would you like coffee? Sorry I didn't ask sooner. Afraid my manners are a little dull. Ever since my wife died, things around here," he waved his free hand at the piles of books everywhere, "go to hell."

Benjamin shook his head. "I've had quite a long drive," he said, "and a *lot* of coffee."

"Something else?" asked Anton. "I think I have prune juice. Maybe even orange juice. I will see." Anton set the coffee down, began to stand up, grunting as he did so.

"No, no." Benjamin waved for him to sit down. "I'm fine, really."

"Um-hm," said Anton, sitting down. He looked again at the briefcase. "You have something so important in there, you can't put it down?"

Benjamin looked down at it. "Well . . ." Now that he was here, Benjamin had no idea how or where to begin. "Mr. Sikorsky—"

"Anton."

"Anton . . . I don't know how long it's been since you've spoken with Mr. Wolfe, but—"

"Excuse me," Anton interrupted. He shifted in the chair, leaned forward. "Sam sends you to me, but doesn't mention our last conversation?" He looked directly into Benjamin's eyes. "Also, he doesn't call to say even 'boo' to this old friend, Anton, the only person can help you? And you come, I think driving maybe all night, by your red eyes?"

Benjamin looked at him, said nothing.

Anton leaned back, exhaled. "How bad trouble Sam in this time?"

"He may be dead," Benjamin said.

Anton nodded. "Told him many times, too fond of whiskey. Drink vodka, I told him. Enough of it, can't hurt you."

Benjamin realized he was joking. But then he turned serious.

"Last time I talked to Sam, almost year ago. Right after his wife died. My wife died too, three years ago now. She never tolerate this," he waved about the room. "Anyway, we commiserate. Told him was worried about him."

"It wasn't anything like that," Benjamin said. "What happened, I mean."

Anton nodded. "But still, you have his briefcase."

Benjamin looked down. "But how do you know this isn't mine?" he asked.

Anton smiled. "Two things," he said. "One, I think if it yours, you not so protective. And two," he pointed at the front, "initials are SCW. Samuel Clement Wolfe, yes? Anyway, not BW."

Benjamin smiled. He made a decision. He was simply too exhausted to be coy with Anton any longer.

He opened the briefcase and took out Fletcher's laptop. Carefully pushing aside some of the books on the oval coffee table in front of him, he lifted its top and pressed the On button. While the computer started up, Benjamin began talking.

"Samuel *has* been working for the Foundation again, but just since last Friday. I was called out there to help him. Well, actually not him, but Jeremy Fletcher, the man who wrote this program. It took us a while to even get into the program because Dr. Fletcher had left some . . . security provisions . . ."

"Left?" asked Anton. "Why past tense?"

In for a penny, thought Benjamin. "Jeremy Fletcher's dead, Mr. Sikorsky. Samuel was called out to the Foundation to investigate his death. Apparently they suspected he'd leaked sensitive information to someone. Once I was there, well, Samuel sort of commandeered me to help him out."

Anton took all this in without any reaction. "And how you help? You said you're historian, not computer guy."

"That's . . . complicated. My area is Colonial American history. Jeremy's work somehow became connected to . . . well, apparently he was interested in a Reverend Bainbridge, who had something to do, perhaps, with King Philip's War, and . . ."

Benjamin stopped, aware he was babbling. His fatigue was beginning to show.

"All right, never mind," said Anton. "Tell me about Dr. Fletcher's work, who you call Jeremy."

This guy doesn't miss much, thought Benjamin. "We were friends, back in college."

"Again, fine. Now, program?"

"Well . . . Samuel thought it looked like nuclear war game theory. But he said it was on a level far above his expertise. He said he wished he could show the program to you, that perhaps you'd have a better idea what it was all about."

He entered the TEACUP password, then rotated the laptop so Anton could see the files displayed.

"This is it," he said. "It's called TEACUP, for—"

"Text Entry, Analysis, Conversion and Utilization Program," finished Anton. "Told you, I know Fletcher's work. Been working on program for years."

Benjamin leaned back, sighed. "I think I came to the right place," he said.

"Maybe," Anton said. He rose from his chair, came over to the coffee table, and, with some effort, squatted down in front of the computer.

"What is files?" he said, pointing to the list on the screen.

"Well, that's one of the things I'm hoping you can tell me. Samuel opened some of them, looked at them. But that's when he said he wasn't certain what it all meant."

"Hm," Anton said, scanning down the list of files. Benjamin noticed a sudden glint of recognition in Anton's eyes when he got to the top of the rightmost list.

"You recognize these?" he asked.

"Maybe," Anton said. He stood up, sighing again. "No way to do work." He looked down at Benjamin. "You look like hell," he said.

Benjamin rubbed at his eyes. "I've been driving all night. If I could just—"

"Take nap," Anton said.

He set his coffee down, picked up a stack of books from the couch, set it on the floor—where it promptly tipped over. He grunted, pushed them aside with his foot.

"Here, on couch. Stretch out. I'll get you blanket." He leaned down and put his hands on the computer, then looked at Benjamin. "All right I take this upstairs, to study?"

Benjamin looked around, nodded. "I guess," he said.

"Good." Anton picked up the computer. "Go on, lay down. I'll be back in minute with blanket. Give me hour or so, see if I can read the leaves of this teacup." He smiled down at Benjamin.

Benjamin suddenly wanted very much to trust Anton Sikorsky; to turn the whole mystery over to him, to fade into unconsciousness, hopefully to awaken to answers and clarity—and perhaps the news that Wolfe was alive.

He leaned his head back against the arm of the couch, and by the time Anton came downstairs with a large, thick comforter, he was already sound asleep.

CHAPTER 27

Benjamin woke up to Anton's face above him. For a moment he didn't recognize him and couldn't remember where he was.

"You've had a nice nap?" Anton asked him. He held out a glass of orange juice in one hand, and in the other he held a plate with some sort of sandwich. "Sit up, eat something. You'll feel better."

Benjamin slowly raised himself on the couch. He rubbed his eyes, accepted the orange juice from Anton. "What time is it?" he asked.

"A little after noon," Anton said. He set the sandwich on the coffee table, then pulled over the armchair and sat down. "You were sleeping soundly, I didn't want to wake you. But then I think, he's not here to sleep all day, is he."

Anton waved toward the sandwich. "It's not much. Something with corned beef, some pickles—you like pickles? Being Polish, I assume everyone likes pickles. Some cheese. Ah," Anton sighed, "if my Liska were still here, she would fix something very nice. She made a lamb sandwich—"

Benjamin took a bite of the sandwich, realized he was very hungry indeed, took another.

Anton watched him chew for a minute. Then he said, "So, now maybe you are ready answer some questions?"

"About Fletcher's computer program? I'm afraid I won't be of any help. It's even more Greek to me than it was to Mr. Wolfe."

Anton waggled his hand. "Maybe yes, maybe no. Come on. Bring food."

With the glass in one hand and the sandwich in the other, Benjamin followed Anton into the foyer and up the stairs.

As they climbed the stairs, Benjamin looked at photos lining the wall. A number were black-and-white photos of Anton surrounded by men, all of them standing in front of blackboards or in offices that suggested academic settings. But in every photograph there were also men in military uniforms—Soviet military uniforms. He recognized those enormous officer hats.

They reached the top of the stairs and turned left, into a small room that might have been Anton's study—except that it looked identical to the downstairs. The shelves were overflowing with books, and a large, heavy antique table held so many even its bulk seemed ready to collapse under their weight.

In a little alcove, Anton's desk was set in the middle of an overarching forest of book stacks. At the other end of the room was a blackboard, filled with equations.

Anton led Benjamin to the desk. Fletcher's laptop was there, the screen up and glowing with a vast, intricate web of equations. Benjamin realized the equations on Jeremy's computer and those on Anton's blackboard were quite similar.

"Now, please, sit," he motioned toward an armchair nearby, "and let me ask my questions."

Benjamin pulled over a captain's chair. Anton sat down in the old wooden swivel chair before the desk, the chair squeaking whenever he turned it from side to side.

"First," Anton began, "what the hell is having happened?"

In broad strokes, Benjamin outlined the investigation he and Wolfe had carried out: his discovery of the TEACUP password, the interest Jeremy had had in Myorkin at the FRN and Orlova at the RCC—and Sikorsky at Georgetown. And he confided to Anton that Wolfe thought Jeremy's death hadn't been an accident, that someone at the Foundation may have killed him to keep some aspect of his work secret. A conclusion, Benjamin said, he'd come to agree with.

"Yes, those clear parts," said Anton, not commenting on Fletcher's possible murder. "But why you? Why history guy, with Indians and Pilgrims?"

Again, Benjamin wondered how much he should tell Anton. But what was the point in asking for his help if he wasn't completely honest with him?

So he told Anton of the mysterious Ginsburg book about Bainbridge and the fake Bainbridge diary at the Morris Estate. He was even about to tell Anton of the strange symbol he'd seen in the Foundation's mural—but once again he feared it would sound outlandish, fantastical, and undermine Anton's faith in him; so he said nothing about the mural.

While Anton was mulling over what Benjamin had said, Benjamin asked a question of his own.

"Have you ever met Dr. Fletcher?"

"Oh, yes, yes. Years ago. Conference, but of smart ghouls, us guys who do this—" he pointed to the blackboard "—get paid to 'think unthinkable.'"

"Kahn's phrase?" Benjamin asked.

Anton looked surprised. "You know Kahn?"

"No, not at all," he said. "But he was mentioned the other night at dinner."

"At that place, no surprise. Almost *everybody* there thinking unthinkable, one way or another." The tone of teasing sarcasm was suddenly absent from Anton's voice; he sounded more than a little angry. Then he seemed to shake it off.

"And you leave after fire?" he asked.

Benjamin wondered if Anton was accusing him of abandoning Wolfe. "I wanted to stay and find out if Samuel was okay, but Gudrün . . . Dr. Soderbergh, she insisted there was nothing I could do, and that I should leave immediately."

"Um-hm," said Anton. "Gudrün Soderbergh. I know this name, too. Rising star. Little bit, how would you say," Anton leaned his head to one side, "bent?"

Benjamin thought for a minute. "Biased?" he asked.

Anton nodded. "Reminds me my old masters. Always knew answer before asked question. Helluva way to do research."

"I saw some photos, in the hall," Benjamin said. "You used to work for the Soviet military?"

Anton frowned. "United States has DARPA, RAND, bunch of alphabet soup guys. In USSR, instead of letters is numbers. My number was 12 Directorate, Ministry of Defense. In Kuntsevo, outside Moscow. Sometimes we get vacation, in Urals, at Kovinksky." He smiled. "Nicer winters." Anton stopped talking for a minute. "You know Russia at all?"

"Not really," Benjamin said. "I've never been there."

"Lucky you," said Anton. "Anyway, *perestroika* come, I go. Americans very happy with my arrival. What the hell for, I wonder. They know everything already. Anyway, here I am. I meet Samuel ten, twelve years ago. We both decide other one is son of a bitch. Get along fine."

Anton sat back in the chair, looked at him. "Now, I have three, maybe two more questions."

"All right," Benjamin said. "If I can answer them."

"We'll see. First question is, who is this Gadenhower guy, with the bees?"

Benjamin smiled. "Gadenhower was a woman. Edith Gadenhower. Her research seemed quite bizarre to us. I have no idea how it fits in with Dr. Fletcher's research."

"Is all right," Anton said. "Think I do." He stopped, squinted. "And you said '*was*'?"

"Yes," said Benjamin, looking uncomfortable. "After we returned from the Morris Estate, I went to her laboratory and . . . well, apparently her bees had escaped . . ."

Anton's eyes widened. "Fletcher *and* Gadenhower?" Benjamin nodded. "And *maybe* Sam?"

"The fire was in her laboratory."

"Yes, big explosion, much chaos," Anton said, nodding to himself. "Sad, very sad." Anton's expression of grief didn't strike Benjamin as quite sincere, but he decided not to question it right now. "But hope for best, yes? Now, question number two: What did Samuel tell you about Fletcher's work?"

"He said he'd been writing about nuclear war theory for years, and that he was far ahead of anyone else with his theories."

"That I know," Anton said. "I mean, did he think it was good or bad?"

Benjamin thought back. "He said it was strange, that the way Dr. Fletcher wrote, he seemed . . . well, that it was almost like he didn't believe the Cold War really happened."

"Happened," Anton said. "I was there. Anyway okay, question number three. This TEACUP program, what did Samuel think it does?"

"Well . . . ," Benjamin tried to think how to put it. "He said something about it calculating probabilities. I guess he meant probabilities of the Cold War being the sort of affair Fletcher described in his other writings. He said Fletcher was looking for flaws in the logic of the whole MAD doctrine."

Anton laughed. "Flaws like crazy bear in room," he said. "Very big, very dangerous, but nobody talks about him."

Anton put his head down for a moment, deep in thought. He stood, stretched his back, walked over to the blackboard at the other end of his study.

"See these?" he said, tapping equations on the board.

"Yes," Benjamin said.

"Three years," he said. He took a piece of chalk from the blackboard, drew an enormous X across the equations. He turned and looked at Benjamin. "All shit now." He came back and sat down, pulled the chair closer to Benjamin, pointed to Fletcher's computer. "Thank you very much, Dr. Jeremy Fletcher."

He settled back into the chair, crossed his hands in his lap, and began to speak.

"Sam wrong about TEACUP program. Or half wrong. Fletcher's TEACUP really does read tea leaves. Cold War tea leaves." He leaned forward now, put his hand on the edge of the computer. "And is really *two* programs."

"Two programs?" Benjamin asked.

"One half calculates probabilities about Cold War."

"You see," Benjamin began, "that's what I don't understand. We *know* the Cold War happened, so how can it calculate the *probability* of it having happened?"

Anton thought for a moment, then asked, "You know how they find planets Neptune and later Pluto?" Benjamin shook his head. "Didn't see them. Too far away. But they see Uranus does not go exactly way it should go. Something making it . . . wobble. They calculate, figure how big such a thing *should* be, where it *should* be. They look there . . . voila! They discover planets. All from the math."

Anton cleared his throat, leaned forward. "TEACUP work like that. For years Fletcher feeding it data from Cold War. Program eats data, spits out analysis. At first what it telling Fletcher not clear. He makes program better. When he gets to TEACUP 6, it's very clear what program telling him." He paused.

"Yes?" prodded Benjamin.

"Is *wobble* in Cold War."

"Wobble?"

"Is something making it go different way than it should go."

Benjamin leaned back on the couch. He wasn't at all sure he understood what Anton was telling him.

"I know," said Anton. "Is confusing. What way *should* a cold war go? But there are things more probable, and things less probable. People like Fletcher, people like me, we calculate such things. What TEACUP tells Fletcher is, things don't add up."

"What 'things'?" said Benjamin.

Anton pursed his lips, blew out air. "From what I read so far, data points at something in sixties. Something very, very strange happen. That *thing*, whatever was, create wobble."

"You mean, this aberration in the course of the Cold War?"

"Sam right, you smart boy. Yes, aberration. Good word."

Anton pulled the laptop closer, began typing. After a moment he turned the screen back so Benjamin could see it.

Displayed there was the same graph he and Wolfe had seen that night in Fletcher's room: the two sides of a rising bell curve, with a missing middle.

"We saw this," Benjamin said. "Samuel called it a . . . a Nash equilibrium?"

"Yes, exactly. He says what that means?"

"Well, something about two sides playing a game, and if each knows what the other will do, they've reached a stalemate."

Anton nodded. "Right again. TEACUP tells Fletcher Cold War at stalemate. In sixties."

"Well, see, that's what I don't understand. Why is that big news? Of *course* it was a stalemate. That's why it was the *Cold* War, right?"

Anton smiled, looking a little smug. "According to TEACUP, such, how is it, standoff shouldn't happen for at least another five, ten years. Or should collapse, you know, go boom. Or even end. Guys who built first U.S. missiles, what you call Minutemen, made them to last only ten years. They figure, by then, madness over."

"But, aren't they still there?"

"Exactly so," nodded Anton. "Rusting in silos. See, in beginning, everybody *know* MAD is, well, crazy. And according to TEACUP, good chance there is something fake about this nice Nash equilibrium."

"How good a chance?" asked Benjamin.

"Eighty percent," replied Anton.

Benjamin remembered: the two incomplete graphs, and above them the blinking red number.

Eighty percent.

"That's . . . incredible." He ran a hand through his hair, felt the fatigue catching up with him again. He wished Samuel were there with them, patiently explaining, coaching Benjamin's thinking in the right direction. . . . He even felt he wouldn't mind a good, stiff shot of scotch right now.

"I'm sorry," he said, "I'm still very tired. And even if you're right, there's still a lot I don't understand. Why would anyone kill Jeremy over this? For that matter, why would they kill Edith? And how does all this even connect with her work?"

"I show you." Anton leaned over to the computer, moved the cursor around and opened one of the files, then turned the screen so Benjamin could see what was displayed. Benjamin recognized it from the Gadenhower file.

"See this?" Anton pointed at the formulae. "All about how bees use enemies to make hive act this way, that way."

"Something Edith called 'swarm intelligence,'" said Benjamin.

"Exactly so," said Anton. "Bees a kind of . . . model. For how people act even when not sure *why* they do what they do. Beehive a kind of conspiracy without little workers knowing *is* conspiracy. Understand?"

Then Benjamin remembered something Edith had said in her lab. "What appears random is really a bunch of small acts, all of them overlapping, interacting, until finally what you get is—"

"Called 'emergent phenomenon.' Too complex to see right away. Looks like chaos, but really strategy. Fletcher talks to Edith, puts that into TEACUP . . . suddenly he calls you, has heart attack, and all hell breaks loose." Anton sat back, making the chair squeak loudly. "Was maybe key TEACUP needed."

Benjamin thought for a moment. "Edith's research is about how what looks like a conspiracy really *isn't*, yes?"

Anton smiled broadly. "And if you turn it around?" He waited for Benjamin to think that over.

"Then . . ." Benjamin looked up. "It would be a model for how what doesn't look like a conspiracy really *is*?"

"Again, smart kid," Anton said. "So smart kid, know plan for end of world?"

"Uh . . . no," Benjamin said.

"I show you."

Anton stood up, went to the blackboard and turned it over to the blank side.

He drew a big circle on the left side of the board and inside it he wrote one word in capital letters: SIOP.

"This is United States plan for nuclear war. SIOP. Single Integrated Operational Plan." He drew many lines out from the circle to little stick figures of planes, missiles, and submarines. "Tells everybody when to shoot, how much to shoot, where to shoot." He tapped the chalk on the blackboard. "Same SIOP since 1963. *Forty years,* still same. Wolfe and me, we tell them ten years ago, when we at Foundation together, time to change SIOP. But noooo, they say. Too expensive, too complicated."

He shook his head, laughed. "Not make sense. Soviet Union is gone. Half of Russian missiles, submarines, bombers? All gone. But *still*, this SIOP not change. Like doesn't *matter* Soviet missiles mostly gone." Anton wrinkled his nose. "Something fishy, yes?"

He moved to the other side of the blackboard, drew another circle. Inside this one he wrote *strategija #1*.

He tapped with the chalk. "This Strategy Number One. Stalin's strategy. Basically, is start war, if anything go wrong, blow up world. But then, thanks god, Stalin dies, Khrushchev comes. Little more sense than Stalin. So," he erased the #1 with the cuff of his sweater, wrote #2, "we get *strategija* #2. Put missiles in Cuba. Big SS-4s, even bigger SS-5s. Spook Kennedy. Great idea."

He turned and faced Benjamin. "Only *not* so great idea. Kennedy not spooked. Why?" Anton smiled at him, a bright twinkle in his eye.

"Kennedy tells everyone, *big* missile gap, Russians have thousand missiles. Ha!" Under the circle he wrote two numbers: 3,000 and 300. He tapped the 3,000. "This is how many bombs U.S. has." He tapped the 300. "This how many bombs USSR has." He looked at Benjamin. "As kids say, do the math."

"So," Benjamin said, "the whole missile gap scare—"

"Big hooey," said Anton. "Cuba episode spooks somebody, yes. Spooks *Soviets*. And," he held up a finger, "Soviets spook *themselves*. Khrushchev sends four submarines, new Foxtrots, to Cuba. Each has nuclear torpedo. U.S. Navy sits on them, like hen on egg. One Soviet captain gets nervous, damn near shoots big fish at U.S. Navy boat."

"How could he have the authority to do that?"

"Ah," said Anton. He pointed to the SIOP circle. "In U.S. plan, president controls everything, even submarines. But," he pointed to the *strategija* circle, "in Soviet plan, tell submarine captains, *you* decide whether blow up world or not. And good luck."

He turned and looked at Benjamin, frowning. "Big problem, yes? So," again he erased the number next to *strategija*, and now wrote in 55, "something change. After Cuba, new strategy. New launch codes, all controlled by Moscow."

Benjamin thought of two questions, asked the first. "But why fifty-five? Why not Strategy Number Three?"

Anton laughed. "Old Soviet joke. In Red Army after Revolution, every officer responsible for his own pistol. All pistols numbered. So, Cheka— Secret Police—line up officers. Ask first one, 'What number pistol?' Officer answers, '23.' Cheka man looks, number should be 32. So bang, shoots officer. Asks next one, 'What number pistol?' Officer says, '34.' Cheka man looks, number should be 43. Bang, shoots again. Asks third officer, 'And what number *your* pistol?' '55,' he says." Anton smiled. "Get it? Number can't be wrong."

"So," Benjamin said, "this strategy 55, it's a joke?"

"Not joke," said Anton. "But not real, either. Nobody *sees* it. It's a *prive-denie*, a ghost."

"Okay, here's my second question," said Benjamin, "and maybe it's dumb, because I don't know Russian. But the name of the file on Fletcher's computer is *Stzenariy 55*, not *Strategija 55*. And Samuel said he thought *stzenariy* meant 'script,' not 'strategy.'"

Anton smiled very broadly. "Samuel right," he said. "Means 'script,' like for movie. Screenplay you call it?" Benjamin nodded. "Very dramatic word. Very . . . *artistic* word. And therefore very *interesting* word. Is KGB-type word."

"I don't see the—"

"KGB guys consider themselves not soldiers, not *apparatchiks*. Great spies. Great *artistes*. Tend to use such words."

"So that name indicates the plan originated with the KGB?"

Anton nodded, made his way to the armchair, sat down again, exhaled.

"Anyway, whether is *strategija* or *stzenariy*, nobody ever see this number 55. Only rumors, then nothing. Instead get *Strategija Chetyre*, number four. But strange, is not much strategy. Mostly propaganda and nonsense." Anton held up a finger. "*And* something else. Americans think 1963 and Cuba closest world comes to big bang, yes? Not so. Was 1968."

"What happened in 1968?" Benjamin asked.

"You don't remember so-called Prague Spring?" Anton asked, looking surprised. Then he answered his own question. "No, too young. Anyway, Czechs rebel, Soviets send in tanks. Everybody in Soviet Union thinks NATO will invade, help rebels. Sit with fingers on buttons for two weeks. But, pfft, big *nothing* happens. Except one small *something*."

Anton tapped at the keyboard again, opened the file labeled "*Stzenariy 55*." *Borba s tenyu* appeared on the screen.

"Yes, we saw that," said Benjamin. "But Samuel had no idea what it meant."

"Click on it," instructed Anton.

Benjamin reached forward, clicked on the text.

A small black border appeared around the phrase.

"It's an image," said Benjamin, "not text."

"Exactly so. Now make bigger."

"How much bigger?" asked Benjamin.

"Much bigger."

Benjamin shrugged, enlarged the image several hundred percent.

What had been the black blocks of text revolved themselves into long columns of numbers and letters. Benjamin saw each column was eight figures wide.

"What on earth . . ."

"Is octal code," said Anton. "Code computer uses for letters and numbers. Fletcher scanned letter into computer, converted words to octal, hid code in picture."

"Letter? What letter?"

"Letter from Fyodor Myorkin."

"My god," said Benjamin. "Are you able to read this?"

"Kids don't know octal these days. Don't need to. But Anton very old," he smiled, "so, yes, I can read.

"Fletcher writes Myorkin because Myorkin wrote about Cold War years, exposed secrets. Made many enemies. Anyway, Fletcher asked him, ever heard anything about something in sixties, in Siberia, something . . . *stranno,* strange? Myorkin writes back, yes, found something in KGB archives in St. Petersburg. About place called Uzhur-4 and something called *Stzenariy 55.* After Prague Spring, KGB all over the place. People arrested, officers reassigned. Big panic. Myorkin says he will go back to archives next week, but first wants to interview one of few officers from Uzhur-4 still alive. And officer's name interesting, I think. Kapitan Nikolai Orlov."

"Orlov?" Benjamin thought. "Why does that sound . . ."

"Female version Orlova. Like, for daughter."

"N. Orlova, at the RCC," said Benjamin. "Then it's a *woman.* And she's somehow connected to this *Stzenariy 55,* which is *somehow* connected to the 'wobble' TEACUP found in the Cold War, which the Gadenhower data *somehow* convinced Fletcher is all part of some enormous conspiracy?"

"Now you understand," Anton said with a mischievous grin, "why I keep saying, is all *maybe.*"

Benjamin leaned back in the chair. He was still processing much of what Anton had told him. He realized he had reached a point where he didn't even know the right questions to ask anymore.

He looked over his shoulder out the second-story window of Anton's study. He could see a narrow sliver of gray sky. He suddenly wished he were back in his small, safe cubicle in the basement of the Library of Congress, his greatest concern deciphering the spelling in eighteenth-century legal codes.

Anton rose and came over to him.

"You need more sleep," he said.

"No," Benjamin answered. "I still have an appointment to keep at the Library of Congress to look for this diary. Though I still don't see how it could possibly fit into all this."

"Ah, like I said, TEACUP *two* programs," Anton said. "First half about wobble in Cold War, yes?"

"Yeah," said Benjamin. "I think I understand that now."

"Second half," Anton said, "is other half of graph, about how find *same* wobble in another war."

Anton waited . . . and then the answer was obvious to Benjamin.

"King Philip's War," he said, half to himself. But then he frowned. "But that was hardly a cold war. Thousands died, whole tribes were wiped out."

"Think he used this king's war as kind of control, test case, time when conditions completely different than Cold War. To compare, understand?" Benjamin nodded. "But then TEACUP finds same . . . aberration. Path different," Anton shrugged, "but wobble same."

"You mean . . . some other invisible influence?"

Anton nodded, then he stood up, stretched again. "But remember, even TEACUP only eighty percent sure. Need two more pieces of data to be one hundred percent. One is this *Stzenariy 55,* and the other is . . ."

"The Bainbridge diary," finished Benjamin.

"Maybe," said Anton.

"Well then." Benjamin stood up. "Sounds like I've got a phone call to make, to a Ms. N. Orlova at the Russian Cultural Center." He looked down at Anton. "Do you mind if I use your bathroom to wash up?"

"Please," he said. "Down hall, on left. Hot water slow, so be patient."

"Patience," Benjamin said as he walked off down the hall. "Heard that a lot lately."

Anton listened to the bathroom door close. Then he rose and went to his desk, pulled the phone there close. He dialed a number, listened until someone answered.

"He's leaving," he said. And then, as the sound of running water came from down the hall, Anton continued listening, nodding now and again. Finally he said, "Helluva plan. Damn risky."

Then, his eyes thoughtful and unsettled, he hung up the phone.

CHAPTER 28

Natalya was exhausted. She'd arrived at the Cultural Center at six o'clock that morning. It was now after noon, and she hadn't had a break during those six hours.

First had been checking that the movers were arriving that morning to begin setting up the tables in the main reception hall; then that the decorators would be arriving shortly after that to begin laying out the tablecloths and silverware, as well as the dozens of flowers, garlands, wreaths, and other decorations that she hoped would transform the Cultural Center into something out of a nineteenth-century Tsarist Russia painting.

She disappeared into the kitchen for a moment to grab something to eat. While she was there she decided to check her phone messages at home. There was only one, but it surprised her.

Her father's cousin Olga had called and left a very brief message, telling her just to call her as soon as possible. To hear from Olga at all was strange— she and Natalya were not that close—but even stranger was *when* she'd left it: 7:00 A.M. Olga probably expected to catch her before she left for the RCC, but since she'd left so early to get ready for the reception, she hadn't been home.

She was about to call Olga back on her cell phone, when one of the assistants came to tell her there was a phone call for her at her desk. *Ah,* she thought as she made her way upstairs, *this must be my father calling to explain Olga's odd behavior.*

"*Alloa*," she said, expecting to hear her father's baritone "*privet*" in response.

"Uh . . . I'm sorry, is this Ms. N. Orlova?"

The voice was clearly American, not Russian.

"Well, this is Natalya Orlova, yes. Who is this?"

"Ms. Orlova." There was a pause on the other end, and she realized the caller was trying to think what to say. "You don't know me. My name is Benjamin Wainwright. I'm a colleague of someone I believe contacted you, perhaps last week. His name was Dr. Jeremy Fletcher."

Natalya held her breath. For a moment, she literally couldn't speak.

"Miss Orlova?" the voice asked. "Are you there?"

"Yes," she managed. She couldn't think straight. "Uh, you said . . . you said he was a colleague?"

"Yes," the voice said. "I . . . it's difficult to explain over the telephone."

Natalya's first impulse was to hang up. But she couldn't quite bring herself to do that.

"Who did you say you were?" she asked, stalling for time to think.

"Benjamin Wainwright," said the voice. "I'm . . . well, I was at the same place where Dr. Fletcher was doing his research. The American Heritage Foundation. In Massachusetts."

Natalya thought back. There hadn't been any institutional letterhead on Fletcher's note, nor any bulk mail stamp on the envelope. She'd heard of the American Heritage Foundation; she knew obtaining any sort of relationship with the Foundation was considered a real coup by the people she'd studied with at Moscow State Institute. She also noticed that this Benjamin had said he "was" there.

"You're not in Massachusetts now, Mr. Wainwright?"

There was a pause. "No," he said. "I'm here. In D.C." Another pause. "I was wondering . . . I was hoping I might see you sometime today, Miss Orlova, and speak to you in person about Dr. Fletcher's research."

"That would be impossible, Mr. Wainwright. I am very busy. We have a reception for the Bolshoi Ballet company tonight, and I have not a minute to spare . . ."

"It's about a file on his computer, to be exact. A file named '*Stzenariy 55*.' Or, perhaps if you don't recognize that, you would know the name inside the file. *Borba s tenyu*?"

Natalya lowered the phone. Her instinct was to put it and this Wainwright as far away from her as possible.

But it was countered by an even more powerful instinct: the same one that drove her to sit in on Yuri's "interviews"; the same one that had kept her digging for years into her family's dark secrets. And that instinct wasn't about to send Mr. Wainwright away, regardless of the shivers she felt down her spine.

"Ms. Orlova?" Benjamin asked. "Perhaps I'm not pronouncing it correctly. I'm afraid I don't know Russian, and—"

"Mr. Wainwright," she stopped him. She looked about her. Everyone was focused on their tasks for the reception, but still, to have him come today would simply be impossible. If she took time away from the preparations it would be noticed, and she didn't want to attract any undue attention. But she also knew she had to see this Wainwright, as soon as possible. There was only one solution.

"Mr. Wainwright," she said. "How would you like to attend a reception tonight?"

CHAPTER 29

As usual, the beauty and elegance of the Library of Congress made an impression on Benjamin as did no other building in Washington, not even the monuments. The ornate Italian Renaissance architecture, the stained-glass dome high overhead, the quiet, majestic glow of light reflected from the polished wood reading tables . . . This was indeed a palace, thought Benjamin. A palace for books.

He stood amidst the murmuring crowd of a tour group, one he'd unobtrusively joined on the library's steps—even though he still had his employee badge, he hadn't wanted to use it to gain entry. He had a floppy fedora hat borrowed from Anton on his head as his meager attempt at a disguise, counting on his colleagues being too busy to really notice him among another knot of visitors gawking at the library's magnificence.

As they'd entered the library's foyer, the guide had begun her spiel—a spiel Benjamin knew by heart.

"The Library of Congress, established by an act of Congress in 1800 . . . The original library was housed in the new Capitol until August 1814, when British troops burned and pillaged it. . . . Retired President Thomas Jefferson donated his personal library as a replacement . . ." (That part wasn't true; Jefferson had *sold* his collection, very reluctantly, in order to pay off a fraction of his enormous debts.) " . . . The library possesses the most comprehensive collection in the world today, with over 130 million items, including the largest rare book collection in North America. . . ."

And let's hope there's one among those rare books they still don't know they possess, thought Benjamin.

He walked through the Great Hall to the staircase, marveling as always at the cherub statues ascending the railing; up the staircase past the names of illustrious authors set into the vaulted coves of the ceiling—Dante, Homer, Milton—past the intricate mosaics inlaid into alcoves along the walls, each with its symbol representing the arts and sciences—Mathematics, Astronomy, Engineering. From the second floor he could survey the eight large statues representing the eight categories of knowledge. He glanced briefly at his favorite, *Philosophy*: *The inquiry, knowledge, and belief of truth is the sovereign good of human nature—Bacon.*

Today above all days, he dearly prayed Bacon was right.

Finally he came to the elaborately engraved bronze doors of the Special Collections room. Every time he passed through these doors, he felt he was entering some fortress, a bulwark against the ravages of barbarians and time. And, if he was even half right about what he expected to find here, fortress was an appropriate image—but not necessarily against the barbarians.

Once inside Special Collections, he headed to a separate, smaller room off to the right that held collections of paintings and prints from the American Colonial period, and where he'd spent many hours researching. He was looking for a particular book, an anthology of prints of American heroes of the Revolutionary War. After a few minutes of searching, he found the book he was looking for, pulled it from the shelves, and took it to a small study alcove set in a corner.

He opened the book and thumbed through to the prints of American generals. After turning a few pages, he found the "hero" he was looking for: Major General Horatio Lloyd Gates, Esq.

He'd been right: this engraving must have served as the basis for the painting over the Morris mantel. Here Gates stood, in major general's uniform, inside a tent; through the opening other tents and cannons and flags could be seen. Obviously it was meant to represent an encampment during the Revolutionary War. Here was Gates's double chin; the thick, pouty lips; the powdered wig. And, as in the painting, his left arm was extended downward, with one plump finger resting on something set on a small table.

But, whereas in the painting that something had been a military map, here it was some sort of manuscript. There was writing on the manuscript, too small to make out with the naked eye.

Benjamin went out to a desk in the reading room and opened a drawer where he knew a magnifying lens was kept. He carried it back into the alcove, trying very hard not to run.

Once he was seated, he leaned down close to the print, the magnifying lens placed over the page. The writing was still illegible—it probably wasn't meant to represent any real writing at all. But there was a symbol at the bottom of the page, and, as he moved the magnifying lens down, it grew in size, until he could make it out.

He sat back with an exhalation. And, just as he had while examining the mural at the Foundation, he reflexively looked over his shoulder, to see if anyone was watching.

It was the same symbol as in the mural.

Or one very much like it. It was so small, so indistinct, he couldn't be certain the tiny details were *exactly* the same.

He checked beneath the engraving for the artist's name. There was none. He turned to the index in the back, found the engraving number. Again there was no artist listed, only the information that it had been published in 1778, under the auspices of one John Morris.

John Morris? John Morris was brother to Gouverneur Morris, and famous for his collection of antique paintings and prints. And books. Books like the ones they'd seen at the Morris Estate.

He returned to the side room and placed the book back where he'd found it in the shelves. Then he crossed to another alcove on the other side. Here, the shelves contained copies of letters from various Founding Fathers and other Colonial luminaries. He searched until he found a collection titled *Diplomatic Correspondence of the American Revolution*.

With that book in hand, he went back to the alcove and flipped through the pages until he came across a collection of letters Franklin had written while he was serving as the minister plenipotentiary to France. He read through them quickly, until he found the one he wanted, dated 15 March 1783, to the superintendent of finance of the United States—one Robert Morris:

> *Honor'd Sir:*
> *Friday last order was given to furnish me with 600,000 livres immediately, and I was answered by M. de Vergennes, that the rest of the 6,000,000 should be paid in quarterly in the course of 1783.*
>
> *I pressed hard for the whole sum demanded, but was told it was impossible.*

Our people certainly ought to do more for themselves. It is absurd the pretending to be lovers of liberty while they grudge paying for the defence of it.

But those "Triangulists" of the recent Newburgh intrigue do no good for our reputation abroad. Any knowledge of such things could hurt our credit and the loan in Holland, to say nothing of sullying our reputation as a true Democracy, and would prevent our getting any thing here but from government.

I hope your disassociation from those rogues is immediate and compleat.

I am & c.

(Signed) B. Franklin.

Benjamin leaned back, then read it again to make certain he'd seen what he thought he'd seen.

There it was: Franklin chastising Robert Morris for his "Triangulist" allies and suggesting that any whisper of the Newburgh conspiracy in the corridors of power in France or Holland, the two major financial supporters of the nascent United States, could irreparably harm his efforts to obtain loans.

He remembered now: he'd read through these letters when he was doing his research on Franklin's pyramid code. He'd seen that reference to the Newburgh conspiracy—but that time news of the aborted coup had reached Franklin in France—as well as the mention of "Triangulists" among the Colonial government.

But at the time he'd interpreted the word "Triangulists" as all Colonial scholars had throughout history: as a sarcastic slap at those in the Congress who'd been less than enthusiastic about formalizing true democracy—full and popular representation in the Constitution—and instead seemed to be maneuvering for a form of government somewhere between democracy and a parliamentary monarchy, as in England. Triangulists, it was thought, were those hedging their bets, people who had either begun the Revolutionary War as outright Tory sympathizers, like Gouverneur Morris's parents, or spent it agitating for appeasement with the British. The delegates so referred to, it was assumed, were the American version of aristocrats. People like Gouverneur Morris and Alexander Hamilton, for instance. And people like General Horatio Lloyd Gates.

He replaced the book where he had found it, then exited the Special Collections room and went to the elevator.

It was while he was waiting for the elevator that he noticed a man who was standing near the railing, apparently taking in the compelling architecture of the library. But something struck him as odd about this would-be tourist. Then he saw it: he was wearing an earpiece cell phone. And such equipment didn't work in the library. Or at least it wasn't supposed to.

When the elevator door opened, Benjamin stepped in and pushed the button for the basement. He saw the man start toward the elevator. Benjamin pressed his ID badge against an electronic scanner on the elevator control panel, then quickly pressed the Close Door button. The doors eased shut just as the man—someone with dark glasses and very close-cropped brown hair—reached the doors. Benjamin saw the look of frustration on his face.

Once the doors had closed, Benjamin took off the hat and leaned back against the brass railing, unsure what to do next. He really hadn't thought about being followed, assuming that, if the Foundation knew where he was, they would simply report him to the authorities. He had to think quickly.

Too soon the doors opened in the library's basement. He looked around. He thought of pressing the emergency or fire alarm button to lock out the elevator, but that would require them to clear out the whole building. And, while he knew places he could hide, they might simply close the library for the afternoon, and then he'd have a tough time explaining himself when he tried to exit and found the place crawling with D.C. police and firemen. Then he thought of another plan.

He went to his old office. He looked for an unoccupied cubicle, used the phone to dial security. He identified himself, and then said he'd seen "someone strange" lurking about on the second floor with an earpiece cell phone. Maybe he had a cell phone camera as well? Those weren't allowed in the library, were they? He didn't want to be a bother, but . . . He was told someone would check it out immediately.

He hung up. Even if security didn't find the guy, still he thought the appearance of several security personnel, all clearly looking for someone, would either delay his pursuer, or perhaps discourage him completely, and he'd wait outside, to pick Benjamin up when he exited the library.

But he had another plan to deal with that eventuality.

Benjamin left the office and walked down the hall to the preservation storage area. There was indeed someone on duty inside, an employee named Larry that Benjamin knew slightly.

"Benjamin!" Larry greeted him—a little too loudly for his comfort. "Back from that think tank already?"

"Sort of," Benjamin hedged. "They needed me to check on something in the storage room, see if it's still here."

"And they sent you all the way down here to do that? Why not just call?"

"Hey," Benjamin shrugged, "it's their dime, right?"

Larry laughed, patted him on the back. "Yeah, wish it was my dime, ya know?"

He unlocked the room, switched on the dull blue lights overhead.

"You know the drill," Larry said. "Knock when you're done."

Benjamin nodded, thanked him, and Larry closed and locked the door from the outside.

And it suddenly occurred to Benjamin: if they had wanted to trap him here, they'd just done it.

The room was essentially a large warren of shelves, the shelves composed of bins, and the bins labeled according to subject, date, and, in some cases, donor. Benjamin thought back: the bin he'd been working on when he'd encountered the diary had contained case history files from some of New England's more infamous asylums for the insane from the Colonial and nineteenth-century millennial period.

But first he went to a small podium set near the door, opened a cabinet, and took out a pair of latex gloves from a box that was always kept there. Many of the documents in this room—where the humidity and temperature were carefully controlled—were sensitive to even the small amounts of acid in human sweat.

Walking carefully past the bins, he tracked down the section devoted to medical records, and then worked backward to the period 1750–1820. Set very far back in the room, almost hidden in the cul-de-sac formed by three shelves, he found the original crate he'd been examining all those months before: documents donated by the American Medical Association. And then, right next to it, just as he remembered, was a smaller crate, with the name MORRIS, S.—1968 written by hand on a small index card and taped to the crate.

Benjamin pulled the crate very carefully forward on the shelf. He peered over the edge into the dim interior. He realized he'd been holding his breath for some minutes. The blue-tinted lights barely illuminated the contents. Regular lighting was too yellow for sensitive paper, and fluorescents were out of the question.

He pulled the crate a little farther forward—and suddenly its weight shifted, and the crate came tumbling toward him off of the shelf. He fell to the floor but managed to stop the crate from hitting his body. He stopped, listening, worried that the sound would bring Larry to see if everything was okay. But after a moment he realized the sound hadn't been nearly as loud as he feared.

He gently set the crate on the floor. He reached in, toward a large clear plastic container, one of the hermetically sealed bags used to contain specimens prior to restoration. There was no identifying information, which was unusual. Inside the bag was what appeared to be shapeless brown wrapping of some kind. Leather—so old it was almost as stiff as cardboard.

He lifted the bundle carefully out of the crate. Very carefully he unsealed the bag and extracted the bundle, then folded back the flaps of the leather.

Inside he could see the first page of a book, yellowed with age and discolored with mildew. In the middle of the page were perhaps a dozen handwritten lines . . . or once had been. Now, the lines were unreadable: faded, smeared, disintegrated. All that remained was a single line of text.

R 6:12—HPB

Just as he'd remembered.

He carried the bundle to a small table nearby, switched on the specially filtered reading lamp, and set it down.

Pulling back the leather wrapping as carefully as possible, he could now see that, while the book had a hard cover of black leather on the back, there was no matching front cover. Examining the spine, he could just make out evidence of a very clean cut. Someone had neatly removed the front cover and first page.

They'd been willing to multilate such a treasure, but not destroy it? Strange priorities, Benjamin thought.

He lifted the book and examined the top edge. He could see that many of the pages were practically melted together with age. To open it at the wrong place would be to tear these pages, or perhaps rip them out of the binding. He would have to be very careful, indeed.

Very slowly, he lifted the first page of the book.

Benjamin's hands were trembling.

He lifted them, watched until the trembling stopped. Then he rose, went back to the podium in the front of the room, and reopened the cabinet. Inside was a large yellow legal pad and several pens. He took the pad and one of the pens and returned to the table.

He sat down and, checking the edge of the page, made sure it was one that could be turned without damage. It was. He turned the page and began to read.

Almost immediately he began making notes on the legal pad. When he was done, again he examined the page's edge, but this one was clearly sealed to the next one. He simply couldn't risk trying to separate them, and he discovered he had to turn to several pages farther on.

Working this way, reading a page or two, then forced to skip several that were inseparable, he continued to make notes. He filled one of the legal pad pages, then another.

And another.

CHAPTER 30

Benjamin sat across from Anton, the small oval coffee table in his second-floor study between them. Spread across the table were a dozen yellow sheets from the large legal pad, covered with notes in Benjamin's tidy, squarish printing—so similar, he realized, to his father's.

Benjamin sat slumped against the back of the overstuffed couch. Ever since he'd returned to Anton's from the library, he'd felt the desperate urge to simply collapse and fall asleep. But his mind was far too excited by what he'd discovered to allow him to do that. And, if he was to attend the reception that evening at the Russian Cultural Center, he needed, somehow, to stay awake.

So he was drinking yet another cup of coffee—or rather glass of coffee. Anton had handed him the tall, flat-bottomed glass set on a saucer, warning him it was "black as the Devil's heart." Benjamin could see a sludge of grounds in the bottom, but he'd tried it anyway, discovered he liked it. First strong scotch, now strong black coffee . . . *What other risky tastes remain undiscovered?* he wondered.

As far as his "tail" at the library, feeling rather proud of himself, Benjamin had explained to Anton how he'd ditched him. Exiting the library when he was finished with the diary, he'd gone straight to the tunnel that ran from the basement of the Jefferson Building, under Second Street, to the James Madison Memorial Building. The tunnel was only accessible to library staff, and he'd known his shadow would never gain entry without identification; probably didn't even know of its existence. Once outside the Madison building, he'd immediately caught a cab to Anton's row house in Georgetown.

"Anyway, it's all there," Benjamin said, waving toward the yellow pages. "That is, everything I could get from the undamaged pages of the diary. But I don't know how you're going to enter it into Dr. Fletcher's program."

Besides the coffee, Anton had brought Benjamin some cheese and bread, but Benjamin hadn't touched any of it. He was simply too tired, and too energized, simultaneously, to even think about food.

Anton began, "Jeremy Fletcher very smart guy. This," he pointed to the laptop, "*Grandiozno*. Genius. Words in, formula out. But explain to me what's here." He pointed to the notes Benjamin had made. "Maybe it make my job little easier."

"Well." Benjamin rubbed his eyes. "You have to understand, much of the diary was too fragile, or too illegible, to read. So I had to piece all this," he waved at the yellow pages, "together, fill in some gaps from what I already know about the period. And make some guesses, which might not—"

"Don't excuse," Anton said, "just say 'maybe.'"

Anton's impatience reminded Benjamin of when Wolfe would interrupt him when he got too "lecturey." He experienced another twinge of sadness over Wolfe's disappearance. He shook it off, realizing he'd have to save such feelings for later, when, hopefully, there would be time for them.

Where to begin? Probably, he thought, at the beginning.

"What you have to understand, Anton, is that the Puritans weren't all the same. As I explained to Samuel, there were sects, factions, rivalries."

"Is always so," said Anton. "Why Puritans any different?"

"Well, one of the strongest rivalries was between the strict Puritans and a group known as the Antinomians. My father had always assumed that Hessiah Bainbridge—Harlan's father—was part of this radical group, because, when Anne Hutchinson and the other Antinomians were banished from Massachusetts in 1638, Hessiah went with them to Rhode Island. And he took his young son and wife."

"Banished?" said Anton. "Sounds like Tsar times, with dissidents and Siberia. And why you say 'assumed'? Your father not right?"

"I'll get to that," Benjamin said. "Anyway, the stricter Puritans considered the Antinomians blasphemers because they believed that each individual was capable of receiving God's grace all by him or herself, without the 'guidance' of the Church fathers."

"Bad for monopoly," said Anton, smiling.

"Exactly. But there was another reason the Antinomians were banished. You see, Harlan's father had been one of the so-called Radicals calling for better relations with the Native Americans. His dream was to build a Prayer Town that could serve as a kind of cultural embassy, where the Natives could learn English and European customs—and of course religion. According to everything my father and other scholars knew about Hessiah Bainbridge, this dream was his driving passion.

"But according to the diary, there was another group among the Puritan conservatives, a group I'd never heard of; a group Harlan names as the 'Congregation of the Eye of Providence.' They were the most doctrinaire of all the Puritans, the most fanatically devoted to the idea that the New World had been given to them by God to create a pure society, free from the corruption of Europe.

"This group considered any plans for peaceful relations with the Indians to be a dangerous threat to their vision of this new society, this New Jerusalem. According to Harlan, they didn't want the Natives converted; they wanted them gone."

"How is it so," Anton asked, "you never heard of these eye guys before?"

Benjamin smiled. "Well, not by that name. There are vague references to the 'Guardians of Purity,' and similar descriptions," Benjamin replied. "No one's ever discovered any declaration of their principles, no sermons that mention them directly, no tracts or stories. Most Colonial scholars thought these references were a joke, a nickname to make fun of the humorless fanatics among the Puritans."

"But now?" Anton prodded.

"These," Benjamin pointed at the notes, "are excerpts from Harlan's diary. And he knew these 'Eye of Providence' Puritans were *not* a joke. He knew they were well organized, absolutely dedicated, and mortally dangerous to anyone they considered a threat. And that they were dead set against any plans to establish better relations with the Native Americans. He knew in fact that they planned to use the Natives as a bogeyman to scare the increasingly secular Puritans back into line."

"And how he *know* all this?" asked Anton skeptically.

"Because his father, Hessiah, was one."

For the first time, Anton looked surprised. "But you said he was be-friends-with-Indians guy?"

"He was what I guess you would call a double agent," Benjamin said. "At first, Harlan was too young to understand. But eventually he came to realize that the Congregation of the Eye of Providence had *planted* Hessiah with the Antinomians to keep watch on them, to sabotage their plans. The irony was, by the time Hessiah died in Rhode Island, Harlan himself had become someone who truly *did* believe in Prayer Towns. He writes about an 'epiphany' he had, wherein God revealed to him that their true calling was to live peacefully with the Natives. To convert them, yes; but also to learn from them and thus build the sort of tolerant new society appropriate to a New World. By then, Harlan had come to hate the Eye of Providence fanatics and everything they stood for, which as far as he could see was merely the maintenance of absolute power by creating false enemies."

Anton snorted. "Very old story."

Now Benjamin was surprised. "You mean, you *understand* them?"

"For seventy-five years," Anton said, looking suddenly serious, "Party keeps power by telling people enemies everywhere: counter-revolutionaries, wreckers, secret conspiracies. Stalin says Trotsky main bad guy, makes everything bad happen in USSR. Trotsky says, if I'm so powerful, how come Stalin's in Kremlin, and I'm in exile?" He laughed. "But nobody listens. People *needed* enemies. Stalin's propaganda tell them what they *already* believe. Is how good propaganda works, yes?" Anton smiled. "*Maybe even in America.*"

Benjamin thought about that, gave a reluctant, "Too true." Then went on.

"Harlan did finally get financing for his Prayer Town, from Henry Coddington, a wealthy merchant. Sometime around 1665 the community of the Bainbridge Plantation was established in western Massachusetts. On the very spot where the Foundation sits today."

"And this not make Eye guys happy, right?"

"Well, at first they didn't seem to bother about the plantation. Perhaps it was too far removed from civilization. And at first the plantation thrived. Harlan writes proudly about one of the first converts—a Native called Wounded Bear, whom they re-christened John Sassamon."

"This name important?"

"Well, it comes up ten years later, in King Philip's War. And though Harlan doesn't come right out and say so, it's clear he came to not completely trust this Sassamon. But by this point Harlan doesn't have time to worry overmuch about that. It seems that the Eye of Providence Puritans finally took notice of the Bainbridge Plantation, decided it posed a threat to their control of the central colonies, and set about to sabotage it."

"How?" asked Anton.

"Food stores burned, hunting parties ambushed, threatening symbols left carved in trees. Some of the plantation's people thought it was the Wampanoags, angry about the plantation's proximity to their burial grounds. But Harlan was convinced it was all due to the 'perfidy of the Puramists.'"

"Pur-who?" asked Anton.

"Puramists," Benjamin said. "It's another name Harlan uses for the Congregation of the Eye of Providence. And sometimes he just calls them 'Triangle Puritans.'"

"Ah," said Anton, "*puramis* is pyramid, yes? But triangle . . . ?"

"From their habit of drawing a little triangle in their Bibles, with an eye at the apex."

"The eye of God," said Anton.

"Exactly. Just as they believed God was watching and judging their every move, they believed *they* had the divine authority to watch over the colonies. Here, look at this."

Benjamin picked up one of the yellow sheets and turned it around so Anton could read it. "It's an entry from the diary. I copied it down verbatim."

Anton leaned over the table and read what Benjamin had written:

> —*Receiving our Guidance from the true Geneva Bible and as Bradford's example a lesson to us all—he that might have possesed himself of the entire Plymouth Plantation, as did Penn or Weldon, and withe his denial sacrificed a greater and reall worthinesse—seek a vertue to sever the serpent of Commerce from Civitas. But that the Civill selfe is the true self, "good with bad," and not the cross of usurpry as well to beare, for that is too much.*
> —*As for Mr. Childham, the new Governor, what passe for his Piety governes the designe whereof Principall is fastned to an artificiall Church, the Church of Businesse—for against this Rule the wheeles of fortune grind out a Soveraignty like dust, filling all the aire, onely to clog an honeste man's mouth and blinde an honest Puritan's eyes.*

Anton looked up. "Which means in plain English?"

"This is Harlan's way of describing the philosophy of the Puramists. To him, they were all about treating not only their civil life but their spiritual life, too, as a business. A business *they* controlled. This idea was blasphemy to Harlan and most of the other traditional Puritans. And this mention of the 'serpent of Commerce' . . ."

"Yes?" Anton prodded.

"It's a curious way to use the word 'serpent.' Usually, in Puritan writings, serpent is a synonym for Satan. But here . . . well, it's just that there was another reference, to 'Satan's trident,' in a letter written by Harlan. And in that letter, he linked it with the Puramists. Clearly he thought they were *very* bad people."

Anton thought that over for a moment.

"*Neveroyatno*," said Anton. "Quite a story. But, how you get from these 'very bad people' to this . . . what is it . . . Newburgh guys?"

"Well," Benjamin shook his head, "it sounds incredible, but I think they're one and the same group."

Anton's considerable eyebrows shot up in surprise. "I thought Newburgh guys soldiers and politicians, not Puritans."

"Actually," said Benjamin, "I think they were all three: soldiers, politicians, *and* religious fanatics. For two reasons."

Anton leaned back, motioned for Benjamin to proceed.

"First, Harlan writes that there were seven major Puramist leaders, a kind of Inner Council. And the name of the leader of that council was one Elias Morriss."

"And this name, is important?" asked Anton.

"Elias Morriss was one of the top aides to Joshia Winslow, and Winslow was one of the most zealous advocates for eliminating the Natives through any means necessary. And they *both* later became commanders in King Philip's War."

"Okay," nodded Anton, "they don't like Indians. But how this connect to an almost-coup one hundred years later?"

"That's my second reason. Their symbol, this triangle with an eye at the apex? It's almost *identical* to a symbol I saw today in the Library of Congress, in an engraving of Major General Horatio Gates. Gates was Washington's rival during the Revolution, and probably one of the ringleaders in the Newburgh conspiracy."

Anton shook his head. "Little triangle maybe too tiny to balance big conspiracy."

Benjamin smiled. "*And,* another of those ringleaders was probably a Gouverneur Morris. Now, granted, that was Morris with one S, and the Puramist was a Morriss with two—but in those days variant spellings of the same last name were commonplace. I haven't done the genealogy, but there's a good chance they're related. So, as you would say, *maybe* . . . ?"

"Ah," said Anton. And now he looked interested. "So you think these Puritan Bolsheviks, these, what you called them . . . Puramists? You think maybe these 'very bad guys' still around one hundred years later?"

Benjamin was about to tell Anton about his discovery in the mural at the manse and his suspicion they may have been around much longer than that; but once again, he hesitated. His only evidence was an indistinct little doodad in that immense painting. And once again, he decided it was simply too fantastic to get into now, and that he should stay focused on what he'd learned from the diary.

"At the very least," Benjamin continued, "it explains why the Morris family had this fake diary created and saw to it the real one was hidden. In 1929, the Morris family and the other benefactors were establishing the Heritage Institute for Good Government, something they hoped would help restore the world's shining hope for democracy. And this was at a time when that democracy was struggling to survive. There were demagogues like Father Coughlin on the right and radicals like the Wobblies on the left. . . ." Benjamin thought for a moment, then nodded. "Yes, I can see how they would have considered it embarrassing to have it revealed that their ancestors had been fanatical racists and antidemocratic conspirators. How they might have even considered murder justified in keeping such a secret. And finally, isn't that symbol just a little too much of a . . . coincidence?"

Anton pursed his lips. "Coincidence just low probability," he said. "Not proof."

Benjamin saw the skepticism in Anton's eyes and began to doubt his own conclusions. Now not just the mural but the whole story began to sound like a paranoid fantasy.

"I don't know," said Benjamin, rubbing his eyes. "Perhaps you're right. How could they have kept it secret for so long, among so many people?"

"Don't give up so fast. *Maybe,* like in Party, most didn't *know* what Eye guys up to. Best conspiracy one you don't tell anyone they're part of."

Benjamin looked up. "Odd you should put it that way," he said.

"What?"

"It's just, that sounds very much like something Samuel said . . . the last time we talked."

"Sam smart guy," he said, trying to sound reassuring. "Maybe smartest thing he do, keep you at Foundation."

"At least all this," he waved at Benjamin's notes on the table, "fill one big hole in TEACUP. If these Eye guys *did* sabotage plantation, maybe even get Indians to destroy it, then explains 'wobble' number one, yes?"

"You mean, they manipulated King Philip's War into happening? That's what the TEACUP program revealed to Jeremy?"

"Or would have," Anton nodded, "if he'd had Bainbridge diary. But still leaves other big hole. Which is *Stzenariy 55*."

"Damn!" Benjamin said, standing up. He looked around for a clock. "What time is it?"

"Oh yes," said Anton, "your date." He looked Benjamin over. "You can't go meet Bolshoi like that," he said.

"Oh, god," said Benjamin, looking at himself in a mirror. What he saw was a very rumpled suit, a wrinkled shirt, uncombed hair, and a dark five o'clock shadow.

He turned to Anton. "Unfortunately, I didn't pack black tie for the Foundation. I'll have to go by my apartment, clean up, and at least put on a fresh suit."

"Not such good idea," Anton said. "Apartment probably last place you want to go."

"Then what the hell am I supposed to do?" Benjamin said angrily. He ran a hand through his hair, rubbed his neck. "Sorry, I'm just tired and cranky."

"Is okay," said Anton. "My son leave some clothes here. Big businessman. I think tuxedo in his closet." He looked at Benjamin. "Older and bigger than you, but fit okay." He smiled. *"Maybe."*

CHAPTER 31

The taxi dropped Benjamin off in front of the Russian Cultural Center on Phelps Place. He climbed the steps, then stood at the back of a line of several people, all of them in elegant evening dress. He felt like something of a clown in Anton's son's tuxedo: the sleeves were too long, the jacket too big, and the pants had been hurriedly hemmed by Anton with pins and tape; Benjamin expected the hem to drop down over his too-large shiny black dress shoes at any moment.

After the guard checked his name on the invitation list, he walked into the building and its lavishly decorated foyer.

There was a large round table with a huge bouquet of red roses in the foyer's center, and red-and-gold banners were draped around its ceiling. On his right in a large dining room, each table had its own centerpiece of red roses and white baby's breath; to his left was an equally large reception hall, dotted everywhere with more bouquets of roses. Dozens of elegantly dressed people stood in groups while around them circulated waiters dressed in red-and-white uniforms and carrying golden trays of champagne.

My, thought Benjamin, *the times of Soviet drabness certainly* are *over.*

The reception hall had a polished parquet floor and stark white walls adorned with rectangular panels and fronted by grooved pillars. Panels and pillars alike were edged with gold gilt filigree. The overall effect was impressively imperial. At one end of the room hung an enormous red banner, with writing in huge gold letters:

Большой & Америка—1776—Bolshoi & America

At the other end of the room was an equally large banner, but this one was white, with green edging to form a continual border of ivy, in the center of which was embroidered, in blue letters:

Let Our Two Nations Never Again Polarize

Benjamin noted that this second banner was in English only.

Light from several large brass chandeliers reflected in a mirror that ran along almost the entire length of one wall; opposite the mirror was a large, white-veined marble fireplace, complete with crackling fire. With all the people in the room, Benjamin felt a trifle overheated and began looking for something to drink.

He walked to a nearby group, where he saw a waiter with a tray of champagne, and took a glass from the tray. Then he realized the group was something of an informal reception line and, before he could move, the first person in the line was extending his hand for Benjamin to shake.

"Ambassador Vasily I. Schastny," the man said. He was tall, with a broad Slavic face and expertly clipped hair. "How do you do."

"Benjamin Wainwright," he said, shaking the man's hand. He noticed his grip was quite solid, and a little threatening. He felt the need to add something to his identification. "Scholar of American history," he said.

"Ah," Vasily replied. He looked a trifle surprised, but said with a bright smile, "An academician." He turned to the woman next to him. "And this is Irina Sedova, director of our little cultural outpost."

The woman turned to greet Benjamin, extending her hand. She, in turn, introduced him to a woman wearing a dramatically low-cut black evening gown and too much eye makeup. "Prima ballerina Leonora Zenova." Madame Zenova held her hand out to be kissed, and Benjamin immediately if a little awkwardly bent slightly and bussed her fingers with his lips.

"Charmed," was the only thing he could think of to say.

And so it went, on down the line. Benjamin couldn't really keep track of the names, though he noticed there were as many Americans as Russians.

The last couple was quite old, the man sporting a very well-trimmed mustache and pointed goatee, and the woman wearing a small silver tiara. They were introduced as "Prince Obolensky and Princess Gagarin." Benjamin wasn't sure whether or not to bow, but he decided that would be a bit too nineteenth century.

When he exited the receiving line, Benjamin felt a bit dizzy from names and titles. And he still needed to locate Ms. Orlova.

Looking about, he saw no one that seemed the sort he could simply walk up to and ask for directions. He finally decided to try a waiter. From the waiter he got another glass of champagne and a suggestion he try one of the security men standing at intervals along the wall. He found one of them— apparently a clone of the man at the door, complete with earpiece but absent clipboard. When he asked after Natalya Orlova, he got an inquisitive look. For a moment he wasn't sure the man understood English.

"A friend of Natalya's?" he asked.

Benjamin didn't know what to say. "No, not exactly. I just . . . she invited me, and I wanted to thank her."

The man smiled. "Look for a beautiful blonde in a red dress," he said, and smiled. "You cannot miss her."

With that advice, Benjamin began circulating. Everywhere he looked, he saw women in elegant evening dresses and men in tuxedos, some of the men with colorful sashes draped across their chests, and one or two of those with some sort of medals. But nowhere did he see a "beautiful blonde in a red dress." He decided to try the dining room.

He walked across the foyer to the dining room, glanced around at people standing about between the tables. He saw that an area at the front of the room had been cleared as a sort of stage. Natalya had told him the reception was for the Bolshoi Ballet, and that after the dinner there would be a brief performance by members of the company. And he'd noticed in the reception hall there had been large photographs of various Bolshoi productions: *Swan Lake,* of course, and others, as no great fan of ballet, he couldn't name. He'd recognized a couple of the ballerinas from the photographs among the guests: very thin, very beautiful women who were the centers of little circles of attention, surrounded by men smiling and nodding and offering to get them more champagne.

At the end of the dining room, serving as a backdrop to the stage area, was an enormous mural painted on polished wood. He walked to the end of the room so he could see the mural more closely.

It was painted in the style of a medieval icon, with much gold trim and flattened perspectives and many bright colors, and divided into panels separated from one another by decorative arches. Within each panel was a representation of what appeared to be cities, their names painted in gold Cyrillic letters. A panel at the center contained the largest city, Москва. At least Benjamin could recognize that one: Moscow.

"Beautiful, isn't it," said a voice next to him.

He turned. Standing on his left was a woman in a strapless, floor-length, red satin evening gown and wearing a glittering gold necklace that emphasized her pale skin. She had very bright blond hair, done up in a French twist. Benjamin saw that her eyes were a curious blue-green mixture; eyes that seemed to shine with a light of their own. Her high cheekbones and small nose made Benjamin think she was Scandinavian, but he'd detected the trace of a Russian accent in her comment. She was, indeed, very beautiful.

"Ms. Orlova?" he said.

"Mr. Wainwright?" she said by way of an answer.

She was smiling at Benjamin, but with a slightly disappointed look. It took him a moment to realize her hand was extended. He shifted his champagne glass to his other hand, took her hand in his, which she shook only briefly.

"How . . . ," he began. His throat felt tight. "How did you know it was me?"

Natalya laughed. "For one thing, you were not talking to anyone. People mostly come to such affairs to talk to someone more important than they are. And for another thing, you do not seem quite," she surveyed his ill-fitting tuxedo, "comfortable here."

"You were expecting someone," he shrugged, "taller?"

She smiled. "Someone older," she said.

"I'm sorry," he said. "I don't even own a tuxedo. I had to borrow this one." He smiled. "And as far as I'm concerned, I'm talking to the most important person here right now."

Natalya tilted her head, her smile faded a little. "Mr. Wainwright," she said. "I thought you were a serious academician, not a fawning diplomat."

Her displeasure made Benjamin very uncomfortable. He turned and looked at the mural. "It is, indeed," he said. "Beautiful, that is."

Natalya turned and looked at the mural. "It represents what is called the Golden Ring. The most important cities around Moscow." She pointed to several of the panels as she translated the names of the cities. "There's Novgorod, Suzdal, Vladimir, Pskov . . ." She stopped and turned back to him. "But then, you are not really here for the Russian culture, are you."

Her comment reminded Benjamin of why he *was* there. He patted the breast of his jacket.

"I brought a CD, Ms. Orlova, of the program I mentioned. Dr. Jeremy Fletcher's program. Perhaps there's somewhere I could show you—" He started to take out the CD.

Natalya reached out and stopped his hand, touching it lightly. "Not now," she said. "I am 'on duty,' at least until the dinner is finished. Afterward there will be a performance, by the ballet. Perhaps that would be the best time to talk further. Until then, I found a place at table number twelve for you. With some diplomats, so be prepared for some very . . . charming conversation. But enjoy the dinner. We will talk later."

Benjamin nodded, and she smiled and then, seeing someone across the room, said, *"Pakah"* and walked away.

For a moment Benjamin didn't move, simply staring at Natalya's pale bare back framed by the folds of her red evening gown. Then he realized he was gawking, took a long drink of his champagne, and went looking for his table.

CHAPTER 32

The tables were numbered from the front to the rear of the room, so he assumed his table was somewhere near the back, for which Benjamin was grateful: he didn't relish the thought of trying to make intelligent conversation with the A-list diplomats and luminaries seated at the prime tables near the stage area.

As he found his table and sat down—he'd been right, it was practically at the entrance to the dining room—a Middle Eastern–looking gentleman with a thick mustache seated next to him rose and extended his hand. Benjamin noticed that he wore a very well-tailored tuxedo, which only made him more self-conscious.

"How do you do," he said. "My name is Nabil Hassan."

"Benjamin Wainwright," he said. They shook hands.

"*Sorirart biro'aitak,*" said Nabil. He saw that Benjamin didn't understand him. "Nice to meet you. Please," and he indicated that Benjamin should sit down.

Benjamin saw that there were already small bowls of caviar, black and red, on the table, along with plates that held semihard bread and soft butter, and others with chopped eggs, onions, chives, and black olives.

Benjamin saw Nabil take a piece of bread, spread butter on it, then use a tiny spoon to scoop a little caviar on it. He followed suit.

Nabil took a bite of the bread and caviar. "Delicious," he said. "The best caviar will always come from Russia."

Benjamin didn't really care for caviar, but he took a bite anyway. And he had to admit, this was certainly better than any he'd had before. As he reached for another serving, Nabil went on.

"Excuse me if I seem abrupt," Nabil said, "but you don't seem like the usual guest for such an affair."

"You're right," Benjamin said, still chewing his caviar. "I'm not."

Waiters began serving the borsch. Benjamin was surprised to see, in addition to the beets, beef, potatoes, carrots . . .

"Ah," said Nabil. "*Real* borscht." He said the word with a pronounced T at the end. "The only Russian soup I prefer to borscht—when it's authentic, that is, like this—is something called *solyanka*. Have you ever tried it?"

"No," Benjamin said. "I'm not really that familiar with Russian cuisine."

"Well, the best Russian cuisine, that of the Caucasus region, is in some ways similar to my own country's. Spicy, and with delicious sauces. Thank god this isn't an event celebrating the food of the Tartars. Then we'd be trying to smile while we ate *kazy*, a sausage made of horse meat."

"Yes, thank goodness," said Benjamin. "Mr. Hassan, you said similar to your own country's?"

"I'm Egyptian," Nabil said. "I'm a cultural attaché with our legion here. Since . . . oh, well, several years now. And you, Mr. Wainwright? To what delegation do you belong?"

Again Benjamin found himself struggling to explain his presence at the reception. He wished he and Natalya had established some sort of cover story. He decided again on a half-truth.

"I'm doing some research for the center," he said finally. "I was invited by a Ms. Natalya Orlova."

Nabil looked at him with a certain new appreciation. "A friend of Natalya's?" He smiled. "A very beautiful woman."

"Yes," said Benjamin. "She is that."

The waiters were already circulating with the next course, the *golubzi*. Benjamin tried his and found it again delicious.

"What sort?" asked Nabil.

"Excuse me?" asked Benjamin.

"What sort of research are you doing for the center?"

Benjamin realized he'd gotten himself into something of a trap, but then he also realized he had a rare opportunity to further his "research."

"This may sound a little presumptuous of me, Mr. Hassan," Benjamin began nervously, "but do you know anything about hieroglyphics?"

Nabil smiled very broadly. "That depends. What sort of hieroglyphics? Aztec? Asian? Polynesian?"

"Well, no, uh, that is . . ."

Nabil smiled. "I'm sorry, that's my little joke. Of course people always assume that only the ancient Egyptians used hieroglyphics for writing, when of course that is very much not the case."

"Of course," Benjamin said. "I'm sorry."

"*Min fadila.* Please, not at all," replied Nabil. "But I assume you were asking about my knowledge of *Egyptian* hieroglyphics?"

Benjamin nodded.

"Well, in that case, yes, I have passing knowledge, though I am far from a scholar on the subject."

"I'm not sure my question really requires a full-fledged scholar," Benjamin said. "In fact, I'm not even certain it concerns *authentic* Egyptian hieroglyphs. It could simply be a facile imitation, something with no real meaning."

"Well, Mr. Wainwright, why don't you describe to me the hieroglyph in question, and I'll try to ascertain its authenticity."

"All right." Benjamin looked around for something on which to write, finally simply pulled the cocktail napkin out from under his champagne glass. Then he realized he had no pen. Saying "Do you mind?" to the woman on his right, he extracted the tiny plastic sword from the orange slice in her emptied cocktail.

He put the napkin on the table and began tracing a symbol on it with the tip of the sword, pressing so as to make an impression.

"It looks something like this," he said. And as he drew he began to describe the symbol he'd seen in the mural in the manse and the portrait of Gates in the library. "A triangle, with an ellipse or an eye at the top, and—"

Nabil reached over and stopped his hand.

"Is this *your* little joke?" he asked. He was still smiling, but he sounded slightly insulted.

"I'm sorry?" Benjamin said.

"This 'Eye on the Pyramid' nonsense? I assure you, Mr. Wainwright, despite all your hysteria over this 'Pyramonster' in American movies and books, there simply was no such symbol in *actual* Egyptian hieroglyphs." He removed his hand from Benjamin's, sat back. "I'm sorry," he said, "but if I hear this *gha 'bi mosh kowayes* . . . this moronic . . ."

He paused, calmed himself.

"Forgive me." He patted Benjamin's hand. "Imagine listening to someone from Cairo ask you about the secret anti-Islamic message of, for instance, 'The Star Spangled Banner.' You would be amused and insulted, simultaneously, yes?" Benjamin nodded. Nabil sighed. "So it is with so much to do with our revered ancestors. In our country, they are almost holy. Like your Founding Fathers. But on your dollar bill, in your films, they become cartoons. You see?"

"Yes I do," Benjamin said.

Now the waiters were serving a baked sole. While Benjamin began picking at his, Nabil continued.

"And when it comes to pyramids, or triangles with eyes, well, they have as much meaning in Christian history as they do that of Egypt."

"How do you mean?" asked Benjamin, eager to keep Nabil talking.

"This eye you mention, this may be traced in Egypt to the Eye of Horus, which was all-knowing. And one can see how this developed. You see, here..."

Nabil extracted a pen from his pocket and, taking the napkin, drew four symbols on it:

"Here are the four Egyptian symbols for pyramid, the Egyptian word for which is *mer*. The first two symbols—the arc and the falcon—represent the light of the Pharaoh's soul as it ascends. But the pyramid *itself* is represented by the last two, the flattened ellipse and the triangle. Move the ellipse to the top of the triangle, turn it into an eye...you see? But this is also a symbol important to early Christians. The Eye of Horus becomes something like..." And then he sketched another symbol:

"In such Christian icons, the three sides of the triangle and the three rays coming from each side represent—"

"The Father, the Son, and the Holy Ghost," said Benjamin.

Nabil looked at him appreciatively. "Yes, exactly."

"And the eye in the center, later Christians called the 'All-Seeing Eye of God.' Or sometimes," and he watched Nabil's face as he said it, "simply the 'Eye of Providence'?"

Nabil nodded but displayed no other reaction. "Exactly so. You know your history."

"Some," said Benjamin. "But I understand what you mean about Masonic nonsense. The fact that it's on the Great Seal stirs up a lot of talk of conspiracies. People seem to forget, or don't know, that this part of the seal wasn't even designed by an American, but by a Frenchman, Pierre Eugene du Simitiere."

Nabil nodded. "If you wish to get truly conspiratorial, Mr. Wainwright, you might mention your own secret intelligence agency, DARPA."

"DARPA?" Benjamin asked. He had no idea what it meant.

Nabil smiled. "The Defense Advanced Research Projects Agency, of your Pentagon. They have something called the Information Awareness Office. Look at their icon sometime. It is a pyramid with a glowing eye at the top." He set the pen down, took up his wine, and tilted the glass toward Benjamin. "See what I mean? Everywhere cartoons."

Now Benjamin nodded. "But in this particular 'cartoon,' there is more than just the pyramid and eye." He held out his hand. "May I?" Nabil handed him the pen, and Benjamin continued with his own sketch.

"You see, beneath this circle or eye at the top of the triangle, there is a line. And then two more similar lines, like this, in each lower corner, to make smaller triangles. And inside both of those are these *other* lines, but with tiny legs at the bottom. And then between them, there's what looks like a snake . . ." But as he was attempting to draw a thick serpent, the pen's point tore through the thin napkin. He turned the napkin so Nabil could examine it.

"I see," said Nabil, looking down at his sketch. "Very interesting."

"So you've never seen anything like this?" Benjamin asked.

"Well." Nabil took another sip of his wine. "Not as a single Egyptian hi-eroglyph, no. But as a combination of different symbols . . ." He studied the sketch for a moment. "You see, these two 'lines with legs,' as you called them, in the bottom corners? These are the symbols for 'enemy.' And this serpent between them, this means 'conflict.'"

He was silent for a moment, thinking.

"Odd," he said finally. "Usually there is no barrier beneath the eye, as you have drawn it here. If there were no such barrier, I would say these were lines of power coming down from the eye. Or not power . . . more like control."

"Controlling what?"

"Why, the serpent of conflict, of course."

"Well, that line, or barrier as you call it, I am certain it was there, be-neath the eye. Why, what could that mean?"

"I have never seen it done so. But were I to hazard an interpretation, I would say it suggested the power or control of the eye was hidden." He studied the sketch for another moment. "In which case, one would say this hidden agency was creating conflict between the two enemies, here in the corners. Provoking them, then sitting back in silence to watch their struggle."

He laughed, shook his head, picked up his wineglass. "But that's all very much guesswork, Mr. Wainwright. Like trying to read ancient Egyptian without a Rosetta Stone." He looked at Benjamin with a very steady gaze. "And where have you seen such a symbol, Mr. Wainwright?"

Now Benjamin was in a quandary. He couldn't possibly explain the en-tire story to Nabil, but to tell him only the part about the mural would seem insane. He decided again to be half honest.

"In my research at the Library of Congress," he said. "I saw it among the details of a sketch . . ." And then he stopped. He wasn't sure he even wanted to share the information about Horatio Gates with a total stranger. "A sketch made during the Revolutionary War."

"Well," said Nabil, "perhaps it meant there was *another* war going on. One less visible to the public." He smiled. "A 'fight behind the veil,' as we say."

Benjamin was about to respond, but then the waiters came with the des-sert: blintzes with fruit served in red wine. Even as they turned to their des-serts, the lights in the dining room were dimmed, and then lights at the front of the room were turned on to illuminate the stage area. And it was at that moment Benjamin felt a tap on his shoulder. He turned.

Natalya stood over him. But before she said anything, she turned to Nabil.

"Good evening, Mr. Hassan," she said.

"*Masa'a AlKair,*" replied Nabil, making to rise.

"Please, do not get up," Natalya said. "I would like to borrow Mr. Wainwright for a moment. Do you mind?"

Nabil smiled. "Of course not," he said. "How could I object to another man's good fortune?"

"You are a true diplomat, Mr. Hassan. *Spasiba.*"

Benjamin stood up, extended his hand to Nabil. "Thank you, Mr. Hassan. You were very helpful. I hope we meet again."

"*Ahlan wa shalan,*" said Nabil. "You are welcome. And *inshaalha,* Mr. Wainwright. If it is God's will."

Benjamin wasn't sure what to say to that, so he merely nodded.

Natalya led him into the foyer, turned to him. Once again, Benjamin felt intimidated in her presence. She was smiling at him, but he sensed the strong will behind that smile . . . and something else—that trace of hostility he couldn't explain. And as before, her striking beauty made him feel like a high school boy too nervous to speak.

"Now, Mr. Wainwright, you said you brought a CD?"

"Yes." He fumbled in his pocket, brought out the disc. "Here." He handed it to her.

"There's a computer upstairs, in my office. Please, follow me."

As they climbed the staircase to the second floor, Natalya held her dress up just a little, so it didn't drag on the carpet.

Benjamin looked again at the elaborate decorations—red-and-gold trimming on the stairway, red roses everywhere.

"Isn't this all a little grand for the former Soviet Union?" he said—but it sounded peevish and he regretted the words immediately.

Natalya replied over her shoulder as she continued walking ahead of him.

"It is ironic, really," she replied, sounding slightly condescending. "This house was built in 1895 for Evalyn Walsh McLean, a very wealthy capitalist who owned, among many other things, the Hope Diamond. The Soviets bought the house in the 1950s, used it as a school for children of the embassy staff. They did not trust American schools. Then it was renovated and reopened as the Russian Cultural Center in 1999. We host all sorts of events, from poetry readings to film premiers. Just last week there was the Tsvetaeva Bonfire."

"Bonfire?" asked Benjamin.

"Not really a bonfire." They'd reached the end of a hallway on the second floor, and Natalya entered an area of small offices. She stopped in front of one with натадья ордова stenciled on the door. "It is a celebration of the poet Marina Tsvetaeva's birthday. And then the week before that we premiered a new Russian film, one of those ridiculous spy thrillers Americans like so much, something called, in English, *Chasing Piranha*. Something about agents and secret weapons. I do not care for such stories myself."

She gathered up her gown and sat down at her desk, turned on her computer.

"*That's* a little ironic, isn't it?" Benjamin asked.

Natalya watched the system start up, inserted the CD into its slot.

"Why is that?" she said, not looking at him.

"Well, with all this," he waved at the CD, the building, the general situation, "it just seems like perhaps you're in such a story."

Now she turned and looked at him. Her blue-green eyes were bright spots in the dim light. Again he sensed the strong will behind her beautiful face.

"I hope not, Mr. Wainwright," she said. "For both our sakes, I truly hope not."

CHAPTER 33

Benjamin and Natalya sat staring at the computer screen. Upon it was displayed the same list of files that he and Wolfe had read that night so long ago—and only forty-eight hours earlier.

"The only thing I see here I understand," Natalya said, pointing to the list of file names, "is *Stzenariy 55*. I spent several frustrating hours yesterday searching for some mention of such a name in our archives."

"Did you find anything?" Benjamin asked eagerly.

"Well." She looked down at her hands, which were folded in her lap. He could tell she was hesitating about being completely honest with him. But then he realized he hadn't told her the whole truth about what had happened since he'd arrived at the Foundation.

"Look," he said, "I understand. You don't know anything about me. I'm simply someone who called this morning asking about Dr. Fletcher. And I think you'd agree, I don't know anything about you, either."

"You know I am a Russian cultural attaché," she said. She looked at him with those bright blue-green eyes, but there was caution rather than hostility in them now. "And that is more than I really know about you, Mr. Wainwright."

"Benjamin," he said. "Benjamin Franklin Wainwright." He smiled. "Now you know the most embarrassing thing there is to know about me." She laughed, and he hurried on. "I have a degree in Colonial American history from Georgetown University, and, until last Friday, I was doomed to spend my life in the basement of the Library of Congress, cross-checking two-hundred-year-old birth and death certificates."

"Well," she said. "So you are indeed an academician, and not some sort of adventurer?"

"Ms. Orlova—," he began.

"Natalya," she corrected.

This made Benjamin feel her hostility toward him was finally fading.

"Until last Friday," he said, trying to respond to the honesty he felt in her eyes, "when I arrived at the American Heritage Foundation, the biggest adventure in my life was when I spent a week in Paris, as a student, and stayed in a fifteen-franc-a-night hotel."

She laughed again. The effect was immediate. He decided to tell her what had happened to Jeremy Fletcher.

"I have to tell you first," he began. "Dr. Fletcher is . . . when I got to the Foundation, last Friday . . . he'd had a heart attack the day before. He was dead."

"Dead?" She looked closely at him. "He was a friend of yours."

"Yes. But there's more," he said. And then it all came out in a torrent, as though he'd been waiting for someone to simply let go with—someone he could trust.

He went on to tell her about Samuel Wolfe, about their discovery of Fletcher's computer program. He told her of their interview with Edith Gadenhower, and their visit to the Morris Estate. When he came to the part about Edith's death, the look on her face changed from serious to alarmed.

He told her about what he'd discovered in the mural at the Foundation, about the fire and Wolfe's disappearance, about his discussion that day with Anton Sikorsky. Finally, he finished by telling her about his visit to the Library of Congress and what he'd discovered there.

Benjamin stopped, afraid that, in his need to finally share all that had happened with someone, he had overwhelmed Natalya. But instead, she seemed to accept it all, to immediately grasp the most significant points. And it was then she began asking questions.

"Then this Anton Sikorsky," Natalya said, "seems to understand this TEACUP program?"

"Yes," Benjamin said. "He said it was very similar to work he did years ago, in the Soviet Union. For the Ministry of Defense. He's the one that recognized this *Script 55*."

She looked again at the computer screen, then seemed to make up her mind about something. She turned back to Benjamin.

"I must apologize, Benjamin," she said. "I was very . . . cold with you earlier."

"I understand," Benjamin said. "As I said, you don't know me, and—"

"It was more than that," she interrupted him. "I told you that I researched our archives for information about all this. I didn't find anything, nothing relevant, that is. Until I checked our own restricted archives."

"Restricted?" asked Benjamin.

"We may be years past *perestroika*, Mr. Wainwright, but there are still many, many secrets too sensitive to reveal. Those secrets are kept in various archives, with names like the Institute of Historical-Archival Studies, and the Russian Center for the Preservation and Study of Documents Relating to Modern History." Benjamin winced. Natalya nodded and said, "It is every bit as difficult to access as it is to say. Anyway, only those with special clearance are allowed to view documents in these archives. But I have another source. My father."

Benjamin wasn't sure how much to tell her about Myorkin's letter. It was the one bit of information he'd held back, not certain how she would react to the implication her father might be involved in all this.

"He was in the . . . security service?" he asked, deciding to find out more about her father first.

She smiled. "No, not him." She shook her head. "My father was in the Red Army, one of the first officers of the Strategic Rocket Forces. His first posting was to a nuclear missile base in Siberia during the Cold War."

Benjamin nodded. "And you're about to tell me he knows something about all this."

"Yes, exactly," she said. "He told me he did not know this name, this *Script 55* and '*borba s tenyu.*' But even when he told me, I did not believe him. And then today, someone called me from Russia. And asked me to do something quite exceptional."

"What was that?"

"To visit. That may not sound so strange, but coming from my cousin Olga, believe me, it is very strange, indeed. When I tried to call my father to ask what this is all about, he did not answer. And I have not been able to reach him all day." She shook her head. "So you see, I was upset about this. It worries me. It worries me even more because he seems to be worried about *me*."

"I have to tell you, Ms. . . . Natalya. I told you Jeremy had written to a

Russian journalist seeking information about this *Script 55*? What I didn't tell you was this journalist, a Fyodor Myorkin, wrote back. And in his letter he mentioned your father's name." Benjamin placed his hand over Natalya's. "Perhaps . . . well, knowing that, perhaps you don't want to be further involved with this. Perhaps you're taking a considerable risk even discussing this."

Natalya's eyes were steady, unafraid.

"From what you've told me about this Foundation," she replied, "so are you."

They looked at each other. Benjamin found himself wanting to tell Natalya everything—about Wolfe's suspicions regarding Fletcher's death, about Gudrün's veiled warnings, about every indication he had that, by getting more deeply involved, Natalya was putting herself at even graver risk than she realized. But he hardly knew where to start, and for a moment neither of them said anything.

The spell was broken when they heard someone approaching down the hall outside her office. A security guard poked his head into her doorway.

"Is everything all right, Natalya Nikolayevna?" he asked. He eyed Benjamin suspiciously.

"Yes, Sander," she said. "Everything is fine."

Benjamin noticed she had quickly clicked the button to remove the window of file names from the screen.

"The performance is over," the guard said. "They've started proposing toasts."

"Thank you, Alexander, I will be down in a moment."

The guard gave Benjamin another questioning look, and then left.

Natalya sighed. "I had better put in an appearance. This toasting can go on for hours, but I think I can slip away soon."

She turned and looked at Benjamin.

"I would like to meet this Anton Sikorsky," she said. "Tonight."

CHAPTER 34

Natalya and Benjamin were in a cab, headed to Anton's house in Georgetown. There had been a light rain during the reception, and the streets glistened, reflecting the streetlamps and car headlights. The tires of the taxi shushed along the wet streets.

Natalya was quiet beside him, huddled into her black fur coat. The collar was turned up, her blond hair down now and flowing over it. What with the thick, dark fur outlining her brilliant blond hair and pale, beautiful face, Benjamin thought her profile was quite regal.

The taxi reached the intersection with Anton's street. While they were waiting to turn right, he heard Natalya ask, "Is Anton's house down there?"

Benjamin leaned forward and looked past her down the street. In the middle of the street, almost exactly in front of Anton's address, there were two police cars, their red-and-blue lights spinning and casting flashes of light against the buildings. He saw a man standing on the sidewalk, talking to one of the policemen; a very tall man, with very blond hair.

"Shit!" said Benjamin.

The light turned green, and the cab began to turn into Anton's street.

"No!" said Benjamin. "Straight! Go straight!"

The cabbie shrugged, spun the wheel, and they headed through the intersection.

Natalya turned to him, her eyebrows raised.

"I'm sorry," he said. "But back there . . ."

"The police cars?" she asked.

"Well, yes that, too. But the man talking to them, he's named Hauser, Eric Hauser. And he's head of the Foundation's security." He let that information sink in.

Natalya thought for a moment. She leaned over the seat and said to the cabdriver, "Take us to Dupont Circle."

"Why there?" Benjamin asked.

"Because that is where I live," Natalya said simply.

Benjamin shook his head. "I don't think that's such a good idea. If they've followed me to Anton's . . . Better if I drop you at your apartment, then go to my place."

"And I think *that* is not such a good idea. You said something about being followed today."

"Well," Benjamin sighed, "yes. But if I don't stay there—"

"We'll go to my apartment and you can call Anton from there," Natalya said. "If everything is all right, you can take the taxi back here. If it is not . . . well, you can stay at my place and we can visit him in the morning."

"Are you sure?"

Benjamin found himself fervently hoping she wasn't merely being polite.

"I am sure," she said, and smiled. "That will give us more time to talk. And I have a feeling there is more you wish to tell me."

Twenty minutes later found them in Natalya's apartment on Dupont Circle. Before Natalya changed out of her evening gown, she'd invited Benjamin to make himself a drink, if he liked. She pointed to an array of alcohol in the small kitchen—"I don't have much of a liquor cabinet, I am afraid, but I believe there is some brandy"—and then disappeared into her bedroom.

He felt like what he needed was coffee, not another drink. He figured he'd had about four hours of sleep in the last thirty-six. But he was afraid that, if he did get the chance to sleep, the coffee would just keep him awake. So he'd poured himself a very small snifter of brandy—the bottle said RUSSIA—KIZLYAR—1885, which surprised him; he wasn't used to thinking of brandy as one of their national products—and then gone to the telephone.

He dialed Anton's number. It rang once, twice, three times. . . . When the message didn't come on after ten rings, he hung up.

Just then Natalya came out of the bedroom. She'd changed into a white pullover and black jeans. Her feet were bare, she'd taken off the necklace and most of her makeup—and Benjamin still thought she was achingly beautiful.

"Nothing?" she asked. She came into the kitchen and poured herself a small snifter.

"No," Benjamin said. "Either he's not there, or not answering."

"Well," Natalya said. She went to a chair by the window and sat down. "Please," she said, "sit down."

Benjamin went to the couch. Before he sat down he removed the tuxedo jacket, folded it neatly over the back of the couch—and as he did, an envelope fell out of the pocket.

He threw the jacket over the back of the couch, bent and picked up the envelope.

"What is that?" asked Natalya.

"I don't know," said Benjamin. "It was in the jacket, which belongs to Anton's son. Perhaps it's his." Then he turned the envelope over and saw BENJAMIN written on the outside.

"Anton must have put it there," he said. "But why?" He looked at Natalya, shrugged, tore open the envelope. Inside was a brief note in the same scratchy handwriting Benjamin had seen on Anton's blackboard. Benjamin quickly scanned the message.

"I'll be damned," he said.

"What does it say?" asked Natalya. "Unless it's too—"

"No, no. Here." He handed her the note.

> Benjamin-
> <u>Maybe</u> you will need this.
> Anton

Below that was a name and address.

> Henri Vielledent
> Crédit Agricole Bank
> Washington, D.C.
> Account Number 07041776

And below that was Anton's signature.

"It seems," Natalya said, "you have a benefactor."

"Apparently," Benjamin said, taking back the note. He felt for his wallet, carefully folded the note, and placed it inside. Then he looked down at his too-long trousers.

"I feel a little ridiculous, still in this monkey suit," he said.

"Monkey suit?" Natalya asked.

"Slang for tuxedo," he said, sitting down heavily, the fatigue—to say nothing of the champagne and brandy—catching up with him. "I didn't bring any clothes from the Foundation, my suit is at Anton's. I feel quite the orphan."

Natalya took a sip of her brandy. "Are your parents nearby?" she asked.

"No," he said. "They're both . . . they were killed in a car accident. About five years ago."

"Oh, I am sorry."

"I miss them," Benjamin said—and was immediately surprised at how quickly he'd admitted such a thing to a near stranger. "My father was an historian, too."

"Another academician," Natalya said. "A family tradition?" She smiled.

"Not quite," he said. "I have a brother who lives out on the West Coast. He does something in Hollywood, I've never quite understood what. And a sister who's what you would have called an 'imperialist exploiter.' She's a stockbroker, in New York."

"These days," she said, "such a person is a hero of the new Russia."

"You don't approve of the new Russia?" he asked.

She looked down into her brandy, tracing the rim of the glass with her finger as she spoke.

"You grow up in one country, you are accustomed to it, whatever its flaws. Then one morning you wake up, that country is gone, and in its place is a country whose people you do not recognize." She looked up at him. "Sometimes since then I feel like an orphan, too, Benjamin."

He liked the way she said his name. "Natalya," he said, "you said your father was a . . ."

"A *rocketchiki*," she said. "That's what they called themselves. It would translate into English as something like 'rocketman.'"

Benjamin laughed.

"What is funny?" asked Natalya.

"Nothing, it's just that there was an American comic book character by that name. Rocket Man." She wasn't smiling, and he continued. "Then your father was one of the men with his finger on the red button?"

"Actually it was a white button," she said. "And yes. He was in the first graduating class of the Kamishinsboye ryssheye artileriyskoye uchilische, the Kamishin Artillery Academy."

"Artillery?" asked Benjamin, confused.

"You have to remember those times," Natalya said. "They disguised their purpose, you see. The only insignia they wore on their uniforms was of the artillery division. Anyway, he was assigned to one of their first underground missile bases. It was considered a posting of considerable prestige. But it was a city in the wasteland of Siberia, a town built practically overnight. It was given the name of a village nearby that had existed for hundreds of years, but the town itself didn't appear on any maps."

"What was it called?" Benjamin asked. He leaned forward and put his snifter on the coffee table, rubbed his eyes, trying to wake himself up. But he couldn't repress a yawn. "Sorry," he said. "I'm interested, really." He leaned back against the couch.

"The village was named Uzhur," Natalya said. "But the military base was called Uzhur-4." She looked down at her own drink, was quiet for a moment.

"Very," Benjamin searched for the right word, "cryptic." And then he remembered something Anton had said. "Uzhur-4, you said?"

Natayla nodded. "Why, you know of it?"

"No, not me. But Anton mentioned it tonight . . . or this afternoon . . ." Again he rubbed his eyes. "Anyway, go on."

Natalya looked pensive as she continued. "It was both a terrifying and a protected place," she continued. "We were surrounded by electrified fences, and there were soldiers everywhere. But on the other hand, we had many amenities other citizens of the 'socialist paradise' could only dream of. I remember how proud we were when a telephone was installed in our apartment, the first private line in the city. Of course, we knew it was monitored. But who was there to call?" She smiled. "When we went on vacation to Sochi, we were flown to the airport in a large helicopter. I thought of it as *my* helicopter. And when we took a train, we always had our own private compartment. Strange," she said, "but for all its forbidding atmosphere, I was happy there."

She looked up at Benjamin. He was slumped against the back of the couch, his eyes closed. He was sound asleep.

Natalya went into her bedroom, came back out in a moment with a blanket and pillow. She lifted Benjamin's legs onto the couch, took off his shoes, then placed the pillow under his head and pulled the blanket over him.

She stood looking down at Benjamin for some time, as though she was balancing some kind of decision. Finally, she turned off the lamp next to the couch and walked off to her bedroom.

CHAPTER 35

Benjamin woke to Natalya's face above him. She was holding a cup of coffee in one hand. The scene reminded him of Wolfe getting him up early, shoving coffee in his face. He preferred this version.

"Good morning," Natalya said. "Did you sleep well?"

Benjamin looked down. Apparently during the night she'd pulled a blanket over him, placed a pillow under his head.

He sat up, accepted the coffee.

"Yes, for the first time in several days," he said. He took a drink of the coffee—it was quite strong, and he winced.

"Too strong?" she asked. "I am afraid I like it very strong. American coffee, well, to me it usually tastes like weak tea."

"No," Benjamin said, taking another sip. "It's good." He looked around for a clock. "What time is it?"

"About seven thirty," she said. "I woke up at six, but you were sleeping so soundly, I decided to let you rest."

"Oh," Benjamin said. He smiled at her. "I'm afraid I dropped off while you were speaking. Sorry to be so rude. These last few days at the Foundation . . . well, there wasn't much time for rest."

"So I understood."

She went to the kitchen, returned with a plate with some croissants and a bagel, a dab of cream cheese, another of red jam. "I was not sure what you would eat for breakfast, so I went to the Starbucks across the street." She set the plate on the coffee table. "But perhaps you would like to wash and change first."

Benjamin was already munching one of the croissants. He looked up at her.

"Change into what, exactly?" he said, his mouth still half full. "This," he plucked the tuxedo shirt, "is all I've got right now."

"Ah," Natalya said, sitting down next to him. "Of course."

"But first," and he stood up, "I think I should try Anton's again."

"Yes, please, go ahead."

While Benjamin went into the kitchen to use the telephone, Natalya sat for a moment, staring out the window. It was a bright, cloudless day, a relief after the gray clouds and rain of yesterday.

She was sipping her coffee and still looking out the window when Benjamin returned.

"Still no answer," he said. "And I didn't want to leave this number on the message."

He came and stood next to her.

"I'm really not sure what to do now. Dr. Fletcher's computer is at Anton's, though I have the CD. We could drive by his house again, but if he isn't answering his phone . . ."

"Does he have the password for the computer?" Natalya asked.

Benjamin thought back. "No," he said. "I started it for him. I never told him the password."

"Well, that is reassuring," Natalya said.

"You mean, you think Anton is . . ."

"A betrayer?" finished Natalya.

"I know it doesn't look good, what with the police and Hauser there. But they might have simply followed me." Benjamin shook his head. "I can't quite believe Anton is on their side."

"Their side?" asked Natalya, raising an eyebrow.

"Sorry," Benjamin said. "I guess that sounds a little paranoid."

"I am a professional paranoid, Mr. Wainwright," she said, standing. "Anyway, why don't you wash up. I need to let them know at the center I will be in late today. If at all."

"I hadn't even thought of that," Benjamin said. He looked at her, an expression of concern on his face. "I'm sorry to have gotten you involved in all this, Natalya." He paused. "I believe I know how Sam Wolfe felt when he last spoke to me."

"Your Dr. Fletcher involved me," she said. She stood up. "And anyway, *chto bylo to bulyom poroslo.* As you would say, it is no good to cry over milk already spoiled."

"Spilt," Benjamin corrected.

"Excuse me?"

"Never mind, I understand," Benjamin said. He looked at her appreciatively. "I think Dr. Fletcher knew *exactly* what he was doing when he wrote to you. Even if we don't yet know *why.*" Then he set his coffee down and went off to the bathroom.

Natalya waited a moment, then went into the kitchen to the telephone. She dialed the number of the Cultural Center. When someone there answered, she asked for Yuri. "All right," she said, "I'll try him at home. Oh, and would you tell them I won't be in for a while today. Perhaps late this afternoon? *Spasiba,*" and she hung up.

She went to the window, stood staring out again, deep in thought.

She was still there when Benjamin came out of the bathroom. He was drying his hair with a towel. He still had on the tuxedo shirt, cummerbund and pants, and black socks. "Are my shoes around here somewhere?" he asked.

"Yes, there," Natalya said, pointing under the couch. "I took them off last night."

Benjamin sat down and began putting on his shoes. "I've decided the best thing for me to do is go to Anton's, see if he's home. And if he isn't . . . well, I'll cross that bridge then."

"To where?" Natalya asked.

"I don't know," Benjamin said. "But I don't think you should be involved in this any further. Perhaps I should just go to the authorities with what I already know."

"Which really isn't that much," said Natalya. "Without Anton's explanation for Dr. Fletcher's program, all you *really* know is that there was some sort of secret group among the American Puritans nearly three hundred years ago, and some odd occurrences at this American Heritage Foundation this weekend. Secretive groups in the history of any country are hardly, well, secrets, are they. And these odd occurrences . . . I am certain such people will be able to explain them to any authorities you contact. Believe me, I have experience with these kinds of people. More than you realize. To deal with them, you must have *kozyr,* an ace up your sleeve."

"Well, yes—," he began.

"And in the meantime, you have stolen property belonging to this Foundation, and no witnesses to back up your version of the story."

Benjamin sighed. "Please," he said, "if this is a pep talk . . ."

"Pep talk?" asked Natalya.

"Uh, never mind," he said. He stood up. "All that may be true, but as I said, I don't know where else to go from here." He began putting on the tuxedo jacket.

She rose and came over to him.

"Mr. Wainwright," she said, looking into his eyes. "Benjamin." She smiled. "I think I do. But you will have to trust me. Do you think you can do that?"

Benjamin looked at her. He'd felt he could trust her from the first moment he'd seen her, but he wasn't sure he could trust *that* feeling. After all, weren't femme fatales always beautiful women you wanted to trust? That's why they were femme fatales.

He started to say something, thought better of it, shrugged.

"All right," he said. "Apparently we're in this together. So, what do we do next, Ms. Orlova?"

CHAPTER 36

Their first stop was at the nearest clothing store, across the street. It obviously catered to the college crowd of D.C., and the best Benjamin could do was some khaki pants, a white button-down shirt, a pullover with GEORGE-TOWN in blue letters on a gray background, and some low Bass Weejuns. Natalya pronounced him "an invisible American college guy."

"I'm afraid," he said, looking at her, "it's a little harder to make you invisible."

"A compliment?" she asked, tilting her head.

"Well, yes, I guess so," he said.

"Ah," she said, "then not the truth."

He started to protest, but she smiled and said, "It is okay," and they left the store to find a taxi.

Once they were on their way, he asked her, "Where are we going?"

"To a friend," she said. "I hope."

"Perhaps you should call this 'friend' first, make certain he's alone?"

"I left my cell phone at the apartment," Natalya said. "It was one issued by the embassy, and, well, under these circumstances, I think it best not to use it. And you?"

Benjamin laughed. "Back at the Foundation, with my clothes."

"Well," Natalya smiled, "let us rely on our wits rather than our technology."

Twenty minutes later found them at an apartment building not far from the Cultural Center. When they exited the cab, Natalya walked up the front steps of the building. She pressed the button with the name YURI ANDROPOV above it. She spoke briefly and they were buzzed in. They took the stairs to the second floor, and stopped in front of 201.

Natalya raised her hand to knock, but before she did she turned to him.

"Let me do the talking, all right?" she asked.

Benjamin nodded. *What else can I do,* he thought.

She knocked, and after a moment a man came to the door. Benjamin realized he'd seen him the night before, at the reception; he was one of the men with an earpiece and a watchful attitude, the one that had told him to look for a beautiful woman in a red dress. Now, he was wearing a bathrobe and looked quite rumpled, as though he'd just gotten out of bed.

The man smiled at Natalya but gave Benjamin the same questioning look he'd used the night before.

"*Vkhoditte,*" he said, motioning for them to enter.

Once they were inside, Yuri and Natalya carried on a conversation in Russian. Of course, Benjamin couldn't tell exactly what they were saying, but it was clear Natalya was suggesting something to Yuri of which he did not approve. Several times during their conversation, Yuri glanced over at Benjamin; once he indicated Benjamin and asked Natalya what was obviously a very pointed question.

"*Nyet,*" she replied. "*Prosto znakomiy.*"

At that, Yuri's resistance to whatever Natalya was asking of him seemed to weaken.

Finally, he sat back, shook his head. "*Te pozhaleyesh,*" he said. Then he rose and went into another room. Benjamin could see through the door that he went to a desk, began looking through a small book he had there.

Natalya turned to him. "I have asked for his help," she said.

"To do what?" Benjamin asked.

"To get us into Russia," she said.

Before Benjamin could ask her about the "us" part, Yuri came into the room and handed a piece of paper to Natalya. He asked her something again, and she replied, "*Spasiba, nyet.*" Then she kissed him on the cheek and they left, Yuri shaking Benjamin's hand on their way out—though it seemed a reluctant shake, at best.

After they'd gone, Yuri walked back into his study. He picked up the telephone, dialed an international number. While it was ringing, he pressed a small button on the side of the phone.

He spoke for several minutes. When he was finished, he hung up, then sat for a long time, smoking and thinking.

Once outside Yuri's apartment, Natalya and Benjamin began looking for another cab to hail. There were several questions in Benjamin's mind; he finally settled on the one uppermost.

"Is Yuri . . . ," he stumbled. "Well, are you two—"

"*Chiort!*" Natalya said with some exasperation. "Men! Do you know, he asked me the same thing about *you*?"

"Oh," said Benjamin. For some reason, Benjamin felt flattered. "But then, what did you ask him, exactly? And what's this about going to Russia? About *us* going to Russia?"

By then a cab had pulled up, and they climbed into the backseat. Natalya gave the driver an address.

"I have a diplomatic passport, of course," Natalya said. "But I think it would be better not to use it, at least not to enter the Russian Federation. And as for you, if there are indeed people following you—"

"I'm going with you, then?" Benjamin asked.

Natalya was still somewhat upset. "Would you rather stay here and wait for your shadow from the library to find you?" she asked, not looking at him.

Benjamin didn't have to answer that. "But then, what was all that about?"

Now Natalya looked at him.

"I told you, Yuri is FSB. They keep track of people who deal with this sort of . . . situation. I explained it was very important that I see my father as soon as possible. Basically, I asked him for a name. A name of someone who could help us."

"A travel agent?" Benjamin asked, trying to make a joke.

Natalya smiled, relaxed. "In a way, yes," she said. "But a very expensive travel agent. Our 'tickets' into Russia will cost perhaps five thousand dollars each, Yuri thinks. So, I am going to my bank, to see if I can somehow—"

Benjamin had an idea. He leaned over the seat. "Wait," he said to the driver. "Do you know where the Crédit Agricole bank is?"

"Yes," said the driver.

"Take us there," Benjamin said.

He leaned back. Natalya was looking at him questioningly.

"Remember Anton's note?" he said. "I don't know how much this will help, but it's worth a try."

When they reached the bank, Benjamin realized he had no idea what would happen. Perhaps Henri Vielledent no longer worked there; perhaps he would insist on some sort of notarized signature from Anton, and they'd simply be out of luck. He didn't relish the thought of looking the fool in front of Natalya.

But in fact Henri Vielledent did indeed still work at the Crédit Agricole—and high up enough in their organization to rate a rather ornate office on the second floor. Benjamin and Natalya were shown in and found behind the desk a rather short man with a goatee and a manner so reserved as to be almost hostile. Benjamin's confidence dropped yet another notch.

But the moment Benjamin mentioned Anton Sikorsky's name, Henri became entirely different. Now it was all "*Monsieur* Wainwright" and "*s'il vous plait*" and "*merci*." And when Benjamin gave him the account number from Anton's note, Henri looked very impressed, indeed.

"And how much would Monsieur Wainwright wish from this account?" he asked.

"Well, all of it, I suppose," he said.

"All of it?" Henri said, surprised.

Benjamin glanced at Natalya. "Well, yes. Those were Mr. Sikorsky's instructions," he lied.

"Let me think." Henri tapped his fingers nervously on his desk. "Do you have a valise, a briefcase?"

"A briefcase?"

"Well, yes," Henri said. "Or were you perhaps planning on leaving with two hundred and fifty thousand dollars in your pockets?"

"Two hundred and fifty thousand dollars?!" said Benjamin. Then he tried to recover his composure. "No, of course not."

The solution they settled on was considerably smaller than a valise. Henri had disappeared for a while, then reappeared with an envelope. He handed the envelope to Benjamin.

Benjamin looked at him, at Natalya, and back to Henri. "And what's this?" he asked.

"A *carte de solvabilité*," said Henri. "It will provide you access to the account from almost any bank in the world. Just use the card and enter the account number."

"And the password?" asked Benjamin.

Henri smiled. "For this type of account," he said, "a password is not required."

They stood and Benjamin thanked Henri, shaking his hand. As they were leaving, Henri said, "When you see Monsieur Sikorsky, give him my greetings."

Benjamin hesitated a moment, then said, "I will, certainly."

Once outside and another cab hailed, Natalya turned to Benjamin.

"A quarter of a million?" she said. "In dollars? I thought you said Anton taught at Georgetown. That seems a bit affluent for an academician."

"I know," said Benjamin, looking worried. "Perhaps it was some sort of . . . settlement from the government. For defecting."

"But from *which* government?" asked Natalya.

Benjamin looked at her. Then, oddly, he smiled. "I see what you meant about a 'professional paranoid,'" he said. "But for now, let's go with the flow."

"Excuse me?"

"Uh . . . let's assume the best," he said. And then Benjamin realized he didn't know where that flow was taking them.

"Where now?" he asked. "Where is this friend of Yuri's with the expensive passports?"

Natalya leaned over the seat. "Reagan airport," she said to the driver. "The international terminal."

Then she leaned back and turned to Benjamin.

"Have you ever been to Nice?" she asked.

Eight time zones away, an old man hung up a telephone and sat back, lighting a cigarette. But whereas Yuri's had been a Camel, this one was a Kosmos.

Had Benjamin been in the room, he would maybe have recognized the old man—from the photos in Anton's hallway. But now, rather than wearing the broad officer hat and wide military epaulets, he was dressed as so many other ex-Soviet pensioners, with no outward sign that he'd once wielded enormous power.

Across the table from him sat another old man, also from Anton's photos, also now without his military garb. They were sitting in an apartment in a huge complex near the Moscow River. In the thirties when it was built, it had been considered among the most luxurious addresses in all Moscow. Only the highest of the Party faithful were given apartments there. Of course, such largess hadn't been entirely without guile, as was everything in those days. Behind each apartment were narrow hallways where the watchers would stand, listening to every word spoken in those apartments. And by the end of the purges, nearly all the original inhabitants had . . . moved.

Out of nostalgia or macabre irony, the old man had appointed the apartment with relics from that time. The table at which they sat—large, rectangular, covered with green felt—was in fact from the old KGB offices in Lubyanka; even the lamp, with its octagonal green-glass shade, was a "signature" of KGB style. He switched it on now, as it was getting dim in the apartment.

"And who was that, Vladimir," said the old man sitting across the table from him.

"A former protégé, Dmitri," said Vladimir. "Yuri Alexandrovich, now with FSB in Washington. He had an odd request. He asked if I could send someone to look after a friend who will be acquiring an illegal passport."

Dmitri looked puzzled. "That doesn't sound so important."

"I'm afraid Andrei did not 'cure' our friend Fyodor Ivanovich quickly enough," replied Vladimir. "The disease has spread."

Dmitri frowned. "But I thought those insufferable American *apparatchiks* had quarantined their problem?"

"Ironic," said Vladimir, "their methods. The more we become like them, the more they become like us. But no, they, too, were too late."

Dmitri sighed. "After all these years . . . you would think the ghosts would be at rest."

"That's the problem with ghosts, Dmitri," Vladimir said, picking up the phone again. "They never rest."

"And now?" asked Dmitri.

"Now we send Andrei on another house call."

"But I thought the *Americanski* wanted them alive, so they could—"

"Their methods are too complicated for this simple old soldier," Vladimir said. "And their *khren* is now in our kitchen." He smiled. "Besides, Andrei deserves this trip. Nice is so much warmer this time of year than Petersburg."

CHAPTER 37

Benjamin couldn't quite believe the view. He was looking out on the incredibly blue Mediterranean Ocean.

It was a clear, bright, even warm morning. He was drinking coffee served in a cup the size of a cereal bowl. Natalya, sitting across the small table from him, looked beautiful and refreshed from her sleep. And perhaps one of the most inspiring panoramas in the entire Côte d'Azur was spread out before him. He could almost forget for the moment why they were here.

He'd been in France before, as he'd told Natalya; he'd even traveled around the countryside of Northern France during that trip, but not the south. In any case, it wasn't so much the exotic locale that left his head whirling, as the speed of the whole affair.

One minute he'd been in a taxi in Washington, D.C.—the next minute he was in another taxi, driving down the Promenade des Anglais in Nice, past some of the most expensive hotels on the whole French Riviera.

Once he'd agreed with Natalya that the most logical, to say nothing of the safest, thing was for him to accompany her to Russia to see her father, they'd gone straight to Reagan airport and booked seats on the next flight to Nice. On such short notice, the tickets had been beyond exorbitant—but the magic *carte de solvabilité* solved that problem. And so, barely twelve hours later, they'd landed in Nice.

Immediately after they'd arrived at the Nice airport, Natalya had called the phone number Yuri had given her. The contact—he gave only his first name, Guy—told them it was too late to see them tonight, and that they should come to what he called his "studio" the next morning.

After the call they'd picked up a taxi. Natalya had asked the cabdriver for a recommendation, someplace quiet they could stay "away from the tourists." And so he'd taken them to La Maison du Séminaire.

La Maison was on the other side of La Chateau, the small hill that divided the town into the two halves: glass and steel and modern on the west side, brick and pastels and centuries old on the east side. They'd driven past Port Olympia, the small port that jutted into old-town Nice and that was stuffed with oversized personal yachts; past the old customs house on the Place Ile de Beauté that had once served as the clandestine bank of Barbary pirates; along boulevard Franck Pilatte; and finally through the front gates of the Séminaire.

La Séminaire was, it turned out, a converted Catholic seminary. When it came time to ask about the accommodations, Benjamin had hemmed and hawed for a moment before Natalya took over.

"Do you have a single room," she'd asked, "but with two beds?"

"A very nice one on the third floor, with an excellent view of the Baie des Anges. Very romantic," the clerk said, giving Benjamin a wink. Natalya had groaned and walked away, leaving him to accept the key with a "*merci.*"

Though their room was anything but luxurious—two beds, it was true, though they were tiny singles, almost cots, and a sink with a curtain that could be pulled around it, the bathroom for the entire floor being down the hall—still the clerk had been right: the view from their small balcony was magnificent. There was a nearly full moon in the sky, reflecting off the vast expanse of gray-black water in the bay. Out at sea, they could see the lights of one of the cruise liners that plied their way up and down the Côte d'Azur; and above, more stars than Benjamin could ever remember seeing before.

"You should see this," Benjamin had said, looking over his shoulder for Natalya.

"We're not here as tourists, Benjamin," she said, lying down on one of the beds, exhausted. "Try and remember that."

Benjamin had gone and stood near the bed.

"Natalya," he'd begun softly. Then, not wanting to sit on the narrow bed, he'd crouched down beside it. "I know you're worried about your father. I understand." She turned her head and looked at him. "But you're doing your best to get there as quickly as possible. Now," he said, trying to look and sound stern, "since we're stuck in this horrible place for the night, come and look at the damn view."

She'd laughed. "Very well, Commissar of Sightseeing," she'd said, and walked to the balcony.

The two of them had stood there for a while, not saying a word, just looking out and across all that darkness, a space that seemed entirely emptied of the tension and menace of the last few days. Standing there, Benjamin had wanted to put his arm around Natalya out of an instinctive urge to protect her from what he suspected was about to come. But he'd fought the urge.

"Did you know," Natalya had said finally, gazing out at that dark sea, "there is a long and deep connection for Russians with this city. There is a Russian Orthodox cathedral here, the Cathédrale Orthodoxe Russe St-Nicolas. It dates back to 1859 and is the oldest Russian cathedral in all Europe."

"I didn't know you were the religious type," Benjamin said.

Natalya laughed. "*All* Russians are the religious type, even during the Soviet times." She turned to him. "Do you know, I was even baptized."

Benjamin looked surprised. "Really? I thought your father—"

"He was," she said. "Not only a Party member, but even a political officer. But that did not stop him from wanting his only child christened into the church. There were a few places people could go, clandestinely, for such rituals. It was dangerous, even for ordinary citizens. For Party members it was doubly so."

"How old were you?"

"Three," she said. "I had never been in a church before. They waited until we were on vacation, visiting relatives in Dubna, far away from prying eyes in Siberia. They took me to a church in a small town outside Dubna, hardly even a village, a place called Ratmino. I had no idea what was going on. All the candles, the ornaments and icons . . . well, when the priest appeared, in his robes and white beard, I turned to my father and said, 'Why is Grandfather Frost here?'" She laughed. "I thought it was an early New Year's celebration."

Benjamin smiled but didn't comment, and again they were silent, looking out into the night with its vault of bright stars and vast expanse of dark sea.

Then Natalya turned to Benjamin. Her face looked sad, but very determined; again, almost regal, Benjamin thought. He sensed for a moment the enormity of secrets with which Natalya was accustomed to living, and felt himself quite young and naïve. He started to say something, but she placed a hand on his shoulder.

"Thank you, Commissar Wainwright," she said, smiling. "You were right." She'd kissed him very quickly, on the cheek, and then said, "So, who goes down the hall first?"

When they were both in their beds and had wished each other a good night, Benjamin had thought he would find it difficult to sleep. But with the salt air coming through the open window and the regular sighing of the surf outside, he'd dropped off almost as soon as he closed his eyes.

Now, early the next morning, they were sitting on the Séminaire's impressive veranda, dotted with potted palm trees. A marble balustrade was seemingly all that separated them from the incredibly blue Mediterranean, which lay just across the Pilatte and a narrow stretch of rocky beach. They had the veranda entirely to themselves.

"Well, despite this view, we have business to worry about," said Natalya. "We are to meet this 'Guy' at eight o'clock."

"And exactly," said Benjamin, "what is supposed to happen at this meeting?"

"We will obtain fake passports," Natalya said, sipping her coffee, as though what she'd suggested was the most natural thing in the world for one's first day in Nice. "And of course you will need a visa."

"Then we'd better stop at a bank on the way there," Benjamin said. "So, just how much is ten thousand dollars in francs?"

"He'll probably want euros," Natalya said. "But we'll need rubles for Russia. A year or so ago, everyone would have wanted dollars. But even money has become an expression of patriotism these days."

After finishing their coffee, they walked the short distance to a bank fronting the port and discovered there that the dollar wasn't doing so well: 10,000 U.S. dollars was barely 7,000 euros. So, just to be safe, Benjamin withdrew 10,000 euros. The teller had had to summon a manager for that amount; and, when he presented the stacks of currency to Benjamin, he also offered a nylon valise in which to carry the money, for which Benjamin was very grateful.

Once outside they'd hailed a cab. Natalya had given Guy's address to the driver, a number on rue Beaumont. The driver had looked a bit surprised.

"Acropolis?" he asked.

"Yes," Natalya had said simply, making it clear he wouldn't get any further information.

Guy's studio proved to be in a block of buildings that had seen better times. Set back in the old town on narrow streets not typically along a tourist's path, it was lined with dented metal trash cans, broken windows here and there, peeling paint on the stucco walls, and a general sense this wasn't a good place to come alone. Not for tourists. Especially not tourists carrying bags of money.

"Ze Acropolis, *là*," said the driver, pointing farther down the street.

"*Merci,*" said Natalya simply. Benjamin paid the driver, who shrugged and drove off.

Natalya led the way. Guy's studio was down a flight of stairs from street level, the number displayed on a very small, very weatherbeaten metal door. There was no buzzer, so Natalya knocked and they waited.

The man that opened the door was remarkable, in several ways. He was very short, very broad, with a wide, fat face. He sported an extremely thin, extremely manicured beard and mustache. His bald head was covered with a few lank white hairs combed over from the side of his head. He wore what appeared to be a velvet smoking jacket that, like the street, had seen better days and, to top it off, a paisley ascot.

"*Entré, entré,*" he said, acting as though he was greeting old friends. "*S'il vous plait, asseyez-vous,*" he continued, acting the perfect host.

The room looked like a small living room set for a stage play, as though the furniture, the paintings on the walls, even the books on the shelves were all props. Benjamin had the thought that indeed Guy's "studio" was all part of a performance; but whether that performance was meant to assuage their concerns, or distract them from whatever was really going on, he wasn't yet sure.

Guy and Benjamin carried on their negotiations in stilted French. Yes, Guy could provide passports and a visa of *la plus haute qualité*; yes, he could accomplish this with what he himself referred to as "*incroyable chargez*" in a few hours' time, so they could pick up their papers that very afternoon.

Guy asked to look at their real passports. He examined them for a moment, repeatedly glancing from the photos to their faces. He spent considerable time scrutinizing Natalya's. Finally he turned to Benjamin and said a few emphatic words.

"What?" asked Natalya. "Is something wrong?"

"He says you'll have to change," Benjamin said.

"Change?" she asked. "My clothes?"

"No." Benjamin smiled. "He says you are far too beautiful, too *extraor-*

dinaire to go unnoticed. And I don't think it is what you would call a compliment. He means it. You just don't blend in, Natalya."

"Should I dress as a nun, then?" she joked.

Benjamin turned and conversed further with Guy. After a few minutes of this, he turned back to Natalya.

"It turns out this is a *complete* studio, indeed. Apparently, besides his work for 'special' travelers like us, Guy uses this place to make certain . . . what he calls *films d'art*. I think you can guess what that means." Natalya nodded, smiling, but Benjamin noticed she didn't seem too surprised. Or too offended. He continued. "So there is a small dressing room, with makeup, hair dye, wigs, other accoutrements of that . . . trade."

"I see," Natalya said. "What does he suggest? Something from the Folies Bergère?" She arched an eyebrow, made her lips pouty. "Like this?"

Benjamin laughed, shook his head. "Much simpler. Monsieur Directeur suggests short, brown hair for you, perhaps some glasses. The blond is just too . . . blond. And the eyes—"

"Yes?"

"Are just too beautiful."

Natalya frowned. "I do not think *le directeur* said that."

Benjamin smiled but didn't answer her implication. "There's something else," he said. "Another of Guy's suggestions."

"And?" asked Natalya.

"Well . . . he asked if it would be all right to make us a married couple. He said that's less likely to attract attention than if . . . well, if some of the people we'll be dealing with think you're single."

Natalya looked directly at him. "And what did you say?" she asked.

"I said, for me, it would be an honor, but that I could not speak for *mademoiselle*."

Natalya didn't respond for a minute, and Benjamin started to get worried Guy had gone too far. But then Natalya nodded and said, "I guess that would make me *madame,* not *mademoiselle*."

It was hard for Benjamin to tell exactly how she meant that, but he turned and told Guy to get started.

The next half hour found them sharing the small dressing room. First Benjamin cut Natalya's hair, trying not to chop it up too badly; then she dyed it with a chestnut-auburn mix she hoped would make her hair sufficiently "ordinary." Then, while the dye was setting, she cut Benjamin's hair, making it very close-cropped and what she called "properly Russian." They found a pair of prop glasses for Natalya—something, Benjamin suggested,

Guy probably used in the schoolgirl fantasy epics, which made Natalya laugh out loud. But at least they helped to dim her brilliant blue-green eyes.

When they exited the dressing room, Guy pronounced their transformations *très magnifique,* and set about taking photos for their new passports. He took down all of Benjamin's information for his visa and then, rubbing his hands together, said there was nothing left to do but settle their account.

"Ah," Benjamin said. He explained that their *ami mutuel* had told them the passports would be ten thousand dollars. Guy looked very sad. He went on at some length about the mounting expenses of this sort of business, the very high risks, the exorbitant costs for bribes . . . finally Benjamin said, *"Combien?"*

"Hmmm," Guy said, stroking his beard as though in deep, deliberate thought. "Twenty thousand?" He held up a finger. *"Euros."*

In fact, Benjamin didn't care how much the passports cost. But he felt he had a certain role to play here, or Guy might become suspicious.

"Fifteen thousand," he said.

Guy shook his head. "Eighteen, *minimum absolu,*" he said, trying to make his flabby chin look resolute.

Benjamin shrugged, tried to look disappointed but resigned. *"D'accord,"* he said. He leaned over and said to Natalya, "For that much money, remember to take the glasses, all right?" Natalya nodded.

Benjamin took the valise into the dressing room to count out the money. He figured he wasn't really concealing anything from Guy, but better to at least appear cautious, or else Guy might feel he was being insulted as insufficiently threatening.

He returned, counted the money into Guy's fat palm, and then added another thousand euros *"pour votre discretion."* Guy smiled, nodded appreciatively.

Guy escorted them to the door, told them to return in two hours' time. Before they left, Benjamin turned and asked Guy another question, to which Guy gave a somewhat prolonged answer. Then they shook hands good-bye, Guy bid them *"Jusqu'à plus tard"* and closed the door.

When they reached the street, Natalya turned to him.

"What did you just ask him?" she said. She sounded a bit suspicious.

"I was curious. I've seen enough films to know such people as Guy use the names of the deceased for fake passports."

"Yes," said Natalya. "Like Gogol's seller of dead souls."

Benjamin laughed. "I also know databases of such names have improved the last few years, and that they're international. Believe me, I've dealt with enough such lists to know. But he assured me he's well beyond such shop-worn techniques, that his methods were thoroughly *moderne*."

"Then where *does* he get the names?" Natalya asked.

"From a friend in the prefect's medical office. But not names of the dead. He uses the names of the *near*-dead—people who are in comas. Still alive, but unlikely to turn up at an inconvenient moment."

Natalya blanched. "You mean, we will be using such names?"

Benjamin nodded. "Try not to be too superstitious about it," he said. "Think of it as giving them a vicarious adventure."

"I will try," Natalya said. But she didn't look convinced.

CHAPTER 38

When Benjamin and Natalya left Guy's studio, they walked west toward the avenue de la République. As they approached the small park set between boulevard Risso and avenue Gallieni, the buildings became older but more respectable, displaying more of the Italian influence in their arches and white stone and carrying their history with a certain grace and confidence. The day was still bright and warm and, as they strolled, Natalya linked her arm through his.

"So, we have two hours to kill," Benjamin said. "*Now* can we be tourists?"

"And will you be my guide, Commissar?" she asked.

"Well, I happen to know there is a museum just down the street, in the place Garibaldi. The Musée d'Art Moderne. It's supposed to be quite a beautiful building. And they have Warhols, Lichtensteins. All the 'old masters,'" he said, smiling.

"Western decadence." She smiled, but then she grew serious. "On such a day, in such a place, I would rather spend what little time we have here outside. I would much rather find a café, sit and have a coffee, and watch the ocean. Do you mind?"

Benjamin didn't mind at all. They continued walking on, through place Garibaldi with its beautiful baroque-style eighteenth-century Chapelle du

Saint-Sépulcre and its famous statue of Giuseppe Garibaldi, the "Hero of the Two Worlds" according to a plaque on the monument. They turned on rue Cassini, with its wine shops and cafés, and followed it until they reached quai Lunel, which formed the western edge of the three-side Port Olympia, where fewer of the enormous pleasure yachts were anchored than the night before, their masters out at sea, taking advantage of the clear and warm fall weather.

They chose a café near the water, ordered two coffees.

"Last night," Benjamin said, "you mentioned there was a long history of Russians in Nice?"

"Well, yes. During the Tsar years, Russians considered Nice the prime spot to vacation, after the Crimea. By the time of the Revolution, there was a large Russian community here."

"And then I suppose many of the Whites came here?" Benjamin asked.

"Not just the Whites," Natalya said. "Even the Revolution has roots here. In 1905, inspired by the St. Petersburg revolution, a rich émigré, Savva Morozov, wrote a will leaving his entire estate to the Communist Party. Then he shot himself. Or at least that is the *official* story. But it did not stop there. His nephew, Nikolai Schmidt, did the same thing."

"Shot himself?" Benjamin asked. Natalya nodded. "How convenient," he said.

"Wait, it gets even more . . . convenient," she said. "The nephew left no will. Now, the bequeathment was to the *entire* Communist Party, but there were factions within the Party: Bolsheviks, Mensheviks, Socialists . . . Each wanted the money only for itself. And each was expecting the others to cheat. Lenin knew this. So, ignoring the Socialists completely, he made an extraordinary proposal to the Mensheviks: they would each send a loyal member to the nephew's two sisters, to court and try to marry them and thus gain their inheritance. If both succeeded, fine, each faction would get half the money. If only one succeeded, well, the luck of the draw, whoever 'won,' that was fate. Understandable?"

"Yes," said Benjamin. "Not particularly admirable, but understandable."

Natalya smiled, continued. "So, our two political paramours make their way to Nice. They find the sisters—who, I believe, were not known for their charm or beauty—and they court them. Then even marry them. Both have succeeded! Both factions will get their share, yes?"

"That was the agreement."

"But for one thing: the Menshevik 'volunteer' was not *really* a Menshevik. He was secretly a Bolshevik, planted in the other faction by Lenin."

"So the entire inheritance—"

"Went to Lenin and the Bolsheviks. You see, they were always like that. Plots within plots within plots. Like *matryoshka,* nesting dolls."

At the mention of plots, Benjamin grew pensive, sat staring out over the ocean.

Natalya reached over, put her hand on his. "Enough ghost stories," she said. "Let's keep walking."

And so they'd spent the next hour strolling along the quai des États-Unis, with its stretch of luxurious modern hotels fronting the white-sand beach, and the Musée Masénna, housed in an ornate nineteenth-century villa, surrounded by elaborate and colorful gardens. Benjamin wanted to go in, but their two hours playing normal tourists was nearly up; it was time to return to Guy's studio and the reason they were really here.

They hailed a cab and were soon descending the stairs to Guy's weathered door. But taped to the door they discovered an envelope, with MONSIEUR BENJAMIN written on the outside. Benjamin took down the envelope and opened it. Inside was a note, in French, with *Guy* in a florid signature at the bottom. Benjamin quickly scanned its contents.

"What does it say?" asked Natalya.

"Well, it says that he is terribly sorry—*terriblement désolé*—but that he had to meet someone in Cannes this afternoon. He asks that we meet him there around three o'clock."

"In Cannes?" Natalya said. "Is he serious?"

"Actually, it's not that far," Benjamin said. "Just twenty-five kilometers or so down the coast. But not actually *in* Cannes. He says there's an island, just off the coast. St. Honorat. He wants us to meet him there, as it's more *approprié* for our kind of business."

Natalya looked suspicious. "This makes no sense. Perhaps it would be wise not to go."

"And then what would we do for passports?" asked Benjamin. "Have you decided to risk using your own?"

Natalya frowned, shook her head. "I think you believe this is as strange a request as do I."

"Yes, I do," he agreed. "But I don't see any option. And I've heard of this place. There's a monastery there, a very old one. It's supposed to be quite . . . scenic," Benjamin finished with a smile. "Consider it another triumph of the Commissar of Sightseeing."

CHAPTER 39

During the twenty-minute ferry ride from Cannes to the island of St. Honorat, Benjamin read aloud from a guidebook they'd purchased, the better to blend in with the other tourists.

"The Isle St. Honorat had begun its long history as an outpost fort, part of the southern coast's defenses against Saracen pirates. The Abbot of Lérins, Aldebert, brought his small flock of monks to the windswept promontory of the island and established a monastery that shared its primitive shelter with a military garrison. The first square, thick-walled fortifications were begun in 1073, built on the even older foundations of a Roman outpost. When the military left, the monks stayed, managing over the centuries to construct an impressive walled monastery at the center of the island. Its interior guards a vineyard where the monks produce an excellent wine, as well as a brandy famous in the region for its sweet taste and high alcohol content. Over the centuries, the twin towers of the original Norman fort had fallen into disrepair, but recently they were partially restored, and now they rise up again, proud reminders of St. Honorat's ancient and rich past."

They looked to the island and saw those very towers: square, blunt, older it seemed than the island itself—and the tallest objects visible for miles. It was easy to imagine Norman soldiers standing guard atop them, watchful eyes turned to the vast ocean beyond.

Benjamin and Natalya disembarked at the small dock on the island. There were paths leading both left and right, and a small building up the low hill where, it appeared, one could buy food and refreshments.

"What now?" Natalya asked.

Benjamin looked at his watch. "We have a little time before our appointment. I suggest we walk around and try to appear like a married couple on vacation."

Natalya took his arm, snuggled up against him, put a wide smile on her face.

"Like this?" she said.

Benjamin laughed. "Perfect," he said. "Now, if only we had a camera."

"Perhaps we can buy one in that shop," she said, pointing up the hill.

Once that was done, they continued on along the path that ran around the edge of the island, edged on one side by a rocky beach and the stretch of the transparent blue waters of the bay, and on the other by groves of Aleppo pine trees. Here and there were the remains of ancient walls and foundations of long-ruined buildings. They stopped now and then, one or the other of them posing before the ocean or the trees, trying in every way to appear like unconcerned tourists enjoying their honeymoon on an exotic Mediterranean island.

But as three o'clock approached and they made their way out toward the promontory with the Norman-style towers where they were to meet Guy, Benjamin felt the knot in his stomach tighten. He had a very bad premonition about this entire escapade. But he didn't want to share his anxieties with Natalya. Better, he thought, to play along with Guy's instructions, but stay vigilant.

Finally they approached the tower where they were to meet Guy. They were about a hundred yards away. The ocean stretched out flat and infinite on three sides, while behind them there was the rocky, sparse ground of the broadened pathway. The bell tower of the monastery was visible in the distance, rising up above the poplars and Aleppos, which waved back and forth in the strong breeze off the ocean.

"Seventy-two steps," read Benjamin from the brochure. "One for every chapter in something called *The Rules of St. Benedict*." He saw the look of skepticism on Natalya's face. "I have an idea," he said. "Why don't I climb all those nasty steps myself. I'll get the passports and meet you back in the courtyard of the monastery. Here." He handed her the camera. "You can take more pictures."

Natalya looked up at him, placed her palm against his cheek.

"Very chivalrous," she said. "But I believe I have more experience with such things than a librarian does."

Benjamin was about to object when a man approached them on the pathway, coming from the tower.

He was tall, quite thin, with old-fashioned wire-rim glasses, wearing a pullover sweater. His brown hair was trimmed very close to his skull—like Benjamin's now—and as he came closer Benjamin noticed he had the most intense blue eyes he'd ever seen. He walked with a certain ease and confidence, as though he were on a holiday lark without a care in the world.

"Excuse me," he said, coming up to them. "Are you friends of Guy's?"

Benjamin wasn't sure what to say. Before he could think of something, the man continued. "He couldn't make it. Held up on business. And in his business . . . well, they don't exactly keep regular appointments, do they."

"I'm sorry," Benjamin said. "I'm afraid I don't—"

"Know what I'm talking about?" the man finished for him. "Of course you don't. And of course you don't know anyone named Guy. Neither do I." He turned and looked at Natalya. "And of course this morning your charming wife didn't have blond hair and perfect vision."

Still Benjamin was silent while he tried to think of something appropriate but not incriminating. His first thought was that this was someone from the French police and that they were about to be arrested.

"Look," Benjamin said, "I don't know you, and I don't know what—"

"But you do know you'll be wanting these," said the man. He held out a manila envelope. Benjamin looked at it as though it were something explosive. "Take it," the man said. "Everything you need is inside. Along with a bonus."

"Bonus?" Benjamin asked, finally accepting the envelope. He began to open it.

"Not here," the man said, stopping his hand. "Just something to perhaps make things easier . . . where you're going." He looked back toward the tower. "I wouldn't bother with the tower," he said. "Those damn steps are a real killer."

And with that, he nodded to Natalya, said, "Good luck," and then continued on down the path, resuming the appearance of a tourist on holiday.

For a moment Benjamin and Natalya simply looked at each other. Then they laughed, and, with a final glance at the tower, turned and headed back down the path toward the ferry dock.

It was some time before anyone else came down the path—this was indeed past tourist season, and St. Honorat was not one of the typical stops even during season. But this couple had come all this way and they weren't about to go without visiting the famous Norman tower, seventy-two steps or no.

And so they made their way through the ruins, found the crumbling steps, carefully picked their way up first one flight, then another . . . until finally they stood at the summit, breathing heavily. They walked to the thick portico in order to get a better view of the wide ocean beyond.

It was then they noticed a man sitting on a stone bench in a cloistered part of the tower. The husband took out his camera, approached the man on the bench—apparently he wanted to ask him to take their picture. But when he spoke, the man on the bench didn't answer. He just sat there, slumped slightly forward. He was heavyset, wearing a blue leisure suit, with a very round face and a stark white streak in his brown hair. He looked almost peaceful, as though he were taking a nap.

"Excuse me," the man with the camera said, touching his shoulder.

At the touch, Andrei tipped sideways and fell off the bench with a thud. It was only then the tourist noticed a bright red spot on Andrei's white T-shirt and a small pool of blood that had gathered beneath the bench.

CHAPTER 40

"Well, it looks like everything is here."

Benjamin and Natalya were sitting on a couch in their hotel room in Cannes, the Hotel InterContinental. It was centrally located, a beautiful example of Belle Époque architecture—and, most important, huge, somewhere they felt they would be lost in whatever crowds were around in the off-season. Spread out before them on the coffee table were the contents of the manila envelope the man on St. Honorat had given them.

There were two passports, both French. Benjamin was now Charles Levebre, born in Marseilles; and Natalya was his wife, Sophia Levebre, née Martel, originally of Lyon. In the passport photo, the brunette hair and glasses made her look slightly older, much more ordinary, and somewhat less intelligent.

"Looking at this photo," Natalya said with obvious disappointment, "I do not know why you ever married me."

"Obviously for your wit," said Benjamin. "And you haven't seen mine." He showed her his passport photo. The bad lighting and shorter hair made him look like a criminal posing for a mug shot. "Why did *you* marry me?"

"For your *carte de solvabilité,*" she said. "Of course."

But he didn't respond. He was examining something else from the envelope. Besides their visas, he'd discovered what the man on St. Honorat had meant by a "bonus."

"They're press credentials," he said, waving the laminated cards at Natalya. "Apparently we work for a magazine in Paris, *La Matrix*."

"It sounds very avant-garde," said Natalya.

"At least we're employed," Benjamin replied, and Natalya laughed—for the first time since their strange encounter on St. Honorat.

They'd found they could take a flight from the Nice airport the next morning to Moscow, then a train to Dubna. Nice was less than thirteen ki-lometers to the east, so they'd decided to spend the night in Cannes. And Benjamin had decided it was time for a distraction.

"Look," he said, "we're in one of the most elegant hotels in one of the most expensive cities in Europe, with an almost bottomless bag of money. Let's see how much we can spend on dinner tonight. Let's be Charles and Sophia Levebre, wealthy honeymooners with a cash gift from their billion-aire Uncle Renault—"

"Is that not a car?" Natalya interrupted, smiling.

"—and forget everything else," he continued. "Just for tonight." He reached over and took her hand. "All right?"

As they quickly discovered, there were any number of five-star restau-rants nearby, any of them equal to the task of making a dent in their fi-nances. When Benjamin—or Charles, as he made sure to have Sophia call him—made it clear that they desired the *highest* in elegant surroundings and that money was absolutely no concern, the clerk looked both ways, then leaned conspiratorially over the desk.

"I should tell you to eat in our own restaurant," he said in French. "But I believe you will find what you're looking for at Gaston-Gastounette. It's on quai St. Pierre."

Benjamin gave him a twenty-euro tip, thanked him, and then thought of something else. He told the clerk that he and his wife had left on their honey-moon *avec la grande rapidité* and without many clothes. Could he recom-mend a good clothing store nearby? Somewhere they could also buy luggage?

The clerk looked at him as though he understood the situation exactly, winked, said something about *affaires du coeur*, and directed them to a nearby store he promised offered the best in haute couture.

An hour and many hundreds of euros later, the clothes and luggage were on their way back to the InterContinental, and they continued on to the Gaston-Gastounette.

The hotel desk clerk had been right: the furnishings were elegant, recalling a time before the glitterati of the film festival years, when the wealthy of the Côte d'Azur came to Cannes to pretend it was still a time of Empires. Even better than the décor was the view: they were able to get a table next to a window overlooking the old port and marina, with centuries-old buildings rising up the low hills, swept back and creating a huge amphitheater around the bay.

Since they'd just been in Nice but hadn't had chance to sample the salad named after the city, they decided to start with *salade niçoise*; and, since they would soon leave the coast for the deep inland of Russia, Benjamin suggested they try the house specialty: tortellini and boiled mussels. When they asked the waiter for a wine recommendation, he told them that, frankly, their cellars did contain what he considered simply the best they'd ever offered, but if price was a consideration . . . *"Pas du tout,"* said Benjamin. Then, the waiter said, there was only the Domaine de la Romanée-Conti Montrachet, 1999.

"C'est bon," said Benjamin, and the waiter bowed, removed their menus, and disappeared most discreetly.

"Guy was right," Benjamin said. "Married couples *do* get better treatment."

Natalya was staring out the window at the sunset over the bay. She smiled, but she was obviously thinking about something else.

"I think your father can take care of himself," Benjamin said. "If that's what you're worried about."

She turned and looked at him. "Very empathetic," she said. "I am not used to that, from Americans."

"What exactly," said Benjamin, *"are* you used to from Americans?"

Natalya studied him for a moment. "Let us just say that my extradiplomatic contacts have not always been positive."

Before Benjamin could answer, their wine arrived, and they waited while it was uncorked and Benjamin was offered the chance to sample it. He sipped it and was very impressed; nodded to the waiter, and both their glasses were filled.

Alone again, Benjamin lifted his glass. "Let's drink to a new *détente*," he said.

Natalya smiled, raised her glass, and they clinked. She tried her wine, and also looked impressed.

"I do not usually like white wine," she said, "but this . . ."

"Worth every euro," Benjamin said. "Ah, the advantages of ill-gotten gains."

"Which makes me wonder," Natalya said, "just how these gains were, as you say, gotten?"

Benjamin frowned, set his wine down. "I only know that Samuel Wolfe trusted Anton."

"And you trust this Samuel Wolfe?" Natalya asked.

"Yes," Benjamin said without hesitation.

"After you knew him for only two days?"

"Two and a half," corrected Benjamin. "And yes, that may sound . . . hasty. But there was something about the man . . ."

"Was?" asked Natalya.

Benjamin realized he'd only mentioned to Natalya that Wolfe had "disappeared" during the fire at the Foundation, not that it was likely he'd actually been in the building and, quite probably, died in the explosion. And he couldn't quite bring himself to suggest that, even now.

Natalya saw his hesitation.

"So there are still some things you are not telling me," she said. Benjamin started to say something, but she stopped him. "That is perhaps as it should be," she said. "You have known me even less time than you did Mr. Wolfe."

Benjamin looked at her. The shorter brunette hair may have dimmed her brilliance slightly, but it hadn't extinguished it. He still thought she was one of the most beautiful women he'd ever seen.

"Tell me about your father . . . Sophia," he said, pouring her more wine.

And so she did. As their meal was served—delicious and quite garlicky mussels in a light cream sauce with tortellini—she told Benjamin a little of how her father had come to be a *rocketchiki*.

"He was a true believer, and to him this was the most patriotic way he could serve the Motherland," Natalya said. "I asked him once, would he actually have pressed his white button, had it come to that?"

"And what did he say?" Benjamin asked.

"He said he could not have reported for duty each week unless he knew, in his heart, that he could do such a thing." Natalya looked into her wine. "In fact, it was when he felt he no longer could answer yes to that question that he resigned."

"And that was after he'd read about the gulags?"

Natalya went very quiet. "Not just read," she said.

"What do you mean?" Benjamin asked.

Natalya looked up, forced a smile.

"We are to distract ourselves, yes?" Benjamin nodded. "Then let us talk

242 | GLEN SCOTT ALLEN

about something else. You, for instance. I know nothing of your past, Mr. Levebre, yet here I find myself married to you."

Benjamin laughed. And so through the rest of the meal it was Benjamin's turn to tell Natalya stories of his childhood: growing up in upstate New York, the son of another "academician" (using Natalya's term), an historian from a long line of historians. "My father used to tell terrible jokes," he said. "He would say, 'History has quite a long history in this family.'" Benjamin smiled. "We would all groan, but he didn't care. He was a very carefree person, for the most part."

"For the most part?"

"There was one subject that would make him go almost nuclear, as we used to say, and that was when he felt someone was exploiting the Founding Fathers to justify intolerance. He thought it was an insult to the Constitution, to everything they'd fought so hard to achieve. 'Don't they *understand*?' he'd say. 'The whole point was to have the freedom to piss each other *off*!'"

Natalya laughed. "I think I would have liked your father," she said. "And I believe you will like my father."

Benjamin looked up, raised his glass again. "Then let's toast to new friends," he said. They tapped glasses.

After dinner, they walked back to the hotel, sticking to the boulevard along the bay. Both of them knew they were trying to extend their little fantasy "honeymoon" as long as possible, to put off the moment when they would have to face the reason they were here.

Once back at the InterContinental, Benjamin immediately opened the French doors to the balcony, went outside, and stood, leaning on the railing and looking out over the ocean. Natalya came out and stood next to him.

"I don't know how to thank you," she said.

"No," he said, "I should be the one—"

Natalya put her hand to his face, turned it to hers. She looked at him for what seemed an eternity before she finally leaned very close and pressed her lips against his. Benjamin put his arm around her waist, pulled her against him, moved his lips from her mouth to her neck.

"Benjamin," Natalya said. Then, very gently, she pulled away from him. She put her hands on his shoulders. "I am sorry," she said. "I just do not think—"

"It's all right," Benjamin said. He was still holding her waist but he made no attempt to draw her close again. "I understand."

"And we need to rise early," Natalya said.

"Yes, we do," Benjamin said. But he was still holding her.

She took his hands, one in each of hers, and moved them apart. Then, without another word, she went back into the room, entered the bathroom.

After that, they wished each other a friendly good night—though it sounded slightly more awkward now than it had in Nice—and went to their separate beds. Once again, Benjamin was sure he wouldn't be able to sleep. Once again, as soon as his eyes were closed, he was fast asleep.

Suddenly Benjamin woke up. He was certain someone was standing over him.

Dim moonlight was coming through the open balcony doors. He could see Natalya above him.

She was naked, her pale skin almost shining in the moonlight. Without a word, she lifted the covers from his bed and crawled underneath them. She pressed her lips to his cheek, his mouth, his neck; her hand traced down his chest, across his stomach, lower.

Benjamin rolled so he was facing her, pressed against her, returned her kisses. He felt himself clearly, sharply awake, and yet wondered whether this wasn't all a dream.

A very wonderful dream.

They made love slowly, without speaking. It was as if a reserve of tenderness, held at bay through the anxious maneuvers of the last couple of days, was suddenly released. When they looked into each other's eyes, they both saw trust and compassion there. Benjamin felt he had never experienced an intimacy so consuming, so deep.

Afterward, they lay for a long while in each other's arms, Natalya's head resting on his shoulder. Finally, Benjamin said something that had been on his mind ever since they'd arrived in Nice.

"Natalya," he said, "I have something to say."

She snuggled closer to him. "You don't have to say anything," she said.

"No, this I do," he said. He turned and faced her.

"What if you were simply to stay here? Whatever will happen in Russia . . . well, it is my adventure, as you called it. I should see it through alone. You could write an introduction for me to your father, and . . ."

"Benjamin," she interrupted. "There is another story about the Russian Revolution and Nice I did not tell you earlier. There was a very famous Bolshevik, Raskolnikov. He was completely loyal to the Party, one of those who put down the sailor's mutiny at Kronstadt. But even he lost faith during the Moscow show trials in the thirties. He fled here to Nice. He lived there seven years, and finally thought he was safe. But Comrade Stalin's agents found Raskolnikov in 1939. Even this paradise was not far enough away from such people."

"Stalin is long dead," Benjamin objected.

"But these people, whoever they are," she said, finally looking up at him, "they might be just as terrible. Such people do not simply forget, Benjamin. If we truly have something they want, or know something they do not want us to know, they will not leave us alone. Believe me," she said, looking into his eyes, "I have known such people. Power is more important to them than anything. Our only hope is to find the truth."

Benjamin looked at her for a moment, then smiled and pulled her close.

"Ah, Mrs. Levebre," he said. "I have a feeling I will not win many arguments with you."

Natalya held him tighter. After a while, she could hear Benjamin's regular breathing as he lay sleeping, but for a long time she lay wide awake, staring out the window at the brightening dawn sky.

CHAPTER 41

Benjamin looked out of the train window at the passing countryside. As they'd left Moscow, the land had grown flatter and less densely populated, and the monotonous, square, gray rectangles of Soviet-era Moscow architecture had given way to the villages of small, haphazard dachas that studded the land between Moscow and Dubna. The closer they got to Dubna, the thicker grew the forests of pine trees.

On the short flight from Nice, and all during the train ride to Dubna, Natalya had said nothing about what had happened the night before. If anything, she seemed more distant than ever. Benjamin wrote it off to her concerns about her father and, for that matter, concerns about their entire adventure here.

Perhaps because of this, or some other reason Benjamin couldn't fathom, much of their trip to Dubna was spent in silence; watching the passing landscape, making small talk about his impressions of Russia, each of them trying not to appear too anxious for the sake of the other's feelings.

Along the train tracks there were stretches of undeveloped forest and of wild land that he thought probably hadn't changed in hundreds of years. There was also the sense of enormous potential, of great power and pride in the land itself, of immense history and possibility. He said something of this to Natalya.

"Yes," she agreed. "That is the Russia no Russian ever truly leaves. My father used to say we inhale Russian history with our every breath, that it is in our blood. It isn't until I return that I remember what that means."

Finally they pulled into the station in Dubna. It was the last stop on the line and so everyone exited the train. There was a light rain falling, and the air was chill with a premonition of frost and perhaps snow.

As they left their car, Benjamin saw a large monument at the front of the platform: a huge red star with an arc over its top and НАУКОГРАД, and in another arc on the bottom, the English words ATOMIC CITY. He asked her what it meant.

"This is where they created the Russian atomic bomb," she said. "For many years, Dubna was like Uzhur, a secret city. Before 1956, it did not even exist on any map. Of course, there was the old Dubna—some say a settlement here dates back thousands of years. But the *new* Dubna was built by prisoners under the NKVD's control during the war."

"NKVD?" Benjamin asked.

"I forget, not everyone knows such things," she said. "NKVD was what came before KGB. Before that it was GPU, and before that it was Cheka. Now it is FSB. The letters change, the job is the same. Understandable?"

Benjamin nodded, and Natalya continued.

"At first, the prisoners stripped the pine trees of their branches up to about thirty meters and built many small buildings, scattered about. They wanted the pine trees to hide the buildings. I have seen photographs. It looked like a summer camp for students. And then they sent their best scientists here. Sakharov, Kurchatov, Kikoin."

"Like Los Alamos," Benjamin said, "out in the American desert, where they sent the American scientists."

"Well, not quite," she said. "Dubna was a *sharashka,* a special camp for scientists. The NKVD was in charge of everything. That is how my grandfather came to be here."

"Your grandfather?"

Natalya looked at him.

"I will explain later. Perhaps." Then she went to a nearby telephone and called her aunt's number. She spoke for a while, then returned to Benjamin.

"Now, we should go to the hotel."

"Won't that be dangerous? We'll have to register."

"Olga said there is a convention of physicists in town, for the Joint Institute of Nuclear Research. It's very famous. They created a new element there, element 105, which they called, of course, dubnium. Anyway, the town is stuffed with scientists from all over the world. Two more foreigners will hardly be noticed."

So they took a taxi to the Dubna Otel. Along the way, Benjamin saw that parts of Dubna were quite charming: rows of forties-style apartment buildings all painted yellow, and many separate houses, some of them rather large and constructed in a classical style not dissimilar to American turn-of-the-century mansions; these were painted in pastel reds, blues, and of course more pale yellow.

At the Otel, the lobby was filled with men and women, all of them looking very academic, and all of them engaged in intense conversations. No one took any notice of them.

At first, the clerk told Natalya there were no rooms to be had, due to the convention. Then Benjamin thought to bring out their press credentials, and Natalya, following his lead, explained they were there to cover the convention for the international press and that their paper would pay a donation to the hotel for finding them space. Once the "donation" had changed hands, an empty room was suddenly discovered.

"Guy's friend was right," Benjamin said, holding up the press credentials. "These are a bonus."

As they were walking through the lobby, Benjamin came to an abrupt stop. He was staring at an enormous frieze on one of the walls. It displayed a forest, obviously meant to represent the surrounding forests of pine trees, but there were also numerous figures and geometric shapes, some he guessed were meant to be people, but others he couldn't interpret.

"What on earth . . . ?"

"Part of Soviet iconography," Natalya said. "It is a sort of map of Dubna. That large arc is the Ivankovo Dam, that circle is the institute, that squiggle is the Volga River, and that triangle, that is the largest statue of Lenin in the world, where the Volga and the Moscow Canal meet."

"How do you get all that from this . . . geometry lesson?"

"It was a very popular kind of Soviet art in the late sixties, when this hotel was built. Now come on, please," she said, tugging on his arm and pulling him toward the elevators. "We should get to the room."

Once in their room they unpacked. Their purchases included parkas, sweaters, and other warm clothing, as well as casual clothes, everything they needed for their dual roles of vacationing newlyweds and working journalists. Natalya changed into a black turtleneck, matching pants, and dress boots. Benjamin was more conservative in wool pants, a white cable-knit sweater, and brown shoes.

"*Trés chic,*" he said, looking Natalya over.

"Not *too* chic, I hope," Natalya said. "The point is to be invisible."

He wanted to pull her to him, to pick up where they'd left off in Cannes the night before—but he sensed that she was in no such mood right now, and so he agreed to follow her down to the hotel bar.

Once there, they elbowed their way to a table with their drinks—he'd surprised himself by ordering scotch, while she'd selected vodka—and sat down. Given the high background noise in the bar, Benjamin thought it was as safe a place as any to talk.

"What did Olga say about your father?" he asked once they were seated.

"We are to meet him tomorrow. But not at his apartment. He has been staying . . ." and she smiled, "in a church."

"Church? Where?"

"Ah," Natalya said, "the very one where I was baptized. In Ratmino."

"Huh," Benjamin said. "And he trusts the priest there?"

"He is being cautious," answered Natalya. "It is his training. Or perhaps it is simply, like history, in his blood." She grew silent again, looked away.

"Look," Benjamin said, "ever since we got on the plane this morning, you've been acting—"

Natalya nodded. "I am sorry," she said.

She looked up at him, placed her hand over his. "It has nothing to do with last night, Benjamin, believe me. It is simply returning here."

"To Russia?" he asked.

"Well, yes," she said. "But more than that, to Dubna."

"I thought you grew up in Uzhur, in Siberia?"

She looked at him for a moment. "All right," she said. "Perhaps it is time to explain a little of my family's history. But if we are going to do that, we might as well order something to eat."

And so they ordered dinner. Natalya asked for *kulebyakas,* pies filled with meat and cabbage, and side dishes of salted cucumbers and sauerkraut. Benjamin decided to try their stroganoff. They also ordered a red Moldavian wine that Benjamin thought tasted almost like a burgundy, only sweeter. And then, with their meal started and the wine poured, Natalya said she was ready to tell Benjamin her family's darkest secret.

"I mentioned that my grandfather—my father's father—came to Dubna, to help build the Russian atomic bomb. But he wasn't a scientist. He was NKVD. He was one of the scientists' . . . supervisors."

"So, he was secret police?" Benjamin asked. "That's the dark secret?"

"Wait. You see, the assignment here was considered a . . . reward. For the work he'd done for the NKVD before the war."

"And that was?"

"Arresting people," she said, looking at him steadily. "Arresting people to be shot." She let that sink in for a moment. "He was a driver of one of the 'black crows,' the dark vans that moved around the streets of Moscow at night during the purges of the thirties. He drove dozens to their deaths . . . and worse."

Natalya took a long drink of her wine.

"Natalya," Benjamin began, "if you feel guilty . . ."

"There's more," Natalya said, interrupting him. Her face had grown grim, her eyes wouldn't look at him. "I said it was my *family's* secret. I meant my entire family. My *other* grandfather was also NKVD. Only he was a prosecutor, in a camp called Magadan, on the Sea of Okhotsk. One of the most terrible of all the camps. Thousands of prisoners died there. My grandfather was responsible for sentencing men to years of hard labor mining gold or building railways. Or to more immediate . . . punishment."

Benjamin was momentarily stunned. He looked at Natalya, at her fierce, bright beauty; it was impossible for him to think of anyone of her family doing such things.

What sort of comfort could he offer to someone suffering under the guilt of crimes committed by relatives so long ago? Crimes she'd had no part of committing?

"When did you find all this out?" he asked finally.

"I myself did not learn of this history until after *perestroika,* after my father resigned from the army."

"And your father? When did *he* know?"

"Only shortly before then. Only when he began to read the books that had been suppressed for decades."

Benjamin was shocked. "You mean, he knew nothing of his own father's life?"

"Benjamin," she said, almost pleading. "You just do not understand what it was like. The Revolution wiped out not just individuals, but whole families, entire villages. History itself. Most people did not want any record to survive of who they had been before the Revolution. My father literally knows nothing of his father's life before 1917. He is not even certain of his father's birthplace. The name Orlov is as common in Russia as is Smith or Jones in America. His father probably took it to replace his real name that was, for some reason, unacceptable. Nikolai knows only that his father appeared in Maikop, in the North Caucasus, in 1918, married his mother . . . and then worked for the security services. He never spoke of his life before the Revolution, and never of his work after it."

Benjamin wanted to offer solutions. "Have you tried searching records?"

Natalya shook her head. "There are no records to search." She gave him a slight smile. "It is not like America, where you simply go to the library and begin to trace backward. In Russia, at some point, all such searches reach a blank wall."

"But your other relatives, they must—"

"They have their own secrets to keep," she said firmly. "That is what you do not understand. For seventy-five years, what happened yesterday or the day before was not just unimportant, it was a threat, something that might be used against you by one of your 'comrades.' And what happened before the Revolution . . . it was another epoch."

"Such secrets . . . they aren't your fault."

"Someone once said, Benjamin, that in Russia, everything is a secret, and nothing is a mystery. The details of my grandfathers' lives are the secret. But *why* they chose the path they did, that is no mystery. For the same reasons millions of others did the same things: to survive."

By now the bar-restaurant had become even more crowded, as there simply weren't that many places in Dubna for people to unwind after a hard day of physics seminars. Their table was surrounded by people for whom there was nowhere to sit. In addition, a small band had begun to play music—which included a balalaika, which Natalya said "drives me crazy."

Benjamin thought of something. "Will they let us take wine to our room?" he asked.

"This is Russia," she said. "The only rule about drinking is to never do it . . . what do you call it? Half-assed?"

Benjamin managed to flag down a waiter, ordered another bottle of the Moldavian wine, paid the bill, and then, using his body as a flying wedge, led Natalya from the bar.

When they were back in their room, Benjamin realized they had no way to open the wine.

"Here," said Natalya, "give it to me. We don't need a bourgeois bottle opener."

She located a pen, asked for Benjamin's shoe, then took these and the bottle into the bathroom. Balancing the bottle over the sink, she pounded the pen into the wine cork using her shoe as a hammer. At an especially forceful stroke, the cork plummeted into the bottle, sending wine spouting up into her face and hair. Laughing, she took a drink directly from the bottle, handed it to Benjamin.

"Now we drink Soviet style," she said.

Benjamin could tell Natalya was forcing herself to drink and make jokes as though they truly were the Levebres, here on holiday, as a way of distancing herself from her confession in the bar.

When the bottle was nearly empty and Natalya clearly half drunk, she crawled across the bed where they'd been sitting and, taking Benjamin's head in her hands, kissed him passionately on the mouth.

Benjamin started to resist. "If you don't—"

Natalya looked into his eyes. "No, Benjamin," she said, "I truly do."

And so they made love again; only this time, Natalya's hands held his body with a kind of desperation. She pressed against him with an ardor that was hunger.

"Please," she said, "let's make love like we are animals. Creatures without thoughts, without words."

Benjamin held her, made love to her. Made love with her.

Later, very late in the night, she was lying with her head on his shoulder and he was stroking her hair.

"Natalya . . . ," he began.

Natalya didn't respond, and he decided she was asleep. But she was breathing softly with her eyes wide open.

Later still, after Benjamin's chest rose and fell with the regular breathing of deep sleep, Natalya was still awake. She looked down at Benjamin, ran her hand lightly over his hair.

"*Ya lyublyu tebia tozhe,*" she said, almost in a whisper.

CHAPTER 42

As their small, rickety, pale blue bus bounced over the rough country road to Ratmino, through ever thicker pine forests, Benjamin caught glimpses of a wide, powerful river beyond the trees.

"And that is?" he asked, pointing.

"The Volga," answered Natalya.

"It's beautiful," said Benjamin.

The bus was crowded, almost entirely with older women, who Natalya had called babushkas. As far as he could tell, Benjamin was the only non-Russian on the bus.

Natalya explained that the church to which they were going—the Sobor Pokhvali Presviatoy Bogoroditzy, or the Church of Our Praised Lady, built in 1827—was more than just a village chapel; it was in fact a cathedral, the largest and most important church in the "oblast." Since the rehabilitation of the Orthodox Church into Russian life, this particular church had received a constant stream of both the ardently faithful and the simply curious.

She was sitting very close to him, holding his hand; he'd noticed all morning that the distance he'd sensed the day before was gone. He didn't know whether Natalya was simply beginning to trust him, or if her feelings ran deeper. As deep as his did, now.

"When Lenin came to power, he had the churches closed, dozens of priests were shot by the Cheka. They destroyed architectural treasures, like the seventeenth-century church of St. Paraskevi. Children were told to bring icons from churches to throw on public bonfires. The rural churches were stripped of anything of value and then turned into storage sheds for vegetables."

"But this one has been restored?"

"It was luckier than most. The local peasants buried the icons and kept their location secret for seventy-five years. Then, after *perestroika,* they dug them up, restored them to the church."

"Remarkable," Benjamin said. "Such . . . endurance."

"It is not just endurance," Natalya said. "The Russian people are perhaps as superstitious as they are religious. The two reinforce one another."

"What do you mean?"

"Well," Natalya said, "here is an example. In June of 1941, Stalin's archaeologists discover Tamerlane's burial site. There was a local legend that it was cursed, that if Tamerlane's sarcophagus was opened, the war god, as he was known, would visit catastrophe on the blasphemers within three days. Stalin pays no attention, orders the sarcophagus opened. A photograph was made of one of the archaeologists holding Tamerlane's skull aloft and sent immediately to Stalin."

Benjamin looked intrigued. "And?" he said.

"That was June 19. Three days later, Germany invaded the Ukraine," she said. "It was a disaster. The Germans moved through Western Russia like a whirlwind." Natalya smiled. "Suddenly, the 'godless Communist' Stalin ordered that the churches in Moscow be reopened, and he invited the Patriarch to the Kremlin for consultation. The Patriarch insisted that one of the most highly valued icons of the Orthodox Church, the Icon of the Mother of God of Kazan, be taken out of 'safe keeping' where it had been put by the Party, and that it be carried from Leningrad to Moscow to Stalingrad in a sort of religious procession; that such a pilgrimage would create a ring of protection around the three major cities, a ring the Germans would never break. Stalin agreed, the procession was made, and none of the three cities ever surrendered."

Benjamin looked at Natalya slightly askance.

"But surely you don't believe the icon had anything to do with that."

Natalya shrugged. "Perhaps. Perhaps not. But you see? Superstition, religion—they are practically the same thing for most Russians. Which is why peasants will risk their lives for a painted statue."

By now they'd reached the Church of Our Praised Lady. There was a small graveled lot that held several buses and cars. Facing them was a white wall with an arch topped with a gold dome and the double-barred Russian Orthodox cross, and beneath the arch a gate, through which they walked to enter the grounds of the church. To every side there were thick groves of maple and birch trees and rows of lilac bushes. Even with the approach of winter, the land all about the church on the banks of the Volga was richly green.

The church was larger than Benjamin had expected, but not what he thought of as a cathedral. The architecture was instead Greek in style with two silver domes that were capped by black onion turrets and rose to points that supported large gold crosses. The church was painted white and a pale yellow color that by now Benjamin was identifying with almost all styles and periods of Russian architecture.

Climbing the few, broad steps to a small, semicircular entranceway, they entered the double wooden doors of the church.

Inside, Benjamin was again surprised: the restoration had been careful and thorough. The large, open space without pews, the arched ceiling high overhead, the stark white walls, the highly polished brown-and-green stone floor . . . all created the effect of a bright space full of energy. Around the edges of the church were carefully lined-up chairs, for the older visitors, of which there were many, and here and there about the floor were waist-high brass incense burners.

Before them was the altar space, with its screen of painted murals, brilliant colors depicting Christ to the right and Mary and Child to the left, with various saints flanking them. On the walls and pillars were dozens of icons: some painted in simple styles on plain wood, others made of ceramic tiles, some in cloth, with the older relics preserved in framed glass.

Natalya began discreetly looking around, obviously expecting to see her father somewhere, but also trying to appear the typical tourist, admiring the brightness and beauty of the church.

About the time Benjamin was beginning to get worried, they were approached by a young man in a priest's cassock. He came up to Natalya and spoke to her in Russian. She answered, and then the priest led her toward one of the doors near the altar space. Natalya motioned for Benjamin to follow.

Through the door, they then descended down a narrow, winding set of steps, to the church's basement. It was a large, open space, though with a series of half-walls extending from one end to the other and with an aisle down the center. Benjamin saw there were bricks beneath his feet, worn with time, and there was a musty, damp smell of a space long closed.

The half-walls created several enclosures to the left and right, almost like stables; in some of these furniture was stacked, in others icons and other art for which there was apparently not room upstairs. In one such space toward the rear they could make out, through the dim light, the legs of someone sitting on a chair.

The priest indicated they should go to that stall, then, taking Natalya's hand in his for a moment, he turned and left them.

Natalya walked to the end of the basement, Benjamin following her. When they reached the last stall on the right, they discovered a man sitting there, looking somewhat uncomfortable on a chair that must have been at least a hundred years old.

He immediately rose and came toward Natalya, saying "Natalya Niko-layevna!" They embraced warmly. Then he stepped back, surveyed her brunette hair, looked surprised.

After they'd spoken a few more words in Russian, he turned to Benjamin and extended his hand.

"Nikolai Orlov," he said in only slightly accented English. "I am pleased to greet you."

Nikolai was slightly taller than Benjamin, slightly thinner. Benjamin guessed he was in his late sixties. He had a long, narrow face, with extraordinarily bright blue eyes—he could see where Natalya had got the blue in her blue-green eyes—and close-cropped gray hair. His handshake was firm, and he placed his other hand on Benjamin's as they shook. Benjamin felt instant respect and trust for the man.

"Benjamin Wainwright," he said, and then added, almost instinctively, "sir. And I am pleased to meet you, as well."

Nikolai turned to Natalya again and spoke to her again in Russian. Then he motioned them to extract chairs from the stacks against the wall and sit down next to him.

Once they were seated, Natalya close to Nikolai and holding his hand, she looked at Benjamin.

"The first thing my father wants to know," she said, smiling, "is what the hell you are doing here."

Benjamin looked surprised, started to say something.

"Is joke," Nikolai said, patting Benjamin on the shoulder. "Sort of. I ask Natashka what brings you together. For your story, I mean. How do you come here in all this . . . *khren*, this mess?"

"Well," Benjamin said. "That's quite a story."

And then, as he had with Natalya, he started at the beginning, with the call from Fletcher to the Library of Congress, his arrival and meeting with Samuel Wolfe, and their subsequent investigation into Fletcher's death. But this time he tried to leave no detail unmentioned, thinking it was important that Nikolai understood the implications of passwords and poisons and sudden, inexplicable deaths. He wanted to make certain Nikolai grasped the full sinister background of everything that had happened to him, to know exactly what his daughter had become involved with.

With Natalya translating from time to time, Benjamin tried to include everything that had happened to him: Fletcher's death, Edith's "accident" with her bees, Wolfe's veiled warnings, his suspicions of a wider conspiracy (though even now he stopped short of including what he thought he'd seen in the Foundation mural)—everything to impress on Nikolai the danger his daughter faced.

Yet oddly enough, it wasn't until Benjamin came to the part about his discussions with Anton Sikorsky that Nikolai showed signs of anxiety, and finally anger, until he and Natalya were engaged in what sounded like a fierce argument, not a word of which Benjamin understood.

"I'm afraid," Natalya said with exasperation, "my father does not trust Anton's role in all this. Especially as he once worked for the Soviet Ministry of Defense. How do *you* know you can trust him, he wonders, especially after he disappeared."

Benjamin started to answer, but Nikolai stopped him.

"Now it is my turn to tell a story," Nikolai said. "Then you will understand my suspicion.

"Imagine," he began, "it is August 1968, at the heart of the Cold War."

CHAPTER 43

From the air, Uzhur looked no different than so many other Siberian villages: ancient houses of blackish brown logs nestled in low, rounded hills and connected to the nearest villages by a solitary, narrow road, a road that wound through the hills and occasional thick pine forests, appearing lonely and alien in this vast landscape.

"Uzhur," in the area's ancient Khakas language, meant "hole in the ground." None of the long-dead tribesmen who named it, and none of its living inhabitants, could know just how ironic that name would prove to be.

But if one could somehow see through solid rock, they would discover what made Uzhur different than the other villages around it. They would see what appeared to be a submarine, or parts of a submarine, buried five hundred meters underground. They would see the secret underground village designated Uzhur-4.

The rooms of this secret village had rounded ceilings and walls, the doors were oval-shaped rather than rectangular and set with large metal wheels in their centers, and everywhere there wound parallel rows of pipes and conduits. But, unlike in a submarine, the hallways bent and twisted at sharp angles, and were constructed of three-meter-thick concrete; beneath the rooms and hallways were dozens of oversized shock absorbers, each a meter wide and driven ten meters into solid granite. The curved, angled hallways, massive walls, and giant springs were all designed to allow the structure to withstand seismic shock waves of up to 500 psi—say, for instance, from the nearby impact of a one-megaton nuclear warhead.

The buried village's inhabitants didn't call it Uzhur-4; they called it, with fierce Russian irony, Solnechnyy Uzhur—Sunny Uzhur. There were only thirty such inhabitants, each of whom visited for a two-week duty shift, after which he returned for ten days to his surface home and wife and children, but as silent and pale as the sterile crypt in which he kept vigil.

And what they kept vigil over were the thirty-three SS-18 intercontinental ballistic missiles of the 39th Missile Division, 33rd Guards Missile Army, Omsk. Each missile was topped by the most powerful nuclear weapon ever created, the R-36M, twenty-five megatons of instantaneous hell. The official manual of the Strategic Rocket Forces labeled the missiles "Voyevoda," a word from the old Russian that meant something like Chieftain, or simply Boss. The name the Americans gave the missile was even simpler, and perhaps more accurate: Satan.

Uzhur-4 was a village of uniformly light gray and green rooms, harshly echoing hallways, shadowless fluorescent lights, unpalatable recycled air, and absolutely inviolate routines. A village whose sole purpose was to destroy a significant portion of the world. A village that didn't exist.

In this village that didn't exist, a group of men in pale blue overalls were sitting in a room with couches, chairs, a Ping-Pong table, a television set—everything that might have made the room a den in someone's home. But the walls were of concrete painted gray, the floor was also concrete but painted pale green, the lights were harsh fluorescents, and the men acted with the controlled ease of soldiers who might at any moment be required to resume rigid discipline. And, even though the room was on the surface, there were no windows, for the room, and the small building in which it was contained, were buried under ten feet of earth, earth that was planted with pine trees and shrubs and therefore, from the air, indistinguishable from the other dozens of small hills around it.

The men were watching television: a news report from Moscow about the growing Czechoslovakian crisis. The stolid reporter was saying that anti-Soviet leaflets were being distributed in Prague, that a radio station had been seized by rebels and renamed "Free Bratislava," and that it was broadcasting calls to the Czech people to resist by all means necessary the "invasion" by tanks and soldiers of the Warsaw Pact. One troop train had already been derailed, and many Red Army soldiers had been killed, some by weapons clearly marked "Made in the U.S.A." Finally the broadcast changed to other news.

"Counterrevolutionary bastards!" said one of the men sitting around the television.

"To think, one hundred and forty thousand brave Red Army men died ridding them of Hitler—and this is how they thank us!"

Another of the men—the name tag on his overalls read ORLOV, N.—turned to a man on the couch next to him, whose tag read LEVEROTOV, V.

"What do you think?" he said. "Will NATO come to the rebels' aid?"

"I think," Leverotov said, putting out a cigarette, "our 'sausages' are a cold compress on the hotheads in the Pentagon. But they are wild Americans." He smiled. "Who knows that they will dare." He looked up at a clock. "Come on, it's time for our watch. And remember, we have a very important drill today."

Saying *"pakah,"* giving a few mock salutes to the other men in the room, they walked out of the room, down a short hallway to a small medical clinic.

After a thorough medical examination, they reentered the hallway and walked to an elevator. There was a keypad next to the elevator, and Leverotov punched in a numbered code. The doors opened and they entered, typed another numbered code on another pad inside the elevator. Its doors closed and it began to descend.

Thirty minutes later found the two men sitting in another room, much smaller, with barely enough space for the two high-backed, padded chairs they occupied, and a huge instrument panel that stretched the length of the room. They sat at opposite ends of the panel. Each of them was holding a small white metal key, and both keys were inserted into identical locks. Their eyes were watching two small screens, each set above the panel, angled down toward them. The screens flickered for a moment, and then each displayed, in an incandescent, wavering green, two words: BATTLE ALERT.

Orlov looked quickly over to Leverotov. "Battle Alert?" he said, his voice rising slightly. "Not Training Alert?"

"Shut up," said Leverotov. "You know the procedure. Follow it." And then he began a countdown. "Three, two, one . . . turn!"

Simultaneously the two men turned the small, white keys. An amber light above each lock went off, and immediately a red light next to it came on. Each man then raised his right arm slightly and positioned an extended index finger over a large round white button. Their eyes were fixed on rows of lights beneath each button, watching closely as the lights turned in sequence from red to green.

When the last little round light had turned green, Leverotov said, "Arming sequence complete," to which Orlov replied, "Confirmed, arming sequence complete."

The words "BATTLE ALERT" disappeared from the screens over their heads, instantly replaced with the words "RED STAR." Both men looked to the binders open before them, traced with a finger down a column of words.

"Firing verification Red Star," said Leverotov.

"Firing verification Red Star confirmed," replied Orlov.

"On my mark," said Leverotov, and raised his finger to the white button, while Orlov, like a mirror image, did the same. "Three, two, one . . . fire!"

Both fingers pressed and held the white buttons. The green lights above the buttons blinked out. The words "RED STAR" disappeared from the TV screens. Still the men held down the white buttons. There was a long moment of silence . . . then a speaker set in the ceiling of the room crackled.

"Fighting watch alpha," said a staticky voice from the speaker.

"Fighting watch alpha aye," said Leverotov.

"Alert canceled. Repeat, alert canceled. Stand down. Repeat, stand down."

"Alert canceled confirmed," replied Leverotov. "Fighting watch alpha out."

He moved his hand to his key, looked over to Orlov, waiting for him to do the same.

Orlov looked over at Leverotov. "That's not—"

"Your key, Captain Orlov," Leverotov said.

Orlov raised his hand to his own key. Once again, Leverotov counted down from three to one; once again, they turned their keys simultaneously, this time counterclockwise, back to Lock.

"Now," said Leverotov, "make your record. They'll be cracking the hatch soon, I want to be on time."

Orlov shrugged, pulled a logbook toward the edge of the panel, began writing down figures. He happened to glance again at the instrument panel. "What the hell?" he said.

Leverotov looked at his own panel. On both sides, a red light was blinking.

The two men looked at each other. Leverotov immediately leaned forward, pressed the button for the intercom.

But before he could say anything, Orlov said, "Wait!" He pointed at the red light in front of him, which had stopped blinking. Leverotov looked at his; it was now off, too.

They could hear the sounds of men on the other side of the oval door, unlocking its mechanism.

"What do you think?" asked Orlov. "Should we report it?"

Leverotov thought a moment. "Let me . . . look into it," he said. "I will let you know."

And then the hatch to the room was opened, and the process of handing over their records and keys began.

CHAPTER 44

The light in the basement of the church had dimmed a little as clouds moved overhead and blocked the sun. Nikolai was leaning back in his chair, while Benjamin sat forward in his. Benjamin realized his body had gone stiff with tension while he listened to Nikolai's story.

"Anton said something about 1968, about it being the time we truly came closest to nuclear war. But in the U.S. we never heard of this."

"Of course not," said Nikolai. "You didn't really care about the rebellion. It was all . . . theater to you."

"And this mysterious red light during the drill, this glitch . . . what did Leverotov find out about it?"

"Before I answer that question, there's something you must understand," Nikolai said.

Nikolai told Benjamin the same thing Anton had: after the Cuban Missile Crisis, a new protocol for the Soviet nuclear forces had been issued. And that protocol changed the way their missiles were targeted. Before that, each missile stored its individual target and guided itself once it was launched. But under the new protocol, Strategija Chetyre, the targeting codes were transmitted from Moscow Center only *after* the missiles were launched.

"That red light," Nikolai said. "It meant the targeting codes were being transmitted then, *before* launch. And next thing we know, new message comes from Moscow. Cancel alert. Stand down. Only 'training exercise.' All damn strange."

Then he explained to Benjamin that his early training at the military academy had been that of an engineer, as were most of the other *rocketchiki,* so he and his comrades were intimately knowledgeable about even the most technical details of their nest of nuclear-tipped ICBMs.

"More than just fingers on buttons," he said. "We must understand fuel, circuits, electronics . . . everything."

He told Benjamin that Vladimir Sergeyevitch Leverotov was someone who knew the insides of the rockets and all the facilities better than anyone. But this particular "bright guy" had come not from the Academy, like Nikolai, but rather from the Ministry of Defense. He'd graduated university as a mathematician before joining the Red Army, and then been assigned to something called the 12 Directorate in the Ministry of Defense.

"Anton mentioned that," Benjamin interrupted. "He said—"

"Please, wait," Nikolai said.

Nikolai and Leverotov had become fast friends. They were both ardent believers in the mission of the *rocketchiki,* which Nikolai described as "guarding the whole planet from the aggression of imperialistic states." Nikolai and Leverotov had had frequent discussions about the importance of what they were doing, about their "ideological certainty" that it was right and, more important, patriotic.

But Benjamin was still dealing with something else Nikolai had said.

"You actually *believed* NATO would attack? Over Czechoslovakia?"

"I know what you are thinking," Nikolai said. "Did we really believe we were the good guys, you were the bad guys?" Nikolai gave him a very serious look. "And would I have used this terrible weapon? The answer is yes, absolutely. We *believed.* And for those four weeks, with Czechoslovakia in chaos, we were very close to edge of making belief into reality."

The Czech crisis lasted another two weeks. By the time it was over, Nikolai told them, everyone of the underground watch group was exhausted, just wanted to go home. Nobody talked about the "glitch." It was considered unpatriotic to even suggest something had gone wrong.

But in the month after that, Nikolai noticed a change in Leverotov's behavior. He seemed preoccupied. He no longer told jokes, didn't participate in the political discussions in the relaxation building. He performed his duties, but something seemed to have dampened his spirit.

"More robot than true *rocketchiki,*" Nikolai said. And after that Leverotov spent more time than ever checking the "sausages," going over their circuits, running tests.

Nikolai said he was used to people lying to one another, hiding their true feelings; that was all part of the system, a part of it he eventually came to despise. But with Leverotov, he felt it was something more than that.

One day, after another drill, they were in the changing room together. Nikolai approached Leverotov, began talking about the drill. Finally he came out and asked Vladimir: Had he lost his belief? If the time came, would he still press the white button?

"You know what he answered?" Nikolai said. "He said, 'Yes, Nikolai, I would, without hesitation.' Of course he would say that. Microphones everywhere, someone always listening. But he is telling *truth*, I can tell. Then he looked very *pechalno,* very sad, and he said, 'But not for reason you would.'"

"What on earth did he mean?" Benjamin asked.

Nikolai shrugged. "Don't know. And never get chance to find out. Because of 'glitch,' KGB comes to investigate. To find somebody to blame. When mistake happens, always has to be a name for Moscow. Understand?"

"Yes," said Benjamin, "I think I do."

"Well," Nikolai went on, "day KGB comes to Uzhur-4, I'm nervous, of course. But I did my job, I think, it's okay. But Vladimir, I guess he didn't think same way."

"Why?" asked Benjamin.

"Because that day, before KGB talks to him, he shoots himself."

Natalya, who had sat silently through Nikolai's story and the two men's conversation, now spoke up.

"I remember something Mother told me," she said. "Something about you being absent for a month, instead of the usual ten days. And I remember, too, she said perhaps a month later, you returned from the base very quiet. You never told her why."

"As I said," Nikolai went on, "Vladimir was good friend. Such a thing, among the *rocketchiki* . . . well, it was very bad. *Very* bad. Of course, KGB talk to everyone, take all his things. Many people reassigned after that, sent to other bases, including me."

"Until you retired," said Benjamin. "Natalya told me about your . . . research."

Nikolai looked down at the floor. "Yes, that was part of it."

"Not all of it?" Natalya asked, coming closer.

Nikolai looked up at her, reached out for her hand.

"I could not tell you, Natashka. I could not tell your mother. I could not tell *anyone*."

"Tell us what?" she asked, taking his hand.

Nikolai stood, went over to an empty chair. He picked up a small metal box, brought it back to them.

He held the box before them and slowly lifted the lid.

"About these," he said. "I call them my relics. And now, in this place, it seems a very good name."

Nikolai reached inside the box, took out two small objects. Benjamin noticed that he handled them as though they were indeed holy relics.

Nikolai held the objects out in his palm.

They were a crumpled, empty cigarette pack and a small wooden box for matches.

After Nikolai explained to them how he'd discovered them in his dress uniform tunic the day after Leverotov's suicide, he let Benjamin examine them.

The cigarette pack was green and blue, with "шипка" (Shipka) stenciled on it in white letters. The matchbox had a red label with a picture of two raised hands, one with a hammer and the other with a sickle, a miniature rocket rising over them.

Benjamin shook the matchbox. Something inside rattled.

"Open it," Nikolai said.

Carefully, Benjamin slid the cover back. Inside, he could see matches, each with a blue tip, except for one.

"Thirty-four," said Nikolai, "counting the headless one. Now remove them."

Benjamin tilted the matchbox and dumped the matches into his other hand. He looked inside.

"What the—"

"Yes," said Nikolai. "Not typical, is it."

"What?" said Natalya.

Benjamin was still looking at the writing and symbols inside the matchbox.

He could make out lines, squiggles, triangles, squares, and other geometric shapes—and in the center of the bottom, the words "*Stzenariy 55*" were written in tiny, precise letters.

"Have you any idea what this means?" Natalya asked. She held the matchbox, still examining the interior.

Benjamin realized he was gripping the matches loosely in his fist, and he quickly opened his hand, afraid he might rub two of them together and ignite the bunch. He handed them to Natalya and then walked away a bit and began pacing back and forth in the opposite stall, his head down, his arms crossed, deep in thought.

"Well," Nikolai said, "there are some interesting points. And I have had considerable time to think it over." He smiled, went on. "You notice, on the matchbox, there is something written."

"Yes," said Natalya. "This number thirty-four."

"Well, maybe coincidence, but that is number of missiles in Uzhur-4 nest."

"But that's also the number of matches in the box," Natalya said.

"Not at first," said Nikolai. "All such matchboxes, they contain forty matches. Exactly. Everything in the nest is counted, believe me."

"Then what about this one?" Natalya held up the headless match.

"Ah," said Nikolai. "When I said thirty-four missiles, I meant there were *supposed* to be thirty-four missiles, when base complete. They built last silo, but never put in its sausage. So, maybe headless match means . . ."

"Empty silo," finished Natalya.

"Maybe," said Nikolai.

Natalya then held out the cigarette pack. "But then why give you this, with no cigarettes?"

"Well, could call Vladimir stingy bastard," Nikolai joked. "Or maybe, is what *on* pack is important."

Natalya looked at the lettering. "Shipka?" she said.

"You remember your Russian history?" Nikolai asked, raising an eyebrow.

Natalya thought for a moment.

"It is 1877. Russian Army defeats Suleiman's Turkish Army at the Shipka Pass, in Bulgaria." She looked at the cigarette pack. "That's the Shipka Monument," she said, "at the pass."

"High marks," said Nikolai.

Natalya shook her head. "I do not understand. Shipka is in Bulgaria. What does it have to do with Uzhur in Siberia?"

"Remember, in my story, there was relaxation area? Building near surface, but covered in dirt and trees, to camouflage? We used to joke, this was where we turn back imperialist aggressors. We called it 'Shipka of Siberia.'"

At that, Benjamin looked up from his pacing and thinking.

"So, Leverotov was telling you there was something *in* that building, something he'd hidden there for you to find."

Nikolai shook his head, frowning. "I look, believe me, before I'm reassigned. And KGB, after Vladimir shoot himself, they go over whole complex with, what you call, thin-teeth comb."

"Fine-tooth comb," said Benjamin, but he'd already turned and bent his head in thought again.

"And these markings inside the matchbox?" Natalya asked.

Nikolai went to her and took the matchbox from her.

"Well, Vladimir engineer. I think these are symbols for electronic circuit. Probably thought I would know what they mean. Some code for wiring, or maybe computer program . . ."

"And?" asked Natalya.

Nikolai looked at her, smiled sadly.

"I don't know. Could never figure them out. For circuit, doesn't make sense."

"What we need," sighed Natalya, "is one of those capitalist treasure maps, with little dotted lines pointing to where the treasure is buried."

Benjamin stopped pacing.

He was thinking of something Samuel had said, back at the Foundation, something about there was no "X marks the spot" to solve this mystery.

Or maybe there is, he thought.

He walked over and took the matchbox from Nikolai, looked again at the tiny symbols.

"Natalya," he said, "remember that mural, in the lobby of the hotel in Dubna?"

"Yes," she said. "But what does that—"

Benjamin looked up at them. He was almost afraid to say out loud what he was thinking.

"You said those geometric shapes were symbols," he said, speaking very slowly. "Symbols for places in and around Dubna. You said it was a kind of art popular in the sixties, but that it was also a map."

He looked at Nikolai. "This all happened in that period, correct? In the sixties?" Nikolai nodded. Benjamin took a deep breath.

"Then what if this isn't some odd circuit diagram that cannot be solved without a special key. What if it's simply . . . a map?"

Natalya and Nikolai exchanged looks of surprise.

Nikolai took the matchbox from Benjamin and looked once again at the drawing inside, walking a few paces away from them deep in thought.

"But why a map?" Natalya asked Benjamin. "Why not just write what he wanted to tell my father?"

"Perhaps he was afraid it would be found, and wanted to put it in a way only your father would understand."

Natalya shook her head, unconvinced. "But he did not understand. And why a map? They were both engineers. A circuit diagram would be much more likely, a reference to something only they knew . . ."

"Perhaps it *is* something only they knew. Some place or—"

"*Tchert!*" Nikolai stopped his pacing. He turned to them. "I am an *idiot!*" He walked back, stood next to them.

"Here, look." He held the matchbox where they could both see inside.

"If this circle, where the diagram begins, is Shipka building—our little joke—then this squiggle *could* be service tunnel from it to . . . and then this would have to be . . ."

He chewed at his mustache, thinking through possibilities.

After a moment he looked up at them—but with defeat rather than triumph in his eyes.

"Yes, I know where this could be," he said solemnly. "Now I understand. And makes perfect sense. It is where *I* would hide something."

"And?" asked Benjamin.

"And it might as well be on the moon."

CHAPTER 45

Natalya and Benjamin looked at Nikolai, stunned.

"But . . . why?" Natalya asked.

"Because is *shakhta* . . . how is in English . . . silo," Nikolai said in frustration. "Thirty-fourth missile silo. Damn headless-match silo!"

"Are you sure?" asked Benjamin.

Nikolai calmed down. "I must look at map of base to be certain. But yes, for now, I think I am sure. This . . ." and he used one of the matches to indicate the final symbol in Leverotov's sketch, "is where silo would be, from Shipka building."

"But if we can't get there," Benjamin asked, "how did Leverotov reach it?"

"From *inside,* where he could turn off alarms. Maybe he thought I would figure it out while still *rocketchiki,* still have access," he said. "Guess I'm not as smart as he thought."

"But that was almost forty years ago," said Benjamin. "And if there's no missile inside, even now . . ."

"Even if no sausage inside, on *outside* is still electric fence, mines, cameras . . . It is impossible to even get close to this silo from outside. Whatever is secret there will *stay* secret there."

Nikolai turned aside, looking angry and dejected.

Bejamin and Natalya looked at each other, neither knowing what to say.

To have come this far, gone through this much, risked everything . . . all to be stopped cold now . . .

"Nikolai," Benjamin said, "you said even he would have had to turn off the alarms, even when he was inside. Does that mean this fence and these mines and cameras on the outside can be turned off, too?"

"Yes," Nikolai said, not turning around. "But as I said, only from *inside* complex. And we would never get inside. There are too many checks, too much security . . ."

"But if we could turn *off* those things," Benjamin continued, "then it would be possible to access the silo from the outside?"

Nikolai nodded. "Yes. What is here is, I think, tunnel next to silo, for equipment. There is hatch at top, can be opened from outside."

Benjamin forced a smile and an optimistic tone. "Then all we need is help from someone *inside* the complex. Someone to turn off those cameras and other things."

Nikolai turned, looked at him, laughed. "Is *all* we need?"

"Well . . ." Benjamin wouldn't give up, not now. "Do you still know anyone stationed there?"

Nikolai thought a moment.

"Well . . . yes," he said, nodding slowly. "Vasily Kalinin. Lieutenant Colonel Vasily Kalinin. I knew him when he was just Lieutenant Kalinin, some years my junior. Now he is in charge of security. He was good man, we trust each other." Nikolai looked up at Benjamin, frowned again. "But what we would ask of him, he would not do."

"But it is just an *empty* silo," Natalya said. "There is nothing there to protect."

"Let me think," Nikolai said. He walked away, then almost immediately turned around.

"Your President Reagan," Nikolai said, "used to say '*doverai no proverai*,' trust but verify. These days, little trust, much verify. Teams there all the time, from United States, from International Atomic Energy Commission . . ." Nikolai smiled again, but now with a trace of wickedness. "Even from newspapers. Perhaps if you knew such people . . ."

Benjamin returned Nikolai's wicked smile.

"And you, Nikolai," he said rather jauntily, "just happen to be looking at two *very* rich French journalists."

After a little more discussion, Nikolai agreed that, yes, there was a possibility, however slim, that they could reach the place designated on Leverotov's map. But he absolutely refused to allow Natalya to travel with them to Uzhur.

They argued for an hour, pacing back and forth in the church basement. Finally, they reached a compromise: Nikolai would fly on ahead to Krasnoyarsk, then take the train to Uzhur and make contact with Vasily. Natalya and Benjamin would take the train from Dubna, through Moscow and on across Russia to Uzhur—a trip that would require four days. That way, he insisted, he would have plenty of time to sniff out the situation with Vasily and determine whether there was any chance for their plan to succeed before they arrived—and before he put his daughter's life in danger.

Just in case something happened to him—he didn't specify the "something," but all of them understood what he meant—he gave them a letter for Vasily, a letter wherein he asked the Lieutenant Colonel to give them whatever help he could, in good conscience, offer.

"I wrote in note, nothing you ask makes risk for Russian Federation," Nikolai said. "He would not violate his duty. But," and he winked, "Vasily is also not hostile to *vziatki* . . . to bribes, if amount high and risk low."

Nikolai also explained that, regardless of their credentials, none of them would be able to enter the "military" Uzhur, and, since there were no hotels in the civilian town, he would contact one of his old friends there and ask him to put them up for a few days. He gave them the phone number of a Boris Silma, a man who had served with him and fallen in love with the wild territory and retired to Uzhur.

"Boris hunts, raises rabbits, smuggles vodka into China. He will welcome you. Especially if you bring dollars."

Benjamin suggested purchasing cell phones for all of them so they could stay in touch. Natalya and Nikolai looked at each other, laughed.

"Unless we stay in Petersburg or Moscow," Natalya said, "they would not do us much good."

"And around Uzhur," Nikolai added, "there is, what you say, blanket. Only military frequencies work. Besides," Nikolai said somewhat darkly, "we either meet there, or we don't."

They left Ratmino separately, Nikolai to make his phone calls—but from Olga's, not his own apartment—and Benjamin and Natalya to gather their things from the Dubna Otel, then take a taxi to a smaller train station outside of Dubna.

Two hours later, Nikolai met them at the small station, where the Dubna–Moscow train would stop briefly; it wasn't really a station, but rather a mere concrete platform with a rusted iron roof.

Nikolai embraced Natalya, kissed her on both cheeks, and told her to be very careful. Then he took Benjamin aside and gave him a small bundle.

"What's this?" Benjamin asked.

"Insurance," Nikolai said. He opened the bundle.

Inside was a compact black automatic pistol with a brown hand grip. A small five-pointed star was embossed in the middle of the grip.

"Is Makarov," said Nikolai. "Good weapon."

Benjamin looked at Nikolai with a mixture of surprise and horror.

"Nikolai," he said, "are you kidding? I've never used one of these. I'm an 'academician,' remember?"

"Is easy," Nikolai said. He quickly showed Benjamin how the safety operated, how to remove and check the clip. Then he rewrapped the gun and gave it to Benjamin.

"I would never get it on plane anyway," he said. "And I feel better if I know you have it."

"I'm not sure *I* will," said Benjamin. But he stuffed the bundle into his parka pocket. Then he shook Nikolai's hand.

"Udachi!" Nikolai said. "Good luck, Mr. Levebre!"

"And good luck to you, too, Nikolai," answered Benjamin.

Then he followed Natalya onto the train.

CHAPTER 46

Benjamin had of course heard of the Trans-Siberian Railway; he just never imagined he'd actually be on it, journeying across three thousand kilometers of Russia to a secret Russian rocket base in Siberia—all so he could perform a supremely unlikely act of burglary.

But those four days of train travel gave Benjamin a better idea of just how vast a country Russia truly was.

Once east of Moscow, the landscape became covered with seemingly limitless pine forests. When there weren't forests, there were fields—immense fields of wheat and barley that stretched to the horizon. At Yekaterinburg—where, Natalya grimly pointed out, the Romanovs were executed by the Bolsheviks—they crossed the Ural Mountains, the divide between Europe and Asia. They were now officially in Siberia. When Benjamin evidenced surprise at this, Natalya explained that, contrary to what most Westerners thought, Siberia wasn't just the frozen north of Russia; Siberia was, in fact, the entire eastern half of the country.

Along the way they passed through the huge oil fields around Tyumen, with numberless red-and-gray oil derricks nodding up and down and looking like the feeding skeletons of prehistoric monsters; through Omsk, a metropolis filled with blocky, white modern buildings nestled against the Irtysh River; through Novosibirsk, Russia's third largest city, famous for its enormous, domed ballet theater, as well as its scientific facilities, both public and secret.

Most of the time they tried not to think about what lay ahead. They talked of their childhoods. Natalya surprised Benjamin by revealing that, as a teenager, she'd been a leader of the Komsomol, the Communist Youth Union. Benjamin said it was difficult to imagine her as some sort of "Commie boss."

"Oh," she said, "I was quite stern. You should see a photograph of me from that time. I look positively sinister."

"But you didn't join the Party?"

"No," she said. "By that time, the thaw of glasnost was already beginning, Gorbachev was breaking up the country, and everyone knew the Party's days would soon be over. And by then my father had made his . . . discoveries. We knew the truth about my grandfathers' work for the NKVD. If I had joined the Party, it would have broken my father's heart."

But Natalya was far more interested in hearing about Benjamin's history. He talked about what he considered his absolutely uneventful childhood.

"It was not nearly so exciting as living in a secret city in Siberia," he said. But Natalya seemed interested in every detail: if he'd been a Boy Scout (what she called the American Pioneers, and yes, he had, making it to Star); who his girlfriends had been in high school (only two, he'd said, which surprised her, but both blondes, which didn't); why he'd never gotten married ("Of course, because I hadn't met you"—an answer she labeled "a blatant compliment").

Mostly, however, they watched the passing landscape, read newspapers they bought in stations along the way, and, inevitably, talked about the whole *khren* in which they'd become entangled.

"I've been thinking about these 'wobbles' Jeremy discovered," Benjamin said one night as they passed through a countryside utterly devoid of city lights of any kind. "It's just hard for me to understand how people, then or now, could manufacture enemies and a war just to remain in power. It seems . . . inhuman."

"Or perhaps all too human," Natalya replied. She was sitting next to him, had been resting her head on his shoulder. Now she sat up.

"Our whole history is of people willing to do anything to stay in power. Everyone was a potential enemy, everything was a possible plot against the Soviet people."

"For years before World War the Second, Stalin had told the people that the Nazis were their enemies. But when Molotov signed the nonagression pact with Germany, in a single day suddenly Germany became our friend, and Britain our enemy. They were told it was all part of Father Stalin's grand strategy. And they accepted this lie without question."

She took a page from the London *Times* Benjamin had been reading, drew a diagram.

"This picture was distributed on millions of leaflets handed out in Moscow and Leningrad."

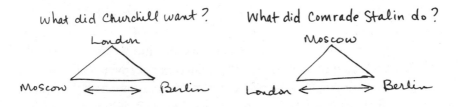

"You see?" she said. "Instead of letting Churchill pit the Soviets against the Nazis, allowing the British to stay above the fray, Stalin wanted people to believe the nonaggression pact forced *London* into that role, leaving the Soviets on top."

"Interesting," said Benjamin, thoughtfully examining Natalya's drawing.

"Understandable?" she asked.

"No . . . I mean yes. It's just that, well, I've seen something before, something that reminds me of your little triangles."

And then he told her about how Nabil Hassan had interpreted the symbol he'd found in the engraving of Horatio Gates: as a secretive power bringing two enemies into conflict, then, he'd put it, "sitting back in silence."

"Whether the Gray Cardinals are from your Revolution or ours," said Natalya firmly, "their methods are always the same."

"I just don't . . ." His voice trailed off.

"What?" Natalya prodded.

"If our Gray Cardinals were behind the Newburgh conspiracy two centuries ago . . ." He paused, then looked up at her. "What happened to them?"

"When the 1905 revolution failed," Natalya said, "most of the Bolsheviks were arrested and exiled. But the ones who escaped went underground. They had struck too soon. They needed to wait for better times. Or, as was the case, worse times." Her eyes became quite steely. "Perhaps your American conspirators were similarly slumbering. Waiting."

Benjamin smiled at her. "You *are* the professional paranoid." He tried to make his voice sound teasing, playful—but it was a distraction.

For at that moment, Benjamin had his first suspicion of what Scenario 55 might have been all about.

And, if he was right, it was monstrous.

Once they reached Achinsk, they had to give up that private compartment and the relatively luxurious accommodations of the Trans-Siberian Railway, and switch to a small commuter train for the final leg to Uzhur.

In Achinsk, Natalya saw a notice that a new, modern express rail service was coming soon to the Achinsk–Uzhur line.

"How things have changed," she said. "When I was a child, even this train was a secret."

As they moved deeper into southeastern Siberia and closer to the Chinese border, Benjamin noticed that the landscape became pockmarked, as though it had been bombarded eons before by giant cannonballs.

"Something like that," said Natalya. She explained to him that modern geologists knew this part of Siberia as one of the densest asteroid impact areas on all Earth. She opined that this was something the oldest locals understood on some instinctive level, for Uzhur had always been considered a place of dark, supernatural power. It was said that he who controlled Uzhur controlled all of Northern Asia.

But for all its supposed mystical power, the civilian Uzhur proved to be a very small town, indeed; one of only 17,000 inhabitants. To Benjamin, it looked like photographs he'd seen of old Western mining towns, with one-story houses and public buildings scattered intermittently, separated by rickety wooden fences and small kitchen gardens. Only the main roads were paved; the rest were rough lanes of dirt and gravel barely wide enough for a single car.

They asked at the train station for directions to Boris Silma's. The stationmaster knew Silma, and it was clear from the look he gave them that, if they were there to see "Bear" Boris, he assumed they were on some sort of illicit business. Looking simultaneously curious and disapproving, he told them that they could call Silma from the station phone; the twenty-dollar bill Benjamin gave him seemed to still his suspicions.

Natalya made the call. She spoke in rapid Russian, and something Boris said made her go very quiet. Then she said a few more words, said, *"Harasho, spasiba,"* and hung up.

She came to Benjamin. She looked stricken.

"Nikolai is not here," she said. "He called Boris from Dubna, said to expect him two days ago. But he has not arrived."

Benjamin held her arms. "Perhaps it's nothing," he said. "Perhaps he just couldn't get a flight, or he was delayed."

"Perhaps," said Natalya, but it was clear she didn't believe him. "I will call him from Boris's house."

They waited for Boris outside the station. It was cold here; not just chilly, but the kind of cold that Benjamin could feel even through his thick parka. There was no deep snow yet—Natalya said the streets would soon be impassable and everyone would move about on skis—but there were patches of snow everywhere and frost on the trees and rooftops.

By the time Boris arrived in a battered and rusting hardtop UAZ Russian jeep, Benjamin was beginning to feel like his face was an icicle. The vehicle clearly had a military past: where there was still paint, it was a drab olive green; where there was not, there was either orange rust or patches of black undercoat.

Boris bounded out of the jeep, swept Natalya up in his arms, kissing her on both cheeks and speaking in a torrent of Russian. Benjamin could see why his nickname was Bear: Boris was over six and a half feet tall, thick limbed, and with a heavy black-and-gray beard.

When Boris was done greeting Natalya—he'd looked slightly askance at her brunette hair but said nothing about it—he turned to Benjamin, removed his glove, and offered his hand. Benjamin removed his as well—he instantly felt the cold work into his exposed fingers—and Boris took it in an almost painful grip.

"Greetings to my country!" Boris said. "Welcome, America!"

"Thank you," Benjamin said, feeling his hand beginning to go numb. "*Spasiba.*"

"Ah!" Boris's face lit up. "*Vy govorite po russiki?*"

"No," Benjamin said. "Two words: *spasiba* and *privet.*"

Boris looked somewhat taken aback, then smiled broadly. "Is okay. I speak American."

He gathered their two bags and tossed them into the back of the jeep. Natalya climbed into the cramped front seat and Benjamin, pushing aside boots and traps and boxes of loose rifle ammunition, climbed into the back.

As they bounced over the dirt roads of Uzhur, and then the even rougher outskirts where Boris lived, Boris and Natalya carried on a conversation. Benjamin couldn't understand specifics, but it was clear they were discussing Nikolai's failure to arrive in Uzhur.

Boris's house was in truth a one-story cabin. "Is only for business," Boris said, removing their bags from the jeep. "Real house in Achinsk." He didn't explain what sort of business he conducted from a wooden cabin in the wild woods far outside Uzhur.

Once inside, he immediately offered Benjamin and Natalya a small glass of vodka each. Benjamin was exhausted, just wanted to lie down, but a look from Natalya told him this was a ritual they must indulge. He accepted the glass, Boris roared, *"Za vashe zdorovye!"* and he and Natalya tossed theirs back in a single gulp. Benjamin started to sip his, and Boris protested.

"Nyet, nyet," he said, and motioned for Benjamin to toss the vodka off as he had. Benjamin smiled, saluted him with the glass, and did so.

The vodka burned his throat, and he bent over, coughing, much to Boris's amusement. And then Boris poured another shot for each of them, pronounced another toast Benjamin didn't understand, and they repeated the procedure.

This time Benjamin didn't cough. And at least, he noticed, he was beginning to feel the warmth return to his hands and face.

It was then Natalya asked Boris to use his telephone.

"Da, da," he said. "But not always work." He showed Natalya where it was, and she went into the other room where it was located.

Benjamin looked around Boris's "business" house. It seemed more of a hunting lodge than anything else. There were bear and fox heads on the walls, and everything was made of either wood or stone. Boris went to the stone fireplace and began making a fire.

Natalya returned from the other room looking even more worried.

"There is no answer," she said to Benjamin. "Not at Olga's, not at his apartment."

While Natalya and Boris carried on another animated conversation, Benjamin looked around the cabin. He noticed a well-stocked gun rack on one wall and a shelf lined, row upon row, with unmarked, clear-glass bottles. There were also numerous foot lockers that looked ex-military, a huge meat refrigerator, a very old television set complete with rabbit ears antenna, and what appeared to be an ancient CB radio.

Photographs were set unevenly along the walls, most of them showing Boris posing with other men over the bodies of bears, deer, and in one case a white-and-black tiger; there were also other, older photographs with Boris in a uniform of the Red Army, standing in groups of men, their arms around each other's shoulders, all of them smiling and looking young, brave, and cold. Upon closer examination, Benjamin recognized one of those men as a younger Nikolai Orlov.

Finally Natalya and Boris finished talking, and Boris turned to the stove and began making coffee.

"I told him we must continue," Natalya said. "Wherever Nikolai is, whatever has happened to him, it is what he would want. What he would insist upon."

Benjamin looked at her. He thought again of how much he admired her strength, her calm resolve in the face of the unexpected. Perhaps Natalya sensed his thoughts, as she came to him and held his arms, looking into his face. He didn't need to say anything; she knew he couldn't but agree with her.

"And so, Monsieur Levebre," she said, "I believe we have an interview to arrange."

CHAPTER 47

"The general says, if the order comes through, he will not hesitate to follow his duty to the Motherland. He will launch his missiles."

As Natalya translated what General Voroshilov had just said, Benjamin scribbled notes, as though he were taking down every word. But in fact he was scribbling nonsense—in French, just in case the general knew more English than he let on.

They were sitting in General Voroshilov's surprisingly cramped office, in the base administration building, which from the outside looked like an average grocery store. Of course, most grocery stores didn't have soldiers patrolling their hallways with AK-47s.

The moment Benjamin had seen the gates of the military base through the windshield of Boris's jeep, he began to regret his decision to allow Natalya to come along. The high fence, obviously electrified; the dozens of soldiers, all armed with automatic weapons; the forbidding expressions on their faces . . . all of it made him want to tell Boris to turn the jeep around. Added to that, Natalya had pointed out the large monument of Comrade Lenin. Benjamin thought he saw a malicious smirk on Lenin's lips, as though he was saying *Who do you think you are fooling?*

At the gate, a soldier took their names, referred to a checklist, then looked very long and hard at their press credentials. Finally, he waved them through, but telling Boris he must park his jeep and wait outside. Boris told Natalya that was okay, there was a soldier's bar nearby where he could wait.

Benjamin asked the questions during the interview and Natalya translated General Voroshilov's answers. The general—a large man with a wide face and a thick neck that the tight collar of his uniform only emphasized, and an easy smile that Benjamin felt wasn't to be taken as quite what it seemed—was obviously eager to praise the dedication and sacrifice of his men, and himself, and at the same time to make it clear that he had under his command the power to devastate large areas of the Western world. He said, looking very stern, that their Voyevoda rockets each had the destructive capacity of 1,200 Hiroshimas.

During all this propaganda, Benjamin looked properly impressed. But finally, Benjamin brought the interview around to the only question he really cared about: What about security? For instance, what if terrorists tried to get to his missiles?

The general looked disdainful, laughed. Even though he was kind enough to entertain two French journalists today, he said, it was not long ago that they would not have been allowed within one hundred kilometers of the base.

And what about the missile silos themselves? asked Benjamin; how well were they protected?

The general spoke at some length, his tone that of an indulgent parent lecturing a child. The entire territory was protected, he said, by cameras and night-vision equipment and special electronic sensors. Each silo was surrounded by an electric fence carrying thousands of volts. He said even the famous Siberian bear wasn't clever enough to cross those fences. Once, one had tried and been "burnt to nothing more than smoking fur." Even the elite Russian Spetsnaz, the Special Forces, had not been able to penetrate their defenses.

As Benjamin jotted down a steady stream of words, his heart sank. This was going to be even more difficult than they'd thought.

Finally, Benjamin said the general had been most helpful. But there was one more favor he could do for them, something to give their article "real spice." He said they would like to interview one or two of the other people involved in the defense of the base, to get some further perspectives on the truly excellent safeguards in place; such assurances, Benjamin said, would go a long way toward quelling Western fears about "loose Russian nukes." Could they, for instance, speak to—and here Benjamin leafed through his notes, as if checking a name—a Lieutenant Colonel Vasily Kalinin, commander of base security?

From the look on General Voroshilov's face, Benjamin was certain he would say *nyet*. But he seemed to consider it for a moment, then smiled, said something that Natalya translated as, "Of course, we have nothing to hide"—which he accompanied with a wink and a chuckle—and then pressed a button on his phone-intercom system.

Suddenly, Benjamin had a horrible thought: What if Voroshilov was summoning Vasily to his office? What if he would insist they interview Vasily there, in front of him?

But it turned out the general was merely finding out Vasily's location on the base. He then summoned the guard outside, barked some instructions at him, and told Natalya that the soldier would accompany them down the hall to Vasily's office. He shook their hands, insisted they send him a copy of their article, which he promised to mount on his wall, and saw them out the door.

The moment they entered Lieutenant Colonel Kalinin's office, Benjamin caught a look of recognition in his eyes. Vasily looked perplexed for a moment, then instructed the soldier to wait outside, and bid them to sit down.

Once they had, he immediately turned to Natalya and said, "Brunette hair does not become you, Natashka. Not even as a French journalist."

Benjamin went cold. But Natalya returned Vasily's look with a steady gaze.

"How are you, Vasily Nikolaevitch," Natalya replied. "My father sends his greetings. And this." And then she handed him the note Nikolai had given them in Dubna.

Vasily took the note, read it quickly. He looked at them, then stood up and went to the window, still holding the note. He read it again. Then he turned to them.

"Is this a theater?" he said. "Some sort of American James Bond movie?" He came and stood in front of them, leaning against his desk. "Or is it a joke? Because if it is, it is not a very amusing one."

"No," Natalya said firmly, "it is no joke. Not when my father has disappeared." She indicated Benjamin. "Not when a colleague of this man has been killed, all to bring us here."

Vasily looked thoughtful. He went back around his desk and sat down, placing the note carefully on the desk before him.

"And what do those events have to do with Uzhur-4?" he asked.

Benjamin leaned forward. "What we need," he began, "is simply to see one of the missile silos."

Vasily raised his eyebrows. "Simply?" he said. "Now you *are* making a joke."

"Not one of the active silos," said Natalya. "Number thirty-four. It is empty, I believe."

Vasily looked at her. "That is something I could not say," he said.

"But if it were," Benjamin said, "and if we just needed, say twenty minutes there. Just to . . . well, look at it." The expression on Vasily's face didn't change. "And if," Benjamin continued, "it was worth, say, twenty thousand dollars for those twenty minutes."

Vasily leaned back in his chair. "Twenty thousand dollars?" he said. "For twenty minutes of 'just looking'?"

"Yes," said Natalya.

"And not to take pictures?" Vasily asked.

"No," Benjamin said. "No pictures. In fact, we don't even wish to see inside the silo—which, if it is full of concrete, as Nikolai told us, wouldn't make much of a picture, anyway."

"Then what—," Vasily began.

"There is an access well," Natalya said, "next to the silo. For equipment. Equipment which was never installed."

Vasily thought about that. "But the hatch to the well is sealed. And there are alarms and mines around the silo, even if it is . . . decommissioned."

"And that seal," Natalya said, "those alarms and mines, they can all be turned off?"

Vasily rocked in his chair. "For twenty minutes," he said, quite noncommittally.

"Exactly," said Benjamin. "That's all we need."

Vasily turned his chair so he was facing out the window. Again he glanced at Nikolai's note on the desk.

"Nikolai was a very good officer," he said. "A good *rocketchiki*. A good friend. He may not have told you, but I owe him a great deal. Perhaps my career."

"And he believed in what we are trying to do," Natalya said. "Enough to summon me all the way from the United States. Enough to risk his own life."

"Twenty minutes," he said again, still looking at the note. Then he looked up at Benjamin.

"Do you know, I am charged with keeping safe weapons that could destroy the world. Each year, I am underground eighty, maybe one hundred days. Since I came here, I don't even want to know how many years that is from my wife. And for this, they pay me five hundred dollars a month." He smiled. "For such a request, I think a thousand dollars a minute is not enough."

Benjamin smiled.

"And *five* thousand dollars a minute," he said. "Is that enough?"

CHAPTER 48

As one followed the main road north out of Uzhur, past the endless expanses of pine trees, about forty kilometers outside of the town one came to a fork in the road: to the left the road was asphalt and continued north to Achinsk; to the right the road was barely discernable and headed off into the menacing, treeless expanses of windswept gray hills, some of them rising in steep, almost impossible angles. If one was brave or foolish enough to take the fork to the right, after another five kilometers even the dirt road soon transformed into frozen marshland. To anyone looking down from on high, it would seem as if the road had simply disappeared into the landscape.

But what wasn't apparent to any such skyborne observer were the tracks that ran on through the now sparsely wooded marshland: two parallel snakes of concrete, each a meter wide and just a few inches beneath the bog's surface. Parts of the tracks were covered in snow, other parts in dust, but if one looked closely enough, one could make out the slight concavity in the surface that marked their path.

After two kilometers of following these tracks, one encountered another road, this one of earth packed under the weight of a dozen steamrollers, then carefully combed with graders to erase its surface perfection. This last leg of one's journey lasted another five kilometers. By the time one reached the end of that road that wasn't a road, one was clearly in the center of nowhere.

It was very early in the morning. The sun hadn't risen yet, though there was a pale light along the horizon to the east. Boris's jeep was grinding slowly along. All three of them were drinking coffee, trying to stave off the bitter cold in the air—especially as the heater in Boris's jeep didn't work.

Next to Benjamin in the backseat, the barrel of a hunting rifle Boris had insisted on bringing fell against Benjamin's thigh. He carefully pushed it aside, wondering what possible good Boris thought it would do them.

Then he remembered the Makarov in his parka pocket. Just as nonsensically, Natalya had insisted he take it along. "Just in case." Just in case what? he'd wanted to ask. In case I'm attacked by a bear?

She had been cold and distant ever since they arrived at Boris's cabin. Boris had kindly given his small bedroom over to them, but when Benjamin turned in for the night, Natalya stayed up talking with Boris in the living room.

"We are going to, how do you call it, catch up on old times?" But there was something in her manner that didn't strike Benjamin as nostalgic.

After he'd turned in, he heard the murmur of their voices for some time, and once or twice it seemed Natalya's voice had risen in anger. But eventually she'd come to bed, snuggled against Benjamin, holding him fiercely.

But when he turned to her, she put a hand to his face.

"I do not wish to make love. Not now. Please, just hold me." The look in her eyes was intense . . . as though she feared Benjamin might be snatched away from her any minute.

And now, in the jeep, she was silent, staring at the bleak, fantastic landscape. Benjamin could only assume she was thinking of what lay ahead, wondering if Vasily would keep his word, would stay bought.

They continued winding their way through the low hills. Benjamin had told Boris he could direct him to the area of silo thirty-four from Vasily's instructions—an offer that clearly insulted Boris.

"Everybody knows where damn holes are," Boris said. "No secrets around here."

The trees had completely given out now. Surrounding them was a vast, barren wasteland, interrupted only by the many small hills bordering the road. Natalya told Benjamin that some of these hills concealed ventilation shafts, even small huts. She had no idea whether any of them were still used, but from what Vasily had told them, they wouldn't need to worry about being observed—not, that is, until they were within half a mile of *shakhta* thirty-four.

The agreement they had finally worked out with Vasily was this: at precisely 6:00 A.M., the control switches for the alarms, fence, mines, and cameras around *shakhta* thirty-four would all experience a temporary glitch, a glitch that would last *exactly* twenty minutes. No more. In that time, Benjamin had to cross the one hundred meters of mined ground, climb the fence, open the hatch to the service well, complete his "looking," and then retrace his steps. After that . . . Benjamin had nodded, remembering General Voroshilov's story about the bear reduced to smoking fur.

Finally, they reached the spot where Vasily had told them to leave their vehicle, behind a low hill that shielded the silo from view. After this point, sensors in the ground would pick up the weight of a truck or jeep, but not that of a single human being.

Benjamin had already decided that he would be that single human being.

They stood by the jeep, shivering in the fierce wind even in their parkas, finishing their coffee and waiting for the hands on their watches to be diametrically opposed. Those hands now seemed to crawl, as though time itself had slowed in this alien landscape.

Finally, when their watches read 5:58, Natalya took Benjamin in her arms and pressed against him. She looked up into his face. The wind was forcing tears from her eyes—or at least Benjamin thought it was the wind.

"Please," she said, "be careful." She kissed him, her lips suddenly warm against his mouth.

Benjamin looked into her eyes—those blue-green eyes that seemed even brighter in the near-dawn darkness.

"Is time," Boris said. "You should go."

Giving Natalya a last kiss on the forehead, Benjamin turned and started off. He went quickly down the road, away from the jeep, around the hill.

Now he could see the silo area. It was absolutely flat, obviously processed by huge equipment to the uniformity of a tabletop. Perhaps one hundred meters away, he could see a chain-link fence, about three meters high, and beyond the fence he could make out the flat, regular shapes of concrete structures.

He stopped briefly at the end of the road. Vasily had told them this was where the minefield began. He made to put one foot beyond the road—then stopped, looked again at his watch. It was 6:01. If Vasily had switched off the mines when they agreed, then it was now safe to proceed; if he hadn't . . . there was nothing Benjamin could do about it.

He ran.

He heard the thumping of his feet against the hard earth and, where there were patches of snow, his boots crunched through the frosted surface. He could feel his breath now, was surprised he was already feeling the exertion. The fence seemed to recede rather than come closer; it was farther away than he'd thought.

And then surprisingly he was at the fence. If the current was still on, one touch would send thousands of volts through his gloves and into his body. There would be a flash, a shower of sparks, and he would be just another "smoking bear" clutching the fence in a death grip.

He thought of throwing something against the fence, wasn't sure that would even work, then realized there wasn't time, anyway.

He grabbed the fence.

He felt only the cold of the metal through the fingers of his gloves.

He began to climb, hand over hand, working the toes of his boots into the gaps in the chain link. He reached the top, pulled himself upright, threw one leg and then the other over, and then jumped down.

Now he could make out the structures more clearly. There were a few small metal boxes; probably, he thought, containing the alarms and other devices Vasily had switched off.

Directly ahead was his target: a rectangular concrete apron perhaps fifty meters long and fifteen wide. And in the center of the apron was a huge, eight-sided concrete slab. This was the lid of the missile silo. He could see the two parallel metal tracks that extended straight out from the lid along the length of the apron; these were the rails that the lid would ride along when an explosive charge sent it violently sliding away from the top of the silo, so that the "sausage" inside could roar up into the sky and off on its arc of death.

Only, for this silo, number thirty-four, there was no explosive charge, no nuclear sausage inside.

But there were still the alarms and sensors on the apron—the ones Vasily had switched off. Or so he hoped.

He reached the apron. The only sound was his breathing and the rush of the wind.

He wanted to look at his watch, but resisted it as a waste of precious time. At the end of the apron, behind the silo lid, he saw a small dome, with a hatch in its center. This was the service well.

He went to the dome and brushed the snow away from the top of the hatch. There was a wheel set in the center.

Vasily hadn't told them about the wheel. Should he turn it clockwise? Or counterclockwise? He decided to rely on the universal thinking of engineers and moved his hands counterclockwise.

It didn't budge.

He tried again. Still, it wouldn't move.

Perhaps it should move the other way after all. He looked more closely at the wheel.

There was a tiny glint of metal just under the wheel: the thread of the large screw device that operated the hatch. He looked at the angle, tried to think: If it was sloping *that* way, wouldn't that mean . . . ?

Over the wind, he thought he could hear his watch ticking. It was the loudest sound he'd ever heard.

Once more he grasped the wheel, tried to turn it, again counterclockwise. But his gloves wouldn't hold a grip.

Pulling his gloves off with his teeth, he grabbed the wheel in his bare hands. Instantly, he felt the frigid cold of the metal against his bare palms. Bracing his feet on either side of the dome, he twisted the wheel once again counterclockwise with all of his strength.

With a creak of protest, it moved, ever so slightly.

He stood, took a deep breath, and bent again over the wheel. This time it turned farther. A few more turns, and he heard a distinctive *click* from inside the mechanism. He lifted the hatch.

Still no alarms.

In the dim light, he could barely make out a ladder descending into the well. Leaving his gloves on the hatch, he backed down the ladder. The rungs were also of metal, so cold they burned his hands.

According to Nikolai, what he was looking for was a small alcove in the well, about halfway down. Had there been a missile in the silo, it would have been filled with electronic equipment. Now it should be empty—except for whatever Leverotov had placed inside.

That alcove was the X on Leverotov's tiny map. And inside that X was a secret buried here for nearly half a century, a secret people on two continents had been willing to kill to keep hidden.

Or maybe that X was empty. Maybe, in the nearly forty years since Leverotov had left the "relics" for Nikolai, someone else had found Leverotov's treasure. Perhaps they'd removed it, thrown it away, hidden it somewhere else. Or perhaps Leverotov had never put anything there in the first place. Perhaps they'd misinterpreted Leverotov's symbols, completely misunderstood the message he'd left for Nikolai.

Benjamin shook off such thoughts, concentrated on climbing down the ladder. Finally, he heard the toe of his boot tap against something metal. He climbed down a few more rungs, peered at the wall.

There was a small metal plate set into the wall, rusted around the edges. It was loose. Benjamin pried at the edges with his fingertips. It came free— and then slipped from his hand and went clattering down into the darkness of the well, until he heard it clang against the bottom.

He held his breath, expecting shouts, alarms, something. But there was only the sound of the wind whistling over the top of the well.

He extracted a small flashlight from his parka pocket, shined its light into the alcove the plate had been covering.

The light reflected off something inside the alcove. About an arm's length away, there was a bright yellow plastic bundle.

Reaching through the rungs of the ladder, he groped toward the bundle. It was almost beyond his reach. Finally, his fingertips touched the plastic. He clawed at it until it moved a few inches toward him. He withdrew his hand, blew on his fingers to warm them. Then he reached in again, stretch- ing his arm to its limit.

He had hold of the bundle.

He dragged it out of the alcove. There was something inside the bundle, something not heavy, but of a rectangular shape with sharp corners. He threw back one flap of the plastic, could see the cover of a flat metal box. On the cover, stenciled in black, was a name.

LEVEROTOV.

He threw the plastic back over the box, stuffed the bundle partially inside his jacket, and began to climb. The bulky package sticking partway out of his jacket made it difficult. Once, his hand slipped on the freezing metal rung, and he hung sideways for a moment, out over the dark abyss of the well. He swung his hand back to the ladder, continued climbing.

By the time he reached the top of the ladder, he was panting, his breath making explosive gray puffs in the air. He climbed awkwardly out of the well. Setting the bundle down, he lowered the hatch, spun the wheel.

His hands were freezing, almost completely numb.

He grabbed the gloves and started running toward the fence, the bundle tucked under one arm as he struggled to pull his gloves on with his teeth as he ran. The cold air was beginning to burn his throat, his eyes filling with tears and making it difficult to see.

By the time he reached the fence, the gloves were over his hands, and he was thankful he didn't have to touch the bare, cold metal with his fingers.

But what if the fence current was back on?

He shrugged off the thought. He'd know soon enough anyway.

Then he realized he had a problem: he could never climb the fence holding the bundle.

He backed up a few feet, tossed the bundle over the fence, then launched himself onto it and began to climb. The only sound now was the wind and the rattle of the fence as he clamored up it.

How much time? his mind thundered. *How much* time?!

He jumped from the top of the fence, fell, picked himself up and went over to the bundle. He bent down to pick it up, then stopped. Only two inches from the bundle a thin metal bar protruded above the light covering of snow. He realized it was probably the trip sensor for a mine.

He reached down and snatched the bundle up, carefully stepped around the mine sensor, and began running again. He felt the Makarov thumping against his side in the parka pocket, could hear his blood pounding in his ears. The tears in his eyes blinded him. He stumbled, went sprawling on the ground, the bundle clattering a few feet away.

He rose up, grabbed the bundle. All about his feet he could see the tiny, dull-gray tips of more mine sensors. And now he was disoriented. Which hill was the right one? Then he saw the faint outlines of the road that bordered the minefield.

He forced himself to run again, sprinting, lifting his feet in their clumsy boots, trying to make himself lighter, faster.

He fought the urge to jump toward the boundary of the road; he didn't have the strength, anyway. His feet were like lead, his chest was burning, the cold air making his throat tight, the wind seeming like a living thing that wanted to knock him down, blow him back toward the fence, back into the mines that must any second now become active.

And then he was across the road.

Benjamin fell to his knees, gasping for breath, the bundle clanging as it dropped from his hands. A light snow was falling now, the flakes landing on his upturned face. A dim grayish glow was appearing in the east as the sun worked to force its light through the low-hanging clouds. For a moment, he stayed down on all fours, fighting to catch his breath, to fight off the numbness from the cold, to still the pounding in his head.

After a minute, he straightened, slid the parka sleeve back from his wrist, looked at his watch.

6:19.

A minute to spare, he thought. He wanted to laugh.

He stood up, bent slowly and picked up the bundle, tucked it under his arm. Then he walked, each step seeming an eternity, along the road and around the hill.

He could see Boris's jeep.

But now there was a truck next to the jeep. And the truck's lights were on, shining into his eyes, blinding him.

Through the glare he could make out three figures in front of Boris's jeep. In the middle was Natalya, and to her left was Boris. He was holding the hunting rifle—and seemed to be pointing it in Benjamin's direction.

And to Natalya's right stood someone very tall, in a dark parka; someone with short, very blond hair.

It was Hauser.

He, too, was holding a gun. But it wasn't pointed at Natalya; it was pointed at Benjamin.

CHAPTER 49

"Thank you very much, Mr. Wainwright," Hauser said, shouting over the wind. "That was very impressive."

Hauser was standing next to Natalya—but to Benjamin's surprise, he wasn't holding her. She was simply standing there, staring at him, with an utterly indefinable expression on her face.

"Boris," said Benjamin, not quite sure if he was asking a question or not.

"He's not the only *predatel,* the only betrayer here, Benjamin," said Natalya.

Benjamin went completely still.

"*You?!*"

Natalya said nothing—as though words wouldn't convey what she felt. Boris merely shrugged, smiled.

"Whatever is," he said, pointing with the tip of his rifle to the bundle under Benjamin's arm, "worth many rubles. I'm just businessman."

"And you, Natalya," Benjamin said, the words biting like acid. "Are *you* just a businessman?"

"Never mind about that, Wainwright," Hauser said. "It's been a helluva ride. I never thought you'd get this far. Congratulations."

Benjamin was still catching his breath. He wanted to stall for time, even if he wasn't sure why.

"You knew?" he shouted through the wind. "All along, you *knew* it was here?"

Hauser laughed. "Hell, no. We didn't know *where* the damn thing was. We didn't know if it really existed. Just rumors, over the years. And it was their problem, not ours. Until Fletcher got too curious."

"And too good," said Benjamin. "So you killed him, then used Samuel and me to track this down."

Even as he talked, he was furiously trying to figure out a way to separate Hauser from Natalya and Boris. Then he remembered the Makarov in his pocket. Boris's rifle was sloping down at the ground, not pointed directly at him. *If I just slip my hand into my pocket . . .*

Hauser chuckled. "And just like a good hunting dog, you brought us right to it. With a little push from that Amazon Gudrün." He smiled when he saw the surprise in Benjamin's eyes. "That's right, bright boy. But I guess not *too* bright, eh?" And then the smile vanished. "Now, set the package down and step back."

Benjamin bent slowly, placed the bundle on the ground, then stood and took a step back. He calculated he was about eight feet from Hauser. But if Hauser stepped forward to get the bundle, and if it took a few seconds for Boris to react . . .

Hauser took a step forward, then turned and dragged Natalya with him.

"And what do you get out of this, Natalya? A promotion?" Benjamin sneered.

She shook her head, even as she struggled in Hauser's grip. "You don't understand . . ."

"Yes, you've said that a lot since we met." Even though Benjamin's chest was rigid with anger and pain, he wanted to keep talking while he moved his gloves toward his pockets, as if trying to warm his hands. "To betray a naïve American, that I get. But your own *father*?"

Natalya bent her head, silent. Hauser stepped closer.

"Ancient history, Mr. Wainwright," he said. "And now that we have Fletcher's computer back, all the loose ends have been . . . snipped off."

"Then Anton is with you, too," Benjamin said. It wasn't a question. Did they also know about the copy of the program on the CD, which was back at Boris's cabin? They had to; Natalya would have told them.

But then, what did any of that matter? He didn't think Hauser was letting them go anywhere.

"Or you've killed Anton," Benjamin said. His hands were inches from his pockets. "Like Dr. Fletcher and Mrs. Gadenhower."

"You have to be committed for the long haul," Hauser said. "That crazy bee lady thought it was all just an idea, just a *theory*. That's how you academics are, isn't it? Big ideas, but when the time comes to ante up . . ." He finished with a shrug.

Hauser had reached the bundle. Benjamin expected him to bend down and pick it up.

"Now, Ms. Orlova," Hauser said, keeping his eyes on Benjamin, "if you would kindly pick that up for me."

Natalya looked back at him, to Benjamin. Then she moved toward the bundle.

Benjamin had to interrupt him, to distract them.

"And what then?" he shouted at Hauser. "You'll kill us all?"

"He just wants package," Boris shouted. "Give it to him, we all go home, nobody dies."

"You're a fool, Boris," Benjamin said, keeping his eyes on Hauser. "They can't let us go. Not now that we know it exists. He'll have to kill you, too, just for being here."

He saw Boris look toward Hauser's back. Natalya, too, turned from where she knelt near the bundle, looked up at Hauser.

"That was not the arrangement," she said steadily.

"Nobody gets killed," Boris said. He raised the rifle a little, moving it toward where Hauser stood. "That is deal."

Hauser swiveled toward Boris and fired before Boris could react. Benjamin saw Boris's head twist to one side, his rifle discharging with a loud roar up into the sky.

Even as Boris fell, Benjamin launched himself at Hauser. As Hauser was turning back toward him, Benjamin slammed into his chest, pinning Hauser's arm and sending them both down onto the ground.

Benjamin heard the explosion of Hauser's pistol and felt the blow in his shoulder simultaneously. It was a searing pain, like a white-hot poker shoved into his flesh. As he flinched, Hauser pushed him to the side. Out of the corner of his eye he saw Natalya crouching, as if about to to leap—*but at which one of us?*

And then Hauser had fought free, was standing over him, pointing his pistol at Benjamin's head.

Benjamin's hand had found the Makarov. He pulled the trigger, firing through his parka.

There was an eruption of fiber and down from Hauser's parka as the bullet creased his arm. Before Benjamin could fire again, Hauser recovered, raised his pistol, aimed it again at Benjamin's head.

There was a tiny puff of snow at Hauser's feet, and a sound, faint in the wind, like a tree limb cracking. Hauser instinctively looked down at his feet. As he did so, there was another crack, this time much louder. Everything seemed to stand still.

Hauser towered over him, like a statue, the gun still pointing downward; Natalya was half crouched, startled and motionless; Benjamin could feel the burning in his shoulder, the warmth of something liquid running down his chest inside his parka, the frigid wind brushing across his face. His vision started to narrow, and he knew he was passing out.

Hauser toppled to the ground like a felled tree. His head was lying on its side, only a foot from Benjamin's own. Benjamin could see a dark red stain spreading across the ground, under Hauser's head.

And then Benjamin *knew* he was hallucinating.

Because, as his vision narrowed even further, he saw Samuel Wolfe bending down over him. And in this hallucination, Wolfe was dressed all in white, like a ghost.

Or an angel.

CHAPTER 50

Benjamin woke up. He tried to raise his head, but it felt enormously heavy.

He looked down. He was covered in blankets. His shoulder felt like a truck had run over it.

He looked around him. He recognized the log walls in the bedroom of Boris's cabin. On a small cot against the wall he saw Boris lying unconscious, a white bandage around his head. Blood was seeping through the bandage.

Benjamin could hear voices coming from the other room.

He felt woozy and weak, but he forced himself to sit up. His left shoulder throbbed. It was wrapped in thick bandages and strapped against his side with a blue nylon sling.

He swung his legs over the side of the bed and stood up. Immediately he felt dizzy and collapsed back down on the bed. But then he tried it again and managed to stay standing. Then, walking slowly and leaning against the wall, he made it to the door and opened it.

Boris's tiny living room was positively crammed with people.

The first one he made out was Natalya, as she stood up and came toward him, a look of concern in her eyes.

"Benjamin!" she said. "You should be lying down."

She came to him, but he shoved past her, pushing her arms away.

Nikolai Orlov was sitting in a chair in front of the fireplace. He smiled at Benjamin, said "*Privet,* Mr. Wainwright," and stood up and came to stand next to Natalya.

Somewhat groggily, he turned from Natalya and Nikolai to the rest of the room. In a chair with his back to Benjamin was Anton Sikorsky. He turned around, looked at Benjamin. "Ah," Anton said, "you're alive. Good." And then there was the third person, standing next to Anton.

It was Samuel Wolfe. And he appeared to be completely substantial, not at all the ghost—or angel—of Benjamin's hallucination.

He was still wearing a white snow parka and white nylon pants.

"Hello, Benjamin," he said. He walked forward. "Let me be the first to congratulate you. And now, please, sit the hell down."

Natalya led Benjamin—he grudgingly allowed her to take his arm—to a worn overstuffed chair in the corner and pushed him down into it. She bent over him and examined his shoulder.

"Is it bleeding?" she asked. "Did you tear the stitches?"

"No," Benjamin said, looking at her. "And why exactly do you care?"

Finally Natalya's composure was shattered. She started to cry, at the same time yelling at him in Russian. Benjamin couldn't tell what she was saying, but if it was an apology, it was a very strange one, indeed.

Nikolai stepped over to him. "She was only protecting me, Mr. Wainwright."

"Protecting you? And he," pointing to Anton, "gave them Jeremy's computer. What the hell is he doing here?" Benjamin looked around the circle of faces. "Would someone mind telling me what's going on?"

"First, we should toast your courage," said Nikolai. He went to the shelf with the rows of clear bottles of Boris's homemade vodka.

"I don't suppose you have any scotch there," Wolfe said doubtfully.

"Only vodka," Nikolai said.

While Nikolai poured drinks for everyone, Natalya brought Benjamin some pills, handed him a glass of water. He took them without a word, then looked at his shoulder. "How long—," he began.

"Eight hours," Wolfe said. "But I think you'll live. The bullet went clean through. And Natalya is quite the amateur physician." He accepted a small tumbler of clear liquid from Boris.

"Nuclear disaster nurse training," she said, fussing over Benjamin's shoulder. "You need a real doctor, and soon."

"How . . . ," Benjamin started. He went dizzy again for a moment, recovered. "How did Hauser know?" He looked at Natalya again, his eyes hard. "You?"

"No," Nikolai said, handing him a glass of vodka. "Was *me* who betrayed you."

Benjamin was speechless.

"Let's everybody sit down," Wolfe said. "You've got some catching up to do."

"But first, toast," said Nikolai. He lifted his glass up, looked at Benjamin, said, "To Benjamin. *Za uspekh!*" and tossed off his drink. The others followed suit, but Benjamin looked at his skeptically.

"Go ahead," said Nikolai. "Vodka contains most amazing healing powers."

Benjamin tossed his back, too. It burned his throat, but the dizziness passed and his head felt clearer. Maybe, he thought, there's something to this healing powers stuff after all.

Nikolai circulated among them, refilling their glasses.

"Now," Wolfe said. "You probably have some questions."

"A few dozen," said Benjamin, "For instance—"

"What am I doing here? Benjamin," Wolfe began looking quite serious, "let me start by apologizing. I'm sorry I had to deceive you. I know you thought I was in Edith's lab when it exploded. I wanted everyone to think that, and if you believed it, well, it would make the sleight of hand more convincing."

"I thought you were *dead*," Benjamin said with some pique. "Why couldn't you let me know you weren't?"

Wolfe leaned back in his chair. "I know you're not military, Benjamin, but let me explain it this way. The best way for a fighter pilot to shoot down his adversary is from behind, on his tail. And the best way to get on his enemy's tail is while that enemy is chasing somebody *else's* tail, focusing his attention forward."

"So I was a decoy?" Benjamin said, with obvious distaste.

"Not at all," Wolfe said. "Everything you did was vitally necessary. And something I couldn't have done myself. They never would have let me get this far. Hauser would have been unchained a lot sooner. As I told you at the Foundation, they were letting us serve as the hounds, to chase out the fox. The fox being Leverotov's journal, if it existed. I'm not sure they believed it did. But with me out of the picture, they gave you your head, let you pursue the leads." He tossed off his vodka, absentmindedly held out his glass for Nikolai to refill it. "And while they were pursuing *you*, I could pursue *them*."

"You mean, you were following me the whole time?"

"I knew you would go to D.C. and look up either Anton or Natalya, or both. And I knew you would visit the library. Meanwhile I could keep a watchful eye on you, make sure they didn't press too close. But you were a shade too clever and nearly fouled that up."

"What do you mean?"

"A friend of mine was keeping tabs on you in the Library of Congress. That was a nice trick you did, giving him the slip."

"That was *your* friend?" Benjamin said with alarm.

Wolfe nodded. "That panicked me for a while, when he called and said you'd disappeared. I thought maybe Hauser had reeled you in after all. But that didn't make sense; you hadn't made contact with Ms. Orlova yet."

"Then you didn't know about Nikolai's 'relics'?"

Wolfe shook his head. "No, *nobody* did. Not even Fletcher. They were the key nobody knew existed. Except Nikolai."

"And I didn't know what lock they are key for," Nikolai said. "Each of us has piece of puzzle, but nobody has whole puzzle."

"A puzzle leading to that box you so heroically retrieved," Wolfe said. "A box of great interest to a great many people—*if* it existed."

Benjamin saw his glass was full again. The throbbing in his shoulder had stopped, so he drank off the vodka. This time it didn't burn at all. Perhaps, he thought, he was acclimating to vodka the same way he had to scotch.

"So that man on St. Honorat who gave us the passports," Benjamin said. "That friend of Guy's. He was really sent by *you*?"

Wolfe looked askance at Anton, who ignored him, then back at Benjamin. "Uh, no, he wasn't one of mine . . . but I imagine he wasn't one of Hauser's, either. Right, Anton?"

Anton looked at him, huffed, and said only one word. "Obvious."

Benjamin thought back, looked at Anton suspiciously. "Hauser said they had Dr. Fletcher's computer back. You didn't give it to them?"

Anton wiggled his hand. "Sort of," he said. "I explain. Samuel calls me, while you driving to D.C., tells me everything, figures maybe I can finish TEACUP program. But without knowing what diary and *Stzenariy 55* are, only get little closer. Samuel decide, make copy of program, let them have computer, then they leave me alone, follow you."

"And how did you do that?" asked Benjamin.

"Well," said Wolfe, "they didn't want to inform the authorities you'd skipped from the Foundation with sensitive information, not unless they could control who found you. But a well-placed phone call, the police show up, find Anton gone, the computer there with the Foundation's name on it . . ." Wolfe opened his arms as if to say "problem solved."

Now Benjamin actually was beginning to get angry.

"Then why didn't you contact us in Dubna? Why didn't you get to Niko-lai, explain what was going on?"

"Ah," said Wolfe. "The best-laid plans. I never imagined Ms. Orlova would be so resourceful." He saluted her with his glass. "It took us a while to track you to Nice, and then Anton came up with her connection to Dubna, and Nikolai, from Myorkin's letter. We got to Dubna, yes, and went to Nikolai's. But he'd already left."

"And that's how I almost betray you," said Nikolai. "In Moscow, when I'm changing planes for Krasnoyarsk, two guys appear, one with FSB badge, beard, dark skin, other very tall, blond hair . . ."

"Hauser," said Benjamin.

"Exactly so," answered Nikolai. "They told me they have my daughter, and unless I tell them what I told you, they will kill her. Like a fool, I believe them. They bring me here, hide me in Uzhur when you and Natalya arrive."

"So Hauser bribed Boris," Benjamin said. "That betrayal I understand." He turned and glared at Natalya. "But yours?"

Natalya looked as though she might start cursing again, but Nikolai in-terrupted her.

"You do not understand. They tell Natalya the same thing. I am here, and unless she helps them get the treasure of *shakhta* thirty-four, they will kill *me*."

He turned to Natalya. "I heard you and Boris talking that night. *That's* what he told you? That they had your father?"

Natalya nodded. "Boris promised they only wanted what was in the silo, and everyone would be safe. Like a fool," she shook tears from her eyes, "I believed them. But when I heard that shot . . ." She lowered her head, then raised it again. "I am very sorry, Benjamin. I . . ."

Benjamin held out his good arm and Natalya came to him, wrapped her arms around his neck, buried her head against his.

After a moment, Benjamin turned to Wolfe. "And Boris?"

"We haven't had a chance to . . . discuss things with Boris. Hauser's shot grazed his head—"

"Lucky bastard," said Natalya with some heat.

"—and he's been unconscious since. Perhaps an overenthusiastic dose of painkiller." Wolfe frowned. "Anyway, all arrows pointed here, where it all began forty years ago."

"*Shakhta* thirty-four," said Nikolai.

"Then *you* were the one who shot Hauser?" Benjamin asked Wolfe.

Wolfe nodded. "Sorry it took two shots. I'm a bit rusty. If you hadn't wounded him in the arm . . ." Benjamin could see that Wolfe had, for the moment anyway, shed his cynical grin. He looked suddenly quite serious— and quite relieved. "I'm very glad you're alive, young man. That was a very brave thing you did."

Either due to the vodka or the medication, Benjamin was feeling light-headed again. He started to stand up, weaved, and fell back into the chair.

"Enough," Natalya said. "You need to rest." And she helped him to stand, walked him toward the bedroom door.

Benjamin stopped her at the door, turned around.

"Oh, by the way," he said, "I've figured out what that is." He pointed toward the metal box with LEVEROTOV stenciled on the cover that was sitting, open, on the wood plank table. "What Scenario 55 is all about."

Wolfe looked up at him. "Have you," he said. He sounded skeptical.

"From what Nikolai told us." But he was feeling weaker, and he could barely get out the rest of his thought. "It was a first-strike plan, so they could seize power . . . But something went wrong."

Wolfe and Anton looked at each other, smiled. Anton turned around in his chair.

"Exact opposite," he said.

"What?" Benjamin started to walk back into the room.

"*Nyet,*" said Natalya, steering him back into the bedroom. "Later."

Once in the bedroom, she helped him to lie down on the bed, checked his bandage again, pulled the covers over him. "First you sleep, then we'll explain everything."

"Explain . . . what," Benjamin said. He could barely keep his eyes open.

She leaned down and kissed him on the forehead.

"Only the biggest fraud in history," she said.

Or that's what he thought she said. He couldn't be sure. Everything was going fuzzy and black . . . and then the warmth of unconsciousness closed over him.

CHAPTER 51

What woke Benjamin the second time was the smell of something cooking, something with beef and onions. He realized suddenly that he was quite hungry.

This time, it was easier to get out of bed and stand up. Boris was still snoring on the cot. Whatever they'd given him, he thought, it must have been a very enthusiastic dose, indeed.

He shuffled to the door, opened it, and went out into the other room.

Through the windows of Boris's cabin he could see it was pitch-black outside, and snow was still falling, now heavily. Inside, the fireplace was casting a warm glow, and there were several oil lanterns set around the room.

Natalya was huddled over the stove, Nikolai at her side. They were arguing about something—apparently the proper amount of spices for whatever they were cooking. Wolfe and Anton were sitting around the wooden table, hunched over a set of papers spread across its surface. As he entered the room, everyone looked up.

"He riseth," said Wolfe. "And looking a trifle sounder. I do believe Boris's vodka is magic after all."

Natalya left the stove, came over to him, guided him to a chair at the table.

"How do you feel?" she asked.

"I'm not sure," Benjamin answered. "I've never been shot before. How should I feel?"

She kissed him. "You're very strong," she said, "for an academician." Then she returned to the stove, leaving Benjamin to muse over the wondrous ambiguity of Russian compliments.

Benjamin looked down at the papers on the table, apparently the material that had been in Leverotov's box.

There was a typed manuscript, in Russian, and next to that a leather-bound journal. The journal was open. Benjamin could see handwriting—very neat, precise Cyrillic—and what appeared to be long lists of numbers.

"I assume that's Leverotov's journal," Benjamin said, pointing to the leather-bound book. "But what are those pages?"

"Ah," Anton said. He swept his hand over them, as if presenting Benjamin with a valuable work of art. "Let me introduce you. Is *Stzenariy 55*."

"Then it exists!" said Benjamin.

"Sort of," said Wolfe, looking up from the pages. "Just not in the way anyone imagined."

"Sam, please," said Anton. "Boy is shot, is on drugs. Don't be coy."

Wolfe leaned back in his chair, stretched.

"Let me get something besides this wretched tea," he said, standing and going over to Boris's well-stocked shelves. He picked one of the bottles, took a glass, then returned to the table, poured one for himself, Anton, and Nikolai—but Benjamin declined; he wanted to stay conscious for a while this time—and then leaned forward, folding his arms on the table.

"Now, let me tell you about Vladimir Sergeyevitch Leverotov, one of the most brilliant people, other than Jeremy Fletcher, that I've never met."

Vladimir Sergeyevitch Leverotov (Wolfe began) joined 12 Directorate of the Soviet Ministry of Defense in 1959, when he was twenty-six—the youngest member of a very small and very elite group of young, brilliant, earnest thinkers; and their task it was to "think the unthinkable": how to prepare for and, if necessary, wage nuclear war against the "imperialist aggressors" in the United States.

As a math prodigy, Leverotov had always been fascinated by the relatively obscure field in mathematics known as game theory. He was among the first in the Soviet Union to read the work of John Nash, an American mathematician who would later become as famous for his bouts with schizophrenia as his radical theories of gaming strategy.

He and his colleagues at the directorate were given a daunting task:

develop an operational plan that would neutralize the ten-to-one advantage in nuclear weapons enjoyed by the United States. They considered the usual ruses common to centuries of warfare: dummy weapons, fake military broadcasts, nonexistent battalions. But such measures seemed like quaint antiques in the modern age of ICBMs and supersonic bombers.

One day, while buried deep in the directorate's archives searching for ideas that might have been overlooked, Leverotov had come across a dusty report written six years earlier, immediately after the first successful test of Russia's hydrogen bomb—what they had called *Kuzkin otets,* the "Father of All Bombs." Apparently the report had been filed away and forgotten.

Its author was anonymous, and Vladimir soon discovered why: the report suggested that, with the coming of weapons so powerful that only a few dozen were needed to utterly destroy one's enemy, and the undeniable reality that one's enemy possessed the same weapons, the greatest threat to both sides would be *fear*: fear of what the other side might do, fear of secrets, fear of being caught by surprise. Since the official Party line was that the Soviet Union knew no fear, it was clear why the author didn't want "credit" for this idea.

The report went on to say that such fear was as strong, if not stronger, for the Americans than for the Soviets. The United States firmly believed that the chief lesson it had learned from World War II and Pearl Harbor was simple: never get caught with your pants down. This fear, the report suggested, would cause the United States to put enormous resources into sustaining a state of "permanent alert": bombers constantly in the air, missiles ready to fire . . . all of which would look quite provocative to the USSR, with its own "master fear" of being surrounded by enemies, all waiting to pounce.

Thus the two fears would fit one another perfectly, becoming a *folie à deux,* a "shared madness" that could only end in catastrophe.

The author of this report pointed out it took only crude statistical analysis to predict that, given all the opportunities such interlocking fears would generate for misunderstandings, it was a matter of a decade, perhaps less, before the two sides would unleash their arsenals, annihilating one another.

But the author of the report had no alternative to offer. He concluded that the best the USSR could do was to build weapons as fast as possible and prepare to survive, in some manner, the inevitable apocalypse.

He wasn't as brilliant as Leverotov, who *did* see another option—one founded on the utterly logical math of game theory.

Leverotov knew from Nash's work that the only stable arrangement in such a "game" was one where both sides knew everything about one another's capabilities and intentions. Only by keeping nothing secret could miscalculation be avoided; only by assuring the survival of the other "player" could one ensure one's own survival.

Leverotov wrote up his own report, titling it *Analiz 55,* after a popular-if-morbid joke of the time, to represent the fact that only by creating a situation where neither side could possibly be wrong could both sides "win."

Though he didn't use the term, not wanting to reveal that he was reading American sources, Leverotov knew such a strategy by another name: a Nash equilibrium.

Leverotov filed the report and waited for the response: praise, condemnation . . . or worse.

But there was no response. Nothing.

It was as if the report didn't exist.

And then Leverotov was suddenly transferred from 12 Directorate and retrained as a rocket engineer. He assumed it was someone in the directorate's idea of an ironic punishment, to be made to now sit with the deadly weapons he'd only theorized about.

And so Leverotov came to Uzhur-4.

But, as a very dangerous souvenir, he'd brought a copy of *Analiz 55* with him.

CHAPTER 52

At this point, Wolfe's story was interrupted by dinner. Nikolai and Natalya set steaming plates of something that looked like stew in front of everyone, accompanied by tumblers of Boris's vodka.

Benjamin tasted his stew. It was very good, but with a flavor he couldn't quite identify.

"Do you mind," he said, "if I ask what I'm eating?"

"Only thing in Boris's freezer," Nikolai said. "Bear meat. Very good, yes?"

Benjamin smiled, dug in.

"As charming as this repast is," interjected Wolfe, "we need to be finishing and getting to town. I want a doctor to see Benjamin, and Boris for that matter. And we need to let Kalinin know what's happened. . . . In fact, I'm surprised he hasn't sent someone out here." He glanced somewhat nervously out into the dark night.

"The phone?" asked Benjamin, wolfing down more of the stew.

"Out of order," said Nikolai.

"Well, as long as we do have a few minutes, would someone mind explaining to me what *Stzenariy* or *Analiz 55* really is, and what it has to do with all this?"

"First understand this," said Wolfe. "At that time, in the early sixties,

American theoreticians like Leverotov working at American versions of 12 Directorate were coming to the same realization he had. They could read the same probabilities and knew one of two things was inevitable: nuclear war, or one side gives up. But this third alternative of Leverotov's, the Nash equilibrium . . . well, apparently they weren't as audacious, or as brilliant, as him. I've read all the literature of the time; there's no mention of it from the American side. At least not publically."

"Sam," Benjamin said, showing his fatigue, "I've been shot, I'm full of drugs and vodka, and now I know how to use a gun. As Anton said, could you stop being coy?"

Wolfe laughed out loud. "Sorry," he apologized. "Professional habit. But Anton should tell this part." He motioned for Anton to continue.

"What I hear is only stories, later," said Anton, sitting back for a moment from his meal. "Rumors KGB had fooled Americans by leaking some fake plan for atomic war strategy." Now Anton looked coy.

Benjamin thought for a moment. "Not Scenario 55, by any chance."

"Hah!" Anton slapped his knee, turned to Wolfe. "You were right, bright boy."

"So we *did* know what Scenario 55 was, clear back in the sixties?"

"No, not really," said Wolfe. "You see, apparently the KGB leaked the plan on purpose, as disinformation, to confuse us. But it had a quite unintended effect.

"Anton showed you how Fletcher had coded Myorkin's letter into octal, then made an image of it?" Wolfe continued, and Benjamin nodded. "But Anton hadn't decoded all of it yet when he talked to you. He did, later. Myorkin wrote that he'd found something else in the St. Petersburg archives, something that seemed strange to him to be in such secret archives because there didn't seem anything secret about it."

"And that something was?"

"Visa applications," said Anton. "For bunch of American academics. To come to Moscow. And then, by train, to Kuntsevo."

Why did that name sound familiar? thought Benjamin. "I'm sorry, I don't . . ."

"Where 12 Directorate was," said Anton, "in 1965."

"Damn strange," Nikolai interjected, "letting Americans come to Kuntsevo back then."

"I can see that," said Benjamin. "But why did Myorkin think it had anything to do with Jeremy's research?"

There was a general pause, and Benjamin could tell a bomb was about to drop. And finally it fell to Wolfe to drop it.

"Because one of the names on that visa list was Fletcher's current boss," said Wolfe steadily. "One Arthur Terrill."

"*Arthur?!*" Benjamin couldn't imagine the slight, precisely mannered academic involved in Cold War intrigue. "But . . . why *him*?"

"Is obvious," said Anton. "American guys, 12 Directorate guys get together. Everybody says, Cuba too damn close. One little slip, boom, *everybody* lose. You want to keep power, we want to keep power. How do we do that? How do we get to Nash equilibrium without blowing everybody up?"

Benjamin realized Anton wasn't asking a rhetorical question, but he didn't have the answer.

"How?" he asked.

"Fake it," Anton said. He took another bite of stew.

Benjamin looked at Anton, then at Wolfe.

"Fake it?" he said.

"Make it so you can't destroy us, we can't destroy you," said Anton. "Everything stable. But public need enemies. Need *almost* war." He looked at Benjamin steadily, as though willing him to understand what he was about to say. "Need cold war."

Benjamin waited for someone to say something else. But no one did.

"Are you saying . . ." Benjamin shook his head to clear it, then realized it wasn't the fog of drugs or alcohol. "Are you saying the Cold War was a *sham*?"

"*Borba s tenyu,*" Anton said, nodding. "Shadow boxing."

"Only with nuclear gloves," added Wolfe. "And how appropriate. Their nickname for this new scenario, for *Stzenariy 55,* was *Borba s tenyu*. The Shadow War."

For a moment, Benjamin couldn't speak. Finally he said, "That's . . . impossible. There would have to be . . . well, thousands of people involved."

"Not at all," said Wolfe. "Just a few. The *right* few."

"In Soviet Union," Anton said, "maybe twenty people in 12 Directorate know nuclear war plan. They give orders, everybody else just *follow* orders."

"And the American plan," said Wolfe, "SIOP . . . well, it's so complicated, there aren't many more than a dozen people who even understand it. It's all under the control of STRATCOM. Not even the president can change it. He just gives the go-ahead. Everything else is automatic. It's a conspiracy he doesn't need to know he's part of," finished Wolfe, raising and draining his glass.

"But . . ." Benjamin thought of something. "But the missiles are *real*. The bombs are *real*."

"Ah," said Wolfe. "That returns us to Comrade Leverotov's journal." He pulled the journal over, pushed it toward Benjamin. "See those columns of numbers?"

Benjamin looked at them. They meant nothing to him.

"So what?" he said. For some reason, he was feeling defiant, angry. He realized deep down he didn't want what they were telling him to be true.

Now it was Nikolai's turn to speak. "Remember, I told you about Czech crisis, about drill where things don't make sense?" Benjamin nodded. "Well, arming codes and targeting protocol *before* Cuba was in missiles. But after Cuba, arming codes and targets come from Moscow. From 12 Directorate. But in drill, red light tells us these codes transmitted. System thought missiles were launched, so sent codes."

"So?" said Benjamin, still defiant.

"Leverotov was an engineer," said Wolfe. "An exceptionally talented one. He knew the missiles would store these codes until they were given new ones. So he decided to check one missile, find out just what those codes had been. And he knew how to translate them. But what he discovered, he simply didn't believe."

"And what did he discover?" asked Benjamin.

"The missile had never been armed. And its target was a spot north of the Arctic Circle. But nothing was there. No NATO base, no submarine patrol zones. Nothing. So he checked another missile. Same thing. And another missile. Same thing." Wolfe pulled the journal back, closed it. "Over the next month, he checked over half the missiles of Uzhur-4. And what he found was that every single one of them, if they'd blasted off, would have been sent straight to the emptiness of the North Pole, there to punch a hole in the ice and sink to the bottom of the ocean like so much scrap metal."

"And," added Nikolai, "if mistake, each missile can be destroyed, *poof,* in the air. From Moscow. From guys in 12 Directorate."

"You have to admit," Wolfe said with grudging respect, "it was brilliant. No outward sign the weapons had been tampered with, and if the 'arrangement' ever collapsed, simply enter real codes, and voila. *Real* MADness."

"I would guess I maybe know two of those 'brilliant' 12 Directorate guys," added Anton. "Dmitri Korsilov and Vladimir Potyminken. Old hands by time I came. Now, who knows where they are—or who they are friends with?"

Benjamin found himself struggling to take it all in.

"But that's just one missile base. What about all the others? What about the submarines, the planes . . . ?"

"In Soviet Union, *everything* controlled by Moscow," said Nikolai. "Not *one* bomb can go off without right signal." Nikolai looked at him, smiled. "And 12 Directorate controls all signals."

Benjamin thought for a minute, came up with what suddenly seemed to him the most obvious objection of all.

"But this," he indicated Leverotov's journal, "is all about the *Soviet* plan. What about the American plan, this . . . SIOP? You said both sides had to know what the other was doing for this Nash equilibrium to work. What proof do you have the Americans were cooperating with this . . . shadow war?"

Wolfe set his glass down. "In the case of the United States we don't need a secret history, we have a very public one." He leaned back in his chair again, directing his full attention to Benjamin.

"In the late sixties, the CIA created something called Team B. It was made up of outside experts, people from a very prestigious think tank, and therefore supposedly neutral. Their report argued that the Soviet strength had been seriously *under*estimated, and they suggested an even bigger American arms buildup. Now, guess who that prestigious think tank was," Wolfe said provocatively, "and who was leader of Team B."

"The American Heritage Foundation," Benjamin said, automatically. "And one Dr. Arthur Terrill."

Wolfe raised his glass in reply.

"Strange thing is," Anton said, "everybody read Team B report said is cuckoo. Including me."

Wolfe nodded. "I've seen it, too. The intelligence doesn't jive with reality. Yet, oddly enough, Team B's *National Intelligence Estimate on the Soviet Union* became holy writ. Then you get Reagan, you get many more billions spent on shiny new missiles . . ."

"Okay now," Benjamin interrupted him. "That's where I just cannot go along with this. Think of those billions of dollars—"

"Exactly," said Wolfe, looking him straight in the eye. "Think of those billions. And then think of who stands to lose if they stop flowing."

Benjamin nodded silently. "Still, to do all this for money . . ."

"And power," interjected Anton. "To some, is more important than money."

"I suppose," said Benjamin. "But there's a mystery neither money nor power explains. Why did Leverotov shoot himself back in 1968?"

"Once he saw numbers in missiles," Nikolai said, pointing to the journal, "he knew everything. He understood fake war. Was *his* fake war."

"His last entries," said Wolfe sadly, "were about how his commitment to defending the Motherland now seemed like some immense farce. And now that he knew the truth, that the world was being held hostage to an enormous lie, he was afraid that the KGB team investigating the missile drill glitch would learn that he knew. So, he decided to hide the evidence, and then eliminate the only key to that evidence: himself."

"I think it is tragic," said Natalya, speaking for the first time. "He must have felt entirely betrayed."

"But had some little hope," offered Nikolai. "That I would understand, would find his journal, and somehow let truth be known. But I didn't. Until now, forty years too late."

CHAPTER 53

Benjamin stood up and made his way to the coffeepot on the stove. He thought maybe some caffeine would make this extraordinary revelation clearer, or perhaps make it go away. Maybe he was still unconscious, dreaming it all.

Wolfe stood up, came over to him.

"We've had a little more time to adjust to this . . . discovery than you have, Benjamin," he said. "Remember what you told me about the Indian wars? That you thought this secret group of Puritans had used them, perhaps even provoked them, to gain power and hold on to it?" Benjamin nodded but didn't say anything. "Well, this is the same idea, only with nuclear missiles instead of bows and arrows."

Wolfe shook his head. "There's still so much we don't know. But I assume once Arthur felt Fletcher's research was showing results, he brought him to the Foundation so he could control those results. Perhaps he even thought they could use that research to better hide any cracks in their forty-year-old cover-up. That's only one of the questions I plan on asking him." He looked thoughtful for a moment.

"I also assume it wasn't Arthur that authorized Fletcher's murder. I think that was our rash friend Hauser's doing, when Fletcher asked to see what he thought was the original diary at the Morris Estate. Anton told me what you discovered at the Library of Congress. What with so much of the Foundation's funding coming from the Morrises, that sort of embarrassment might have put the kibosh on this contract with the State Department even after all this time. The Foundation couldn't have that." He sighed, as though suddenly feeling the weight of so much betrayal and revelation. "But once it was done, what better way to still discover whatever other cracks might exist in their cover-up than bringing me in to investigate? And once I brought my findings to Arthur, well then . . ."

"They'd eliminate you?"

Wolfe didn't answer.

"I still don't understand," said Benjamin. "Forty years of fear? Of scaring the whole world with this nightmare of a nuclear Armageddon? An Armageddon that was a fake? Why not just admit the fallacy of the whole thing? Why not just negotiate?"

"Ah, Benjamin, you idealist you. They didn't do this out of any fondness for the Soviets. They did it because the only alternative was détente. *Real* détente. They needed an enemy with nuclear teeth, but one that couldn't really bite."

Natalya came over to the counter, put her empty plate in the sink. "Lenin once said that 'even the Devil is an acceptable ally if it means staying in power,'" she said.

Benjamin shook his head. "But all those *people* . . ."

"Who kept doing exactly what they would have done anyway," said Wolfe. "As far as anyone outside the small group of conspirators knew, it was *real*. On both sides. They thought they were working for the Cause."

Wolfe looked out the window into the apparently infinite darkness outside.

"And when you think about it, Benjamin, if there hadn't been such a conspiracy, the two political structures probably would have acted much the same way. Each needed an archenemy to keep their respective citizenries frightened and in line." He placed a hand on Benjamin's shoulder. "In the final analysis, it almost doesn't matter whether there was a conspiracy or not. We all got the cold war we needed."

Then Benjamin had another thought.

"But all of this, everything you've discovered, it still doesn't *prove* that the Foundation is involved, only Arthur and Hauser."

"As to that . . . ," began Wolfe.

At that moment, there was a small *pop,* and a tiny hole appeared in the window in front of them. At the same instant, the oil lamp on the table shattered. The spilled oil was immediately ignited by the heat of the lamp, and a small river of flame spread toward the papers on the table.

"The journal!" Wolfe shouted.

Then several things happened simultaneously: Wolfe crouched down behind the counter, pulling Benjamin with him; there was a second *pop* and the window shattered. Something struck the fireplace, sending out slivers of stone. Natalya threw one of the coats over the flames from the lamp even as Nikolai reached for another of the oil lamps and pulled it down from the table.

"The other lamps," hissed Wolfe. "Put them out!"

There was yet another crash, this time of some of the vodka bottles on the shelf. Clear liquid flew from the shattered bottles onto the floor, where it touched some of the burning oil. The vodka ignited with a wavering blue flame, and soon there were two fires: one on the table, and a second spreading across the floor.

Now all of them were crouched on the floor. Anton was yanking journal pages from the table, beating them on the floor to extinguish their burning edges; Natalya was trying to smother the fire on the floor; and Nikolai had reached the other lamps and turned down their flame, so now the only light was from the fireplace and the burning oil and alcohol.

"Is anyone hit?" asked Wolfe.

"Bastards don't need to hit us," said Nikolai from the floor. "Just burn house down."

"Or burn book," said Anton. He was sitting on the floor next to the fireplace, Leverotov's journal clutched to his chest.

"How many?" said Wolfe to Nikolai.

"One, maybe two," answered Nikolai. "But they probably have night scopes."

"Who the hell is out there?" asked Benjamin.

"I would guess some old friends of Anton's from 12 Directorate," Wolfe said. "They've got as much a stake in keeping this secret as the Foundation. Maybe more." He was looking around the cabin. Then he spotted Boris's gun rack. "If only there was a way out of here other than the front door."

"There is," said Nikolai. "In bathroom, hole in floor, little tunnel. For when militia come."

"All right," Wolfe said. "Benjamin, you and Natalya and Anton, stay put. And stay low."

He crawled across the floor to the gun rack. Reaching up, he grabbed one of the rifles by the stock, pulled it down from the rack. Even as he did so, another bullet struck the gun rack, splintering the stock of the remaining rifle. Wolfe slid the rifle across the floor to Nikolai. He pulled his automatic pistol out of his parka, began crawling toward the bathroom.

"Come on, Nikolai. If they think we're still inside, perhaps we can sneak around them."

Nikolai crawled from the table, and both men moved slowly across the floor and into the bathroom. There was the sound of a section of the flooring being removed, and through the open doorway Benjamin could see the two men drop down through the floor to the ground beneath.

With both fires out, the only light now came from the flickering fireplace. Benjamin wasn't sure what to do. He crawled awkwardly across the floor to Natalya, trying to keep his shoulder from bumping into things in the dim light.

"Are you all right?" he asked, reaching her.

"Yes," she said. "Are you?"

"I'm okay," said Benjamin, cradling his shoulder.

"Me, too," said Anton from the fireplace, "if anyone asking."

"I should be out there," Benjamin said. "They don't know how many there are."

"With that arm in a sling, what could you do, except make a fine target?"

"I don't know," Benjamin said. "Something. Anything. But I feel like a coward, hiding here."

"Benjamin," Natalya said. She put her hand to the side of his face. She looked into his eyes. "What you did at *shakhta* thirty-four was not the act of a coward." She put her arm around his neck, pressed her head against his chest.

Benjamin smiled, but immediately winced in pain. "I was almost useless. If Samuel hadn't shown up—"

Suddenly there was the sharp crack of a shot somewhere outside the cabin, followed in quick succession by two more.

"If only the other rifle hadn't been hit," Natalya said, "at least we could defend ourselves."

It was then Benjamin remembered the Makarov pistol in his parka. He looked around the cabin.

"Natalya," he said, "where did you put my parka?"

"That's it," she said. "On that chair."

"Natalya, can you reach it?" he asked.

She began crawling toward the chair, keeping close to the floor. There was another crack of a rifle from outside, then the higher-pitched snap of another gun in response, and the cry of someone in pain.

"My father!" whispered Natalya.

"Just stay down," Benjamin said. "Your father's pistol is in the parka pocket. Throw it to me."

Natalya was at the chair. She reached up, felt in the right-hand pocket of the parka. "There is only a glove," she said; then, "No, wait, I think . . ."

Suddenly the front door to the cabin was thrown open. Against the dark backdrop of the night sky, littered with the white dots of snowflakes, there was the silhouette of someone tall, someone in a white snow parka and pants. In the dim light they could see he was dark skinned, with a black beard.

The figure began to raise its arm. And then Benjamin noticed that there was some sort of helmet on the man's head. In the flicker of the firelight, he saw the reflection from lenses set in the helmet, with a faint green glow behind them.

Now the figure moved its arm to the side—toward where Natalya lay, under the table, her hand inside the parka pocket.

A sudden shaft of bright light was cast into the room. Benjamin turned his head, saw Boris standing in the doorway to the bedroom, the light flooding out into the room.

"*Kagogo Diavola?*" Boris said.

The figure in the doorway raised an arm in front of his face, blocking out the sudden glare of light that must have blinded his night vision; at the same moment he fired a quick shot in Boris's direction. Boris jerked back as the bullet struck his thigh.

And then the figure was swinging his arm back toward Natalya.

Suddenly there was an eruption from the pocket of the parka over the chair—and the figure at the door staggered back as if hit by a fist in the chest. His gun discharged a bullet into the ceiling.

But he didn't go down. As he was lowering his arm, aiming again, Natalya fired a second time.

The figure lifted its arm weakly—but the pistol dropped from his hand. And then he fell backward, out into the snow, and lay still.

"Anton!" Benjamin shouted. "Anton, put out the fire!"

Anton moved from the fireplace, jerked a coat down from a rack on the wall, patted it over the fire in the bedroom. Boris lay on his side, groaning. Natalya crawled over to Benjamin.

"Are you all right?" she said, clutching him. She still had the smoking Makarov in her hand.

He nodded. "Yes, I'm all right." He gently took the gun from her with his good hand, then put his arms around her.

"I am now tired of people shooting at us," said Anton, smothering the last of the flames.

"I think it's over," Benjamin said.

Suddenly there was a thunderous sound overhead, and a blinding white light that made the trees stand out in bold relief.

As the roar grew louder, the light moved back and forth on the ground, then angled off beyond the front of the house, to the meadow across the dirt road from Boris's cabin.

Benjamin started to get up, and Natalya helped him to rise. Together they walked to the doorway, looked out onto the landscape turned into blazing white by the light from overhead. Benjamin realized it was a searchlight, and the deafening *whomp-whomp-whomp* was the sound of a helicopter—a huge one. As they watched, its dark bulk settled slowly onto the meadow. It was painted in olive drab and black camouflage.

A door in the helicopter's side slid open, and men began to tumble out, dressed in white snow-camouflage uniforms. Soon there were a dozen of them in front of the helicopter, each of them armed with an assault rifle.

Then someone else jumped from the helicopter. But rather than white, he was wearing a green officer's tunic and hat.

"Thank God, it is Vasily," Natalya said.

Lieutenant Colonel Kalinin shouted orders and pointed, and the men began fanning out into the woods—then stopped as two figures emerged from the trees. One was also dressed in a white parka and pants, but the other was in a dark parka and was grasping his upper arm.

"Nikolai!" shouted Natalya. Benjamin held her back.

The soldiers raised their weapons, pointed them toward the two men—then Kalinin shouted something, and the men lowered their guns. Kalinin approached Wolfe and Nikolai, spoke with them for a moment. Then he sent two of his men into the woods, and the rest of the group approached the cabin.

"If he's here to rescue us, he's a little late," said Benjamin, looking at Natalya and smiling. "You've already done that."

Natalya helped Benjamin back into the cabin and into a chair at the table, where Anton was sorting through the burned pages of the journal and *Analiz 55*.

"Saved most of it," Anton said. "But don't know yet which most."

"That's not a problem," said Kalinin from the doorway.

Wolfe and Nikolai entered, Nikolai cradling his left arm, and also sat at the table. Immediately Natalya turned to Nikolai, started to remove his parka so she could check his wound. Nikolai looked at Benjamin, smiled broadly, said "We match!" then accepted a glass of vodka Wolfe handed him and tossed it back.

Now Kalinin entered, telling his men to wait outside. He glanced down at the tall man lying in the doorway, cocked an eyebrow appreciatively.

"I see one here," he said, "and I sent two men into the woods to search for the other."

"Could you see from the air?" asked Wolfe, watching Kalinin very closely. "Are there any more?"

"No, I don't think so," Kalinin said. He went to the fireplace, removed his gloves and began warming his hands. He barely glanced at Boris, lying unconscious on the bedroom floor.

"And what means 'not a problem'?" asked Anton. He held up the burned journal. "You have any idea how important this is?"

"No," Kalinin replied. Then he turned around. "Nor do I want to know."

"Then you won't mind getting these men to a hospital," Wolfe said.

Kalinin didn't answer immediately. He walked to the shelves of vodka, took down a bottle, removed the cork and sniffed it, frowned, put it back.

"This is contraband," he said. "It will be confiscated." Then he walked to the table, held out his hand to Anton. "As will all contraband."

Anton, mouth open, looked to him, then to Wolfe.

"Is joking?" he asked.

"No," said Wolfe, watching Kalinin. "I think not."

"Then, you're here to finish their job," Benjamin said, struggling to keep his voice steady.

Kalinin, his hand still out, turned to Benjamin.

"I'm an officer in the Army of the Russian Federation," said Kalinin coldly. "Not a hired killer. My duty is to keep secrets of the Motherland safe and secure, not to punish foolish young adventurers." Then he faced back to Anton. "Please?" he said.

As though giving up the Holy Grail, Anton placed the singed journal in Kalinin's hand. "And those," Kalinin said, pointing to the pages from *Analiz 55* spread across the table. Anton began scooping the pages together.

"Vasily, if you only knew what was in those pages," Nikolai pleaded, "you would understand, it is *they* who betrayed *us*."

"I don't think Vasily is interested in the truth," Wolfe said.

"Truth?" Kalinin shot back. "Today, two American agents, a runaway Russian diplomat, and an ex–Red Army officer tried to breach the security of a Russian nuclear missile base, after impersonating journalists and bribing officials." Kalinin smiled. "You mean *that* truth?"

"But *we* know the truth," said Benjamin. "We know what is in those documents, even if you take them. We'll tell—"

"Who will you tell, Mr. Levebre? And without these," Kalinin waved the pages in the air, sending loose ashes floating about their heads, "who would possibly believe you?"

CHAPTER 54

The next few days were a blur to Benjamin. Once Vasily had confiscated their "contraband," he'd acted as though they were merely tourists who'd wandered astray. He'd arranged for them to be transported to Krasnoyarsk— all except Boris, whom Vasily had indicated would be busy for some time answering questions about his "business" dealings. Whatever Boris's other failings, Benjamin made sure Vasily knew that, at the last minute anyway, Boris had been unwilling to participate in Hauser's cold-blooded murder plan.

As for the events at *shakhta* thirty-four and Boris's cabin . . . apparently Vasily would obtain a medal for thwarting a terrorist plot to infiltrate the Uzhur-4 base; and it was implied Nikolai would share in that medal, as well as an increase in his pension . . . as long as he went along with Kalinin's story.

From Krasnoyarsk they'd flown to Moscow, and then, rather than to D.C., to Nice, for a brief rest all of them needed.

It was in Nice that Wolfe had told Benjamin of his intention to go back to the Foundation, to confront Arthur Terrill and give him the chance to fill in the remaining pieces of this forty-year-old puzzle. Benjamin had insisted on going with him, whether for moral support or because he wanted to see the Foundation through new, wiser eyes, he wasn't sure.

He'd also insisted that Natalya wait for him in Nice. Things still needed to be smoothed over with the Russian embassy, and for a while she'd be better off out of the country. He assured her the trip to Massachusetts would take a day or two at the most, then he'd join her in Nice and they could enjoy it properly, like the tourists they'd only pretended to be before.

Now, on the plane from Nice to D.C., Benjamin and Wolfe spoke of what would happen with the Foundation's all-important contract. Benjamin was certain it would all lead to an investigation of the Foundation.

"Once I go back to the library and get the real Bainbridge diary, reveal what Morris's ancestors were up to and how they've been covering up ever since . . ."

Wolfe turned to him, smiled indulgently. "Benjamin, your commitment to optimism astounds me. What on earth makes you think the diary is still there?"

"I concealed it fairly thoroughly after I was done. Besides, this is the Library of Congress, not the Morrises' private estate. How could they . . ."

Wolfe shook his head. "Haven't you learned anything about the reach and fanaticism of power from what we've been through? The Morrises aren't just backers of the Foundation; through Montrose and his contacts they have friends in nearly every branch of government. Especially with this administration. Once they learned the diary still existed, they'll have had the library scoured for it. And without the diary, you have only your notes for evidence of this huge conspiracy, the notes of a young postdoc fellow who fled the Foundation in possession of secret government property, entered the Russian Federation on a false passport, and was involved with a known smuggler and other shady characters in a plot to steal nuclear materials and sell them to terrorists."

"What!" Benjamin shouted. Wolfe shushed him, indicating the other passengers around them. "That's not what happened," he continued, lowering his voice to a near-whisper.

"No," said Wolfe. "But I bet that or a similar version is just waiting to be spread all over the Internet, should you make a stink about the diary." Wolfe patted his knee. "Whatever results will be far more subtle. Enjoy our first-class ride," he said. "Anton's paying for it."

Benjamin decided, for now, to take Wolfe's advice. He summoned the stewardess, ordered some champagne, tilted back, and tried to focus on Natalya waiting for him in Nice.

A day later, they were driving up the winding, graveled road to the manse. Benjamin was eager to confront Terrill. And he was angry.

The day before, while in D.C., Benjamin had gone to the Library of Congress, to see if Wolfe had been right.

There had been no trace of the diary. And no record of a crate of books from the Morris family.

So now the only remaining evidence for all the intrigue they'd uncovered was on the walls of the manse at the American Heritage Foundation.

"When we get to the manse," Benjamin said to Wolfe on the drive out, "I'll show you that damn mural, and you can tell me then if you think I'm insane. It's just too much of a coincidence. First King Philip's War, then the Newburgh plot, then Arthur's little arrangement with the Soviets. And the Foundation is connected to them all, one way or another."

Wolfe looked just as skeptical now as he had when Benjamin first told him about the mural.

"Coincidences are just an improbable alignment of events," Wolfe said flatly, echoing Anton. "Not evidence of collusion. And think what you're suggesting. While I might allow that some of your Puramists survived to the Revolutionary War, and perhaps even had their own agenda, to suggest they continued for another *two hundred* years . . ." He shook his head. "The Morrises are an old and powerful family. Of course they have connections throughout American history. But that doesn't mean they're at the center of some arcane conspiracy." Wolfe pulled through the Foundation's gates. "Just show me this sinisterly suggestive mural of yours, and we'll go from there."

As they drove through the Foundation's gates, Benjamin thought back to how he'd felt two weeks before, passing through this same portal. He recalled his burning eagerness to be admitted through those gates and into the world of power and privilege of the Foundation; how, in Arthur Terrill's office, he'd thought of the Foundation as a sort of magnificent theater, one in which he desperately desired to know the machinery behind the stage. Now, that theater seemed to him like a papier-mâché façade concealing not tantalizing secrets, but brittle fossils.

They parked outside the manse—once again Benjamin was struck by the almost preternatural stillness of the Foundation's grounds—climbed the portico's steps, and entered the manse's foyer.

And came to a dead stop.

The mural was gone.

From floor to ceiling, the walls had been painted a universal thick, bright white. There wasn't a trace of the mural visible anywhere.

Benjamin could only stare in silence, but Wolfe harrumphed. "Well, now," he smirked. "A preservation project?" He turned to Benjamin. "I apologize. Apparently there was more to that mural than met my eye. Let's see if Arthur's wearing a false beard and dark glasses."

He led the still-stunned Benjamin to Terrill's office, opened the door without knocking.

Arthur was sitting behind his desk, rifling through papers, just as when Benjamin had first met him. Only now Arthur didn't look confident and officious; he looked gaunt and harried.

"Mr. Wolfe and Mr. Wainwright," Terrill said tersely. "I must say I'm surprised but pleased to see you again."

They walked to Terrill's desk, neither choosing to sit down.

"Pleased?" Benjamin said with skepticism.

"Any results of this entire misadventure that would prove fatal were, as far as I was concerned . . ." And then he seemed to run out of steam and slumped back in his chair.

"Unavoidable?" offered Wolfe. "God, Arthur, what *happened* to you?"

Terrill looked down at his desk, began to straighten papers, stopped himself.

"I'm not sure you would understand, Samuel." He looked up at him. "I'm not sure you've ever really *believed* in anything that strongly. Which is why you never really . . . fit in here."

"Oh, you're wrong there," Wolfe said. "But now I know there's nothing more dangerous than believing the ends justify the means."

Terrill's eyes went bright. "But if those ends are *vital* to the survival of your country—"

"And if those means change the very *nature* of that country?" Wolfe said. "What survives then?"

Terrill didn't respond, and Benjamin spoke up.

"I'd like to know one thing," he said. "How did Jeremy become involved in all this?"

Terrill sighed, looked down at his desk. "Old colleagues from RAND recommended him. We gave him money and his head. He'd already written brilliantly about nuclear war and game theory. . . ." He looked up. "When he started to report the preliminary results of this TEACUP program . . . well, I was against letting him continue. But others saw an opportunity. There'd always been concerns about possible . . . fault lines. It was felt by some that Dr. Fletcher's work might reveal those fault lines so that we could better . . . repair them."

Wolfe snorted. "Don't you mean *conceal* them?"

"Do you really think, Samuel," Terrill said to Wolfe, suddenly energized again, "that the average person *wants* to know all this, *wants* to understand how . . . insane it all was? If we'd told them we couldn't protect them, that no matter how many bombs we had they would be no safer . . . Do you think they *wanted* to hear that truth? But by creating an enemy they could understand, we provided our people with unity, with purpose—"

"And stability," said Wolfe sarcastically. "I know the speech, Arthur. From the thirties and in another language. And it's no more convincing now than it was then."

"But surely even you, Samuel, can see that this . . . arrangement made the world safer—"

Wolfe shook his head emphatically. "You only made the terror *acceptable.*"

Terrill's eyes darted about, as though seeking an answer.

"There were traditions to defend," Terrill said, almost pleading, "ideals to sustain—"

"Ideals?!" said Wolfe, finally losing his temper. "Tell that to Jeremy Fletcher. Tell that to Edith Gadenhower, and who knows how many others." Wolfe calmed himself. "You weren't upholding ideals Arthur. You were merely clinging to power by any means necessary."

Arthur looked at Wolfe with a mixture of resentment and resignation.

"And we noticed the 'renovation' work in the foyer," Wolfe continued. Still Arthur didn't say anything. "It won't matter, Arthur. Not in the long run. I would guess there are other 'fault lines' waiting to be stumbled upon, as Fletcher did."

"I wouldn't look for them, Samuel," Terrill said. Now he looked . . . frightened.

"Oh, I'm beginning to suspect we're not the *only* ones looking."

Now Arthur's eyes flashed, as though Wolfe had struck a nerve, but he said nothing.

"You could still salvage something from all this, Arthur," Wolfe said, his tone changing to that of an old friend giving unwanted-but-wise counsel. "*You* could tell the story. Let people decide for themselves. Isn't that one of the ideals you did all this to sustain?"

Terrill smiled ruefully. "You don't understand, Samuel. Not even now."

And Benjamin realized that Terrill looked not like an arrogant conspirator, not even like the director of a powerful institution . . . but rather like a man who'd received news he'd been found guilty and would pay the price.

Wolfe hung his head, sighed. He turned to Benjamin. "We should go,

Benjamin. I believe Arthur has some . . . sorting out to do." He looked once more at Arthur. "Good-bye, Arthur," he said.

And then he and Benjamin turned and walked out of the room.

Just as Wolfe and Benjamin were driving out of the Foundation's gates, there was a sharp, short noise from the manse that echoed across the Foundation grounds. The noise sent a flock of crows in the tree outside Terrill's office scattering into the gray afternoon sky.

CHAPTER 55

Reagan airport was crowded. As Benjamin looked at the faces of all the people hurrying to their destinations, to business meetings and vacations and everyday lives, he wondered: Would they behave any differently if they *did* know the truth?

He realized this sounded slightly cynical, like something Wolfe would ask; and he wondered if more than Wolfe's fondness for scotch had rubbed off on him.

He and Wolfe stood together at the entrance for the security line. He found himself searching for something to say, something equal to the incredible experiences of the last two weeks.

"It's infuriating," he said finally. "Here we know about the biggest fraud ever perpetrated in modern times, and we can't say anything about it to anyone."

"You're an historian," Wolfe replied calmly. "So of course you want to set the record straight. But believe me, if we tried to tell this story without the proof to back it up, even those who weren't in on it would oppose us. Nobody wants that kind of . . . revelation. Not now, not with these new enemies without flags or borders."

Benjamin didn't look convinced.

"Besides, I think you're making an excellent decision decamping to

Nice. Whatever happens here, better to watch from the sidelines. And I can't think of better sidelines than the south of France or better company than Ms. Orlova."

Benjamin smiled. "And you?" he asked. "Are you going to sit on the sidelines somewhere?"

Wolfe looked serious. "Not quite. There are still too many questions I need answered."

"Such as?"

"Such as . . . did it ever strike you as strange, Benjamin, that we got as far as we did?"

"I thought you said Terrill and Hauser *allowed* us to get that far, that it was all part of their plan?"

"Oh, I'm sure that's how it started," Wolfe said. "But there were too many other . . . coincidences along the way. I feel the presence of more than one invisible hand in everything that's happened."

"What do you mean?"

"Well," Wolfe said, obviously weighing his words carefully, "we have Arthur and the Foundation and 12 Directorate all working together to keep this secret, the Gray Cardinals in all this . . . but why should they have been the *only* group working behind the scenes?"

"You mean some other group who *knew* about this arranged nuclear standoff? What," Benjamin thought, laughed, "something like . . . the *white* cardinals?"

"Why not?" Wolfe replied. He saw the look of doubt on Benjamin's face. "I wouldn't be so skeptical if I were you. After all, I believe you met one of them."

"*Me*?" Benjamin said in shock.

"On St. Honorat," Wolfe said. "The man who gave you Guy's passports? I told you, he wasn't a friend of mine. I didn't even know you were there. And I have a strange feeling he wasn't one of theirs, either."

"But then who—"

Wolfe displayed his trademark half-charming, half-infuriating smile. "*That* is one of the first questions I will put to Anton. I intend to have a very long and frank discussion with my old friend. There's a good deal about all this he either guessed or already knew. I think my search is far from over, that there may be other murals out there not yet covered up."

"So you'll go looking for these . . . white cardinals?" Benjamin asked.

"For the truth," Wolfe said. "Whatever it is, wherever it leads."

"Why Samuel," Benjamin teased. "You sound almost idealistic."

Samuel frowned. "There's no need to be insulting."

"No, it suits you," Benjamin said. "And thank you, Samuel, for everything." They shook hands awkwardly, what with Benjamin's arm still in a sling; then he remembered something.

"I'm afraid," Benjamin said, "we were rather liberal with Anton's bank account." He started to reach into his jacket for his wallet. "But I think there's still something in the balance . . ."

Wolfe stopped his hand. "Anton told me to tell you to keep it, especially if you're setting up housekeeping on the Côte d'Azur. He said to consider it a reward from a grateful people."

"What people?" asked Benjamin.

"That's another of my questions for him," Wolfe said. "As for you, besides sharing a life of leisure with a beautiful woman, what else are your plans?"

"What else can I do?" Benjamin shrugged. "I'm going to write a book."

Wolfe looked skeptical. "But I already explained, with Arthur dead, *Stzenariy 55* locked in some Russian vault or destroyed, and the diary god knows where . . ."

"Oh, not a book about our . . . adventure," Benjamin said. "I'm going to finish my father's book, about the Puritans."

"And I think your father would be quite proud of you," Wolfe said, and then he added mischievously, "Benjamin Franklin Wainwright. And in the meantime get married, sit in the sun, and drink good French wine. And I would strongly advise you to learn Russian. You'll need it to keep up with that extraordinary woman."

Benjamin smiled, then turned to check the line and saw it was time for him to enter security.

He turned back to ask Wolfe when he and Natalya would see him again—but Wolfe was gone, vanished into the jostling crowd. Like a ghost; or, Benjamin thought ruefully, a spook.

Benjamin turned, juggling his carry-on bag, wallet, and boarding pass with his one good arm, shuffled forward, and soon he, too, disappeared through the security portal.

A man sitting nearby lowered the newspaper he'd been reading as Benjamin entered security. He was tall, quite thin, with old-fashioned wire-rim glasses. His brown hair was trimmed very close to his skull, and he had intensely blue eyes.

He watched closely as Benjamin walked off down the hallway to the boarding gate. Then he rose and headed down the concourse, in the same direction taken by Samuel Wolfe.